WITH SLEEP CAME THE DREAMS, THE HAUNTING TERROR OVER AND OVER AGAIN . . .

. . . the wagon stood there, the horses snorting and stamping in their traces. The body of his father lay face down in the soft, white dust of the trail.

A big man jumped from the back of the wagon, dragging Theo's mother with him. She struggled to her feet crying and the man slapped her down again. Three other men walked from behind the wagon and jeered. The big man stood above her, grinning. She looked at him, pleading.

Theo heard his mother scream, and while he watched, he whined lowly to himself unable to accept the horrid thing he saw. His security was being destroyed. His father was dead and his mother . . . Theo was old enough to know rape . . .

Theo the boy had witnessed horror. Theo the man would stop at nothing to avenge his parents.

Tor books by W. Michael Gear

Long Ride Home
People of the Wolf (with Kathleen O'Neal Gear)
People of the Fire (with Kathleen O'Neal Gear)
People of the Earth (with Kathleen O'Neal Gear)
People of the River (with Kathleen O'Neal Gear)*

*forthcoming

A TOM DOHERTY ASSOCIATES BOOK
NEW YORK

LONG RIDE HOME

Cover art by Maren

A Tor Book
Published by Tom Doherty Associates, Inc.
175 Fifth Avenue
New York, N.Y. 10010

ISBN: 0-812-51392-4
Library of Congress Catalog Card Number: 88-50633

First edition: November 1988

Printed in the United States of America

0 9 8 7 6 5 4 3

To
Kathleen O'Neal Gear
for your courage
for your love
for your respect
and for your appreciation

ACKNOWLEDGMENTS

A debt of gratitude is owed to several people for their input during the writing of this work. First and foremost, I would like to thank my exceptional wife, Kathy, for it was she who urged me to expand on the original draft and concept. She was willing to dump two highly successful careers to pursue a dream. To Dick Wheeler, my friend and advisor, go heartfelt thanks for hints, criticisms, encouragement, and constant feedback. I would like to acknowledge my agent, Sharon Jarvis, for finding the right place at the right time after seven rejections. And to Wanda June Alexander and Tor Books, a special appreciation for their thoughtful comments and suggestions.

PREFACE

When Owen Wister published *The Virginian* in 1902, the gunfighter was given a shining romantic image which has grown over time. Writers, including Zane Grey, Max Brand, Louis L'Amour, and others, have continued to build upon this image of an American folk hero. Few authors of Western fiction have cared to delve beyond the realm of legend and portray the sort of man from which the romantic figure was derived.

In writing *Long Ride Home* I have attempted to create a more accurate profile of such a man. Theo Belk becomes more than a romantic figure. He is a man who deals with the world through a unique perception of reality—a reality forged and tempered by his personal tragedies, joys, goals, and experiences.

From the traumatic moment when his parents are brutally murdered, he constructs a very different understanding of the world in which he interacts. It is a reality of strength, violence, and harshness which must be balanced by his personal concepts of justice derived from a Judeo-Christian cultural background.

Theo Belk cannot be the typical hero we have come to associate with Western fiction. His personality is more akin to that which can be constructed for people like Jim Courtwright, Wes Hardin, and Tom Horn, all men who were molded by violence, war, and the necessities of survival on a hostile frontier that—as in the case of Theo Belk—constantly changed and left them out of place and beyond social acceptance. It is from such a world that Theo Belk comes, a world totally alien to our modern one.

Theo Belk is neither good nor evil when judged by such standards. He is simply human in his reaction to the forces that molded him—a child of his times. He is tormented by emotional disturbances and haunted by dreams which reflect his feelings of justice, guilt, and responsibility.

If the reader identifies with Theo Belk as a human being, this book will have fulfilled its purpose by depicting the gunman as he was. As most biographies of such men suggest, they were deviants who suffered from neuroses, psychoses, and flaws of character which handicapped their relationships with society. Theo Belk is such a man.

An attempt has been made to place Theo Belk in a background that reflects historical reality. The places, people, and events are reconstructed with as much accuracy as can be expected within the bounds of fiction. Buildings such as Essington's Hotel, Ida Hamilton's House of Mirrors, and Bullock and Wards are real and existed in Theo Belk's time.

While Theo Belk, the Moores, Tom O'Connell, Louis Gasceaux, and Ruby are fictional characters, they interact with men and women who are historical figures. Colonel Dye, Walter Cheesman, Kelly, and Ham Bell along with others were actual people who helped build our land.

Many of the events depicted in the book are factual

or have a factual base from which they are derived. Immigrant journals talk about their fear of white thieves dressed as Indians, though most such events took place closer to the settlements. The shootout in Ellsworth is based on the Tuttle Dance Hall massacre in Newton 1873, and to this day no one knows who the man was who shot ten men in as many seconds.

There were definite antagonisms between the Jayhawkers and the trail herders. The conflict of cultures was not only that of red and white. It included differing life-styles which often ended in violence between mountain man and Mormon, cattleman and farmer, and as today, minorities had their own troubles.

It is the belief of the author that historical fiction should be more than fantasy. With this goal in mind, this book is an attempt to take the reader back to another time and place him in the harsh frontier world as it was, constantly in flux, constantly evolving and emerging as it became part of America and the pageant of our heritage.

CHAPTER 1

THE GUSTING WIND BLOWING OUT OF THE BLACK NIGHT whipped the tail of the horseman's mount, almost staggering the animal with each icy blast. Theodor Belk sat hunched on the horse, his body giving slightly to the wind as he stared longingly at the small town that lay below the rocky ridge. Yellow light from the windows reflected on the cold, white drifts of snow.

Another gust jerked impatiently at the man's coat and fluttered the brim of his snow-encrusted hat. The horse blew softly and shifted his back to the wind and the stinging sleet.

"Ho, shuh. Easy boy," Theo coaxed to the frosty ear that swung his direction. The sorrel vented a sigh as if in reply and sniffed futilely for the warm stable he knew lay below.

Theo Belk was tired. He was well bundled in a worn army greatcoat. His soogan provided protection from the ever-curious wind and snow that worried the loose wraps of his clothing. Ice rimmed the bandana that pulled the brim of the battered felt hat down over his ears.

"There she is boy. Down there in that house with the pretty red shutters. She married a no-account storekeeper. That's what they told us over to Radersburg." He emphasized the last with a stream of brown tobacco juice that stained the crusted snow.

"Said she wanted to marry a man that would stay at home. Said she couldn't marry a man who had shot someone. Wanted a name in the community, and a family, and . . . Ah, hell!

"Let's make tracks, horse." Theo flicked the reins and prodded the sorrel into the wind and blowing snow, away from the beckoning lights of the town below. His body felt empty, while his emotions churned. He felt the desire to go down there and shoot that damn storekeeper but he knew the townsfolk would hang him.

The thought of how warm and soft her body had been crept in around the edges of his consciousness. He remembered the feeling evoked by her delicate hands and the soft look of her eyes.

It had been the first time in his life that he had allowed himself to get close to another human being. Prior to Liz, Theo had never known there was a deep emptiness in the tough shell of his body. Now she was gone and Theo felt the void—deep, lonely, and bottomless. He had been vulnerable and it scared him.

Snorting at his thoughts he rationalized, "Yep, she done got herself a name now and a nice tame store-keeper to boot. Not half-bad for a line girl from Sylvia's Place." A grim smile played crookedly about his lips and cracked the ice that rimmed his mustache and beard.

The sorrel picked its way carefully down the deeply drifted slope, feeling for purchase among the dark shapes of rock that thrust through the dimly lit snow. Finding better footing in the drainage, the sorrel stepped out, making better time and glad to be moving in the biting wind. The clouds were breaking to the west and soon a thousand stars watched them pass through the cold empty night. They entered the breaks of the river and ghosted between the shapes of cottonwoods that thrust black branches to the dark sky.

Theo pulled up and sniffed the wind, watching the sorrel's reactions. The red horse had better senses than he and any warning would be relayed by the animal first. Seeing no sign of worry on the sorrel's part, Theo nudged the mount into his camp.

The small fire he had left hours ago was down to a deep bed of coals that shimmered in red waves with the shifting wind. Two packhorses whinnied their greetings as the man swung coldly from the saddle and cared for his horse with stiff fingers. Theo blanketed the animal and made sure of the picket pin before throwing a few more branches onto the dying fire.

"I guess I'm a fool for going up there," he muttered. "You'd think even a damned idiot would learn after a while."

Theo batted snow from his hat and coat before stooping to brush it from his bedroll. He placed the bedroll feet first toward the fire and, pulling off his icy soogan, crawled between the blankets.

"Reckon there's times a warm house and a lard eatin' job wouldn't be half-bad," he growled. "Women! Hell's full of women!" His eyes grew heavy as his body warmed in the blankets.

The next morning he started south. By afternoon he'd picked up the rutted trace of the Bozeman Trail. Leaving the Yellowstone, it skirted the defiant slopes of the Pryor Mountains and the Big Horns. The days were cold, stark, and clear, marred only by the incessant wind. Then the sky clouded and the snow fell in fine flakes while the wind rushed wraiths of snow across the frozen drifts. Four days after his departure from the Yellowstone, the sun came out and the wind ceased. That night, cloud cover gone, the temperature dropped.

The only excitement on the long trip came in the form of a sleeping Sioux village nestled in the breaks of the Tongue River. The man slowly wended his way through the foothills, giving the conical lodges a wide berth. The red brethren were still angry about the white man's roads and forts.

Working his way south, Theo stopped at Piney Creek and stared thoughtfully at the few charred timbers that protruded like blackened limbs above the crusted snow. Here lay the gutted remains of Fort Phil Kearny. The Sioux, after driving the hated white army from their lands, had set fire to the structure. The Bloody Bozeman had been closed at an awful expense of red and white lives.

"Carrington was a fool," he mused aloud. "Damn stupid to put a fort here in the first place, and damn stupid to break the treaty in the second."

The sorrel swiveled an ear to listen. Theo spoke periodically to the horse. They had traveled together for years, covering the empty, windswept steppes of what would become Montana, Wyoming, Idaho, and Colorado—sole companions in the quiet land.

"The army taught them how to march in straight lines," Theo continued. "Taught them how to fill out forms, build buildings, dig ditches. Taught them how to fight, too. Taught them how to fight armies of their own people. But they never taught them damn martinets how to live with the wind, the snow, the rain, and the heat. They sure never taught them how to fight the Sioux. Book soldiers!"

Working his jaws under his frozen beard, he squinted, looking around at the high, rolling grass- and sage-covered ridges blanketed in the white mantle of winter. The Big Horns rose to the west, stolid, silent guardians of the lonely graves of fallen soldiers.

From the time John Jacobs and John Bozeman first staked the trail in 1863 until Red Cloud drove the army away in 1868, war had been the constant companion of the Bozeman traveler. The land had been granted to the Sioux in the Treaty of 1851. Until gold was found in Montana, no one had a need to cross these last barren hunting grounds.

The wind picked up as Theo headed the sorrel and his pack animals south down the drifted trail. The sorrel took the lead, the packhorses following, the first led by a strap, the next tail hitched.

The second day after leaving Phil Kearny, the slopes of the Pumpkin Buttes rose in the east above the gently rolling grasslands. Theo scowled at the sandstone-capped prominences, aware that Sioux scouts haunted the excellent points of vantage.

Crossing ice-choked Crazy Woman Creek, Theo made camp in the breaks. The low sagebrush fire provided little comfort for the weary man. While the wind whimpered, the horses pawed the crusted snow in search of last year's grasses.

Morning brought low clouds and wisps of snow. Theo growled as he threw the frost-encrusted saddle onto the sorrel. He fumbled with the cinch with frozen fingers. The air warmed and the snow began falling in fluffy white flakes. Taking to the trail, he led the horses down the frozen Bozeman.

Theo was a tall man, wide through the shoulders. His hair was black and hung thickly from his head, falling over the collar of his coat. His beard was long now, unkempt from the lack of attention necessitated by winter. His eyes were blue and cold—cold as the land he surveyed. Framed by deeply etched crow's-feet, his face was lined to belie his age. The weathered skin was blackened from the bite of sun and wind and from squinting out over glaring deserts and snow-fields.

As the morning progressed, the trail grew dim from the accumulating snow. The horses began to labor as the ceaseless wind sculptured drifts. Theo hunched in the saddle, twisting his head to maintain some protection for his face in the lee of his hat.

He crossed Ninemile Creek and wound up the breaks, following the trail more by feel than from the vanished visual evidence. By late afternoon they reached the crossing of the Powder River. Theo pulled the sorrel off the trail to flounder up to the burned buildings that marked the wind-blasted site of what had been Fort Reno. Burned rubble looked down from the steep bluff to the river.

This post, too, had been abandoned by the military. Originally called Camp Conner, it had been rebuilt and renamed by Colonel Carrington as a post to protect the Bozeman road. While the fort had not received the beating Fort Phil Kearny had, life had been bloody here, too.

Red Cloud had seen the white man coming, building his road through the last pristine hunting ground of the Sioux Nation. He had been angered by the perfidy of the devious whites who had broken their word and regarded the Treaty of Fort Laramie as so much paper—the words, those of old women.

They had built their road and called in the weak Sioux beggars that cadged handouts from the soldiers along the Medicine Road or Oregon Trail. They made a new treaty with the wreckage of Sioux manhood and called it binding on all the great chiefs and their warriors.

That had been in 1866. By 1868, Red Cloud, Sitting Bull, and Crazy Horse had enforced the treaty of 1851 and the fight over the Bozeman road was over.

A cocky captain named Fetterman had said with pride that with eighty soldiers he could ride through the middle of the Sioux Nation. He finally got his chance; he made all of seven miles.

Men froze in the snow. They died of thirst in the hot sun. They died of dysentery from the water. They died of Sioux bullets and arrows. But beyond the wailings in Sioux villages, beyond the words the chaplain called out over mutilated bodies in mass graves, the government found that war on the Bozeman cost too much money for the depleted treasury to bear. The Bozeman road was closed. Peace with the Sioux and Cheyenne was made; the whites left.

Theo shook his head at the thought and looked over the few standing timbers, blackened by Cheyenne fires as Phil Kearny had been. Then with cold eating through his clothes, he stepped out of the saddle. Ice and snow cracked from his soogan as his numb feet hit the ground.

Stamping, Theo kicked his way to a looted dugout and entered. In the dim light he could see dry wood stacked in a corner. Slapping circulation into his stiff hands, he put together a small fire and warmed his fingers before forcing himself to take care of the horses. Rubbing them down as best he could, he hauled his packs into the shelter and prepared a stew of pemmican and jerky. Satisfied with a warm supper, he rolled out his blankets, checked the horses one last time, and crawled in, falling into an immediate deep sleep.

With sleep came terror. It was the same haunting dream. He saw again—as countless times before—the shining waters of the Blacks Fork River. The Uinta Mountains rose cool, blue-green, and inviting to the south while the gray-and-white-banded spires of the Church Buttes shot up above the terraces of the river. The sky was crystal blue with occasional white clouds.

He was a boy of eight. While he played, his father was busy rearranging the wagon to make the crossing of the ford easier.

Theo let himself pretend to stalk some wily Indian through the low dunes capped with prickly greasewood. He carried a stick that served his young imagination as a rifle. A cottontail rabbit shied and ran for its hole—Theo in hot pursuit.

The rabbit made its burrow and Theo, with the magic little boys invest in their toys, turned the rifle into a shovel and began to dig the cottontail out for supper. The sand made digging easy and before long he had scooped out the hole to the point where he could squirm in to scrape out the wet, cool sand. It was then that he heard the staccato of shots.

A final shot was fired—then there was silence. In panic, he wiggled out of the hole and ran blindly for his parents. His mind pictured howling, screaming Indians besieging the wagon. He stumbled and fell, sliding on the deflated, cobble-covered hardpan between the dunes. His nose was bleeding and he was crying. Rushing up the last dune, he stopped in terror.

The wagon stood there, the horses snorting and stamping in their traces. The body of his father lay face down in the soft white dust of the trail. His old blue shirt was stained crimson in the bright, morning sun.

A big man jumped from the back of the wagon, dragging Theo's mother with him. She struggled to her feet, crying, and the man slapped her down again. Cowed, she whimpered on the ground. Three other men walked from behind the wagon and jeered. The men stood and laughed at her before turning back to their looting. All, that is, except for the big man who stood grinning at Theo's mother, leering. She pleaded, her voice panicky with fear.

He laughed and reached down, grabbing the loose fabric of her dress. Cotton ripped loudly. Theo heard his mother scream. Then she screamed again as the big man lowered himself onto her.

As Theo watched he whined lowly to himself, unable to accept the horrid thing he saw, comprehending but refusing to understand. His security was being destroyed. His father was dead and his mother was being forced. Theo was old enough to know rape.

"Louis," one of the men called as he jumped from the back of the wagon. "*Sacré*, Louis Gasceaux. Women, zey be zee death of you yet, non? Hurry, someone may come! Let us go quickly!" The rest of the men were removing sacks of goods from the wagon and unhitching the team. Louis stood, buttoning his pants.

"The hell with you, Sabot," Louis cursed. "She's almost done in anyway. Still, she has now known true pleasure. Louis Gasceaux is good, non, cheri?"

Theo's mother whimpered while Louis took three steps toward his companions then absently pulled a pistol, turned, and almost as an afterthought, blew the woman's jaw off.

The boy lay on the low dune, frozen with terror. His sobbing breath was choked in his throat. Spasms of fear began jerking his limbs. He felt the warm rush as his bladder let go, fouling his legs and pants.

The men walked their horses to the wagon and began strapping the loot onto packsaddles. Sabot had turned from this chore and walked to Theo's father. He casually stripped the body and—with his knife—mutilated it beyond recognition. Theo watched muttering incoherently to himself, his teeth clattering fear while tears streaked his dirty face.

Sabot then moved to his mother. She shuddered and cried as the knife slid around the top of her skull. Sabot pulled the scalp loose and cooed as he stroked the bright, blond hair. He laughed and kicked her hard in the side. She gurgled through her bloody, frothing, broken mouth, clutching spasmodically at the dusty ground. Then Sabot used the knife again on her still living flesh, slicing deftly until the whimpers ceased and the blood ceased to spurt from the dismembered limbs.

Theo willed his muscles to work and crawled away from the hideous shrieks rending the still, clear air. Below the dune crest he got hesitantly to his feet, mumbling with terror. He sprinted back the way he had come. Though by chance, he passed the rabbit hole he had dug at so earnestly. Gasping in shock, he pulled himself into the hole, mindless of the stinging of the greasewood, and tugged one of the bushes down on top of himself. In the darkness, he shivered and vomited from horror.

With a start, Theo Belk awoke in the dark shelter of a frozen dugout. Sweat was pouring down the sides of his face. He almost cried as he pulled and jerked the blankets away from his body before stumbling out into the snow.

Shaking, he drew in deep breaths of the cold air. The sorrel stood, back to the wind, watching him with wide eyes and pricked ears. The horse whickered softly and took a step toward him before stopping, unsure. Theo waded through the drifts to the sorrel and with a cry buried his head in the animal's neck.

The next morning the sun was shining over a rolling sea of blazing white. Theo ate the last of his pemmican and jerky. He led the horses to the wide floodplain of the Powder River and kicked aside the snow so the animals could feed on the rich bottom grass. Stamping his feet to keep warm, he watched the change in colors as the sun shimmered pink on the Pumpkin Buttes to the east.

Tightening the cinches, he swung into the saddle and checked his rifle. The action on the worn Springfield was crusted with frost. Theo broke it open and extracted the cartridge. Inspection showed no ice in the chamber or bore. He reinserted the brass and worked the hammer and trigger. If game showed, Theo would eat. Reining the horse, he proceeded south, following the whiter patch of snow that indicated the trail.

He was moody, as always, after the dream. It

seemed so clear and vivid, just as it had happened that day so long ago. Theo felt empty, drained. No matter how hard he tried to forget, no matter how he tried to push the memories of that horrible day into the back of his mind, the dark hours would come to haunt him when he was deep in sleep and defenseless against the ghosts. The horror lived in him, eating away at the edges of his consciousness, frustrating his desire for peace, and devouring his nerves. The memory drove him now as it always had, to beat death as he had done that day at the Blacks Fork.

It drove him to seek and to hunt. From that horrifying day, his life had been geared to one goal: find and kill Louis Gasceaux! He had hunted for years and over thousands of miles. Now, the trail had gone cold in Montana. The only thing that had ever warmed his lonely life had turned cold in Montana, too. Liz had left him for another man. He had been betrayed by the love he had wasted, betrayed by time lost in his hunt for Louis Gasceaux.

There had been other periods of slight warmth. They had been ephemeral and somehow hollow. Ever since that day on the Blacks Fork, Theo Belk had been alone, haunted, at war with the world that was his reality and the hell that was his memory.

Liz. The name left a bittersweet feeling in Theo's breast. Theo had been hot on Gasceaux's trail when he met her. In Liz's arms he had forgotten for a while. The dream had not come.

"It was a trick the demons played on me." His voice was a gruff snort as the sorrel swiveled an ear his direction. It was a lesson he had not learned before. Now, no matter what sort of temptation would be offered in the future, he would not stray from his course. He could track Gasceaux down only by perseverance, dedication, and strength.

Liz had worked at Sylvia's, but that was of little concern to Theo Belk. Most women in the rugged little frontier communities were line girls. He had fallen in love. For the first time in his life it appeared that someone cared for him. He had begun to trust her. It shook him a little; trust had been a mistake.

She was blond, tall, and handsomely built. Some of her mannerisms reminded him of his mother. He felt a pang in his chest as he remembered running his fingers through the wealth of golden hair that cascaded from her head. He remembered the soft talk as they lay in bed, spent from their lovemaking.

"And I killed that bastard who took you away from me!" he growled. Toddy Blake had been dapper, intelligent, and witty. He had been smooth, bringing Liz flowers and small gifts. Theo had watched her attentions begin to shift. Then one night he had the dream again.

The next day, Toddy Blake bled his life away on Sylvia's packed-dirt floor. Theo left on the run to avoid a vigilante hangman's noose but he remembered the fear, revulsion, and pain in Liz's eyes. Toddy Blake had been lowered into the frozen, rocky ground, and she'd married the storekeeper while Theo ran for the Bitteroots.

"That's where we met that old Blackfoot, horse," Theo whispered, his eyes darting around the bleak land. "Said ol' Louis lamed 'im with a bullet. Said it whar Louis who stole his hosses an' left him for dead. Said his medicine saw it and come an' told him while he was a waitin' ta die." He repeated it over and over like Shasty, his Ute foster mother, had taught him, making it truer in his mind.

"That ol' Injun had med'cine," Theo whispered.

"He saw the demons a followin' me. Don't ne'er mistrust a man's medicine. He was gimp'd with rheumatism, horse. His eyes was blinded with them white spots, but he seen true. His medicine tol' him Louis done it an' headed south!" He nodded soberly.

And Theo followed, trusting in the word of the Blackfoot and to the prompting of the devils that lived in his mind. Fort Fetterman lay to the south, and beyond that Fort Laramie—the only place a man with Gasceaux's wants and desires could head in this cold empty land. At Fort Laramie, Gasceaux would find warmth and companionship, and maybe he would find Theo Belk, too.

Louis Gasceaux waved a mittened hand at the figure trudging his way through the drifted snow. The man's tired steps indicated he'd walked a long way, a pair of well-oiled saddlebags swinging on his shoulders. He wore an army coat and the chevrons of sergeant stood out on the sleeves.

"Sergeant Huffman! You made it, my friend," Louis called, his grin cracking his white-frosted beard.

"Whew!" Huffman puffed a long, frozen breath. "I should have stole a horse." He walked up to Louis and slapped his hands together to restore circulation. He looked back down the frozen bank of the North Platte, eyes nervous.

"It might have been noticed." Louis reached for the saddlebags and worried the buckles open. "It's all here?" He raised a black, bushy eyebrow as he studied the contents.

"Seven thousand," Huffman said with a happy smile. "You were right about how easy it would be. That's payroll for a lot of men. We'd better get a move on."

"Relax, my friend." Louis laughed in his deep baritone. "They will not miss it. I have learned a lot in my life, sergeant. I jumped ship in Galveston and worked the waterfront. When that got too hot, I moved to the mainland. I learned to hate Texans. They had no money, only women, kids, pigs, and corn." Louis laughed again. "Texans do not like their women molested."

Huffman tilted his head, appraising Louis with new eyes. "What happened?"

"They chased me into the swamps." Louis grimaced. "Texans shoot very well and I did not like running shits, cottonmouths, and alligators, but I made it to New Orleans alive."

Louis smiled at the memories. It had been a good life, he'd taken up his old occupation of garroting drunks. "I did well there."

"So why'd you leave?" Huffman asked, skeptical.

"I ran into another Texan!" Louis snorted. "I had to run with a ball in my back! I stowed aboard a riverboat and had to work it upriver." He shrugged. "I remembered then how much I hated work. Saint Louis was where I got off." He and Huffman had begun to walk upstream, past a long reach of bare willows.

"So how did you get to the West, Louis?" Huffman asked, trying to keep from shivering in the cold, winter air. Night was falling with the temperature.

"Saint Louis was right for me. There were many Americans leaving for Oregon. Many were wealthy." He looked at Huffman and smiled wickedly. "Many had beautiful wives. I went with them."

"I don't understand." Huffman seemed suddenly uneasy after the mention of the women.

Louis seemed to ignore him. "There was a storekeeper I traveled with at first. It didn't take much to sow the seeds of discord in his wagon train. Then, at Fort Laramie, that very post we have just fled, I met Sabot, an old trapper. Together we went west with the wagon. He taught me many things."

Louis waved an arm ahead of them. "Out there is an open, empty land. Many things can happen out there. Wagons are lost. There are many Indians. The storekeeper died. His money disappeared. His wife got to know my pleasure before she, too, passed from this world."

Huffman had stopped dead in his tracks, his face shocked. "You killed them? After traveling all that way with them you murdered the man and raped his woman?"

Louis acted shocked. "But of course! Where is the difference between that and what you have just done to your comrades in arms? You have taken their back pay!"

"Yep," Huffman said hesitantly. "Reckon we're partners from here on out."

"Ah, but I agree," Louis's voice soothed. "But what is a woman here and there? Does it make a difference, when they will die anyway?"

"Guess not," Huffman muttered. "How long you rob wagons?"

"Five years. Long enough to amass enough money to go back east and buy a plantation." Louis watched his frosted breath rise in the evening breeze, the snowfields were turning blue with the night.

"Have any regrets?" Huffman asked, looking sideways at Louis.

"Two." He barked a short laugh. "The last wagon bothered me. It was owned by a man named Belk. His wife was very beautiful." He smiled as he remembered her golden hair and how she had been tight with fear as he entered her. "I left a loose end; I did not find the child."

"Child?" Huffman asked, darting him a look.

Louis tried to shrug it off. "Many things happened to the little brats on the trail. They are bit by rattlesnakes. They die of coughs. Some drown. Others fall off and the wheels roll over them. Who knows? He was not with the wagon."

"And the other regret?" Huffman asked, his face pinched from thought.

"The war," Louis said easily. "I once owned a magnificent plantation in the Carolinas. Mine was a life of leisure. Sherman burned everything to the ground. Now I am here to rebuild. I shall have a life like that again." Louis worked his left hand into the big pocket of his buffalo coat.

Huffman came to a decision. "I guess we'll do all right, Louis. I ain't a saint either."

"Very good, partner." Louis smiled. "The horses are up ahead. Let's shake on it one more time. For the future, eh, my friend?" He reached out his right hand.

Huffman grinned happily. "For the future!"

Louis grabbed the hand and shook as his left snaked out. The Smith & Wesson's roar was muffled against the coat. Huffman's body jerked under the impact; his eyes widened in his surprised face.

"Why?" Huffman whispered in disbelief as he pitched forward. Louis kicked away the hand that pawed for a holstered pistol.

"Seven thousand dollars split in half is thirty-five hundred." Louis pulled a knife from his belt. "Your life is worth considerably less to me. The army will be looking for you, sergeant. They will not look for me."

Dropping to one knee, Louis slit the man's throat.

He heard the soft footfalls of horses and looked up to see Sabot leading the animals up. The old trapper spit into the snow before he carved Huffman's scalp loose.

"You were veree quiet, mon ami." Sabot grinned in the darkness, spitting again.

Louis nodded with satisfaction. Old skills died hard. He pulled himself onto his horse and tied the saddlebags in place. The army owed him at least that much.

Dolly Moore stepped over an ice-covered puddle, thankful that the streets of Denver were frozen hard. When warm, the foul mud—reeking of urine, waste, decay, and manure—squished through the holes in her worn boots. She pulled her shawl tightly about her, shivering as her frosty breath rose around the tips of her bright red-blond hair where it stuck out from her bonnet.

Mr. Adams had been nice—even if he didn't like dealing with a woman! He'd taken a loss for her though, knowing the worth of his wagon, unable to make a profit on a pretty young woman in need. She'd seen it in his eyes, but she was desperate. Another month, and Denver would kill her father. That or she'd have to go to work and that, too, would literally kill the old man. It would be but one more reflection on Henry Moore and his ineptness in this new land.

Wagons were plentiful in Denver just then and Adams was shrewd. Dolly smiled proudly. Well, so was she! All those years watching Paw care for the gear had paid off. She'd looked the wagon over with a critical eye to see the bed was solid, the frame uncracked and sturdy, the axles strong and sound as were the true wheels. The tongue didn't look like it would take much more and the traces were worn, but with limited finances a woman couldn't have everything.

"And Adams gave in in the end," she whispered to herself, feeling her stomach fall. "Damn, Paw. It's the only way!"

They had to get out of Denver—out of Colorado—and away to the East where the climate and the work and the men ceased to take such a toll on her aging father.

"Oh, Paw!" she whispered under breath, fearing the meeting to come. Why had he let himself get suckered into that tarnal poker game? He'd been picked clean and fleeced! These weren't men! They were wolves, animals, predators like the coyotes they'd seen crossing the plains.

Predators that preyed on everything! She dropped her eyes as a tall man smiled and tipped his hat. Women were rare in Denver. Oh, Market Street was full of cribs and bordellos, but real women were few and far between. She stopped to look at herself in the window of a clothing store. The imperfect reflection showed a tall redheaded woman with a full figure. Her eyes were serious, her nose delicate and straight. Her face was well formed, capable of gracing the cover of *Godey's.* Only now there was a haunted worry there. What if Paw died? Well, there was marriage or some labor or . . . She swallowed and forced herself on again, knowing the wagon purchase was going to hurt her father even more. He'd see it as yet another of his failures.

She stepped up on the rickety boardwalk and found their rooming house, such as it was, hesitating as she stared up the well-worn steps that led to their tiny room. Well, no longer would they pay such atrocious rent! Biting her lip, she started up, feeling the stairs shaking under her feet.

The rattly doorknob was like ice in her fingers, and the hallway only a little warmer. She kept away from the rough-cut lumber that would snag and snare even the worst of her clothes and drew a deep breath at their door. With dread, she entered.

"Hello, Paw!" she called, looking nervously to the dim back of the small room and feeling the chill in the unheated air. The lumber was unevenly cut, the boards blackened with soot from the small smoky stove that refused to draw well. A crumbling of gray ashes had accumulated around the stove legs, barely visible in the dim light. The ash box needed to be emptied, too.

"Where you been?" Henry Moore asked, looking up from the magazine he was reading. His eyes had that uncharacteristic dullness she'd become so used to. His gray-white hair hung collar length, untrimmed now despite her attempts. His beard bristled long and white and hid the tightness she knew had grown about his lips. The slump in his posture had only become pronounced since they had come to Colorado last fall. In that time, Henry Moore had lost most everything down to his respect. Now that, too, was ebbing like their finances.

His lanky body was stretched on the fragile cot he maintained while she had the bed behind the blanket divider in the small room.

"I swear, Paw!" she scolded. "You'll freeze to death in here!" She turned to stoke up the stove and saw the empty wood box.

He hesitated and she could see the anguish as he bit his lip, looking at her sideways, chewing his gray mustache. His face was thinner now, the lines deeper. Once again, she noted that Henry Moore looked old and her heart went out to him. "Well, run down and get some . . ." Her voice faded away and she cocked her head. "What's that?"

Henry's eyes shifted away from her face, looking at the clapboard wall. "It's a rifle, girl."

She stifled the cry. Rifle? Seeing the upset in his face she swallowed her protest and asked, "Well, why didn't you get some wood for the stove?" Rifle? What for? Confusion began to lead to anger.

"Well, now, girl, don't you go a gittin' all het up, now, hear?" Henry shook his head, sitting up and gesturing with the magazine in his gnarled old hand. "Ya see, I read me this article in the *Harper's* magazine! Did you know that—"

"Paw!" She turned to face him, hands twisting nervously. "I bought a wagon, Paw. Used fifty dollars I kept back a couple of weeks ago when you got fired from that mine up in Central City." She drew a deep breath, seeing the way his mouth turned down at the corners and the lines on his forehead went deeper.

She plunged ahead. "Colorado's killin' you, Paw! When them gamblers fleeced you of all but that last bit of money, I made up my mind! Now, you always said I was headstrong, but—"

His nod was so slight she almost missed it. "Good!"

Her mouth went open. That was the last thing she'd thought he would say! Her voice was drowned by her confusion. "Good? Why I . . . I mean I thought you'd be . . . Oh, Paw, I love you! I just want to get you away from this awful place to somewhere where you can use your skills! I want to get us to someplace where men don't kill each other all the time. I want us to go back home or maybe to Missouri or Iowa where you can put a freight outfit together again. I—"

He smiled, his eyes weary. "I know, girl." His eyes shone and he sniffed slightly. "You know, you look more and more like your Maw everyday, bless her soul."

She bit her lip. "Then you're not mad at me?"

He laughed softly, chiding, "Shouldn't hide money, Dolly. Money is a man's bizness. Women shouldn't be—"

She let a smile dimple her cheeks. "I don't play poker, Paw!" She shook her head and shivered, changing the subject at the hurt look on his face. "What's the rifle for?"

His eyes brightened again. "Your future, girl! That's why I'm glad you bought the wagon. You see, I been reading! There's a fortune to be made. Buffalo hides, girl! Yes sirree! Three dollars and fifty cents a hide! So I bought this here rifle and a hunert rounds of .44 bullets. One shot a buffalo and that's a sizable return on the outlay! Why, we'll be rolling in greenbacks afore fall!"

"How much, Paw?" she asked, settling down on the little stool. Her heart sank. They were out of wood; she'd spent the last dime on the wagon and team. They had to pray she and her father could keep the harness spliced until they were east again.

"Fifteen dollars and thirty-five cents!" Henry smiled. "I tell you girl, it was a steal! This here's a Henry lever action! Get me in the middle of a bunch of buffalo and—"

"What are we gonna do to stay warm and eat in the meantime?" she asked, feeling a sudden tightness about her heart. Denver was an expensive place to live!

He had stopped, his mouth still partway open. "Oh,

something will come along, girl. Trust your Paw, now!" He gave her the warm smile that had always reassured her as a young girl. Now it was a hollow mockery.

"Oh, Paw," she sighed, feeling the cold creeping in around her dress. The dim room seemed even darker. As she looked, she could see his expression falling again and she felt like crying. His eyes lowered and he worked his mouth, knowing he'd failed her again.

"I love you, Paw," she whispered walking over to him, putting her arms around his thin shoulders, and feeling him tremble as he fought to still the tears of frustration.

"I'm trying, Dolly girl. I'm trying so hard!" His voice was heavy, shaky as he fought for control. "It's just that nothing seems to go right for an old man no more!"

"I know, Paw. We'll make out. We always do!" God, how she wished she could believe that!

CHAPTER 2

FROM WHERE THEO SAT HIS SORREL, HE COULD SEE THE outline of Fort Fetterman on the high bluff south of the North Platte River.

"You damned fool," he muttered to himself as he stood in the stirrups and stretched his tired back and stiff legs. "You never thought that after the army abandoned the forts, they might not have any use for a full-time ferry, now did you?"

Theo stared glumly at the partially frozen river. Rivulets of dark water showed through holes in the ice. He could not trust the rotten ice to hold his weight, let alone the sorrel and the packhorses.

With a heavy sigh he turned his animals to the east, following the old Child's route of the trail. It was that or make the long trip upriver to Platte Bridge, a hundred miles out of his way. Travel along the north bank was no more difficult than on the Oregon Trail, but there would be no warm meals except those he could shoot and cook.

Two days later, at dusk, Theo rode into Fort Laramie. The ride had been long and tiring. While the snow had held off for the last couple of days, the wind had not let up for a second and he rode in a perpetual ground blizzard that dusted him in powdery snow, which found every gap in his clothing. Worse, one of the packhorses had split a hoof and was limping badly and he had found a body.

Pulling up at the livery, Theo left his animals in the care of the hostler. He batted the crusted ice from his coat and hat, feeling weary to the bone. His feet were numb from cold and his breath had frozen in his beard. Wearily he clumped his way into the headquarters building. As he opened the door a blast of warm air massaged his frozen face.

"Can I help you, sir?" a young corporal asked formally. The man was seated at a battered hardwood desk where he had been squinting at reports in the dim light.

"Are you missing a soldier? A sergeant?" Theo asked, awed by the sudden warmth.

The man became wary. "We are. Do you know where he is now?"

"I should smile, I do," Theo granted. "An' he ain't a going nowhere either." Theo grimaced as his face began to thaw and a tingling sensation burned his cheeks. "He's laying on the north bank, about three miles up from the bridge."

"Sergeant Huffman is dead I take it?" The man was cool and appraising in his inspection of Theo.

"I reckon," Theo agreed with a grin. "Cause he's frozen solid. He was scalped while the body was warm and it wasn't any Indian who did it, either. He have any enemies here who might want him out of the way?"

The corporal's eyes had narrowed. "Please wait right here, sir. Colonel Dye will want a few words with you." The man jumped out of his seat and left at a run. Theo backed up to the stove.

When the corporal returned he had a gray-haired man in tow. "I'm Colonel Dye," the elder man announced. "What do you know of Sergeant Huffman? I understand you found his body?" There was the tone of command in his words.

"Just what I told the corporal here." Theo paused, noting the intense scrutiny he received. "I passed his body on the way in. I couldn't bring him in. One of my packhorses has a split hoof and I'm about done in myself."

"I see." The colonel frowned as if he really didn't. "Who are you?"

"Theodor Belk, colonel. I'm headed south as soon as I can get recuperated and fix what's broke in my outfit."

"Are you the Belk involved in that shooting in Montana?" the colonel asked, noting with annoyance the water dripping from Theo's beard to the floor.

"Yes, sir, that's me. It was a fair shooting, colonel. He had a gun out and I figgered he'd use it." Theo gave the colonel a hard, measuring glance. He felt his legs tingle as they started to warm up. Theo moved closer to the glowing stove and stamped his feet, adding to the puddle of water that spread under him.

The colonel seemed to dismiss the shooting incident. "You say Huffman was scalped by Indians?"

"No, sir, not by Indians," Theo returned thoughtfully. "I never seen an Indian job done this way. It's messy like the man didn't know what he was doing and didn't know how to pull the scalp loose. He carved it off."

Colonel Dye turned to the corporal. "Send a detail out to retrieve the body. Have the surgeon take a look at it and bring me his report. I also want the scout to look over the trail." The corporal left again at a run.

Then he turned to Theo. "What did you find near his body? Any equipment, a saddlebag perhaps?"

"Nothing, colonel, just some tobacco stains in the snow. Not only that, but there wasn't anything there before. The snow was drifted some, but there were old tracks and they were disturbed since the coyotes have been at him."

"I see," Dye said thoughtfully, as if he did this time. "Mr. Belk, I'll take your word on the Montana shooting. I want no trouble here. Do you understand? Further, there is more to the death of Sergeant Huffman than you appear to know at this time. You will remain on this post until the surgeon has investigated. I will send word when you are free to go."

"I understand, sir. I'll be around if you need me." Theo extended his hands to the stove, hating the feeling of returning circulation.

"I guess we were wrong about Huffman," Colonel Dye growled as he turned for his office. "Oh, Mr. Belk, help yourself to the coffee." The door closed behind him.

Theo gratefully poured himself a cup and frowned as he thought about the dead man and the apparent interest the colonel had shown in him. What could the sergeant have been involved in?

The coffee was delightful. It was a delicacy he had

not enjoyed in some time. A different corporal entered and continued going through the reports on the desk, pointedly ignoring Theo.

After having warmed up for the first time in months, Theo strolled over to Bullock and Ward's mercantile. The lights were warm and yellow through the windows of Old Bedlam, the officers' quarters. He made it through the door as the clerk was about to lock up for the night. Quickly, he rattled off a list of things he needed, sending the clerk scurrying through the aisles. While the man piled wares on the counter, Theo noticed a rack of new Sharps rifles. He picked one up and ran his hands down the smooth lines of the weapon. Dropping the block he eyeballed the polished barrel. From his experience, it looked good.

"Nice gun, isn't it?" The clerk startled him.

"Sure enough. I had one during the war. Shot good, too. How much is this thing worth?" Theo added absently, absorbed in the feel of the rifle.

"Twenty dollars," the clerk replied offhandedly.

"Twenty dollars!" Theo cried. "How about I make a trade?"

"What have you got to trade? I'll warn you now that muzzle guns don't sell so good anymore," the clerk told him.

"I'll trade an Allen-conversion Springfield. She's 50-70 rimfire. The gun is a little nicked up but she shoots straight." Theo worked the action of the Sharps.

"Make it fifteen dollars and the Springfield and you have a deal," the clerk decided. "That's a brand spankin' new Model 69 Sporter you have there."

Theo threw the clerk a sour look and let his hands caress the wood lovingly. He shouldered the rifle and sighted across the room. "Says .45 caliber on the barrel. Forty-five what?"

"That will be the new 45-70 center fire. Pretty good cartridge. There's talk the army will be adopting it, so ammunition will be plentiful."

"Just a minute." Theo hated to put the gun down as he went to his pack outside the door and retrieved a small bundle wrapped in tanned buckskin. Theo laid the bundle on the counter and slowly unwound the leather. The clerk peered close to see. Eight giant claws lay exposed on the counter.

"Holy Moses!" the clerk interjected. "I'd hate to see the bear you got those off of."

"He was a mean old coot," Theo assented. "Caught him up in the Bitteroots in Montana. Never seen a bear that big before. Most claws don't run anything close to this size. He damn near got me, but I got him first. Took the last shot in that old Walker pistol before he went down."

"You want to trade them claws, too?" The clerk was interested.

"Yep, I'll swap the Springfield, the claws and six dollars for the Sharps. Some of those emigrators come through next summer and they'll give ten dollars for them claws, not to say what some Indian might come up with to get claws that big," Theo challenged.

"Done!" The clerk grinned. "And, I'll even throw in a box of cartridges for you." The clerk swooped up the claws and tested them against the ends of his fingers. "Lordy, what a bear that feller was!"

Theo grinned and worked the action on the Sharps. It was smooth and crisp. He picked up the box of cartridges and opened it. Lined up inside were fifty shiny brass cases.

"I think you'll like that rifle, mister," the clerk added prying his eyes off the claws. "They are using a lot of them down south hunting hides."

"You sold yourself a rifle. If it don't shoot straight, I'll be back in the morning and you'll get it right back," Theo warned. He paid for the rest of his purchases and stared glumly at the fifteen dollars left in his possibles.

A meal and a place to stay cost him another forty-five cents. A hot bath was extra so he skipped it. The bed made him uneasy and he dreamed of Liz.

In the morning he received the message from Colonel Dye that he was free to go. He found he had picked up lice from the bed. Grumbling, he broke a hole in the river ice and stripped for a bath. He was shivering afterward and actually sprinted for the fort to find a cup of coffee. The same clerk manned the store and coffee came free for a valued customer.

After he warmed up and listened to the talk, Theo wandered down to the rifle range to sight in his new gun. It took him a while to figure the elevation, but the gun shot straight and consistent.

Picking a four-hundred-yard target, he worked out the trajectory his old 50-70 shot and was happy to see the new gun shot flatter. When he had satisfied himself, he had only two cartridges left.

The clerk smiled when he entered the store. "How did it shoot?"

"Shoots fine, now I need more ammunition." Theo grimaced as he paid for another fifty rounds. "One thing about that Sharps I had in the war," he muttered, "I could make my own bullets."

"You can with this gun, too. All, that is, but the brass and powder." The clerk was smug. "You have to buy the proper equipment for it and you can reload the brass, unlike that old rimfire."

"How much is the equipment?" Theo inquired

dryly with a sinking feeling in his gut.

"That'll be about eight dollars." The clerk grinned at the expression on Theo's face. "But relax, we don't have the reloading materials in stock right now. Have another cup of coffee."

Theo chuckled his thanks and poured.

That afternoon, he took a close look at the pack-horse's foot. The split was bad and the animal would be going nowhere for a while. Making the best deal he could, he swapped straight across for a swaybacked plug he guessed was about fifteen years old. Finally, he packed his outfit and was ready to leave.

"Where you headed?" the stable hand asked.

"South to Denver, I guess."

"At least you pay your bills," the hand granted. "That French feller what was here a while back sure left me in the lurch. He just lit out in the middle of the night. I never did like him. He smiled too much and didn't have no bottom to him. I figgered he was pretty mean. He left just before the robbery."

"What robbery?" Theo demanded. He had absorbed every word about the Frenchman.

"Didn't you hear? They thought Sergeant Huffman made off with seven thousand dollars until you found his body up the river. Now they don't know who did it."

"This Frenchman, did he say what his name was?" Theo asked softly, his eyes narrowing.

"Said his name was Robideaux, but I got a hunch it ain't." The hostler scuffed the toe of his boot in the manure of the stable. "Seemed to be kind of a cultured fella, but like I say, mean underneath."

Theo nodded. "Did he say which way he was going?"

The hostler looked at him with knowing eyes.

"Uh-huh, he said he was headed north to Montana. Said that he'd never been there afore, but you know he was lyin'. I'll bet he never went thataway."

"Where'd you learn so much about people?" Theo snorted.

"From knowin' horses," the hostler replied with a sly grin. "And from knowing that no man comes from anyplace but up north ridin' a horse shod with Hudson's Bay Company shoes. He was stringing us all about Montana."

Theo rode out that afternoon, making camp along the Cheyenne-to-Fort Laramie road. The next morning he made moderate time. The farther he got from Fort Laramie, the more obstreperous the old black mare became. She shied at harmless sagebrush and refused to pick a path through the brush and willows, her legs locked and her eyes rolled.

"Where the hell have you been all your life?" Theo demanded of the balky mare. "It wasn't Wyoming Territory, that's for damn sure."

After tying his handkerchief over the animal's eyes, better time was made. Three days after leaving the fort, the mare tried to follow a northbound caravan of freighters. In desperation, Theo almost shot the horse. As a final measure he lip hitched her and travel proceeded rapidly, if painfully.

Finally, his horse problems more or less solved, he was allowed time to ponder the murder of the Sergeant Huffman. The devils whispering in the back of his mind told him it was Louis Gasceaux. The scalping was his style. There had been enough snow to tell that the body had been there for days. After the wolves and coyotes had made hash of the tracks, there was little chance to pick up a trail.

Gasceaux liked people. He tended to end up where

there was companionship and better food than trail grub. Cheyenne and Laramie were still small places with little to draw a man besides the railroad. Beyond them lay Denver and the Colorado goldfields. Denver would be wide open for a man like Louis Gasceaux. Gold meant wealthy men, and wealth drew a leech like Gasceaux.

Reaching the bend of Chugwater Creek, Theo made camp in a low overhang of sandstone. The black mare was picketed, hobbled, and side lined. The fire crackled warm in the dry overhang and out of the unremitting wind. Theo watched a jackrabbit brown over the coals. The roof of the shelter was blackened by eons of smoke from campers, Indian and white. The towering cliff rose above him in the dull, evening light.

The rabbit finished to perfection, Theo shuffled the hot meat from the fire and fanned his hands from the heat. He sucked his toasted fingers for a second and, pulling the large bowie from his belt, sliced off one of the hind legs.

Blowing on the meat, he cooled it before sinking his teeth into the juicy feast. The taste reminded him of that long ago night when the Shoshoni band, led by the wise old Chief Washakie, had found him cowering in the sand dunes beside the Blacks Fork.

He'd been shivering from the cold and burning with fever as he darted through the dunes, starving, crying, and whimpering while he babbled incoherently to the newly born voices inside his head. Theo grinned sourly, remembering his prostrating fear. "Never again," he whispered hoarsely, looking up at the white stars.

"They told Washakie to leave me to die," Theo almost cackled. "Told him I was trouble. Then the old chief looked at me and saw the *Buhagant* had reached into my mind and given me power.

"Washakie had still been mad at Pocatello for saying he stole little Nick Wilson from the damn saint Mormons. But Washakie read the sign." Theo nodded soberly to himself. "He knew what Gasceaux had done. He didn't leave me to die. Washakie, he's a great man even if he's got too much of a soft spot for an Injun!"

Theo's face tightened fiercely as he remembered how he had shrieked gibberish and tried to throw hands of dirt at the Shoshoni warriors who'd grabbed him. They'd wrapped him in a blanket and securely tied him so he wouldn't hurt himself. That night, in the lodges of the Shoshoni, Theo had eaten his first food since that terrible day: rabbit, like this.

Now Theo savored the sweet meat and remembered the concern and respect in old Washakie's eyes as he watched the boy wolfishly devour the tender meat. If Washakie ever had a fault, it was that he loved children too much.

"So they took me and gave me to old Jim Bridger," Theo snorted and wiped the grease from his beard with a filthy coat sleeve. "He was half-dead of grief for that daughter of his, Mary Ann was her name. The Palous killed her and them Whitman missionaries on the Waiilatpui."

The Blanket Chief, Old Gabe, mountain man, guide, trapper and half owner in Fort Bridger, teller of tales, Bridger had taken a liking to the boy and through his antics and stories, Theo Belk had returned to the world his whispering mind had caused him to leave. Bridger had liked the lad but found him to be somehow different, always quiet, with something deep inside smoldering. At night Theo cried in terror in the dark and listened to the demons rustling in the back of his mind.

Finally, Bridger sent Theo to stay in the lodge of Fletch and his Ute wife, Shasty. Fletch was a mountain man who had worked in Bridger's brigades. Fletch had proved to be a fair father for the boy even if he didn't set a good Christian example. It wasn't that Fletch didn't have his heart in the right place, it was just that he had been in the mountains since his teens. Often, Fletch and his good friend Skin would leave for weeks to trap and hunt in the mountains.

Shasty would stay at the fort with Theo. That wasn't the woman's real name but it was as close as Fletch could come to the Ute pronunciation. She was kind to Theo and a little awed by the stories the Shoshoni told of his relationship with the spirit world.

He knew that she loved him in her own strange way. He learned Ute proficiently and picked up fluency in Shoshoni, too. Under her teaching he learned how to find roots, herbs, seeds, and berries. He soon knew the best way to snare rabbit and how to knock sage grouse down with a stone.

"Good woman," he said to himself.

Theo cracked a long bone in his teeth and sucked the marrow out. "So long ago," he muttered, using a bone fragment to pick his teeth, his blue eyes seeing back to a skinny kid sitting in a smoke-browned lodge. He was twelve then, still waiting until he could kill the man who had destroyed his life and given him the dreams.

Fletch had sat there, his grizzled gray beard wiggling as he worked his mouth. His battered brow was scarred from a Blackfoot war arrow, his nose twisted from being broken time after time. Finally, the old man spoke. "Louis Gasceaux done pulled his stick, boy. He done took out'n this part o' the country after he kilt yore folks. Sabot's still around, but ye ain't about ta get a shot at that ol' coyote. He's some, that Sabot is. Been in these mountains from the first. He whar hyar afore I come out with Ashley in twenty-three. If'n I git the chance, I'll put a galena pill in 'im m'self."

"Why doesn't anyone talk about it?" Theo demanded.

"Fraid ye'd git kilt," Fletch muttered. "Fraid ol' Sabot'd sneak in some night an' slit yore gullet wide open t' keep yore damn mouth shet. Yore the only one as could finger him."

Fletch continued, "Reckon come daybreak we'll round up old Skin an' go do us some trappin'. Yore larnin' needs some work, boy." After the old man spoke, he knocked the dottle out of his pipe and rolled up in his robes.

The valley of the Green River had been Theo's path to manhood as it led north to the mountains. The Wind River Range rose impetuously to the crystal, blue sky in the east. The ragged gray spires of granite were capped with white crests of snow, while the lower slopes were girdled with a belt of green. The horses' hooves struck the cobble surface of the terrace along the river and Pilot Butte marked their passage north. Then the Wyoming Range lay to the west and soon the Gros Ventre Mountains began to rise in the north.

That summer, Theo learned the wilderness of nature and found it as harsh as the wilderness of his mind. He learned to shoot. He learned tracking, stalking, to kill and butcher. He learned how to make a fire, find water, build shelter, make clothes, and collect food. He learned the value of patience and how to bear hardship and adverse conditions.

Fletch and Skin were among the best. They had graduated summa cum laude from the college of the West and had advanced degrees from the school of hard knocks. Neither institution is acknowledged by the Ivy League but the final examination is severe—passing is survival.

"Now that child jist takes all," Skin muttered one night. They were camped on the banks of the Musselshell River in what would one day be called Montana. Theo was feigning sleep.

"Reckon he's some all right," Fletch agreed. "Wonder who 'is folks was?" He glanced at the sleeping boy.

"Emigrators!" Skin spat.

"Must o' had 'em a head though," Fletch pointed out as he pulled his beard. "They done born'd a right smart child. No lard eater, this un."

"He'll do," Skin said softly as he listened to the sound of the wind. "Hope he don't find Sabot though. Sabot's canny. Wouldn't want any piece of 'im m'self."

"The boy has a devil in 'im," Fletch granted. "Reckon if'n he got around folks very long there'd be hell ta pay." Unconsciously, Fletch blew smoke to the four cardinal directions.

Theo shook himself to be rid of the ghosts and stripped the last of the tender backstrap with his teeth, dropping the well-chewed backbone into the coals. Fletch was many years dead now, killed by his old nemeses—the Blackfeet. Theo tried to make sense of it as the demons murmured among themselves.

Later, after a good bowl of tobacco, he rolled into his blankets, tired, bone weary, but his memories had stirred the demons until they would not let him rest. The dream came to haunt him again. Screaming himself awake, he blinked, wondering why he never dreamed like other people. The only times he dreamed, it was of the terror. Never did he dream of other places, other faces, or feelings. His only dream was of the Blacks Fork and the whispering of the demons.

"Aw, I hate to see you go," Mabe Adams admitted as Dolly made a final check of the wagon. She cataloged the flour and coffee. Not much for the length of the trip ahead of them, she thought. At the same time, the money Paw'd spent on that cussed rifle might fill the larder just enough.

"Here," Adams said, lifting a half-frozen elk hind quarter in to her. "I picked this up for almost nothing. Shod a feller's horse. It was all he had to pay with."

"Oh, we can't!" Dolly protested, struggling with eighty pounds of frozen meat and bone.

Adams waved it back vigorously. "No, take it. I mean it. Listen, you're headed for the elephants' backyard!" He hesitated. "Look, why don't you stay —at least until spring if nothing else. The grass will be up then. Who knows, maybe you'd find somebody headed that way. You'd have company in case anything happened."

Dolly sighed, looking at the meat, feeling the raw chafing in her belly. Her mouth began to water as she thought of the thick rich red steaks they could carve off that wealth.

She shook her head smiling. "We'll take the meat, Mr. Adams. You've been a saint. But we have to go. Paw is a proud man. He used to own his own freight company. It hurts his pride to have to stay here. Bless you for letting us sleep in the straw, Mr. Adams. I can't say how much we appreciate that. But Paw, well, it breaks his heart to know he's here on charity."

Adams scratched his bulging belly. "Well, it ain't exactly charity, Miss Dolly. He's been a regular whiz at keeping the place clean and keeping the wagons and stock. Never saw a man who was so good with stock! I mean, you're more than welcome here. Why don't you stay on? Gosh, it's still winter out there!"

She chuckled softly. "Oh, I know. It's foolish to go on now. But Paw has to. We ran a crack freight outfit in Virginia so we know you've been feeding us busy-work. We're a drain on your hospitality. You don't need the burden of another two mouths to feed, and Paw and I know it."

She sank onto the flour barrel and looked at him, smiling into his big, bluff face. "It's Paw. Well, he's fretting. He's a broken man here, Mr. Adams. If I don't get him away, he'll do something dumb. I just can't stand to see him slinking around here avoiding people! Maybe we can shoot some buffalo or I can get him back to civilization where he can start clean again." She raised her hands helplessly and dropped them.

Adams nodded, his black eyes thoughtful. "Yeah, I know. Why, if we had the space you and Henry would be more than welcome to share with Amy and me. We'd enjoy having you—"

"I know," Dolly protested. "We can never thank you either. Paw's just . . ." She sighed and looked up at the stained canvas over her head.

"A man, Miss Dolly. Yep, he'll do. Get him the right breaks and he's got it in him to make it work. I seen men, Miss Dolly, all kinds of 'em. Sometimes the breaks just come wrong—and Henry's had that happen to him here. He thinks it's a jinx of some sort. Yep, get him out and away and he'll come through.

Just don't leave now!" Adams jammed his hands into his pockets, his eyes pleading with her.

She nodded. He was right. But how long would it take before Paw's spirit was so low he caught chill or picked up pneumonia? How had they managed to stay healthy for so long, shivering each night in the loft over the livery? No, the trail was their salvation. Besides, it was almost spring. The days were getting longer and grass was greening on the south sides of the buildings.

At that moment, Henry entered leading the two draft animals. They were old but seemed healthy. Henry had nodded when he saw how they moved, his critical eye on their gait and the way they placed their big hooves. Under his care, their coats had begun to shine and take on a new luster.

"How 'bout it, girl?" Henry called. "You ready to get this outfit on down the trail?"

"Aw, Henry, I was trying to talk her out of it," Adams called. "You could git kilt out there! Why, big storm blow in and you'd freeze! Shucks, what if you run smack dab inta a big band of Cheyenne or 'Rapaho out there?" He raised his arms, his blunt face lined with worry.

Henry chuckled. "I got me a Henry rifle and a hunert rounds of ammunition, Mr. Adams. We'll do'er."

Adams nodded. "I don't like the thought of a lone wagon out there."

Henry backed the horses in and settled the hames. He checked the tugs and traces with a rattling of the singletrees as his quick, sure fingers made the buckles fast, his practiced eye seeing that nothing bound or chafed the horses.

"Yep, we appreciate that, Mabe. Reckon though

we'll be off. In the words of these here miners, 'I dun bin round these diggin's too long. Grass's growing under my feet.'" Henry laughed nervously at his words and looked around hastily, failing to meet Mabe Adams's eyes.

Dolly took up the reins and crawled out onto the worn seat.

Mabe Adams reached up and took her hand in his big one. "You take care out there, Miss Dolly."

Henry shook his hand and added as he climbed up, "We'll send you a letter from Kansas, Mabe." He dropped his eyes as he settled in the seat, staring dumbly at the horses in front of him. "I owe you a lot. Reckon thanks is a pretty thin word at times."

"Naw, you take care Henry. Don't be shy on coming back. There's always a place for you here. You know that."

"Yep. Well, take care, Mabe." Henry slapped the ribbons and clucked the horses. "C'mon, you critturs, let's go. Kansas is a waiting out there!"

The wagon jerked and rolled, Dolly leaning over the side, waving and calling good-bye. Adams waved in return, his face a mask of concern.

Beyond the big doors, the weather was a cold gale. Dolly pulled her shawl tight around her shoulders, her red hair creeping out from where she'd pinned it. The west wind sought them, creeping into every fold of their clothing.

"I don't know, Paw," she said softly, shuddering from the cold.

"Aw, we'll be all right." Henry hawked and spat off the side into the street. "Stock's solid. We'll be there afore the grass is up enough for the Injuns to be out and about."

Dolly looked at the buildings they passed. Most

were rough-cut lumber, hauled from the mountains. Some hadn't even had a coat of paint. Even in the light of morning, Denver looked uncurried and unkempt. It was a dirty city full of trashy streets and trashy people. But here and there some, like Mabe Adams, were making homes for their families and betting on the future. That tarnished lure had drawn her father and her so far from warm Virginia.

Dolly looked to see the firm set of her father's jaw, tight through the mat of his beard. His nose was running in the cold, and his eyes were squinted with determination.

"What are you thinking, Paw?" she asked.

"Aw, it's good ta git outta this place, gal. Reckon I sure done wrong a commin' here. Shoulda listened to you. I'll make it up to you, Dolly. I swore I would. I'll make it up. I promise, gal. I sure do promise." His voice had an odd quaver. "Yep, just over the horizon is a wealth in hides!"

They banged along the frozen streets, the wagon shuddering and shaking over the frozen ruts. Two men, wrapped in brown buffalo coats, rifles over their saddles, walked weary head-hanging horses toward them. One was big and burly with a full, black beard; the other slender, his face thin around a wicked, sharp nose. They looked dangerous, wild, fierce, and deadly, with their guns gleaming.

Dolly dropped her eyes at the big man's stare and sudden lusty smile. She felt as if her soul was punctured by his hot black eyes. The fellow and his smaller partner rode past, stares pinning her, as if the big man's very glinting eyes could strip her naked. The old trapper riding beside him shot her a hungry wolf look and he laughed, the black quid of tobacco in his mouth exposed along with a few snaggled yellow teeth.

"A pretty one, eh, Louis?" she heard as they passed her. The big man's laugh was loud and his voice echoed, "Oui, mon ami, but there are others here for us, non, Sabot?"

Dolly felt herself color and, swallowing nervously, shot a glance at Henry, afraid he'd heard. But he was lost in his thoughts, his eyes gleaming as a pack train of mules followed a dirty man on horseback. One by one, the animals passed, heads down, ears flicking wearily this way and that as they plodded under load after load of frozen buffalo hides.

"Yes sirree," Henry was muttering to himself. "Hides, gal. We'll make it yet!" He looked at her and winked. "Three dollars and fifty cents a crittur. And, why, we gits ta eat what we shoot, too!"

She nodded to herself, remembering the big bearded man who'd leered at her and left her feeling ravished and weak and violated. Indeed, it was time to get out of Denver. Time to get away from this West with its rude men and wild ways.

The wagon rumbled and banged over the frozen ruts as the sun rose in the eastern sky. Dolly turned and looked back, seeing the squalid city, bare and brown behind piles of cans and bottles, with occasional dogs nosing through the rubbish. Smoke rose from countless stoves as morning fires heated eggs, beef, antelope, and coffee.

Yet, there was a glory, too, as the sun reflected from the jagged magnificence of the Rockies rising to the west in violation of man and ambition. The snow-capped peaks were stark against the incredible blue of the sky—overlords, dwarfing the miserable doings of

Denver and its mulling human heartbeat. The sight took away her breath, and she had to physically tear her eyes away. Her heart pounded as she thought of the power and majesty of those mountains. If only there were some way! No, she was done with the West and its burly, unwashed men.

Closing her eyes, she willed the wheels to turn ever eastward toward a safe land—a land where they didn't need to worry about what fate had in store for them around the next corner. Maybe there she would find a man who was strong and who would keep her and her aging father safe.

Who would he be, this savior, this powerful prince who could lift them from so much misery and defeat? She dreamed of him—powerful, strong, handsome and majestic like those mountains behind them. He would be like them, wild and untamed except by her love. He would hold her in his strong arms and never again would such as that Frenchman leer at her! She opened her eyes and looked over the brown rolling grassland. Yes, he was out there, somewhere, waiting for her.

CHAPTER 3

CHEYENNE WAS A DUSTY TOWN MOST NOTED FOR THE UNion Pacific Railroad shops and Fort D. A. Russell. The city had grown on the heels of the railroad that spanned the continent, linking East to West. The UP was the only reason the raucous little city had established itself on the endless sea of grass.

Theo rode up to a ramshackle building on the main street. The sign proclaimed, SALUNE—FIRST AND LAST CHANCE—TOM PURCELL, PROPRIETER. Theo stepped off the sorrel and pulled the soogan over his head. As usual the wind was blowing and the February morning chilled to the very bone.

Theo ducked through the rickety door. A wagon tailgate had been nailed onto two water barrels to make the bar. A stack of boxes lying on their sides was nailed together to make shelving behind the bar. A fat man with three days' stubble on his cheeks and a drooping walrus mustache was propped in a chair under grease-streaked blankets, snoring loudly. His boots were propped on the bar next to a line of unwashed glasses.

"Morning," Theo offered.

The fellow started and blinked. Then he yawned, showing gaps between his brown teeth. "Mornin' yer seff," came the mumbled reply as the man dug a dirty knuckle into his sleepy eyes.

Theo watched as the big man lumbered to his feet, shivered, and began to build a fire in the little wood stove. "Fell asleep an' fergot the stove," he muttered apologetically.

"Happens," Theo agreed calmly.

"Excuse me a minute." The man retreated out the back, probably to relieve himself. Theo walked to the stove and adjusted the dampers as the fire caught.

The man returned, wiping his nose with his fingers. "Name's Purcell," he offered. "What can I get you?"

"A good stiff whiskey, something to cut the cold," Theo grunted.

"Looks like you've been riding a ways," Purcell returned as he poured a glass full.

"A ways," Theo agreed. He gulped the cold liquor down and put the glass on the bar. The stuff lit a fire in his belly, making him feel better. Slowly, it began to creep out to his limbs.

"Another?" Purcell asked.

"No, that's enough for now. Might need my senses later. There been a French man through here recently?"

Purcell frowned. "No, not in my place, but you

might ask the girls down on the line. If anyone went through, one of the girls would remember."

"Thanks, I'll do that. I got a horse for sale. A black mare. If you know of anyone interested, send them to me." Theo turned and placed a coin on the bar. Purcell was settling himself in the chair and placing his feet on the bar as Theo left.

Cheyenne was growing. Brick buildings were rising down the street and the wall tents that comprised most frontier towns were spreading out onto the grassy plains. The train tracks glistened in the morning sun, the line of cinders and ties blatant against the brown background of dead grass and the white patches of snow.

Leading his horses, Theo followed the street toward Ida Hamilton's House of Mirrors, built two years before. Madam Hamilton's brothel had the sort of reputation for finery that would immediately draw a man like Gasceaux after his ride from Montana.

Theo stopped to look at the UP building that had been under construction for several years. It would soon be the largest building in Dakota Territory.

When Theo entered Ida Hamilton's, he stopped in amazement. No place he had ever been, including the mansions he had seen in the East during the war, compared to this. Opulence graced the room like it was the house of a Persian king.

"Could I help you?" Theo turned to see Ida herself smiling at him. Embarrassed, he pulled his hat from his head and wished he had at least beat the dust from his boots.

"Just after some information, ma'am." He grinned. "I don't reckon I can afford anything else." He stared at the rich carpets under his run-down boots.

"Nevertheless, I would be glad to help in any way I

can. What do you need to know?" came the cultured reply. Theo saw she was smiling openly. She was quite an attractive woman, with the bearing of education. Theo realized he was blushing. She was unlike any other prostitute he had ever met.

"Uh, ma'am, I'm looking for a fella. Uh . . . an old friend, if you will. I heard he was in this part of the country and he would have come to a place like this. That is . . . well, I think so. Knowing Louis like I do." Theo put on his best grin.

"There is more than one Louis; could you perhaps describe him?" She was still pleasant which allowed Theo to relax.

"Big fellow, ma'am. I'd say about my height, with some gray in his beard. The thing is, he always talks with a French accent. Most likely he has quite a bit of money, too. He'd—" Theo had let his eyes wander around the room but he caught Ida's tightening squint.

"This man is a friend of yours, you say?" Her voice had become cool. It caught him off balance.

"Well, not exactly. I've been meaning to have a short discussion with him for some time," Theo added pointedly, his eyes hardening.

Ida Hamilton nodded, a faint, knowing smile crossing her lips. "I see. The man is not welcome in my establishment. He got a little rough with one of my girls. The man I refer to called himself Henri Clement. Perhaps . . ."

"That's probably him, seems to change names about as often as most folks change shirts. Where can I find him?" Theo's eyes were smoldering.

Ida Hamilton nodded as he talked. She evidently understood. "I believe the man left town several days ago. As to where he is, I have no idea. I can, though, add emphatically that he will *never* enter my place again!"

"Well," Theo drawled, "if I find him, I can guarantee that he won't. Sometime . . . uh, when I'm on my uppers . . . well, I'd like to pay your business a visit, ma'am." Theo pulled his hat onto his head and, nodding to Ida, left.

A freighter told Theo he had passed a man meeting Gasceaux's description on the Denver road three days before. The man had a surly attitude and had been in a hurry.

Three days! Never before had Theodor Belk been so close to his quarry. Selling the black mare to an Easterner for the unheard-of price of thirty dollars, Theo bought a new packhorse, saddled the sorrel, and followed the rutted road south toward the town of Denver. Gasceaux would be there by now. Theo smiled warmly to himself.

Theo spent the night at the Rock Forts. The limestone deposits gave shelter from the wind and had been used by many travelers. The only fuel was grass and dried manure, so he ate a small dinner and bedded down out of the wind in a cold camp. The weather had somewhat ameliorated.

Lying in his blankets, Theo watched the stars and the cold white moon. The final showdown was coming. His body was growing tense. For so many years he had followed the trail. Through his captivity among the Mormons, through the long trip east, through his time in jail in Ohio, even through the war, he had followed, heedless of the passing of time, dedicated to the search. But every time he came close Gasceaux slipped away. Wryly, Theo remembered the stories of Tantalus he had been forced to read in Salt Lake City.

No matter, Louis had been gone after the war. He'd

never surrendered to give his oath of allegiance. Some said he turned renegade along with the Missouri outlaws; some said he was dead. Theo believed none of the stories. He had other ideas about where Louis would go to rebuild his fortune. Deep down inside he knew Louis had returned to the West. The whispering demons told him so as they urged him to ride the endless trail.

Theo was on the move before the sun came up, not being able to sleep. He crossed the Cache la Poudre, the Big Thompson, the Saint Vrain, and finally followed the South Platte into Denver late that night. It was the first real city he had seen in four years.

Staying in a stable on the outskirts of town, he rode in the next morning. Denver was bustling. Men and boys walked rapidly through the frozen, muddy streets. Packs of dogs growled, fought, and played around mountainous piles of tin cans and bottles. Urchins came to beg and thought better of it from the rough look Theo gave them. Smoke billowed from stovepipes above the wall tents and soddys that lined the street.

Saloons in tents, buildings, or wagon backs sold rotgut to any that passed. Several ladies sat in front of their cribs smoking cigars and propositioning the men. A pack of dogs was worrying the bloated gut of a dead mule. Civilization had come to the plains.

Theo realized his temper was rising. He grew tense as the sorrel walked slowly down the street. Louis Gasceaux waited somewhere in this city; the long chase was winding down. Ahead along Larimer, Wazee, and Champa streets, red brick buildings were rising. Once through the outskirts of town, the air of prosperity was vibrant.

Theo left his horses off at a livery. "Howdy, I'm

Mabe Adams! Where'd you come from, mister?" the hostler asked jocularly, extending his big hamlike hand.

The demons goaded Theo's answer. "Shut your mouth, friend," Theo warned. The man swallowed and nodded, stepping back. Theo realized his heart was beating faster and he was breathing deeply. "Sorry," he added, flipped the man a coin, and left.

Hell, he thought, the fellow didn't need to be so damn nosy. The tension increased as the demons chanted in the back of his mind. His step seemed lighter; his senses alert. On impulse, he took the thong off the hammer of the big Colt. The Sharps rested easy in his hand as he scanned the faces for a glimpse of Gasceaux.

"I'm gonna kill you!" a young boy called to one of his friends. Theo spun on cat feet, dropping a lightning hand to his pistol. The urchin, oblivious, chased his companion down a tin-can-filled alley.

Theo's heart pounded as he tried to unwind. Never in his life had he felt so jittery. Slowly, he willed himself to relax. He was too tight. Taking deep breaths, he continued down the wood plank that kept the citizens from the squalid mud of the street.

"Lookin' for someone?" a rouged prostitute asked demurely.

"Yep," Theo responded in a wooden tone.

"Well, here I am. Three dollars buys you more than you can handle," she teased.

"I'm not looking for you, miss. But it would be worth something if you can tell me how to find a French feller that rode into town a few days ago. Flashy, big man with a gray-streaked beard and money." Theo watched her intently.

She paused and frowned. "No," she said, shaking

her head, "I don't know who he is. If you got any other interests, I'll make it two dollars." She cocked her head and smiled. "I'll make you—"

"Maybe later." Theo thanked her and walked on. After four hours he was no nearer to finding Gasceaux. The pressure was building. For too long he had walked around strung tighter than a catgut fiddle.

Tension and anxiety had become a tangible thing, as if another mind had grown within his, pounding behind his eyeballs. His empty stomach churned and twisted. He jumped at sounds and caught himself several times at the thin line that separated prudence from action when the dark forms of men passed in the growing twilight. The demons chittered to themselves in a hushed whisper.

Feeling as if he would burst at any moment, he realized his mouth was dry and his hands were shaky. A slow pain was building in his head, stabbing like a white-hot fire in the back of his skull. The shrill noise of the street irritated him. The demons began to scream in the back of his mind.

A sudden thought shook him. What if Louis was not in Denver? What if the Blackfoot had been wrong? What if the whole cold trip had been for nothing?

"No," he muttered to himself, frantic. "Gasceaux's here somewhere. He's . . ." The demons waiting behind his thoughts laughed.

Angry at the milling crowd in the street, Theo looked for a saloon. The hour was late and he was getting nowhere. Several leads had ended up with the wrong men. He had come ready to kill and now there was no release for the frustration of pent-up emotions. A drink would settle his nerves and cool his rage.

Theo pushed his way into the Citation Saloon. Monte, poker, and faro tables were going strong.

Several large men dressed in the fashion of miners stood along the bar. More miners were singing Irish songs in the back of the dimly lit tavern.

Theo pushed his way roughly to the bar and ordered a double shot of rye. Feeling foul, he wondered where Gasceaux had got to. He had seen the men who matched Louis's description, but none had been him and none knew where such a man could be. All he knew was a man had been in Cheyenne the week before. Could he have followed a false lead? The thought returned to gnaw at him.

Theo felt heat rise in his body. He clamped his jaws and ground his teeth. Damn all these people! They were in his way! If he hadn't had to sort through all this riffraff, he could have found Gasceaux. Angrily he glared at the jostling crowd. He was used to the lonely trail and few people. The constant shoving and the smell of the crowd built the rage inside to a fever pitch. The hot stinking bodies were packed around him like fish in a tin.

Theo did not see the bent figure that slid through the door. It belonged to an old man with filthy gray hair. Grease-blackened leather clothing hung on his skeleton frame. The gnarled hands were hidden below a dirt-shiny blanket. The old eyes had not lost their sharpness though, as they scanned the room they cataloged each face. Finally, the stare rested on Theo Belk. As the man studied the broad back, the lips curled up in a wicked smile, exposing a black quid of plug tobacco and two yellow incisors, the only teeth still in his head. The man began to weasel through the crowd of bodies.

Theo wrestled with the thoughts in his head. Could he be as far away from Louis as he had been in North Carolina?

A miner shouted loudly as he fell over a chair. Damn them! Damn them all, even these stinking drunken miners! Damn the whores who told him that Gasceaux had come this way! Damn the hostler who had thought he had come south! Damn the whole stinking lot!

Theo heard a roaring in his ears that was his muffled heartbeat. The muscles in his shoulders bunched and rippled. He gripped the glass as if to break it and stared at the tendons that jumped from the back of his hand. Damn them all! he whispered to himself, euphoric from the surge of rage that thrilled every fiber of his tingling body.

Angered further by the sight of his empty glass, Theo turned and threw it against the wall. At the smash and flying glass fragments, the miners quit their singing. One large fellow howled a curse at Theo.

"Damn you, too!" Theo hurled back, and turning, ordered another rye. The skin of his face was hot and sweaty.

The bartender placed a new glass and poured, watching Theo closely, swallowing, afraid to meet his eyes. As Belk reached for the glass, a rough hand clasped his shoulder and spun him around. The drink spilled.

"Who the hell d'ya think ye are?" the big Irish miner demanded. "Ye coulda put me eye oot!" He was burly, with wide shoulders and clear green eyes. His red complexion had been battered by a hard life. Now the friendly eyes were hostile.

"Get your stinkin' hand off my shoulder, Paddy!" Theo roared. Something black and foul broke loose in Theo's mind.

"Aye, so ye be a tough mon, now?" Irish asked with a slight smirk. "A tough, tough—"

"You buy me another drink or you're dead, Paddy," Theo gritted, feeling release flooding through his body, his senses were extraordinarily clear. "Buy it or die." Rage was building to a new crescendo. "*Buy it!*"

"Laddy, I come here to drink in peace and sing wit' me friends. That don't include no thrown glasses. Now laddie, hold yore peace or begone wit' ye. We don't loike nasty drunks here. If ye canna hold yore whiskey, now, ye should'na be drinkin' in the first place." The brogue soothed. "Now, hold—"

"Buy, damn you, you coward. You damned potato head!" Theo's voice cracked like a whip in the suddenly silent room.

"Coward!" cried the Irishman. "Ye'll not be callin' Irish O'Connell a coward for long!" He swung a huge right hand at Theo's head.

Before it landed, Theo shucked the huge Walker from the holster and shot. The big gun roared and the giant miner staggered under the impact of the .44 bullet, his eyes wide. He stepped back and looked quizzically at Theo. "Fer . . . the price o' a drink . . . ye'd kill me? Mon, what sort o' . . ."

Theo did not answer. Calmly, he cocked and triggered the gun again, feeling the euphoria of killing. The first bullet would have done the job, the big Walker backed lead with 55 grains of FFF Dupont powder. The second shot took Irish O'Connell between the eyes and blew the back part of his skull over the rough-cut boards of the ceiling. Theo put two more shots into the man's chest before he hit the floor.

"Anyone else in on this?" he asked evenly, eyes searching the room. No one spoke, the fight had come too quickly. The men in the room were ashen faced; one young lad turned green and swallowed convulsively.

"You'd better go," the bartender said softly. "That was Irish O'Connell. He has a lot of friends in town. I don't want more trouble in my place."

"Leave me a path out of here," Theo ordered. As if by magic, the crowd melted away to the door. Theo picked up the Sharps in his right hand, holstered the Walker, then slowly and arrogantly left the silent room. After he walked out the door the kid vomited profusely.

"Who . . . who the hell was that?" the kid asked, wiping his mouth.

"Calls himself Theo Belk," one of the men offered. "Said something to me earlier today about trying to find some French fella he's been tracking."

"I'll tell you what boys, the way he pulled that damn Walker, that French fella better light fer the high country an' once he's there, he'd better not come back." The bartender shook his head slowly, eyes on the corpse bleeding on the floor.

No one noticed the old man who slipped to the back of the room and pulled a pistol from under his greasy blanket before reholstering it. The old man silently ghosted out the door. Looking down the street, he could see no sign of Theodor Belk.

In the Citation, the bartender wiped his hands on a now-gray towel. "Shady, you and Bill get Irish outa here. Kid, clean up where you puked. Come on boys, the night is young." Then he scowled at the spattered remains on the ceiling and shook his head in disgust.

Outside, the old man halted on the plank walkway. Sabot spit a stream of tobacco juice into the mud. He sniffed the wind coming down 17th Street. It smelled of night earth, manure, vomit, and stale whiskey. He could see Dave Cook, the town marshal, coming easily along the buildings. Shootings brought people like that these days. Sabot slunk away. After seeing Belk in action, he would be very cautious the next time they met.

Louis Gasceaux relaxed in Molly's big brass bed. Smiling, he poured himself another glass of the fine bourbon. Sabot had ridden ahead from Cheyenne to hear the news. Louis was no fool. He had hit the army for over seven thousand dollars. He had covered his tracks after killing Huffman, but wariness never hurt the wolf. Sabot had brought him to Molly's. It was safe.

With some of the army payroll, Louis had bought fine whiskey—a rarity in Denver. While Sabot prowled the streets in search of news, Louis lounged in Molly's bed and sipped his whiskey. It would do well to know if anyone was asking for him.

Louis did not allow himself folly. That canny X. Beidler had been watching him too intently. Unlike his friend Henry Plummer—deceased—Gasceaux had departed for a warmer climate. And he hadn't been thinking of brimstone either.

A soft tap at the door admitted Sabot. The grizzled trapper grinned, exhibiting his yellow teeth and black gums.

"I think you have a follower, mon ami. He was asking about a man who speaks like the French. He asks about a man who might 'ave ridden in from Fort Laramee, about a man such as yourself."

Louis swung himself off the bed his eyes narrowing. "Who?" he asked.

"Zee name eez Theo Belk." Sabot grinned wickedly. "He eez very good with zee peestol."

"Where is he now?" Gasceaux asked. He watched Sabot like a hawk. Many years had passed. How well could he trust his old comrade?

"No one knows." Sabot shrugged. "After he shoot O'Connell, he runs. Ah, he ees wise. Irish O'Connell, he 'as many friends, indeed, many friends. Hees friends, weell—"

"What was he told of me?" Louis asked, checking his pistol and making note of the disposition of his belongings within the room.

"Nothing. No one knows you are 'ere. No one knows 'oo you are. No one knows where you come from." Sabot grinned again.

"Ah," Louis sighed. "Perhaps you could have killed him?" He raised his eyebrows suggestively.

"Oui, I would 'ave tried, mon ami. But before eet eez possible, he peeck zee fight with O'Connell. Then poof, he eez gone into zee night, like smoke, no?"

There was a long pause as Gasceaux thought, stroking his chin.

"Therefore, mon ami," Louis said, smiling smugly as he came to a conclusion and reclining on the bed, "if I do not say who I am or where I am from, no one will know, eh?"

"Oui," Sabot answered simply.

Theo cursed himself again, keeping the sorrel to a trot, the pack animals following behind. If pursuit was coming, he would need the horses in a condition to run, and the pack animals would make that difficult.

What had happened to him? Shooting that miner was the craziest thing he could have done! He had gone to Denver to find Gasceaux and kill him. He had not gone to kill Irish O'Connell. He hadn't even bought supplies.

Hunger gnawed his belly. There had been nothing to eat since the camp in the Rock Forts, and the growing populations along the Front Range had shot out most of the game to feed Denver and the teeming mining camps.

Climbing the uplands west of the South Platte, he stopped to watch his backtrail. Fortunately, the moon had come out from behind the clouds and given him fair visibility. No riders followed in his wake. He had purposely traveled off to the side of the Golden road. That little town lay about ten miles ahead of him behind Table Mountain.

The killing fever had left him. In its place came hunger, a sapping desire for sleep, and a deep-felt frustration with himself over his recent actions.

The killing he had done in the war had taught him how easy it was. He'd killed to escape jail in Ohio—to avoid serving for horse theft—but in the war he had learned to enjoy watching a man die. It gave him a feeling of power and security. One minute there was a warm breathing man before him. The next he pitched on his face—clay-cold flesh—seeping life into the bloody ground.

He, Theo Belk, the child who had shivered in the dark below the Church Buttes, had the ultimate power. With his skill, he could take a man's life. It made him strong and it kept him from fear. It made him someone. He would survive while others did not. That was God's cardinal rule. Survival was God's reality and to hell with what the damn Mormons had tried to beat into him.

The world was a hard, calculating place; there was no difference between the morality of war or peace. Theo could see beyond the distinctions made by most men. Live was live and dead was dead—war or peace, it mattered not.

Perhaps he had been close to Louis Gasceaux.

Perhaps there was some divine plan spun by God or the Fates. He smiled slightly at the thought of the old Greeks. In Salt Lake he'd read the Greek myth that a man's life was spun, woven, and cut off by three immortal women called the Fates. Was his search for Louis dictated by some such mystical beings? Gasceaux was close, Theo could feel it deep in his mind. The demons snickered, agreeing.

Yes! Louis Gasceaux was in Colorado somewhere; it must have been the work of the devil or the demons that had made him doubt. He would not have been so vulnerable if he hadn't known Louis was close. He'd let some unseen, malevolent spirit make him kill the wrong man! Another lesson was learned.

He was being led through trials so he would be ready for God's greater purpose. He was meant to learn that certain forces could influence him away from his goals. Liz had been an example and so had Irish O'Connell. Now, as he swayed on the horse, almost asleep, he realized his whole life had been directed to shape him for some great service. Grimly, he smiled. He would be ready!

The town of Golden was nestled between South Table Mountain and Lookout Mountain, the vanguard of the Front Range. Like Denver, Golden was wide open, booming with prosperity and the flotsam it inevitably collected. Men walked the streets even at this late hour. The cribs, saloons, and gambling dens were in full swing.

From what Theo could see, the population was mostly drunk and staggering through the streets, their pants shoved into scuffed boots. They were singing songs and telling jokes. Languages from around the world greeted his ear.

Stabling his horse, Theo found an all-night restaurant and ordered a cup of coffee and a plate of beans and meat. After eating, he was surprised to see the sun rising in the east, poking its red-gold rays between the hills.

The town was coming to a different kind of life as the merchants opened their stores and the revelers made it back to their camps and rooms. Exhausted, Theo made a deal with the hostler for space in the loft and rolled into his blankets to sleep.

Later that afternoon, refreshed and unplagued by the dream, Theo began his quest for Louis Gasceaux in the slim hope he might be in Golden. He could still feel the man's presence in his mind. When night began to fall, Theo had made no progress. He was referred to several Frenchmen, but none proved to be his quarry.

Over a meal, Theo felt the returning pangs of doubt. Could he have followed a blind lead? Had he missed the trail? Could Louis even now be riding the rails to the East? The demons inside whispered no. Louis was close.

Later that day, someone recognized him as the man who shot Irish O'Connell. The notoriety was discomforting. Theo saddled the sorrel and his packhorses and followed the Floyd Hill road into the mountains. He had exhausted the potential for locating Louis in Golden anyway.

First he followed the trail to the gold camps at Central City, then Idaho Springs and Georgetown. He rode lonely trails and heavily traveled roads choked with ore wagons and freighters. The towering peaks thrust into the sky and often he rode above cloud level. The northern slopes were somber in a green blanket of fir, spruce, and lodgepole pine deep in snow. The southern slopes were barren, colored in browns and grays from last year's brush and grass. Outcrops of schist and gneiss stood belligerently on the hillsides, overlooking dark slopes of lichen-covered talus.

Theo was running low on cash. During his stay in Breckenridge, he took a week off to do some hunting. It paid better than any work in the mines, and he was good at bringing in meat. It really paid when, returning from South Park with loads of elk, deer, and bear, he located a copy of *The Rocky Mountain News* in the restaurant he sold to. The paper mentioned a gold-brick deal in Denver. The demons in Theo's mind told him he had found his prey.

It seemed a wealthy investor had come to Denver with the idea of investing in mining stocks and several new businesses in the area. The victim, a Mr. Jakes, had been approached by a large black-bearded man who offered to sell a sack full of gold coins for greenbacks, which he stated he could get a better return for in the East.

When Jakes spread the gold coins out to count, he found he had purchased a sack of lead. Mr. Jakes was offering a substantial reward for information leading to the apprehension of the swindler. The only information Jakes had been able to dig up was that the man called himself Phillip Giourard. He claimed to be a French noble returning to France. He spoke French fluently and had been seen headed south with an old trapper known only as Sabot.

Theo cursed his luck and saddled his animals. By night he was well down the trail.

CHAPTER 4

IN THE MOUNTAIN TOWN OF EMPIRE, A SMALL FUNERAL party entered the fenced cemetery lot bearing a large pinewood coffin. The party numbered about twenty people—all men, wearing white gloves and leather aprons over their rough mining garb.

The last physical remains of Irish O'Connell were about to be lowered into an oblong, rock-lined hole that had been hacked into the frozen ground. A bearded man in his late twenties knelt at the side of the grave while ritual words were said. A white apron was draped on the coffin before it was lowered on bristly hemp ropes; and last, a sprig of evergreen was dropped in the grave. Rising to his feet, the young man nodded to the grizzled somber faces. With care they took turns shoveling rocks and dirt into the grave. The sodden thumps seemed to shake the young man with each impact.

Tom O'Connell sighed and looked to the west at the cloud-capped peak of Ball Mountain. The wind blew streamers of snow from the heights, swirling them in an aerial dance before letting them settle into the valley three thousand feet below. The sound of Clear Creek blended with that of the wind in the fir trees and the hollow sound of dirt cascading into the new grave. It was the sound of the final dirge to be played for Irish O'Connell. A solitary tear drifted down the side of Tom's face to lose itself in his mustache.

"That'll be it Tom," one of the men said at last, looking at the new mound of the grave.

"Tell me again how it was," Tom ordered softly.

"Was a fight in the Citation in Denver, Tom. I guess Irish had some words with a man over a thrown glass and the price of a drink. Irish tried to talk Belk into settling down a bit. Belk told him to buy another drink. Irish refused; then Belk called him a coward. You know how Irish reacted to that." The man rubbed his hands together and interlaced his fingers, watching Tom with concern.

"Aye," Tom breathed. "For the price of a drink. Who is this Belk?"

"I saw him in Golden," a third man put in. "Heard there he was called Theo Belk. He was staying at the stable. Seems he was trying to find a man—a Frenchman named Louis Gasceaux. Um . . . a con man of a sort, so I hear. Big fella, with a beard."

Tom knelt at the grave again, nodding slowly as he absorbed the information. "We come a long way, brother," O'Connell crooned. "From County Cork we crossed the seas. We come t' build this new land. We made us a strike . . . an' a good one, too!

"Do na' worry aboot the woife and the little ones, brother. I'll see them clear o' worry and bring them here to grow strong and straight. An' by th' Old Gods, I'll gif Mister Belk the same thing we gif the Bloody King o' England!"

Tom stood, another tear on his face. "Gintlemen, the Shamrock moine is . . . is fer sale." Tom turned and walked slowly to his horse and stepped into the saddle. He gave the lonely grave a last look and, turning the horse, trotted toward Lyon's Gulch.

"And what did he mean by all that talk of England?" one hardy asked.

"You don't know why the O'Connells came here? They were run out by the English for causing trouble. What he just meant was he's gonna do the same thing to Belk that they did to them English soldiers—and that, friend, boils down to a drubbin'."

"Dunno . . . Peter O'Connell was a big man. Belk killed him when he wasn't wearing a gun. I hope young Tom is up to it. I just . . . well . . ."

"Irish Peter O'Connell was big and he was strong," the man agreed, "but Tom has the edge." The man paused, thinking, and spit onto the frozen ground as he thought. "Tom's smarter. Being smart now makes all the difference in the world, and by God that lad has a lot of sand in his craw. For my money I'd . . . well, I'd hate to be Belk when Tom O'Connell catches him."

"Paw!" Dolly called looking up. The sun was breaking through the clouds.

"Yep!" Henry shivered as he looked up from where he'd been checking the horses' feet, careful of cracked hooves and sore frogs.

Dolly pointed. "The sun shouldn't be on our right. It's almost dark! That way's got to be west!" She stood on the wagon seat, looking out over the cold grassy knolls blending forever with other knolls until they met the sky so far away.

Henry stood up and stretched his back muscles, his eyes darting nervously to the sun then the horizon. He worked his stiff white beard and hitched his thumbs into his belt. Hidden in his eyes was irritation and . . . what? Worry?

"Aw, well, probably just got a little turned around, girl. Following the contours, you know. Saves on stock that way." Henry smiled up at her and climbed tiredly into the seat. His cold hands grabbed up the reins and slapped them. Obedient, the horses turned away from the setting sun and Dolly felt the wind hit them from the side.

Henry shoved his hand into his threadbare coat and grinned, unaware of the frost on his mustache. "Cold one today, eh?"

She shivered, snuggling next to his bony frame for the warmth she could find there. "Yes, Paw." She didn't say the rest. How many times had she found them to be going the wrong way?

Looking over her shoulder, she took a look at the elk quarter bumping about in the back of the wagon. The thigh bone had been stripped clean. They were down to the stringy, gristly lower leg now. How much of the flour was gone? A third of the small keg? She looked back at the horses, noting their ribs, visible now. How long until the animals wore down?

They camped that night in a dry creek bed. Henry found a crusty snowbank from which he filled the little tin pot. Dolly's fire was a small thing, made from handfuls of brush and grass. The fuel was a godsend after all the barren, short grass they'd crossed.

Henry was whistling to himself as he hunched near the fire, his cold fingers working a needle through thick leather—harness mending, the eternal chore of the trail. "Yes sirree, we got good grass for the animals tonight. That and they got that snowbank to chew on. Be good for 'em."

Dolly looked into the little pot, noting the grit that floated in it. Using all her restraint, she dropped some of the shavings she'd hacked from the frozen elk into the warm water and added a little flour.

"Food's running low, Paw," she said softly. "We're gonna need something to eat in a couple of days."

Henry's eyes were haunted when he looked at her. "Don't worry none, girl. Why, we're almost into buffalo country now! I'll shoot us a couple dozen and we'll skin 'em and cook some of that right fine hump meat. You just watch yer old Paw do'er up right, gal! Yes sirree! Right!" He tried to give her a smile of reassurance, the crow's-feet at the edges of his eyes deeply etching his weathered face. It didn't work anymore. She could see the desperation and worry he couldn't hide.

"Yes sirree!" Henry repeated. "You jist wait, gal!" His tone conveyed purpose, as if by saying so, he could make it true.

Dolly took a breath of the frigid air and watched her breath curl around her nose and up into the night. How cold was it? Five degrees? Maybe ten? Overhead the patchy stars were brilliant, sparkling gems in the blackness of the sky, where blotches of clouds didn't hide them. Was tomorrow going to be another dreary, gray day? Was the future nothing but gray? The wind howled and ripped past in a sudden gust, sandblasting Dolly's back, scattering the little fire, blowing the thin sticks that fed it out over the sand.

Henry was on his feet, stamping the glowing coals where they stuck in little tufts of grass. Dolly scrambled frantically as she tried to save her tiny blaze. It was no use; she didn't have enough fuel to keep it going. Blackness settled around them.

"Want me to go find more wood?" Henry asked, stamping at the last of the sparks. "Hell, what am I worried about? Ain't 'nuff burnable out here to light a ceegar!"

Dolly closed her eyes and fought the tears of frustration as another icy blast of cold air ripped through their cold, dark camp. It took all her courage to control her breath and say, "No, Paw. Stew's almost done as it is. Let's eat it and I'm going to bed. It's warmer under the blankets anyway."

So, huddled in the dark, they ate the lukewarm broth, the flour heavy in the bottom while the meat was still raw. Shivering, Dolly stepped behind the wagon to relieve herself in the brunt of the wind before climbing into the back, pulling her boots off, and climbing dressed beneath the frozen blankets.

She was shivering wretchedly when Henry crawled in next to her. Her father snuggled under his covers, shivering like a round-bottom water pot on a hot stove.

The cover overhead rippled and snapped as the wagon trembled and quivered in the blast of air. Dolly buried her head under the covers and pulled herself into a miserable ball. Had she ever been this cold this long? Her toes felt like blocks of ice, and she fought the sobs that choked her.

Where were they? Lost! They were lost out here so far from anything. The tears were warm and they came with a rush. Her memories of Mabe Adams's livery were of chilly nights, true, but they'd been warm there during the day when Mr. Adams had his jolly, round heatstove going.

If they tried to go back, could they find Denver again? If the sun didn't come out, how would they know which way they were going in this featureless land of grass and wind and drifted snow?

She shuddered to herself as the wind worried the wagon again, jingling the trace chains. The hopelessness of it all tore at the treads of her mind. Not even at her mother's death had she felt so incredibly miserable. She let herself cry and cry until she could cry no more. Her dreams were of warmth and food and bright, sunny days. Only, as she began to find happiness, something black and cold would steal it away.

She jumped at the sound of the shot, clawing her eyes open and peeling herself out from under the layers of smelly blankets. Wool scratched her cheek as her heart stopped dead in her chest. Indians? Were they even now being killed!

She jumped from the warm blankets, cold air like a brisk slap to her warm flesh. She frantically pulled on her boots as a second shot echoed into the distance.

She tripped and fell, banging her knee as she caught herself on the back of the wagon. The sun was bright on five inches of new snow. Blinded by the glare, she stumbled into the day, hiding her eyes behind a shading hand as she tried to gather her wits and stop her thumping heart. Turning, she looked in vain for her father.

"Paw?" she cried out, feeling herself on the point of hysterical tears again. "Paw? Where are you?" Would the Indians come now? Desperate, she ran for the wagon, losing one of her unlaced boots and stepping in cactus hidden under the soft cushion of snow.

Gasping frustration, she scrambled awkwardly up

the seat and ripped the canvas back—only to find the rifle missing!

She swallowed, feeling her heart pound. Closing her eyes, she forced herself to think. Her foot started to throb with cold and the cactus needles stung. Frigid air was burning her throat as she gasped it in big gulps. A fierce shiver overwhelmed her, and she clutched herself to still it.

The trip back to her boot was misery. Hopping one-footed, she made the back of the wagon and pounded the snow from her boot. One by one, she picked the cactus spines from her foot. After three tries, she found her boot hook and pulled the laces over the fasteners. By the time she finished, Henry was walking over the low crest of the ridge. Rifle hanging loosely from his hand, she could tell from his posture that yet another calamity had befallen them.

He didn't meet her eyes as he stepped up on the wheel, slipping the loading tube aside and shaking the cartridges from the gun.

"Paw?" she asked, fearing to hear what he'd shot at. Indians? Her eyes still sought the horizon, looking for feathered headdresses.

"Tried to shoot us an antelope, girl." His voice was eloquent in tones of defeat and despair. Henry bent his neck back, looking up at the blue sky. "Missed, girl. Hell, they wasn't more than fifty feet away! I just missed." He lowered his head, the brim of his worn felt hat hiding his eyes. "Let's fix something to eat and get on our way. Maybe t'day we'll find buffalo." He fingered the dashboard absently, his knobby fingers feeling the texture of the wood as he avoided her eyes. "I'll get the stock together."

She patted him on the shoulder as he walked by, but he acted as if he didn't feel it.

The sun held for them that day and they made moderate time, ever eastward. Henry's spirits seemed to pick up toward nightfall, and Dolly couldn't help but feel things might improve. The snow had melted and the wind warmed as it changed to come from the southwest.

The next day they cut wagon tracks. "Buffalo hunters!" Henry decided, dropping down to study the place where the iron tires had cut the thin sod. Henry walked along, finding a spot where the dim imprint of a horseshoe could be made out. "Before the storm, I'd guess." He fingered his beard. "Let's foller 'em. Maybe they can tell us where the hide hunting's best at."

"Paw," Dolly shook her head. "You don't know who they are or where they're going! I think we'd best stick to heading east. These people were going north!"

Henry couldn't tear his eyes off the faint track. "Buffalo hunters," he muttered under his breath. As if an afterthought, he looked at his daughter. "We're running low on supplies, girl. Why, if'n we ketch up to 'em, they'll have lots of buffalo. We could dicker for some, now, gal! You just trust your old Paw!" He smiled his happiness and whistled to the team, setting out on the dim track.

Dolly took a deep breath, clenched her jaw and looked miserably up into the clouding sky. What sort of men would they find at the end of this trace? Would they be rough and smelly and leering like those two in Denver? Did she want her and her father at the mercy of beasts like those? If only they had someone to help them! If only there was someone to keep them from trouble. The faint image of her hero stayed shadowy in the back of her mind. Would to God that someone strong and handsome and brave loomed soon on their horizon! After all, the storybooks always ended that way. Couldn't it happen for real just once?

She noticed the similarity first. A slow, dull ache began to form under her heart. She checked for the signs they had left—the places where she'd taken care of nature's duty and where she'd walked to see the stars. It was the same.

"Paw, we ain't following no buffalo hunters." Her voice was wooden.

"Huh? Why, how do you know, girl?" Henry looked at her, his eyes sullen, afraid. He was chewing his cheeks, his pipe clamped in his teeth.

She pointed. "Cause we camped right down there five days ago, Paw!" It was true. She could see the sheltered low spot where they'd parked the wagon. She could see the grassy patch where the horses had grazed and the marks they'd left in the snow bank. "We been following our own tracks, Paw!" She couldn't stifle the tears this time. All of a sudden, it was just too much to take.

His arm was around her, comforting. "There, there, girl. It'll be all right. We just lost a little time is all," his soft voice soothed as it always had. "I love you, girl."

"I . . . I love you, too, Paw," she sniffed through her tears. "It'll be all right. I know that." She wiped her eyes and looked up at him, seeing the devastation in his eyes. "Let's head back east again. Can't be too much farther."

He nodded hesitantly, his eyes reflecting misery. "Yep, c'mon, horses. Back to the east. Let's find us some buffalo!" Henry called, his voice strained in an attempt to be cheery.

Dolly gave him a forced smile and bit her lip. Somewhere up ahead there had to be someone who could tell them how to get to safety.

* * *

Theo rode wearily into Denver. As usual he was tired, dirty, and hungry. Nevertheless, he pulled up before the Broadwell House Hotel and dismounted. From the desk clerk he got the room number of Mr. Jakes. The clerk glanced suspiciously at the rider's worn clothing—but Denver in 1870 was not a place to make much of a man's dress. The run-down prospector who crashed through the doors might be worth a million dollars.

Theo took the stairs three at a time. Finding the room, he tapped. A florid, portly gentleman opened the door a crack and looked hostilely at Theo. "Yes?"

"You Mr. Jakes?" Theo met the glare with hard eyes.

"I am. If it's about that con job, forget it. I'm tired of telling the story to everybody and their brother. Read the paper. Or is this another scam to get the money back for a small fee?" Jakes started to close the door but found it impossible with Theo's pistol barrel in the way.

"It's about the man who did it." Theo pushed his way in, Jakes backpedaling as he stared at the huge Walker. Theo holstered the gun.

"I . . . I don't have any money on me! Please just . . . just leave." Jakes swallowed rapidly, a thin line of perspiration forming on his fleshy lip. His eyes were frantic, almost pop-eyed, as they watched Belk.

"Mr. Jakes"—Theo sat easily on the bed and interlaced his fingers over his knee—"I'm not here to rob you or try and take you for more money. I want to find the man who did it. You didn't seem to want to talk and I need information."

"I see," Jakes sighed, relaxing a little. "This West is just so . . . so different from New York. What is your interest in this man, Mr . . . ?" Jakes turned and began pouring drinks, partly to still his nervous hands.

"Belk, Theo Belk. I've been trying to catch Louis Gasceaux for years. We have a matter to settle between us."

Jakes handed Theo a glass of bourbon. "I thought perhaps you might be a brigand, but perhaps you're from the Pinkerton Agency?"

"No, sir, are they involved, too?" Theo sipped the bourbon; it was good stuff.

Jakes seemed to have recovered. "It seems some of the money involved was stolen from the army up north someplace. Given the nature of the crime and possible government involvement, I put the agency on retainer just in case anything should get sticky.

"I have been taken by one of the oldest tricks in the book, Mr. Belk. I was trying to get something for less than its intrinsic value." Jakes looked tired as he lifted his glass to his lips.

"I reckon that makes you human, Mr. Jakes." Theo grinned. "In a similar circumstance, I might have done the same."

"At least you are honest." Jakes laughed.

"Describe how Louis looked. What did he wear and how did he act?"

As Jakes recounted everything he could remember about the con job, Theo nodded. It had to be Gasceaux! He'd been in Denver all the time! The demons chortled.

"I've also heard there is a federal marshal looking into the case. You might run into him and you may be of some help to each other," Jakes continued, speculating on the wolfish, quiet man.

"Makes sense," Theo agreed. "He didn't do such a

good job of covering his tracks at Fort Laramie. He must have run into Sabot recently. Sabot did all the scalping."

"I beg your pardon? Scalping?" Jakes was puzzled.

"Huh? Uh . . . talking to myself again." Theo grinned sheepishly. "I'll see if I can't get your money back for you. I just want Gasceaux, nothing more, nothing less. How much did he hook you for?"

Jakes scowled and looked at the rug. "Six thousand dollars. The money was going to make me a substantial investment here. I still have a large sum from the company; that was not mine to invest . . . thank God."

"Well"—Theo cocked his head and looked at the older man—"I'll just see what I can do. If I get the money back, how do I get in touch with you?"

"Here is my card. I'll be headed back to New York when I finish my business here. Do you really think you will catch this Louis Gasceaux?"

Theo nodded slowly, his eyes on Jakes. "If it kills me."

Jakes studied him as he finished his drink. "Yes . . . yes, you just might."

"Thank you for your time, Mr. Jakes." Theo nodded as he reached for the door.

"You're very welcome Mr. Belk. When you apprehend this blackguard, I shall be more than willing to testify." Jakes smiled.

"That won't be necessary." Theo grinned back. "I'm gonna kill him first."

Jakes turned white as he watched the door close. Quickly, he poured himself another glass of bourbon. He had heard the name Theo Belk before. The man was disconcerting. It was apparent that he truly did mean to kill Louis Gasceaux.

Later that afternoon Jakes was in the hotel bar listening to the conversation and thinking about how these Western men could take killing each other so indifferently. He heard Theo Belk's name mentioned.

"Theo Belk?" Jakes inquired. "Do you know the man?"

"Not me, an' I don't want to. That fella is pizen mean with a gun," the loquacious old miner told him. "Kilt a feller over to the Citation saloon last month. Just blew his brains out for the price of a drink."

"Well, I don't know that Mr. Belk would . . ." Jakes felt his stomach grow queasy. Could this be the same man who had talked to him so politely earlier? Then he remembered the pistol holding the door open and the cold blue eyes. Jakes squirmed in the chair. He'd had a murderer alone with him in his room! His stomach began to churn while he gulped his drink.

"Beggin' yore pardon, Mr. Jakes," a heavy Irish brogue interrupted Jakes's scattered thoughts. "Didn' ye mention Theodor Belk jist now?"

Jakes turned to see a stocky, dark-haired miner confronting him. "I . . . well, I've met the man. We're not what you would call—"

"An' where moight he be?" the Irish lad insisted.

"To be frank, I don't know. He saw me this morning about some money I had stolen from me. He was after the man who swindled me and said he would try to get my money back." Jakes was puzzled and was having a hard time pulling his scattered thoughts together after learning Belk had killed a man. It was all so . . . different!

"Ah, an' who moight he be tryin' ta foind?" The Irishman's eyes were intent.

"It is my understanding that the man who swindled me is called Louis Gasceaux. I would imagine that if you find him, Theo Belk will be close on his trail." Jakes smiled at the man. He seemed to be a nice fellow, albeit Irish.

"Aye, now that be a foine bit o' information," the young man said with satisfaction.

"Who might you be?" Jakes asked pleasantly, liking the sincerity in the man's face.

"I be Tom O'Connell, sir." The young man tossed down the drink he had been holding and placed the glass on the bar. Wiping his beard, he turned to leave.

"Just . . . just a minute, young man." Jakes placed his hand on the fellow's shoulder. "I'm interested in Mr. Belk. I'd like to, well, know more about him. I . . . I mean, well, without prying, could you tell me your business with him?" Jakes took a sip of his drink.

Tom O'Connell looked into Jakes's eyes, his voice soft, intent, leaving no doubt as to his sincerity. "Aye. When I foind 'im, I'm going to kill him," O'Connell replied evenly, then turned to walk away. Jakes was gagging on his whiskey as Tom went briskly through the door.

At that same moment, a line girl named Molly was glaring at Theo through eyes almost swollen shut. Her face was mottled with bruises. From the information Jakes had provided, Theo had managed to locate her upstairs room off Market Street. She hadn't wanted to talk at first. Theo had felt his blood rise in a black rage.

She'd talked.

"I hope he kills you!" she snarled through her bloody lips.

"I hope he tries," Theo returned darkly. His fist

made a hollow, smacking sound as he hit her one last time. She bounced off the wall and sagged limply to the floor. She spit one of her teeth out along with a thick clot of blood. Smiling, he left as she stared dull hatred at him.

He rode out into the brown, grassy, rolling plains east of Denver, following the trace of the trail eastward. He turned south off the track that followed the old Smokey Hill Trail and headed into the vastness. The sorrel stepped out easily, refreshed by a bait of grain, the packhorses trotting behind.

By the time Theo had beat the story out of the woman, he had learned that she had overheard them talking of the buffalo camps and the money to be made skinning the hide hunters. Sabot had said fortunes were being made in western Kansas.

"The time has come to get him," Theo announced to the sorrel. A red ear swung back to listen. "Maybe this time, huh?" The horse shook his head and worried the bit in his mouth. Theo laughed and patted the side of the horse's neck.

"I know, I've said it before. He's still out there—waiting. That's what he's doing. He's waiting for us. Reckon we've learned everything we had to to get him? This country ain't that big. Hell, he can't keep ahead of us forever." Theo scanned the short grass hills.

Realizing there would be no more talk, the red horse pricked his ears ahead and worked the bit again. He was happy; the land was flat and the footing was good. The horse liked the open country. He was on the trail again and the man, his friend, seemed in better spirits than in previous months.

They continued late into the night. The April moon

shone on the few remaining drifts of snow that hid along the walls of the arroyos, where the ever-warmer sun did not reach. By midnight, clouds had rolled in from over the Rockies and the horse had been sniffing the now-cold wind. The sorrel pranced and shook his head with misgivings.

"You thinkin' what I'm thinkin'?" Theo asked with a soothing voice. The man turned to sniff the wind himself as the sorrel snorted in agreement. There was a smell of snow racing behind them in the blackness. The temperature continued to drop. Theo pulled his soogan from the latigos and donned it.

"Spring blizzard," Theo guessed distastefully. "Let's find us a hole." He searched the darkness for a sign of shelter. The low, rolling hills could no longer be made out in the inky blackness.

"Hell, horse, you see better in this stuff than I do. You find us a place to cache now," he ordered, letting the horse have its head.

The sorrel, given free reign, stepped out. The first flakes began to fall, pushed by the wind. Soon they were sticking to Theo's back. The sorrel abruptly stopped and whickered lightly. Theo, half-asleep in the saddle, kicked loose and dropped to the ground. He could make out the dark line of trees before him.

Satisfied, he led the horses forward. Ahead of them in the dark, a horse whickered a loud greeting. With a silent oath, Theo grabbed the sorrel's nose in time to throttle him. The packhorses, without such restraint, whinnied with equine familiarity.

"Hell," was all Theo could mutter under his breath. Tying off his animals, he checked the load and cocked the big hammer of the Sharps. Taking the thong off his Walker, he began to work into the trees, feeling his way through the thick grass and fallen cottonwood branches. It would just be his luck to have fallen in with a village of Cheyenne who were still feeling the injustice of Custer's mad attack on the Washita. Theo heard a stick snap as an unknown foot was placed in the dark.

CHAPTER

5

THEO CROUCHED IN THE DARK, SCARCELY BREATHING, HIS ears searching for the slightest sound. The hunting fever rose. There was that lift of spirit and sharpening of the senses. He felt light, ready for action. He and the night joined together.

There came a crashing sound as brush gave way before awkward legs. It took no effort to follow the man's path through the tangled blackness. Theo ghosted behind the bumbling man, smelling tobacco. Another crashing sound followed a thump and grunt as the shadow fell over something unseen. Muttered curses greeted Theo's ear. Theo choked on ridiculing laughter; it had to be a tenderfoot pilgrim!

The man stumbled to his feet and from the sounds,

almost fell again. Grunting, he went back the way he had come, with Theo on his heels. The fellow walked incautiously into the light of a large fire. A wagon stood in the clearing. Turning, he screwed up his face in distaste as he glanced back at the trees, an old Henry rifle in his hands.

Shaking his head he called to the wagon. "'Twarn't nothin' out there. Just the tarnal wind in the trees."

"All right, Paw," a female voice called back. "I'll go back to sleep. If'n you were smart you'd get some, too. Is it still snowin'?"

"Yep, reckon it won't last though." The old man winced and rubbed his hip, evidently the one he had fallen on. "I'll be in in a bit," he called. Then to himself, "Someone autta keep the fire up though."

He was gray haired, with a wizened face. He looked to be of medium stature and had a slight bulge of belly over his belt. His boots were worn, like the old coat he wore. His hat was of gray felt, battered and dirty, with a hole in the crown. He was bearded and a pipe waved at the corner of his mouth.

Theo shook his head in amazement and sighed. There were times when immigrants could be all-fired amusing. A cold gust of wind howled through the trees, reminding Theo of the coming blizzard. Well hell, he could use a little company.

"Hello the camp!" Theo called loudly before shifting his position. The man spun and bent, squinting into the dark with fire-blinded eyes. He watched the place Theo had called from.

"Tarnation! There is someone out there! Come on in, mister!" the old man called. Theo noted he held the old Henry by the barrel. It was no way to hold a rifle—no way he could get it into action if necessary.

The old man still stared at the spot, looking a little

uneasy now. He jumped when Theo walked in from his left.

"Howdy, tell the other fella he can come in, too." The man gestured toward the trees.

"There's no one else," Theo said wryly. "That was me who called."

"Then why'd you call from over there and walk out here?" the old man demanded, pointing at the trees and watching Theo, suddenly suspicious.

"That was in case you were hostile or shot at sounds," Theo reproved. "And another thing. Don't smoke your pipe when you're out scouting. I smelled it a long way back. If I were a Cheyenne, I'd have your topknot by now."

"Topknot?" The man stared at Theo.

"Scalp. But I heard you long before I smelled you."

"That's the Lord's truth!" the old man sputtered. "I ain't no hand at this playin' Injun in the sticks."

"Huh!" Theo snorted. That was obvious. "Well, getting serious, I could have had your scalp a couple of times and you'd never have known I was there. The Sioux, Cheyenne, and Arapaho don't play games. You could wind up in a heap of trouble and I don't think you'd want to leave your wife out in this country all alone."

"It ain't my wife," the old man sulked. "It's my daughter."

"At least you're armed," Theo pointed out.

"Yeah, there's that. 'Course I don't keep no bullets in it." The man nodded seriously.

"You what?" Theo shouted incredulously.

"Hell, mister!" The man stood belligerently with clenched fists. "The thing might go off an' I'd shoot myself. Then wouldn't I be in a pretty fix, clear out here away from everybody!"

"Damn!" Theo groaned, rubbing his eyes. All of a sudden he felt very tired. "Here, take my rifle. It's loaded so don't shoot yourself and most of all, *don't shoot me when I come back!* I've gotta go get my horses."

Handing the man the Sharps, Theo walked away. The last the old man heard was Theo's muttering, "Pilgrims! I don't believe 'em, damned if I do!"

A chastening voice called from the wagon, "I told you, Paw." The old man just grunted, holding the big Sharps gingerly.

Theo walked his animals into the light after calling and began stripping his packs off and rubbing the animals down.

"What are you doing out here this time of year anyway?"

"Goin' buffalo huntin'." The old man grinned ear to ear. "I hear tell hides are selling for $3.50 apiece now that they figgered out how to make good leather out'n 'em." He tucked his thumb into the strap of his suspenders.

Theo threw him a curious glance. "You plannin' on shooting with that old Henry?" He cocked his head while he grinned at the thought.

"You bet, young feller." The man nodded positively. "Hell, it's .44 caliber, ain't it?"

"You need a bigger gun," Theo said dryly.

"Why, I killed a horse with this once. One shot and it was down. Buffalo ain't no bigger than horses, is they?" the oldster insisted with a touch of pride.

"Uh-huh," Theo grunted. "From how far away?" Theo pulled the knot tight on the picket line.

"I'd guess about a foot. Why?" the man demanded, chin stuck out.

Theo walked to the too-big fire and squatted down to warm his hands. "A foot, huh?"

"Give or take an inch," came the reply.

Theo ventured mildly, "You gonna be able to walk up to within a foot of a buffalo?"

"Never give it no thought. But I read in a magazine that folks shoot 'em out of railroad cars with pistols."

Theo was silent. He looked skeptically up at the man. Exasperated, he sighed and tipped his hat back. The snow was falling faster.

The lilting voice from the wagon called, "Paw don't think much anymore, but I love him anyway." There was warmth in the voice. Theo cocked an eye at the old man, who had chuckled at the remark.

"Damn women!" the old man said under his breath. He turned to Theo with a twinkle in his eye. "You lookin' fer a woman? I got one fer cheap! By the way, call me Henry Moore."

"Paw!" the cry was indignant.

Theo shook his head, his eyes sparkling. "Reckon I got enough trouble right now. Them horses is more than enough bother for any man. I'm Theo Belk."

"Men!" the girl retorted with disgust. There was a rustling in the wagon.

The old man shook his head sorrowfully. "Lordy, now you gone and done it. Son, you'd better just hightail it back into the dark and don't light 'til you come to Chicago or Mexico or someplace like that."

The canvas parted and the girl stepped onto the wagon seat before dropping spritely to the ground. She was redheaded, tall, and quite attractive. Though her coat hid her figure, Theo let his imagination fill in the details.

"I'm Dolly Moore." She smiled saucily and offered

her hand. Theo, uncertain, took it lightly and nodded briefly.

"My pleasure, ma'am." He let go of the hand and took Henry's strong grip. "I hope you're not planning on traveling soon. From the smell of the wind we have quite a blizzard coming in."

"Hell!" Henry spat. "It's the middle of April. Shouldn't be more 'n a spit of snow this time a year."

"Can you really smell snow?" Dolly asked, blue eyes wide.

"You can smell it," Theo assented. "I'd say this one's big. Maybe a foot or two."

Henry was shaking his head. "Not that much, it's too late in the year. Why the sun's—"

"How long have you been in the West?" Theo turned his ice-blue eyes on Henry Moore.

"We went to Denver last year. Started from Richmond last spring. I was going to start a store in Denver. Well, I was, uh, foolish enough ta get involved in a poker game and got fleeced. Then I made some bad minin' deals what fell through.

"About a month ago I heard about this here hide huntin' and by jing, it sounds like just the thing. Figger'd I'd give it a whirl. Fer the money it can't be beat. I bought the rifle and a couple o' hunert cartridges. Figger one buffler per bullet an' that makes a fair investment. Can't fool me, I know bizness. Why, time was—"

Dolly broke in, "Mr. Belk, we had a freight business in Richmond. After the war, the Reconstructionists made any sort of comeback difficult. We came west 'cause Virginia is a lost cause for anyone who had anything to do with the Confederacy. It just took Paw longer to realize that than most."

Theo was still studying Henry. "You have any idea

of what hide hunting is like?" These people astounded him.

"Couldn't be any worse than mining," Henry pointed out. "That was some of the hard—"

"It sure could!" Theo cried. "An' it damn sure ain't the place to take your daughter. Hell, man, after you shoot, you work twenty-five hours a day to skin 'em. From what you tell me, I get the sneaking hunch you never skinned a rabbit let alone a buffalo! Skinning a two-thousand-pound bull ain't my idea of fun!

"Not only that but you had just better consider the Cheyenne, Arapaho, and Kiowa. They consider them animals to be theirs, given to them by God. Those Indians are bad enough, but you get farther south and you run into Comanche. Comanche will raise your hair first then they'll haul your daughter off, and even if she gets away afterward, most white women can't live with the memories! Have you ever had a good stiff Indian fight, Henry?" Theo threw up his arms in desperation.

Henry looked cowed. "I reckon I had a Cherokee that worked for me once. He was—"

Theo roared frustration. "*Henry, these ain't Cherokee*! Maybe you'd better go on back to Denver and find something more suited to your abilities. You stay out here and you'll be wolf meat within a month."

Dolly stared at Theo with wide eyes. Henry rolled his lips back and forth and looked at the ground, now white with snow. The falling flakes were swirling between them. Worried, Dolly threw another branch of wood on the fire.

Henry looked up stubbornly. "I've got to do it, Mr. Belk." The snow was clinging to his already-white beard. With a callused hand the man brushed it off.

"Guess that's your business, Mr. Moore, but I

suggest you get a heavier rifle. Better load the one you've got while you're at it," Theo said softly with a shrug.

The snow was much thicker now, coming down in sheets. Theo gathered brush and built himself a shelter. Dolly and Henry stood by the fire talking in low voices. Weaving the branches together with skill Theo completed the shelter. Dolly walked over to inspect it.

"Looks right cozy," she admired.

"The Ute build 'em this way when they are out on a war party or hunting trip. In a heavy storm like this snow builds up and creates a pretty fair shelter. Granted, a tipi is better, but they're too bulky when the men want to travel light; gives 'em more mobility."

"You know a lot about this country." Dolly looked at him intently. "I'll bet you've been here for a while."

"Raised out here," Theo murmured. "Been here all my life except for the war." She was easy to talk to. Usually, with a woman who didn't work the line, he was tongue-tied and nervous.

"Paw tried to fight. They said he was too old. He got so mad he tried to fight for the North. That didn't sit well with folks that lived around us. Paw's pretty headstrong. I guess that's why . . . well, we had such a hard time in Virginia," Dolly admitted.

"I'd say it's about midnight. You'd better get some sleep," Theo said softly. "Don't worry about getting up in the morning. Nobody's going anywhere for a while. I guess we got about three feet of snow coming if we got an inch."

"Thank you, Mr. Belk. Thank you for all you told Paw. I . . . I love him a lot, but he doesn't always understand what he's letting himself in for. Thinks that anything he puts his mind to, he'll conquer, just like that."

"That's what it takes to live out here," Theo observed, "but you have to have an understanding of the country and the people first. Guts are one thing, and brains another; without both you don't survive here. The strong and the smart live, Miss Moore. The weak and the stupid die."

"I think that's true anywhere, Mr. Belk," she responded.

"Uh-huh, but in Virginia a mistake may cost you some money or maybe a spell in the chain gang at worst. Here it means starvation, freezing, thirsting to death, or a bullet. Not much room for mistakes."

"You're a study, Mr. Belk." She squinted in the flickers of the fire. "You talk like a man who's well schooled, and yet you walk and act like I'd think an Indian would."

"Mormons kidnapped me," Theo grunted. "I was running the Green River ferry for my fa—, uh, a friend of mine, when Hawley, Thompson, and McDonald showed up in 1853 with that Mormon charter. Scar Face Bill and some others ran 'em off with what they called a Green River charter. You see, that was a Hawken rifle balanced over a cottonwood log.

"I went scoutin' their camp one night and they caught me." Theo's eyes went grim. "They taught me letters, to figure, to read and write. There wasn't much else to do but look at four walls and try and get out."

"That sounds awful," she whispered, watching him closely.

"Wouldn't do it again," Theo agreed, suddenly uncomfortable. She dropped her eyes while he wondered why he liked talking to her.

"Will you talk to Paw some more? I'd take that real kindly, Mr. Belk. I don't think he's, uh, going to give up this idea about buffalo hunting. Maybe you could tell him some things that might save his life. I know he'd listen to you. He's a smart man despite what you may believe on first impressions. He learns fast. This is just a new world for him."

He could see the sincerity in her eyes. It touched something deep inside him. What would have happened if his father had had a guide instead of bulling off down the trail by himself?

"I reckon we can talk about it tomorrow," Theo agreed as he rolled out his blankets. "I'll see you in the morning."

"Good night, Mr. Belk, and thank you again." She turned and walked slowly to the wagon.

The dream did not come that night.

Theo awoke warm in his blankets. From where he lay he could see the sorrel watching him, snow and ice thick on the horse's back. The red horse whickered a light greeting, flaring its nostrils and snorting frosted breath his direction.

The windblown snow curled and looped down through the trees, falling in stringers of icy crystals. The cottonwoods swayed and moaned as gusts whipped through them. Drifts were built and torn down again, the snow rippling and eddying over the ground.

Cursing, Theo got up and attended to the horses. Then he started to make his shelter a little larger and with the shovel on the side of Henry's wagon, built himself a small fire pit. When Henry crawled out, Theo had coffee on and a pemmican and jerky stew boiling.

"I never would've believed it could snow like this. Why right now as we are talking, there's leaves on the trees and flowers all over Virginia." Henry shivered his way up to Theo's little fire. Henry ducked into the shelter and remarked at the warmth.

"Be thankful you have the trees around," Theo gestured, pouring Henry a cup of coffee. "Think about how miserable you'd be out in the open."

"I can make a fair guess," Henry agreed. "You was right about this here blizzard." A gust of wind obliterated the world in a white haze. "If a man was walking out there—he'd be killed!" Henry muttered, shaking his head.

"It happens." Theo nodded. "And not just to greenhorns like you, either. This country is said to be hell on horses and women—but it ain't any too easy on the men at times."

"Well, Mr. Belk, Dolly said you and she had a talk about this buffalo huntin' idear o' mine. She said that you really didn't think it was such a good idear for a fella my age. I still gotta try it." Henry paused, studying the coffee in his cold hands, frowning.

"You got a daughter, Mr. Belk?" At Theo's negation, Henry continued, "It makes a difference. If I can't make me a stake now, why then . . . well, what will happen to Dolly? She's all I got! If'n I was to die, what would she do? I lost most everything I had in Virginia . . . then lost the rest in Denver. Way I see it, I got nothing to lose in the hide huntin' bizness. Besides, I promised Dolly's mother before she died that I'd, you know, leave Dolly well set."

Henry sat staring at the fire while Theo digested his words.

"All right, Henry, man's got to fulfill his obligations. Mark my words though, you'd be better off headed back to Denver. Don't underestimate the girl. She'll make do."

"I know that, Mr. Belk. Still, I don't want my daughter having to scrape to get by. Sure, she'd do just fine. Got a good head on her shoulders. But, damn, she's *my* girl. You understand what that means to a man?" Henry was getting worked up.

"Reckon I do, Mr. Moore. I can hardly remember my folks. Hmm! I did my share of scrapin' to get by. Makes a man strong, but I ain't sure about women." Theo's mouth curled slightly.

Dolly came slowly out of the wagon and kicked her way across to the little shelter. "My Gawd," she whispered, "it's warmer in here than in the wagon!"

Theo's eyes twinkled in amusement. "I got another cup here, it's been used some, but it's all I got." He poured the girl coffee and noted with approval that she didn't flinch when he handed her the stained cup.

"My word, I needed that, Mr. Belk." She sipped the coffee and huddled near the little fire. "How come this fire is so much warmer than our big one?"

"Injun fire," Theo granted. "You make a big bonfire like last night, and it's so hot, one side fries while the other freezes. Now the Injuns make a smaller fire you can sit right on top of. Course you smell like smoke, but you do stay warm. Dig the fire into the ground. It keeps the heat concentrated and the wind don't blow the sparks around. Fill the pit with rocks, too. Cooks more evenly that way."

"You know a lot about this country," Henry mused. "I take it you've shot buffalo afore?"

"Time or two," Theo granted dryly.

"Mr. Belk," Dolly asked, "which way are you headed?"

"Western Kansas," Theo told her.

"Paw, what do you say we ask Mr. Belk to join us? He knows how to hunt buffalo and he knows the country. We sure don't. I think it would be a smart thing. Maw would approve." She sipped her coffee again, pensive eyes on her father.

Henry watched the fire speculatively. He frowned and pulled at his beard. Theo sat back and thought. These fool pilgrims would slow him down. Still, anyone hunting buffalo would be where Louis was going to be. The question was, would Louis set up in a town or be out on the plains? It came to him that with Sabot, they'd probably stick to the plains where Louis could prey on greenhorns just like these. Louis'd do Henry and Dolly the same as he had done Theo's mother and father.

"Mr. Belk, you interested?" Henry asked.

"Might be," Theo offered.

"I reckon we go fifty-fifty to start," Dolly suggested. "Then if you decide to do something different, Paw could buy you out. I don't want you to feel you're being pushed into this."

Theo said firmly, "I might have to ride off of a sudden. I got some things I gotta do. I don't want in if I got to stay in one place. I'll do what I can for as long as I can and we split the profits when I pull my stake. That way there's no papers and no obligation other than what's fair. Just don't start dependin' on me bein' around, that's all."

"Sounds good to me," Dolly agreed, her face reflecting satisfaction. "Paw?"

"Reckon I got a lot to learn about this here country to start with—an' buffler huntin' fer seconds. I never had a partner in anythin' but I guess this, uh, makes sense. I won't hold you when you want to go, Theo.

You'll get what's your fair share, I give you my word." Henry swallowed the last of his coffee.

Theo pulled a tin pan from his pack and dipped the pemmican from the little pot. Blowing on it, he sipped some. "All right, I'm in for a while at least." He looked Henry in the eye. "If I give you an order, I want it obeyed. There's folks out here that will mean to kill you Henry—red and white. There's things that'll kill you just as dead as a bullet, like this here storm. You think you can live with that?"

"I reckon," Henry granted. "You done made a lot o' sense already. I may be stiff-necked, but I can see when I got to pay my dues."

"I'll see that he does, Mr. Belk." Dolly grinned. "May I try your stew?" She drained her coffee and dipped some out. A strange expression crossed her face. "What is this?"

"Pemmican. Made of buffalo fat, dried meat, and crushed berries and roots. It'll keep you alive." Theo filled Henry's coffee cup from the bubbling broth.

They spent the day talking about the country and Theo told stories about places he'd been and men he had met. Dolly seemed to draw him out.

"So I ran with the Shoshoni kids when I could get away from Shasty. I heard the tales that can only be told in the dead of winter. Then Fletch and Skin took me off to learn trapping and hunting. Shot my first buffalo at twelve." Theo smiled at the memory.

Henry sat enraptured as Theo spun his yarns.

"When's this gonna break?" Henry asked a day later, slogging through two feet of wet snow.

"I'd say sometime tonight from the pattern of the clouds," Theo answered, watching the flakes falling from the gray sky.

"Don't see how you can tell what the cloud patterns

are through all this stuff," Henry growled. "Then what? Do we freeze for another couple o' months?"

Theo chuckled. "The sun will be so bright tomorrow morning you won't be able to stand it, Henry. I'll bet it's fifty degrees by noon tomorrow."

"Damn strange country," Henry offered. Theo shrugged.

True to Theo's prediction, the sun rose the next morning in a cloudless blue sky. The world was a white wonderland of drifted snow sculpted into fantastic shapes. Theo put his outfit together as the Moores hitched up their horses.

A short distance from camp, Theo dropped a deer at three hundred yards with a well-placed shot. Henry was amazed and Dolly's eyes glowed.

"Not bad shootin'," Henry mumbled. "Not bad a'tall."

"I think we done good, Paw. I think Theo Belk is just about the best thing to happen to us in quite a while."

Theo said nothing as he dumped the deer carcass in the back of the wagon, but he was conscious of her eyes on him.

Belk took the lead, breaking trail while Henry's team followed, making tough work in the deep drifts. As the sun rose higher and the wind warmed, the snow on the ridge tops retreated, making a morass of mud over the frozen substratum. Mud clung to the wheels of the wagon and the horses' feet. Leading the animals on foot, Henry cursed as he kicked gobs from his feet.

Stopping to rest the animals, Henry remarked, "Reckon you could make better time without us."

"Yep, sure could." Theo trimmed some tobacco from his plug and put it in his mouth. When he got it juicing, he spat a brown stream.

Henry didn't try to push conversation. He was becoming aware that Theo only spoke when he was in the mood. It wasn't the right time.

That night, Dolly was cheerful as she roasted venison over the tiny fire. Theo had shown them how to skin out the deer, letting them do the work. Dolly proved better at it than Henry, who tended to buttonhole the hide.

The night was warm and the snow continued to melt. They said little that night; Henry sought his blankets early after having fought the mud all day. Dolly seemed to want to talk so Theo answered her questions about the land, the weather, and the buffalo.

"You have any family, Mr. Belk?" she asked as she poured him another cup of coffee.

"Might," Theo admitted somewhat uncomfortably. "Reckon I had some somewhere. After my folks was gone I didn't have much of a way to find them. I can remember Ohio as a kid. I'm not sure just where we was from. I think I remember an uncle and grandparents."

He also remembered another Ohio where they locked him up for trying to steal a horse. After escaping the Mormons, he'd gone east trying to find Louis. His horse had broken down and he'd been jailed when he stole another. The feeling of his stolen knife sliding between the guard's ribs when escaping stirred the demons resting in his subconscious.

"Have you ever gone to see them?" Dolly settled herself on a pack, unaware of his thoughts.

"Nope, never had no desire. Don't reckon there'd be too much to talk about. That was a long time ago an' I been over the mountain and down the creek since then." Theo sipped the coffee, retracing his pursuit of Louis Gasceaux. He'd seen a newspaper clipping in Salt Lake. A French nobleman had bought a plantation in North Carolina. The tintype had looked like Louis.

"How about . . . a wife, Mr. Belk? Do you have someone, someone waiting for you somewhere?" she asked softly, eyes on the fire.

"Nope, ain't nobody but me and the horses." Theo was far away, hardly aware of her questions. But war had broken out while he was in prison. The obvious way to find Louis—then a Confederate captain—was to enlist. He hadn't any idea how big a war could be. His concepts had still been Western in nature.

"Reckon I'll turn in. Gonna be a long day tomorrow." He smiled absently.

"Good night, Mr. Belk," Dolly whispered. "Sleep well."

Theo nodded and went to his bedroll. It had been a long time since he was with people who were so easy to get along with.

Sure, they asked questions they shouldn't; but they listened to everything he told them. It made him feel important. No one had ever depended on him before. Curious emotions stirred within his breast.

Henry was striding next to the horses the following day as Theo walked along beside, leading the sorrel. The arroyos were running bank-full of muddy brown water as the snow retreated. Somewhere a meadowlark was trilling its welcome to spring.

"Never heard such a pretty bird song," Henry said with a smile. "Warms my old sour soul."

"That it does," Theo agreed. "Meadowlarks mean spring and warm weather. Shoshoni kids wait all winter to see who the first is to hear one."

"Dolly said you was educated by the Mormons." Henry cocked his head. "Some trainin' you got. Injun and white man knowledge."

Theo worked his chew in his mouth. "That Mormon education wasn't exactly my idea. Every time I run off they sent them damn tame Utes of theirs to bring me back. If I didn't learn, I didn't eat."

"Looks like you got away in the end." Henry looked out over the gently rolling grasslands.

"Only because the army was riding in under Johnston's command. Mormons shipped me out to a farm just before the United States invaded. With them burning all the fields and falling back into the desert, why, I couldn't turn down the chance to go."

He didn't add anything about old man Jones. He'd pinned him to the wall of the barn with a pitchfork as a token of his esteem and for all the beatings. His name was probably still on a death list somewhere in Utah.

"I went east then, Henry. Got there in time for the war. Fought all the way through till the end. Went with Sherman to the sea and right up through the Carolinas. Saw a sight of the East—enough to never want to go back."

"It was different before the war," Henry averred.

"Wouldn't have made any difference to me, Henry." Theo spat. "It's all . . . settled." He looked up into the blue sky, seeing the wheeling shapes of eagles. To his left a jackrabbit bounced and sailed. "It ain't free back there," Theo added softly. "A man needs to move, to go where he wants with no one saying yes or no. No man can tell me I'm on his land out here. This is where life is, Henry. I'd die back there."

Henry seemed perplexed. "I'm not meanin' ta be pryin' at you, but where are you goin' anyway? Why's a man like you just roamin' 'round the country?"

Theo fixed his cold eyes on Henry before he spoke.

The demons chattered in his ear. "I'm lookin' for a man. He's somewhere ahead. I have to find him . . . that's all. Been on his trail since I was little."

"Who is he? Can I help?" Henry's honest eyes met Theo's.

The blamed fool was sincere! Amused, Theo smiled thinly. At the same time, a little panic started to build. The last thing he needed was interference from some damn greenhorn. Hell, Henry didn't realize he had to kill Gasceaux!

Feeling his panic spread, Theo started to anger. The demons rustled darkly in his mind. Still staring at Henry, he stepped into the saddle of the sorrel and kicked the animal to a trot with the pack animals behind.

Henry stopped in his tracks and shook his head. Then he cursed and caught his pace next to the wagon as it rolled by.

"What was that all about?" Dolly asked from the seat.

"Damned if I know." Henry spat into the mud. "Just asked him what he was doing out here." Henry paused in thought.

"Such an interesting man," Dolly said to herself as the now-distant figure topped the horizon. Henry threw an appraising glance at his daughter and thought some more. Why did he get that feeling of unease when Theo looked at him just so? There was a wild, untamed feeling of invincibility about Belk. In his presence, Henry felt small, somehow silly, but at the same time Belk represented a way to succeed and secure Dolly's future.

As the sun sank into the west, Henry began to worry. Theo Belk did not return.

CHAPTER 6

FROM THE WINDSWEPT RIDGE TOP, THEO LOOKED DOWN into the swale. The grass was greening nicely, but the white streak of snow was almost blinding in the morning sunshine. Henry's wagon was canted at a ridiculous angle. Moore had no doubt misjudged the snow, not realizing there was an arroyo underneath.

A pile of belongings was growing as Henry shoveled, trying to lower the box. His team stood in slumped boredom, awaiting the command to try pulling again.

"Reckoned you was takin' too long, Henry," Theo granted wryly, leaning over the saddle horn. Fifteen minutes later, the wagon was free and mostly reloaded.

"Glad to see you back. Hoped you'd not gone on," Henry admitted as he scraped mud off his soaked britches.

Theo looked around the horizon before replying. "I guess I'd hate to see you come to any grief out here, Henry. You're a good man, but you and the girl don't know enough to be chasing around loose."

Theo lowered his voice. "Hell, that man I'm trying to find will take time to set himself up. He'll be in or around Dodge when we get in. If that's where he's got to. If he's not there, I'll pick up his track. I've done it before." Theo watched Dolly climb into the seat and cluck the horses into movement.

"You a lawman?" Henry's eyes got wide.

Theo laughed. "No, Henry, it's personal business that goes back a ways. Now keep mum about it," Theo warned. "A man's personal doings are his and that's all."

"Uh-huh," Henry said slowly. "I figger'd you fer a rough one, Mr. Belk."

They stood silently for a while, each lost in his own thoughts before Henry said, "Had to shoot me a man once. I was a kid then. We had us an argument over Dolly's mama an' we settled it one morning. I ain't never gonna fergit him a layin' on the ground coughing up blood. Guess that's why I never liked guns too much afterward."

Theo was still silent, seeing in his mind all the men he'd killed. The glazed eyes looked at him with accusation. The demons stirred. Henry looked at the muddy ground where the wagon had been stuck and shrugged. "Dolly don't know that. I never wanted to tell her."

"Reckon I didn't hear it then, Henry." Theo swung onto the sorrel and took off in the wagon's lead.

The sun warmed during the following days and the drifts became ghosts along the arroyo walls and north slopes before admitting defeat to the relentless sun. They sighted their first buffalo. Henry was immediately set to ride into the middle of them shooting with his old Henry rifle. Theo put his foot down.

"Theo!" Henry cried. "Lookit 'em out there. Must be a million dollars afore our eyes." Henry waved his arms at the distant bison.

"Uh-huh, an' you'll ride right into the middle of them an' start shootin'. Then after the stampede, Dolly and I won't find enough of your body to put in an oyster tin. Whatever give you the idea that you ride right into the middle of a herd? That takes a lot of savvy and a horse that's been trained for years!" Theo concluded with a gasp and exasperated sigh.

"Saw the pictures in xHarper's magazine one time," Henry said, swelling to his full five feet and six inches and glaring at Theo.

"Hell! *Harper's* magazine!" Theo stomped around. Dolly was watching them trying to stifle laughter. "You sit here, Henry! You sit here and watch what I do. You hear? Dolly! You make sure this plumb fool idjit stays put. If he makes one move toward that herd . . . *shoot 'im!"* Theo jumped into the saddle and trotted out on the sorrel.

"Told you, Paw," Dolly smirked.

"Quiet, woman," Henry growled as he muttered under his breath to himself.

Theo rode toward the herd at a slow pace, keeping the wind to one side. He skirted a low ridge and ground hitched the sorrel. Pulling the Sharps, he crawled on hands and knees to the crest of the hill and waited nearly forty-five minutes until the herd had drifted closer.

When the animals had moved as close as they would get, Theo shot an old cow. As she fell, a younger cow walked up to sniff the body. When she turned sideways, Theo shot her. In a like manner he killed another two animals before rising to his feet and sauntering back to his horse. The buffalo continued to drift past the dead.

At Theo's wave, Dolly and Henry drove the wagon up to the bodies. Theo had retrieved his horse and started skinning the animals.

"You only shot four!" Henry cried watching the herd move off. "You could'a kilt a hunert!"

"Henry," Theo said woodenly, "get off your duff and get down here. You're gonna see once and for all just what you got yourself into!"

By dark they had skinned the four animals and staked the hides out. Henry collapsed by the fire. He didn't even eat, but fell soundly asleep on the spot. Theo, under no such compulsion, ate heartily of hump roast and slightly cooked liver. Dolly cringed when he poured bile over the bloody stuff.

"That has to taste horrible," she moaned.

"Keeps you fit. Too much red meat colics a man. There's tales of greenhorns who only ate lean meat. They got sicker'n Hob if they didn't eat the lights, too. Indians say it makes up for a lack of greens during the winter."

Dolly just nodded, still looking grim. Henry started to snore and grunt in his sleep.

"Thank you for having so much patience with him," Dolly said lightly. "He tries so hard sometimes. I know that he's all ambition and no experience, but he's learning."

"He's a good man," Theo agreed. "I can't help but like him. He'll make do. I reckon today did him more good than anything. He sure pitched into the work and by jing he stuck with it till it was done."

"He doesn't give up." She smiled at the sleeping man. "We've had to do so many things the last four years. Paw just pitches in and gives it the best he's got. He never learned to give up. He has to be kicked real hard before he'll admit it's time to do something else."

"Makes a man a success," Theo said positively.

"How about yourself, Mr. Belk? Do you consider yourself to be a success?" She watched him as she sliced meat from the bone and chewed it thoughtfully.

"Now that's a question if I ever heard one." Theo grinned. "I'm alive. That's about all the success I guess a fella can count on. I see the sun come up in the morning and go down at night. I rely on myself and don't have nobody to tell me what to do. Bein' alive is the test of success."

"That's an interesting way to measure success, Mr. Belk." Her eyes held his for an electric moment before they dropped.

Theo cleared his throat awkwardly. "I'm a hunter, Miss Moore. Sure, I could build me a house—and a fine one to boot! But then what? I'd have to live in the blamed thing. Me? Stay put? Naw, there's too much of me in the trail. Only time I had to stay put, the damn Mormons made me. Poor doin's that!"

"Don't you ever want a wife and family?" She looked puzzled. "Everyone needs to be loved . . . sometime."

Theo sat back and sighed, remembering. "I loved someone once," he said softly.

She was startled at the pain in his eyes, then they turned hard and cold as he got to his feet and walked off into the night where his bedroll lay.

Dolly picked up the dishes and cleaned up around the fire. Then she towed Henry to bed and lay awake thinking of the things Theo Belk had told her.

Hours later she heard Theo cry out and peeked out past the canvas. He was bolt upright in the bedroll and she could see sweat glistening on his face in the pale moonlight. He was gone the next morning.

Two days later, wondering if they would ever see Theo Belk again, Dolly and Henry pulled up at the sight of thousands of buffalo scattered over the grass before them. Henry was pulling his rifle out when Theo rode up.

"You ready to shoot a buffalo, Henry?" Theo asked offhandedly.

"Uh-huh, I shore am, Theo. Glad to see you back. You tell me what to do this time an' I'll do it." Henry smiled. He was coming to accept Theo's peregrinations. Dolly was quiet and watched Theo with a puzzled frown on her face.

"Let's go!" Theo turned the sorrel and, stepping down, tied it off on the tailgate. Since Henry didn't have a saddle horse, they walked to the nearest group while Dolly followed slowly with the wagon.

Theo showed Henry how to use the wind and they made a stalk on the small bunch. "Shoot that old cow." Theo pointed to an animal and handed Henry the Sharps. He adjusted the Lawrence sight and hunkered down next to Henry.

Theo called the shooting at four animals. Henry could at least shoot straight. Only one old cow needed a follow-up shot from Theo. The skinning chore started all over again. Both Dolly and Henry remarked on the fact it hadn't gotten any easier.

The hides scraped and pegged out, camp was made and fresh, lean buffalo placed over a chip fire to roast.

Theo had cut off the humps and taken the tongues. A long string of intestines went into the red coals and sizzled as they swelled with steam. He didn't notice Dolly and Henry excuse themselves, nauseated, as he started eating the fresh-roasted boudins.

Later over coffee, Henry and Dolly were both scratching. "Fleas and graybacks," Theo told them with a grin. "You'll get used to it."

"I must have blood all over!" Dolly stared miserably at her soiled, blood-stained clothing. "Paw, this hunting may make money but it's hard as all get out on clothes. Then Theo tells me I have fleas!" She looked at the men with desperate resignation.

"I reckon we can find a creek sometime soon," Theo said with a laugh. "Then you'll be in fine shape . . . till next time."

"I can hardly wait," Dolly groaned.

"You know, it sure seems a shame to waste all that meat." Henry scratched as they listened to the coyotes yapping around the carcasses.

"There's lots more buffalo," Theo grunted.

On May 20, 1871, they drove into what used to be Buffalo City. Now it was known as Dodge City—after the fort on its outskirts. The state of Kansas hadn't liked the old name since it conflicted with another community called Buffalo farther east. Many of the community's inhabitants kept the old name, especially the hunters who claimed the town as their own.

Like many another boomtown of the era, Dodge City was wide open and catering to the nomadic male population of the plains. Buffalo hunters—or runners as they called themselves—liked their amusements. Stiff drink, games of chance with long odds, feminine companionship, and brawls were readily available.

There were no restrictions outside those imposed by "Colonel Colt's" law.

A dozen rough, frame houses lined the street. A similar number of soddys and a score of wall tents and dugouts composed the dwellings of the more stable of the fluid population. The itinerants lived out of open camps, wagon boxes, and tipis. The grandest building in the new metropolis was Essington's Hotel.

Feeling good about the sale of their green hides, Henry proclaimed a celebration dinner. Drooling in anticipation of a real, cooked, sit-down-at-the-table meal, Henry led the way. Dolly received more than her share of stares from the mostly unwashed collection of soldiers and buffalo hunters as they walked through the restaurant.

Theo had sold his share of the hides while Henry and Dolly had twenty-four for themselves, many of which Henry had shot with Theo's Sharps. Their covered freight wagon had changed appearance considerably from the wagon Theo had found in Colorado. It was now stripped of most of the bows and the canvas had been modified into a tent. The box that had held supplies was now rid of fragrant hides.

"By God!" Henry cried as they sat at a table. "Civilization! I'm gonna have me real vegetables, with potatoes and gravy and maybe a whole roasted chicken, or maybe a ham steak, or maybe even beef stew! Lord, how I've been looking forward to this day!"

"What will it be gentlemen and lady?" Essington asked after they were seated.

"What 'ave you got?" Henry grinned at the man, smacking his lips.

"Well, we've got buffalo, buffalo and beans, and just plain beans," Essington replied, ticking off his fingers.

"Two house specials," Theo ordered, indicating himself and Dolly. Essington nodded.

"Hell of a choice!" Henry cried. "That all you got in this here big fancy restaurant? What kind of a place you runnin' here anyway? I want real food. I been eat'n buffler for weeks now!"

"What do you expect? Lobster in Kansas?" Essington roared back, glaring at Moore. Then he smiled. "We do have pies."

"Pie!" Henry's face lit up. "Now there's something! Bring me a pie. I want the whole thing!"

"Hey, Hank!" Essington hollered to a man across the room. "This man wants pie. You want to do the honors?" A fellow in a buckskin jacket left on the run, a grin spreading on his face.

"Now that's more like it," Henry said smugly. "Place like this ought to have good pies. Buffler, fer Gawd's sake!" He grimaced at the end.

Essington returned with two heaping plates of buffalo and beans for Dolly and Theo. He grinned maliciously at Henry.

"Where's mine?" Henry demanded.

"We are heating it up, sir. I don't like to serve cold pie in my fine restaurant," Essington replied with a flourish.

Five minutes later, Hank strode in with a large dish covered by steaming towels. The other diners were looking on with obvious enjoyment.

"Better be game to what's coming off," Theo whispered to Dolly.

Hank set the steaming plate on the table and handed Henry a napkin and a fork.

"You will need these, sir. Our pies are very juicy. We have to send special teams out to import the ingredients. I can guarantee, sir, you will find no other restaurant in the region—hell, the whole country—that serves the like. You are about to sink your teeth into an Essington specialty."

Hank paused for effect. Then, with great ceremony, as Henry looked on, he pulled the towel away. Moore started to drive his fork into the contents only to find two steaming buffalo chips resting in the bottom.

"What in hell?" Henry looked up, stricken.

"Yes sir," Essington replied with a smirk. "That there is genuine buffalo pie!" The entire room broke into a pandemonium of approval and delight.

Henry began to turn red. "Reckon I'd sort o' take a plate of meat and beans," he grumbled miserably.

Theo asked Essington to join them. At first Henry fidgeted, but Essington was a hard man to hold a grudge against.

"I guess I stepped right into that," Henry finally admitted.

"Oh, no, Mr. Moore. If you had, you'd have it on your boots instead of your plate." Essington had a satisfied look on his face.

"We've got a good start here," Essington told them later. "There's no problem in starting a business. The trouble is keeping it supplied. To illustrate one of our problems, Rath has over two tons of flour sitting in his store. The freighters, Long Brothers, can't find a single can of baking soda for him in the whole state! The way things sell here, if Rath could get that baking soda, he could sell every loaf of bread he could bake—and at a healthy profit!

"The railroad will be here any time now, and when that happens, the prices will drop for everyone. As it is, everything in town has to be freighted in in wagons from the End-of-the-Tracks. It costs money, and that's only when you can get the supplies you need. We're growing like mad as a result of the hide business and the commerce from the fort. Of course, a lady like Dolly will find the surroundings a bit, uh, crude, but that goes with the country. It's just the nature of any new town out here."

"So good money can be made on hides?" Henry was thoughtful.

"If you have the right kind of outfit." Essington nodded. "The arrival of the railroad will help a lot, too. I guess you've found out how cumbersome it is to transport green hides. When the railroad comes to Dodge, the hide market will bust wide open and business will be extremely lucrative. But keep in mind that you have to keep your money," Essington finished darkly.

"How's that?" Henry asked.

Essington smiled and shrugged. "Most of the boys around here are buffalo runners for the express purpose of making a good haul so they can come to town and blow the profits. They just don't give a da—, er, excuse me, Miss Moore. They plain don't care.

"They go out on that prairie, freeze, fry, thirst, starve, get shot at and scalped, suffer dysentery, work like dogs, and make a fair enough living just to come to town and blow the whole proceeds in one night of fun and drink. Crazy if you ask me, but by jinks, they load up the next morning, broke as beggars and pop-skulled 'til Hob won't have it, and ride out again to do it all over. Craziness!"

Henry looked sober. "I see, but I'm too old for that kind of nonsense. Besides, I have to take care of Dolly here. That's why I'm out here in the first place. And thank God Theo came along when he did. I learned more from him in the last two months than I could have learned after years in Denver. I'll leave with money, Mr. Essington. You just watch me."

"With that attitude you might," Essington agreed. Then he looked at Theo. "How about you Mr. Belk. Do you think you'll get out of the game ahead?"

"Might." Theo nodded. Then his eyes narrowed. "Mr. Essington, you must see just about everyone that comes through here. Do you remember a feller who may have arrived in the last couple of months? Big man with a full beard, talks with a kind of French accent. He's strong as a bull. He's flashy and likes to spend money. Last I heard he was traveling with an old trapper named Sabot. I don't happen to have the name he's using these days. Sort of changes it on impulse."

Essington thought for a bit then looked up. "You might mean Dupree. He was in about a month ago. He bought an outfit and went out to run buffalo. He was with an old man, a trapper, I think, who claimed to have been a mountain man. The old man chewed tobacco like it was candy.

"Dupree spent a lot of time down on the line. If those are the men, I'd say they'll be back. There's not much of anyplace else to sell hides around here." Essington paused at the wolf look in Theo's eyes.

"Good. They're old friends of mine. It would be fun to surprise them. I'd appreciate it if you didn't say I'd been in." Theo looked like the cat that got the canary. He was trying to look casual but he knew Henry had drunk in every word of it. Essington was no fool either. Dolly, looking at him thoughtfully, knew there was more than curiosity in his request.

"Yep," Essington continued. "I hear that he's going after hides. He bought an outfit, then the night they were leaving he was relieved of a rather large sum of money over in George Hoover's saloon. They had words and this man Dupree came pretty close to calling Hoover. George is no greenhorn. He has house men all over that place. Dupree backed down and left that night for the buffalo ranges."

"So the old wolf got fleeced." Theo laughed louder than he should have. "Mr. Essington, that makes me warm all over. I appreciate hearing that. Why, you never know . . ."

Dolly was studying Theo again but she kept her thoughts to herself. Henry sighed, looking worriedly at Theo, but Belk was oblivious to them all. Lost in his private amusement, he sat in the chair smiling to himself.

Leaving Dolly to her own ends, Theo and Henry walked back to Rath's store, where they had traded their hides and resupplied. Theo managed to find enough cartridges to fit his rifle and also picked up one of the reloading tools, primers, powder, and lead.

The prices were high, with corn meal twice the cost of a pound in Denver. Moore traded his old Henry for a new Remington. The reoutfitting cleaned out their earnings from the first trip.

Being broke, they rounded Dolly up and made the decision to go back to hunting the next day. Theo just nodded when Henry asked if he was going to continue with them. Out there, somewhere, was Louis Gasceaux. For the first time, Theo had a chance to make money while he looked for his nemesis.

The next morning, early, they hooked up the traces and pulled out, the wagon rumbling and banging in the dusty, rutted streets. The weather was wonderful as they started west along the Arkansas River bottoms. A southern breeze was blowing in the scents of springtime. The rolling grasslands were verdant in new growth and wildflowers made a many-colored carpet on the spring grass. The brush along the creeks was leafing out, as were the cottonwoods. It was a good day to live.

Dolly cantered up on the horse she had spent her earnings for. Belk was riding the sorrel in advance of the wagon. "Theo!" she cried. "It's so beautiful. Do you think we'll have luck finding the buffalo?"

"Sure," Theo met her grin. "Keep in mind though, if we find a big herd, we won't make a big haul. We shoot what we can skin. There's just the three of us. You know how much work we had skinnin' those others on the way in."

She nodded. "We can build though. This time we get a little ahead. Then we invest in a bigger outfit and go back for more. I'm so glad you decided to come with us again, Mr. Belk. Looking back, I don't see that we could have made it as far as Dodge without you. Paw has been learning, too. I think he needed someone like you to come along. You are our godsend, Mr. Belk."

Theo thought about that last. A godsend? Him? Thinking about who and what he was, he managed a small chuckle.

"Don't go relying on me too much," he warned. "I might just take a notion someday and pull my stick for other waters."

"But you can't!" Dolly cried. "What would we do without you? You have come to mean an awful lot to us, Mr. Belk. Paw and I like your company. You're a walking classroom on the country. Tell me what we'd do if you left?"

He looked into her deep, blue eyes and felt something rising inside him. They were pretty eyes. The notion came that he could look into those eyes for a long time.

"Get along, I reckon." Theo was casual. The girl's words bothered him. He'd almost quit these greenhorns more than once. Something he labeled curiosity kept bringing him back—usually just as they were headed for some sort of trouble or other.

He remembered how he had felt that first time he brought a deer to camp. Dolly's eyes had been wide with praise. It made him feel good to provide for them. Why? What new thing was he supposed to learn about himself, and how did it fit into the hunt for Louis Gasceaux? Was this the work of some sinister unknown force like he had experienced with Liz and Irish O'Connell?

Perhaps this, too, was a test of vulnerability? Men had been made to stand on their own two feet, as he had since that day on the Blacks Fork. It was one of God's laws. Was he here to teach that lesson to Henry, or to learn for himself? Puzzled, Theo tried to make sense of the whole thing.

It was law that those who could, made their own way in the world. They did it through fortitude, strength, and knowledge. The others would perish or become obstacles to the survivors. Was Henry an obstacle, or a man learning to be a survivor? Mystified, Theo searched for the answer.

Henry and the girl had been quick studies as he showed them how to survive on the plains. He had taught them where to go to dig the right kind of roots to supplement a meat diet, and how to make a fire that didn't blow away in the wind. He'd taught them how to find water and how to keep the horses from being stolen by wandering red men. Some part of himself had been touched by that. Now he questioned why and wondered what was happening to him.

These people were so different from the other

immigrants he had met. Or were they? They had to be. They hadn't tried to tell him about the Bible or the Christian way of doing things. Dolly wasn't at all like the dour-faced women that went to carve new homes out of pristine land.

He liked the girl. He enjoyed knowing that she was watching him as he went about his chores, and had caught himself doing things more than once just so that she would notice him. To his mind it made no sense at all.

"And I'm a godsend," he muttered. Grimly, he wondered what she would think if she knew how many men he'd shot. Then came the memory of Liz and the look of disgust she had given him when Toddy Blake had fallen limply to the floor, stinking with his fear of death. Theo glanced at Dolly and watched her bright eyes taking in the country. He didn't want to see that look in her eyes.

Those men he'd killed hadn't been strong like he was. They were weak and ineffectual. He had survived and they had all needed killing. It made the world a better place for the strong. Just like sick elk and buffalo were weeded by the wolves. The same laws of nature worked for men. He was a wolf, but would Dolly understand?

"We might have already died without you," Dolly reminded him seriously, her eyes almost luminescent.

She tossed her red curls so he could see the creamy white of her neck. He swallowed hard.

Theo appreciated the way she sat the saddle, astride rather than sidesaddle. Another trick Theo had taught her—to Henry's displeasure. What good was Eastern propriety when clinging to a horse might mean the difference between life and death in flood or Indian fight?

Dolly was much more attractive than Liz had ever been. Dolly was bright, soft, unsullied, and kind. Liz had been a child of the Montana gold camps and she made her way on her own. Dolly had never been pushed. She reminded Theo of a flower: delicate, colorful, and pleasing to the sight, touch, and smell . . . and she needed him!

He shook his head slightly, drawing Dolly's attention. No one had ever needed him before. It was a weakness, he reminded himself, to need anyone. At the same time it made Theo Belk feel good. The demons muttered sourly.

"You look serious, Mr. Belk," she said lightly. "You do that a lot. Is there anything you want to talk about? I'd listen if you wanted to tell me."

"Nope, just ruminatin'," he mumbled, still trying to sort out the conflicting thoughts. How was a man supposed to place any kind of order to such thoughts? Where was truth in this mess of need, strength, and appreciation? Where was survival? Which way led to Louis Gasceaux?

How in the name of the Almighty was a man to know? Why in the name of Hob did his world have to keep getting so cluttered? His quest for Gasceaux—so simple in essence—could get so twisted and contorted. What was right? What was he supposed to learn now?

He turned to look at the girl. She met his stare and her mouth opened a little, showing him straight white teeth. There was interest and curiosity in her eyes, as well as strength. She gave him a slight smile and her eyes were challenging. A little color was rising along her neck. Theo wondered what that meant.

"I would like to know what you were thinking," she

continued softly, the tone of her voice holding no threat. Theo held back. How did a man tell a woman about truth and strength and survival?

"Been thinkin' about buffalo, Miss Moore. When you ride to hunt you've got to put yourself in the animal's place. Try to figger on what they're doing and where they'll be. Tough to do in the spring when the new grass is up. Buffalo can go just about anywhere." He could tell it sounded awkward.

"I understand, Mr. Belk," she said looking around the horizon. She knew he was fibbing, he realized. There had been a twinkle in her eye, and even now he could see the ghost of a smile playing at the corners of her lips. "How many do you think we'll get?"

"I'd say we'd do best to pick up about three a day when we get into buffalo. More would be a waste of ammunition. That's about enough to keep everyone busy without runnin' ourselves and the stock into the ground."

"I heard that Tom Nixon shot a hundred and twenty in forty minutes," she said dreamily.

"Uh-huh, an' how many of 'em did his skinners get before they moved on?" Theo drawled, shifting his gaze to watch her.

"I don't know." She looked at him with cool, appraising eyes. There was still that look to her eyes, as if she knew something he didn't. It was worrisome.

"Got forty-five of 'em," Theo continued. "That's bad business. It means seventy-five rotted. Tough part is if the Cheyenne or Kiowa hear about it, somebody will die for it. They don't hold to that kind of thing. They don't mind runnin' a thousand head over a cliff, but they consider them to be part of their spiritual world. When we kill 'em, the medicine ain't right."

She threw him a cool look. "You always seem to be right, Mr. Belk. That's impressive. Don't you ever make mistakes?"

"Hah," he snorted, remembering how he lost his head in Denver. He'd sure made a bad one when he shot O'Connell. "I guess I do, Miss Moore, but I'm alive and that means I'm doing something right. Never had anyone say I was impressive before."

She looked away with hidden thoughts in her eyes. He couldn't understand it. No woman had ever treated him this way. Did she want something from him?

"Maybe you are, Mr. Belk. You seem so sure of yourself; you always know what to do. I know that Paw is impressed by you and I am, too. I'm so glad you are with us," she said pensively.

Theo felt the conflicting emotions in his chest. Her words pleased him while they also made him self-conscious. Why did it seem that he and the girl were supposed to know something special? The feeling of confusion came back to haunt him.

"Sure wish old Skin could hear you say that, Miss Moore," Theo joked to get his mind off it.

"I'd like it if you'd call me Dolly, Theo." Her eyes were warm. What was he supposed to do? He felt lost.

"All right, Dolly. I guess a partnership is a lot less formal than Sunday go to meetin'." Theo felt choked up, still trying to sort out his feelings. The girl wasn't making it any easier.

"Have you thought about what you are going to do after we finish buffalo running?" she asked.

"Nope, not yet. Dolly, I reckon that I'll ride on ahead and scout out the trail some." He could see disappointment rising in her eyes. "Don't get too far from the wagon and make sure Henry's got that new Remington of his loaded."

Leaving the girl behind in his urgent need to flee from the throttled emotions building in his breast, he remembered the almost frustrated look that had been in her eyes.

CHAPTER 7

THAT NIGHT, THEO CAMPED IN A DRY DRAINAGE CHANNEL. He slowly fed sticks and branches into the small fire while his rabbit cooked. The Sharps glistened in the flickers of yellow firelight. The moon overhead had been obscured by dark clouds and Theo could smell the coming rain.

As he ate the rabbit, his mind worried at his confusion. Why did these pilgrims bother him so? He just plain liked them and there wasn't anything wrong with that. Henry and Dolly were his friends. Startled, he realized he had never called anyone his friend.

"I'll be damned," he muttered. "Must be what that fool girl was talking about. I'll just be confounded if that ain't what this is all about!" Theo began to laugh.

But, was there a trap in friendship? What did it have to do with Louis Gasceaux?

His thoughts kept straying back to Dolly. He hoped they would be all right in the storm, and he had a sudden urge to ride back and make sure Henry hadn't got himself into some sort of trouble. No, he steeled himself. The land was flat; they could follow the trail and he hadn't seen any Indian sign.

His thoughts kept returning to the freckles on the girl's face and her hair glinting red-gold in the sun. He heard her voice and remembered the look in her eyes. He saw her beckon to him and as he walked close, she opened her arms to enfold him. He hugged her tenderly and breathed in her fragrance. Slowly, he bent down to kiss her full lips. The demons in the back of his mind screamed. The dream exploded. A cold drop of water splatted on his hand. It began to rain.

Matching his suddenly dark mood, the wind kicked up and the heavens opened. Theo stood and checked the horses. Satisfied, he returned to the arroyo and crouched under the bank out of the storm.

His soogan on, hat pulled low over his head, he watched the water fall from the dark heavens. The rain continued to pick up and large drops battered their way into his slight shelter, thudding into the ash of his fire, raising little puffs of steam.

Brilliant streaks of lightning slashed across the sky, flashing on the landscape to be followed closely by banging crashes of thunder. In the flare of lightning, Theo sullenly watched the streamers of rain. The creek had begun to run.

Angry with himself and nature, Theo left the creek bed and scaled his way up the muddy bank. He stood on a terrace and watched a wall of water roar through the overhang where moments before he had sheltered.

He howled and cursed at the sight. That trick was an old one. Never stay in a creek bottom when the rain is fierce. The night became one of misery, loneliness, pain, and terror as the demons giggled and lightning cavorted overhead.

It was late afternoon the next day when Theo topped a low hill and rode down to the wagon.

"Where you been?" Henry asked curiously, with a slightly concerned look.

"Scoutin', Henry, just scoutin'," Theo replied laconically.

"Well, all right. What did you see?" the old man asked as he set the brake on the wagon and dug the makings from his bag. He stuffed his pipe and tamped it. Striking a sulphur match, he puffed contentedly while he watched Theo.

"Saw a buffalo," Theo returned lightly, kicking his foot from the stirrup and hitching a knee over the saddle horn. He took out his plug and shaved some tobacco. Working up the quid, he spat a stream. Dolly was watching his every move.

"Saw a buffalo, eh?" Henry took the pipe stem from his mouth. "Did you shoot it?"

"Nope, just let it go." Theo looked casually at the horizon.

"Damn, Theo," Henry snorted. "Why didn't ya shoot him?"

Theo shook his head, looking helpless. "Well, Henry, if I'd a known you was goin' ta be so upset about it, I would have." Theo gave the old man a wry smile. "But then we'd a played hell tryin' to catch up with the rest of the herd!"

A knowing glint was in Henry's eyes. "Uh-huh, that's what I figger'd." Henry took another pull on his pipe. "You know, Theo, it scares the plumb hell outa me, but I'm startin' ta know how you think."

Theo continued to scan the horizon. "Now, Henry, that don't scare you near as much as it scares me." He laughed openly.

"I worried about you last night out in the rain, Theo," Dolly added. "Are you hungry? I could fix you a little to eat."

Theo sidled the sorrel over to the water barrel and dipped out a drink. Wiping his beard he speculated on the girl. "I guess I can wait until later. Had a whole rabbit for dinner last night and finished up with jerky this morning," Theo drawled.

Her eyes were making him feel funny again. Trying to look unconcerned, Theo started to study his thumbnail absently.

She sighed. "There's times Paw and I wish you wouldn't ride off like that. It always makes us afraid you won't come back."

"I reckon Theo can take care o' hisself, girl," Henry rumbled, watching Theo study his thumb with more intensity and chuckling to himself.

"Well, I'm still in one piece," Theo declared, scanning the horizon again. "Henry, there's a little creek about a mile ahead. It'll make a good stopping place. If that herd don't drift we'll get a shot at them first thing in the morning. I'll go keep an eye on them and see you at camp."

With that, Belk spurred the sorrel to a canter and left, raising dust. Henry puffed his pipe and switched his gaze from Dolly to the horseman, the crow's-feet at the corners of his eyes crinkled in merriment.

"Wonder what's botherin' him?" Henry goaded. "Probably got him some Injun squaw he's been seein' on the side out there. They say they make a man right pert company."

Henry laughed outright at the look of shock and dismay as Dolly's face contorted. He flicked the reins and the wagon banged and clattered on its way to the creek.

Theo rode into camp at sunset, confident that the buffalo would not move much in the night. Belk caught Dolly's eyes on him more than once and Henry seemed unusually content. Theo said little during the evening meal. After leaving his plate in the wash pan, he rolled out on the far side of the fire; the rain had not let him sleep well the night before.

That night he suffered through the dream. Once again, he cowered on the dune and watched Louis Gasceaux commit the act. Again, he saw that leering face. But this time as he watched, the face of his mother was replaced by Dolly's. Screaming, Theo awoke and sat bolt upright. Forcing his heart to calm, he stared into the dark.

"You all right?" Henry called from his bedroll.

"Bad dream," Theo sputtered as he wiped the sweat from his face.

"Happen often?" Henry asked mildly.

"Too often." Theo nodded in the dark as he tried to stop the shaking of his hands.

"You sleep. It'll be better in the morning," Henry soothed.

"It always is," Theo agreed with what he hoped was confidence. Hours later he still stared into the dark, fearing a return to the world of dreams.

The next morning, Theo shot four buffalo. They all jumped into the skinning while Theo showed them how to pull the hides off with the help of the horses. The added strength of the animals made the job much faster and more efficient. The tongues were cut out and dried while the hides were scraped before being pegged down to dry.

Theo went out to shoot more. At the rate they were going, they would be able to process seven animals a day.

As the sun set, Theo sat the sorrel and looked below the little hillock where the pink-red carcasses were drying in the sun. The bloody flesh had none of the majesty of the whole beast. They were just dead meat. Already, the magpies and flies covered the bloating bodies. The sight affected him and he felt saddened though he could not say why. There were more buffalo—so many that these few animals would never be missed.

He could see the gray-brown shapes of coyotes slinking toward the feast. They had begun to congregate on the ridges and yapped tentatively to each other. Later, there would be choruses of yips and howls and barks as the little prairie dogs feasted.

What the hell, Theo thought to himself, it's money. Still, his mind was uneasy. He knew how the Indians felt about this kind of hide hunting. The whites didn't know the link between the animals and God.

The Brulé Sioux had cleaned out most of the buffalo in southern Wyoming to trade hides at Fort William for white goods, but they used the animals to feed their families, and *Wakantanka* blessed them.

Taking one last look at the naked dead that had been the lords of the plains, Theo reined the sorrel. He'd need a stake to go after Gasceaux. A few dead buffalo were nothing to him. The demons shifted and he choked his thoughts away and growled at himself for being weak.

As time passed they worked their way along the

Arkansas River, the load of hides growing. On occasion they camped with other outfits.

Dolly was a sensation. Women, let alone decent women, were scarcer than hot days in January. This was more than true in the buffalo camps. The only other woman Theo had heard of was a squaw who worked with a lone hunter south of the Arkansas.

At each camp, Theo asked about Gasceaux. Had anyone seen a man that matched his description? A few claimed to have either seen him or seen someone that sounded or looked like him. From the gleanings of information he compiled, Gasceaux was working his way along the river with a big outfit.

Camped one night with the large outfit run by Josiah Mooare—no relation to Henry—Theo started out amused by the young men who tried to enthrall Dolly with their virtues and charms. They told the girl about fights they had been in; how they had killed Indians and saved young ladies' lives. At first they were so obvious he wasn't bothered.

Then Dolly began to listen with admiration. Theo felt restless as she continued to admire the stories of the daring young hunters. He began to feel hot in spite of the breeze and there was a nervous energy that flowed in his tired body. He was becoming irritable. He thought of seeing just how tough these young bucks were. Leery of what had happened with Irish O'Connell, he fought down the impulse.

The camp was suffocating him. What if the girl was talking and laughing with the boys? Why should it mean anything to him?

Grabbing up his Sharps, he stalked away, unaware that Dolly watched him go with a slight smile and a twinkle in her blue eyes.

In the cool dusk he climbed the truncated bluff west

of the camp and sat on the round cobbles. Silently he watched the darkening blaze of red in the western sky. He ground his teeth as he tried to sort out the anger that smoldered in his breast. The passion was blending with an unaccountable sorrow. He felt hurt, snubbed, and vulnerable. How could a few strange boys make him feel that way?

He almost got up to go back but forced himself to stay still. He should have learned from the O'Connell shooting. The young men sparking Dolly had to be a test. If he shot one of them, Louis might get away again.

But it hurt, damn it! He shouldn't even care what they said to Dolly. Was he weak? The thought left him shaken. Since the Blacks Fork, he had been a fortress, unassailable. Why was he becoming so vulnerable now? Were the demons testing him?

His anger flared.

The wind whimpered through the grass as Theo scratched his beard. Damn lice! They all had them now. It came from working the hides. Fleas and lice were constant companions to the trade. A man worked the hides for a couple of days and he scratched and itched and fought vermin for weeks. Blood, grease, stink, and graybacks were the lot of the buffalo hunter.

"And women!" Theo growled. "Hell's full of women!" He felt his britches; they were caked with dried blood, sweat, and grease. So was all of his bedding and clothing. His whole outfit reeked of dead buffalo.

Dropping to his belly, he crawled out to the edge of the bluff and looked down at the dark waters of the Arkansas below. The water swirled and gurgled along the river grasses, gnawing at the bank.

The oily waters were almost invisible in the fading

light, but he could hear them. The rushes swayed with the gentle evening breeze while the leaves of the cottonwood clattered softly. He could smell the trees through the damp musk of the river. Inhaling deeply, he drew in the mild scent.

Gasceaux was out there somewhere, surrounded by the same night. Perhaps his old enemy was also hearing these same sounds, feeling the warm dark, cursed by the same bites and itches from vermin. Any day now he would cross Louis's path. Perhaps tomorrow he would stand over Louis's lifeless body.

In his mind he saw it: Gasceaux, lying in the hot sun, pink, defenseless carrion, just like the bloating bodies of the countless buffalo they had passed and left in their wake. Only, the leering face would stare blankly into the glaring sun as the eyes dulled and grayed with the shine of death.

Something whined around Theo's ear. He slapped at the little insect and cursed. There would be more soon. As the sun sank, the mosquitos came in swarms. Another of the little beasts began humming around his other ear. Feeling foul, Theo growled his frustration; it had been such a peaceful night.

Theo swatted the blood-sucking insect only to hear others. It was no use; they would not leave him in peace. Frustration from his futile hunt for Gasceaux added to his anxiety, and quivering from the anger engendered by the young hunters seeking Dolly's favors, Theo rose to his feet. The demons in his mind screamed in delight.

Damn them all, Theo thought blackly, emotions flaring. He'd kill the first buffalo skinner who didn't watch his step! They could just bear the consequences and to hell with that twist of fortune that had sent him Irish O'Connell!

He felt rage burn loose. He started back to camp on cat feet. His senses were heightened by his emotions. He felt cool and calm, expecting combat. His throat was tight from the bursting fire in his breast. He could feel the blood in his veins. The thrill of invincibility surged through his taut body.

Thought he was vulnerable, did they? Make him weak by talking to the girl? Not Theodor Belk. He'd shoot the first young jasper that looked at him cross-ways.

Theo began to think of what he'd say to Dolly. She needed a good stiff lecture about how to act in front of men.

His foul mood did not blind him to the figure creeping through the tall grass. Theo stopped short and cocked his head to listen and watch. He squinted into the darkness. The shadow moved again. Theo dropped to a crouch, bringing up the Sharps. He waited, sniffing, watching, listening for the slightest sound that would give the shadow identity. His mind was suddenly clear with the challenge of the chase.

The shadow moved again. It was a boy—an Indian boy! The young Comanche slipped forward on silent feet, all of his attention on the fire and the men around it. He was working his way slowly toward the picketed animals. Horse thief, Theo thought, as he slowly eared the big hammer on the Sharps back. He kept his finger on the trigger so the tumbler wouldn't click.

The Indian took another step, his head silhouetted by the light from the fire. Theo settled the front bead on the boy's skull, sure the bullet would fly clear of camp. The youth froze as if he suddenly sensed danger.

Theo felt himself smile as he tightened his finger on the trigger. The world disappeared in a bright flash of fire and sparks, which melted into the bang and recoil of the heavy rifle. Theo was blinded by the bright spots left by the flash. Quickly he changed his position and crouched.

He could hear men calling as they rushed around the fire. Slowly Theo's vision came back and he could make out the form of the boy on the ground. Covering him with the pistol, Theo checked the body. He was dead. Light from the campfire glistened in the blood. Grinning, Theo called out and grabbed a foot to drag the boy into camp.

Men were crouched behind the wagons, rifles ready, peering into the darkness. If other Comanche were around they'd find the pickings tougher. Two men were leading the horses into the confines of the camp.

Theo felt good. The black thoughts were gone.

"What you got?" Josiah Mooare asked as Theo entered the light of the fire.

"Horse thief!" Theo grinned. "Doubt he's gonna steal another. Seems his career got shortened a bit."

Henry came running up with Dolly behind him. The girl stopped short at the sight, staring, her mouth open. She put her hand to her throat and looked away, breast heaving.

"It's a youngun," Hansen chimed in. "Good shot, Mr. Belk. Plumb shot the back of his head off."

"Yep, in the black of a moonless night to boot," Mooare agreed. "Somebody throw what's left of him in the river. Double the guard on the horses in case there's others out there. We don't want to get caught with our britches below our arses."

"I don't think we'll get hit," Theo speculated. "It just don't feel right. I think the kid's on his own. Probably trying to pay for a wife."

Josiah Mooare just grunted and walked off fingering

his beard. Theo noted that someone had scalped the lad before he was dragged to the water's edge and pitched in.

Theo felt euphoric as he walked over to Henry's wagon. The old man had resumed his seat by the glowing coals of his fire and was pulling at his pipe, eyes lost in thought. Dolly sat down and fumbled absently with her hands. She had a queer, strained expression on her face.

She refused to look at him and with a start, Theo realized she had probably never seen a man killed before, even an Indian. If she stayed very long, she'd see a sight of dead men.

"I don't think the wagon will take much more weight," Henry offered, to break the silence. He stared somewhere far away, his calm face belying the activity of his mind. A babble of excited voices still came from the other camp.

Theo swatted a mosquito on his hand.

"Reckon we got us a load," Henry continued. "Might be good to head back to Dodge and sell what we got. Maybe the railroad will be built that far by then. We'd better travel slow though. The wagon is some overloaded."

"Sounds like the ticket." Theo squatted on his heels and poured a cup of coffee. "We're about out of supplies and I need powder and lead. Old Josiah didn't have any to trade."

Dolly didn't say a word for the rest of the night; she just watched, doe-eyed, while Theo smiled and hummed to himself. He felt fine.

The dream didn't come that night.

The next morning they started back. Dolly was surrounded by men who wished her well. Several of them gave her small gifts. It didn't bother Theo at all.

He grinned at how mad it would have made him the night before. Now he just chuckled to himself.

The weather held warm and dry. They had an even hundred green hides piled on the groaning wagon. Henry kept stopping to soak the wheels to keep them swollen in the increasing heat. When it came to wagons, Henry knew his business.

Meeting another party they picked up an extra team from a broken down outfit to help with the load. That had taken no little haggling for animals were scarce, but their load was worth $350. More than Theo had ever seen in his life.

The trip back was slow. The overloaded wagon couldn't make good time. One steep hill required half-loading to make the top. Then the wagon tongue broke and a makeshift one had to be manufactured from local cottonwood. The replacement broke the next day.

"Poor wood," Henry moaned shaking his head. "I figger we'll be replacing tongues every two days. Cottonwood don't take the strain like ash or hickory."

Dolly said little, subdued by the Indian shooting. Theo wondered at the change, unable to understand the girl's emotions. There seemed to be a rift between them. It made him try harder to make her laugh. Finally, Theo chided her about being courted by hide hunters.

"What do you know about courting?" she asked with a slight quaver in her voice. She turned away.

"Huh? What do mean by that?" Theo was surprised. "Henry, what's she talkin' about?"

"Figger it out yerself, knothead," Henry sighed as he whittled on another replacement tongue for the wagon. "Fer somebody who reads trail sign like you do, you can have all the sense of this here block of wood."

"Just never mind, Paw," Dolly said shortly, and glared at the old man.

Theo shook his head watching the girl before he turned and walked into the darkness of the night.

From then on he spent more time on the trail and away from Dolly. Baffled, he said little and sat by the fire late into the night. Daily he rode wide in search of Indian sign or perhaps Louis Gasceaux. The few travelers he talked to said they thought Gasceaux had headed for Dodge City. Theo began to fret over the delay caused by the wagon. The demons were whimpering louder.

As time passed, Dolly became more like her old self. She seemed to have made some sort of resolution about the Indian kid. Or, at least, it seemed so to Theo.

What was it about this woman? He had caught himself daydreaming about the way she walked, seeing her eyes on him, imagining her warm arms around his neck. But the old days of her doting wonder were gone.

"Did I do something wrong?" Theo asked her once.

"No, why?" she responded, showing interest and confusion. "I can't think of a single mistake you've made."

"Well, I was just thinkin' that we don't talk like we did before. Thought maybe I did something wrong is all. Must be the heat. Probably got us all worn." Theo nodded.

"Probably," she agreed with a nod. Her eyes pained, then hardened.

They were some distance from the wagon. Henry had disappeared. Theo shook his head. "You sick or something?"

She closed her eyes and took a deep breath. "No, Theo, I'm fine." It was voiced as a challenge.

"Then what's wrong with you?" His eyes burned into hers.

She squinted an eye at him and tilted her head. "What do you know about women?" she cried. "Didn't it ever occur to you that maybe I care about you? Theo, what makes you the way you are? One minute I see you smile and laugh. You're strong then, sure of yourself. The next minute, you're someone else! It's like there's two people inside that head of yours."

Completely confused, he couldn't put his thoughts together. "I'm just me," he said defiantly.

"And who is that?" Dolly asked, her eyes pleading. "Why won't you let me know who you are? Why won't you let me talk to you, Theo? Maybe I can help! Did you ever talk to another human being about what you were feeling?" She put her hands on his arms. "Something bothers you. Together maybe we can lay it to rest!"

The passion in her voice touched him. His heart was pounding and his body shook as he took her in his arms and bent down hesitantly to kiss her firmly on the lips. Her body went rigid and she hugged him fiercely.

He wanted her desperately, his lust growing. He was gasping for breath as she pulled gently away. Theo whispered, "My God!"

"Oh, Theo," Dolly almost moaned. Her face was flushed red and her breast heaved.

What had he done! The demons screamed at him. A

sudden tightness built in his chest, making it difficult to breathe. He was drowning.

Dolly seemed preoccupied. "If only you hadn't shot that Indian boy, I'd be so sure!" Her voice was fervent.

Frightened by his emotions, Theo started with surprise. "I gotta go," he decided, finding the words hard to speak. Panicked, he fled.

Theo fought a rash of different emotions. Good Lord, it wasn't like he was in love with the girl—or was it? The thought hit him like a thrown rock.

No, it could not be! There was no time in his life for a woman like Dolly. She was good and kind, warm and friendly. She needed protection, stability, and a home. "Not this hoss," he growled. "A wolf don't turn into a dog! Why in hell's she so concerned about that damn Comanche?" he puzzled.

He thought about it again the next day as the sorrel stepped out on the trail. The wagon was a little distance behind him. The sorrel pulled up and halted, bringing Theo back to the real world. Cursing, Theo realized he'd been dreaming. Such nonsense would have to quit or he'd end up stopping a Comanche bullet.

The sorrel pricked its ears and snorted softly. Theo tested the wind and smelled smoke. He pulled the Sharps and checked the load. With rifle across the saddlebows, he prodded the sorrel forward.

Moving through the trees he could see the bodies of men scattered on the ground. There was a jumble of harness and equipment strewn about. Two burned wagons still smoked in the afternoon sun.

His senses at a pitch, he stepped off the sorrel and walked around the perimeter. He waved for Henry to hold up as the wagon came within sight.

At last he found tracks, but not those he expected. They were wagons, heavily loaded. His eyes narrowed. An attempt had been made to hide the deep cuts made by the iron tires.

Theo moved to the bodies and studied them. They had been mutilated and scalped. The manner of mutilation was not Comanche. The job looked like Sioux—all the throats had been slit. Theo allowed a grim smile to come to his lips; the pattern looked familiar. There were still a few green hides smoldering on the burned wagons, too few to account for the tracks the wagons made coming in. Other wagons had been here, too.

"Come on in, Henry," Theo called. "Looks like we got buryin' to do."

The outfits had been rifled. Saddlebags were torn open and the contents scattered. Rings had been cut off fingers.

Henry was pale as he looked at the carnage. Dolly had closed her eyes and was talking softly to herself. Theo found where the other wagons had stood. Carefully he probed the dust that had been sifted over the tracks. They had left heavier than when they arrived.

"Damn Injuns!" Henry spat. "Damn them all to hell!"

"Easy, Henry," Theo said softly. "It wasn't Indians. Come look."

Theo pointed out the tracks and how the bodies had been made to look like they'd been killed by Sioux. "You see, Henry, Injuns would've taken different articles of clothing. See that mirror. No Sioux would have left that lay."

"Well, skin my hide," Henry muttered, then his eyes turned black. "If I catch them snakes, I'll kill 'em. There ain't no reason fer this!"

"Uh-huh, reckon you're right." Theo nodded.

Dolly had got down from the wagon and walked over. She listened intently as Theo talked. In spite of the smell and sight, she had a fire in her eyes. "Never thought I'd see the likes," she said firmly. "For the first time in my life, I could kill a man."

"Does kind of affect you that way." Theo was wry, his thumbs in his belt.

"Theo, don't smirk at me. Let's get to buryin'," she ordered. "Sooner they're in the ground, the better I'll feel." She strode for the wagon and shovel, her activity showing her agitation. He could tell she was trembling underneath despite the stern image she portrayed.

"How long ago did this happen?" Henry wondered, grimacing at the stench. "Couple o' days?"

"No more than three from the looks of things. Bodies bloat fast in this heat. The crows and coyotes haven't made that much of a mess here."

Dolly was back with the shovel. "I'd sure like to know who did this," she gritted, fighting for control.

"Well," Theo drawled. "Looks like I found my man again. This here was done by Louis Gasceaux and Sabot. Reckon this time I'll catch him."

CHAPTER 8

FOUR HOURS LATER THEY PUT THE MANGLED BODIES IN shallow graves. The wolves would dig them up later, but Henry and Dolly didn't need to know that. Henry read some words over the graves from his dog-eared old Bible while Dolly stood with her head down.

"Let's move down the trail a ways," Dolly suggested. "I don't think I could sleep well here."

As they put the shovel away, Theo went through the scattered materials, collecting anything they might need. He stuck an old pot and a sack of flour under the wagon seat. A box of 45-70 cartridges and some .44 rimfire were spilled on the ground. The rest wasn't much use.

"I don't know, Theo"—Dolly eyed the flour—"I'm not sure I could eat a dead man's food."

"Won't taste any different." He untied his horses and checked the cinches on the pack animals.

"Where you goin'?" Henry looked worried.

Theo adopted a wry smile. "The way I figure it, Louis Gasceaux can't be ahead more than three days' travel with those wagons of his. That's a hard day's ride. I got three hours of trackin' light left. I ain't wastin' it."

Dolly shook her hair over her shoulder. She was scared. "I wish you wouldn't go, Theo. I'd feel a lot better with you around. It ain't goin' to be easy to sleep tonight as it is. I wish you'd wait a day so this could settle a little."

"Thanks Dolly, but he's close, real close. He's got to be stopped." Theo legged into the saddle and pulled his plug from the pack.

"It's Louis's style. I've followed him long enough to know how he works. He's done the same thing in Wyoming for years. Take a party by surprise an' kill 'em. Then Sabot takes and covers the tracks. Makes it look like Indians. There's enough people in this part of the world who'd rather believe that than think a white man done it. Makes a good cover . . . if a man knows how to use it. Sabot taught ol' Louis that trick years ago."

"Go if you have to, Theo," she said bravely. "You once told me that Paw an' I'd make out if we had to. I guess we will. We'll be all right."

He could hear the fright in her voice. "Yep, that you will, Dolly. I'll meet up with you in Dodge, or else on the trail somewhere." He nodded at the girl, thinking he ought to say something else, but he wouldn't let himself. He'd made up his mind. There wasn't any chance for the two of them together. The killing of the hunters had cinched it.

"Henry," Theo called as he started the horse forward. "Don't fergit to load your gun. I reckon you know what I mean by now."

"Ride careful, Theo," Henry called as he rode out.

"Why does he have to do it?" Dolly whispered to herself. "Just hope he . . . comes back in one piece. I just wish . . ." She bit her lip.

Theo rode warily. A wily prey like Gasceaux might have left someone on his backtrail.

Judging from the sun, it was about six that evening when Theo heard the cry. Instantly he kicked loose from the sorrel and hit the ground running, the Sharps tucked tightly.

The sorrel trotted a short ways and stopped, watching the trees along the small creek. Theo wormed his way through the grass and pulled up behind a log. Instead of looking over, he peered around the side. The sorrel studied the creek with interest. His manner did not indicate an Indian. The packhorses walked slowly, one dropping its head to graze while another kept an eye on Theo.

Nothing happened. Theo waited patiently. He heard the low gasp of pain again. He got to his feet before darting behind a tree; he had pinpointed the source of the sound. It came from the creek. The sorrel whickered slightly.

Theo flanked the creek. From where he crouched he could see the man. He was lying on his back in the cool water. There was a nasty bullet wound in his right breast. Blood had caked around the man's mouth; it was obvious the bullet had struck a lung.

He was stocky, with long, dark brown hair and a full beard. From his pain-drawn face, Theo guessed him at about twenty-five. Theo circled wide, checking for tracks. He found where the man had crawled, leaving a frothy blood trail. There was no ambush.

Carefully, Theo pulled him from the cold water and laid him on the grass on the bank. With his knife, he cut away the coat and shirt to study the wound. The man's eyes fluttered and he mumbled before coughing lightly.

"What happened?" Theo asked gently.

"Mffzzaaat," the man muttered before passing out again.

Theo growled to himself as he built a fire and pulled a pan from a pack. He waved the flies from the wound and dropped a handkerchief over it to keep the pests away. Then he boiled water.

With care, he washed out the wound. There were broken fragments of bone in the torn hole. The bullet was in deep. With a grunt of disgust, he pulled his little flask of whiskey from his stores and poured it liberally into the ragged wound. The victim bucked in pain and gasped, but the wound was already coagulated and didn't start to bleed again.

The man gave a groan and opened his eyes again. Theo gave him some water. He croaked a couple of unintelligible words.

"Easy," Theo soothed, "you're doing better than could be expected. Don't move fast. Better yet, don't move at all. Relax and rest. You're in pretty bad shape. I don't know where the bullet is, and I ain't sure I can get it out without killin' you."

The man nodded limply. "Where am I?" he gasped weakly.

"About a day's ride from Dodge City."

"Water. Water, please?"

Theo bent the canteen to his lips. The man spilled

some down his front. He wavered on the edge of consciousness.

"Am I going t' die?" he asked.

"Reckon not. But you don't have to be a bullheaded son of a bitch and prove me wrong. I've got a wagon coming. They outta be here sometime tomorrow. After what they've just seen, I'll bet they make good time."

The man was not listening. He started muttering. "I've got to foind 'im. Gotta foind 'im. Bastard killed Peter, killed me brother. Gotta foind. . . ."

He passed out again. Theo made sure he was in the shade before backtracking him. He found where the man had been shot. Circling, he saw where a horse had come within sight of the man and pulled up. After a lengthy search, he located a bit of brass, the cap from a muzzle-loading gun. The tracks had continued on at a canter.

Theo was groggy the next morning. He'd spent the night keeping the wounded man from moving and feeding him water and broth. It seemed as if the Irishman had lived only by Theo's willpower. He'd brought water, covered the man with his only blankets, and cleaned his fouled pants.

Imagining Louis's escape, Theo fretted over the waste of time. When would Henry get there? The sun began to climb the sky.

The next morning, Henry finally drove the heavy wagon into Theo's camp. Theo waved wearily and stared with his bleary eyes. "Don't look like I made it too far, eh, Henry?"

"Is he hurt?" Dolly cried jumping from the wagon before it rolled to a stop. She came up to Theo. "Are you all right?"

"Well," Theo greeted her, "this feller here, he's

damned near dead, got a hole in his chest you can drive a wagon through, but aside from that, he's plumb chipper! An' me, I'm fine. I was just a sittin' here wishin' for ten hours o' sleep." He smiled haggardly.

She bent down and placed a hand on the man's head. "Pretty high fever, Theo," she said, her voice betraying worry.

"Can he travel?" Henry asked as he came over. "Where we gonna put him?"

Theo scratched at a persistent louse in his beard. "I guess on top of the hides. If the trip don't kill him the smell ought to. I just don't guess that we got much choice, now do we, Henry?"

Henry sighed with a nod and began fixing a shelter from green hides. Theo put together a litter from poles and blankets, and they gingerly lifted the man to the top of the wagon. The ride would be a little easier than an open wagon box.

"What took you so long?" Theo asked at last. "Figgered I'd have that fella healed and gray headed afore you showed up."

"Wagon tongue!" Henry spat shortly. He didn't need to make any further statement regarding that. "You know who that fella is?"

"The couple o' times he was awake he was talkin' Irish. Other than that, I got no idea. He may be a tracklayer from the railroad. I hear they had a bunch of 'em got tired of driving spikes and lit out for the buffalo range."

"Well," Dolly added, "whoever he is, he's sure in for a heck of a ride now."

"Let's hope he makes it." Henry looked at Dolly. "You'd better ride up top and keep him stabilized. I don't reckon him fallin' off that load o' hides would do him any good. I'd feel real bad if'n we lost him when I hit a gopher hole."

"Keep this in mind, Dolly." Theo was serious. "He may have been tied up with the bunch that hit that buffalo camp back yonder. If he comes to, watch him till you know."

The man regained consciousness long enough to ask for water. Theo went in search of rose hips. They were still green and nowhere near ripe. He hoped they'd be of some help. Mixed with broth, Dolly fed it to the man.

"He's a tough one," Theo granted as he lay down for a nap. "By rights, he should'a been dead when I found him." Henry just nodded as Theo fell asleep.

The next morning, refreshed from a full night's sleep, Theo had finished saddling the sorrel when Dolly called from the wagon. Theo climbed the stack of hides.

"He's awake," Dolly said.

"Who shot you?" Theo asked firmly.

"Dupree," he muttered weakly. "Henri Dupree."

"You work for him?" Theo's eyes had hardened.

"No . . . no . . . He camped with us. Shot us up. . . . I ran . . . ran hard. Got to the trees . . . Sabot followed. Sabot . . . shot . . . shot . . ."

"Sabot shot you," Theo prompted.

The man nodded his head. He blinked his glazing eyes. "I'll foind 'im Peter. I promised. I'll get 'im. Murderer . . . Killed ye . . . Peter. Shot ye o'er the price o' a wee drink." The man began to drift off again as Dolly crooned.

Theo shook his head. "That's one tough hombre. I'd hate to be the feller in his way. I reckon though he's just plain outa luck this time, 'cause I'm gonna beat him to it. He's got sand but I got a prior claim." He met Dolly's eyes.

She nodded slightly as she bathed the man's face. "I know," she admitted. "Theo, be careful. Louis Gasceaux is dangerous. I don't like you going after him but it's got to be done. I just wish you had some help. Won't the men in Dodge help you?"

He heard the concern in her voice and could see the worry in her eyes. "Nope, I got to do it myself, Dolly. It goes way back. Reckon it's . . . it's just me. Things a man—"

"You going after Dupree now?" she asked flatly.

"Uh-huh, an' I'd better be ridin' or he'll get away again. The way I figger, you an' Henry have less than three days of travel unless the wagon tongue breaks again. If Gasceaux is in town, I'll get 'im." Theo smiled. "'Course, I been this close before and he got away. Maybe this is my lucky break."

"Theo," Dolly said in a whisper. "Be careful. I want you back alive, you hear? If you don't get him, well, someone else will. I'll . . . I'll be waiting for you." She laid her hand on his.

"Yes, ma'am." Theo grinned. "I'll be back. Might not find such a good cook in the next outfit." He touched the brim of his hat and jumped lithely from the wagon.

"Take care, Henry," Theo called. "An' another thing . . ."

"Yep, I know," Henry waved him down. "The gun's loaded."

Theo laughed as he jumped into the saddle and spurred his animals down the trail.

"You know what you're doin'?" Henry asked pointedly as he watched the rider disappear into the shadows of the cottonwoods.

"I sure hope so, Paw." She shrugged. "He's a violent man. I know that just like you do. Then there's the times that he's all fun and smiles and his eyes get that warm humor in them. He's so strong, Paw. If he just didn't have that dark side and whatever's hidden in that dream he has at night. I love him, but he sure scares the daylights outa me every now and then."

"Uh-huh, I reckon I know what you mean, gal. There's times he looks at me an' my gut turns cold." Henry pulled at his pipe and blew smoke at the sky. "Dolly, one thing's sure. There's blood in that man's trail. There's blood behind him and sure as Hob's tail, there's blood ahead of him."

"There go the last of the hides." Louis fingered the side of his nose as the Kansas Pacific huffed into the darkness, sparks flitting redly from its stack.

"Eet was good to sell zem at dusk," Sabot agreed. "No one weell see zee marks on zee hide until Kansas Ceety or Mizzouri. Zen eet weell be too late."

In the three months he had been on the buffalo plains, Louis had shot only four animals. Sabot had done the rest. The rest of the hides had been obtained by less distasteful means.

Small camps of hunters were easy prey. A good dose of poison in the camp coffee made short work of four or five unsuspecting men. After that it was a simple matter to bury them and take their hides. The horses would be let loose and unwanted wagons were rolled into an arroyo. No one would be the wiser.

"That last group almost outsmarted us," Louis remarked. "That Tom O'Connell got wind of what was going on and raised the alarm." Gasceaux patted the .44 Smith & Wesson at his hip. A fast-shooting pistol indeed. It had saved his life.

"I track heem." Sabot shrugged. "Zee buffalo runners come on zee run when zee camp eez found. Zey worry about zere scalps too much as eet eez. Zee army goes out and patrols and poof, zee dust settles, non?"

"Belk is still on my trail." Louis frowned. Belk, a man Louis didn't even know, was still asking questions about him. Belk, a man reportedly fast with a gun. Could this be a relation from the old Belk train in Wyoming? Impossible! Who could have known it was he who had ambushed that wagon?

Louis studied Sabot, seeking an answer. "Is he the kid from Church Butte? If so, where was he during the attack? How did he survive the empty Wyoming wilderness? There was no settlement closer than forty miles from the ambush site! The boy couldn't have walked all the way to Fort Bridger!"

Sabot shrugged.

Small odds or not, a man named Belk was on his trail. He had been involved in a shooting in Denver. He had asked about Louis's path from Montana to Colorado. It had worried him so much he had rushed the Jakes swindle and come too close to being caught. It made him uncomfortable. Louis did not like being rushed. He was convinced success came from carefully laid plans. When a man was rushed he made mistakes.

"You 'ave another two thousand dollars, mon ami. I 'ave money for wimmen and whiskey. Zee hide business eez good." Sabot showed his two teeth.

Gasceaux did not like living in the open. Worse, there was no way to stay clean. He, Louis Gasceaux, had lice and fleas! The vermin that infested the hides crawled into his hair, clothing, and bedding. It was enough to drive a man of culture to the brink of insanity.

These new inhabitants of the wilds he had to associate with were another irritant. For starters, they had no women. They were uncouth, uncultured, unwashed, ignorant, and they'd fight at the drop of a hat. When they did fight, they were damned good.

"Have your fun, Sabot. In the meantime, I have an account to settle. Cover me." Louis grinned.

"Oui, zen I 'ave to work thees night." Sabot shrugged and melted into the shadows.

Louis turned his steps toward Hoover's. To have lost three thousand dollars of his original stake in Hoover's had been a blow to Louis's pride. He had made a stupid mistake and almost demanded satisfaction. Louis knew he'd have been dead in a minute. These saloon men did not play by the old rules of honor. He'd been looking down the barrel of a Navy Colt before he could utter a challenge. The eyes behind that Colt had left no doubt about the outcome. Louis smiled; the gambler was still in town.

The train whistled. Louis had the sudden urge to ride the rails east. He had enough, he could start over again. He shook himself and grinned at his foolishness. There was much more money to be made here. Perhaps he was being too careful. Was it advancing age? A man without initiative would go nowhere in this world and Louis wanted to go places. He desperately wanted to return to the life he had lived in North Carolina.

Louis was whistling as he walked into George Hoover's saloon. The room was crowded with men and soiled doves. His gambler sat at the back of the room. Sabot slid in the door behind him, looking unobtrusive with the old blanket he carried. Louis joined the game, the gambler met his eyes with recognition, and Louis grinned back with deadly intent.

An hour later, the man lay dead on the floor, a .44 hole in the middle of his head. This time Louis had witnessed the cheating and called it to the attention of the others. There had been silence as he gathered up his winnings, covered by the Winchester that had suddenly appeared in Sabot's hands.

"Good evening!" Louis called pleasantly to Hoover, and walked calmly from the room. After Sabot had backed out, the house noise rose to the same fevered pitch as before the shooting. Whistling happily, Louis headed for Ruby's crib.

The lady had a tent in the line out behind the buildings. She was unoccupied when Louis arrived. Sabot had gone off to his job at the hotel. Ruby's busy sign was placed outside for the rest of the night.

Essington was washing glasses when Theo walked into the hotel; he strolled down and leaned on the bar, looking Theo up one side and down the other. "What can I do for you?"

"Hello Essington." Theo nodded. "Pour me a glass of your best." Theo allowed himself to grin through his dusty beard.

"I do have good stuff now that the railroad is here. Good Tennessee sour mash and rye as well as regulation rotgut." Essington looked smug.

"Sour mash," Theo decided. "It's been a while since I had that much class."

Essington laughed as he reached down a bottle and poured. "How'd you do in the hide business?"

"Henry is bringing in a hundred hides. Not a big haul, but enough to outfit right." Theo tasted the whiskey and raised his eyebrows in approbation.

Essington agreed. "Should make you a pretty good outfit."

"Uh-huh, but it's a sight of work for an old man, a snip of a girl, and lazy old me." Theo squinted warningly.

"You mean that girl works hides, too!" Essington cried.

"She's game, that one is. You ought to see the muscles on that gal." Theo chuckled.

"She's a looker, too," Essington agreed, a fleeting smile passing his lips. "Seriously, Theo, you ought to latch onto that one. She looks to be a lot of woman."

"Nope, but thanks, Mr. Essington. You gotta realize she's out of my class. I've been over on the rough side for too long. I wouldn't know what to do with a—an honest woman if I had one. That girl's good all the way through, and if I ever hear anyone say different, he's a dead man." Theo was sober in his analysis.

Essington shook his head. "Theo, I've heard that before from you boys. Out here, why, it don't cut much water one way or the other. Seems like I can think of some pretty rough hombres that got hitched up with real ladies. I guess women just expect their men a little on the wild side out here. You might—"

"Uh-huh," Theo grunted. "And she's got a bunch of them young buffler runners hot on her trail, too. Why, you shoulda seen them young galoots. Them ornery cusses was a bringin' her flowers and tellin' lies like old Gabe himself. They was so straight an' proper it'd make a dead man cry. They was even goin' down the creek an' takin' a bath a day. How's that for a hide hunter?" Theo laughed at the memory.

"Maybe there's some hope for them fellas after all," Essington mused.

"Oh, that ain't all," Theo continued. "There was one fella that fell all over hisself. There she is, all blood and grease after a day of skinning and fleshing, and up walks this one towheaded kid. He's so nervous he's fallin' all over his feet. He up and hands her a bunch of . . . *posies!*"

"I reckon I'll keep that story for later." Essington nodded happily. "I ought to get a lot of mileage out of it."

"My friend Dupree in?" Theo asked casually. Essington caught the change in his voice.

"Came in four days ago. Sold twelve hundred hides right off the bat. Then he sold his outfit. He killed that gambler over to George Hoover's. Made up most of his losses and called the gambler for cheatin'. Shot him down before George could do a thing. He's fast and that pistol was out before Ace knew what was comin'. Get me right, Theo, Cameron was a good hand with a gun and Dupree beat him. The man's fast. Dupree shot him between the eyes quicker'n cat scratch. He—"

"Must a been practicing," Theo muttered to himself. "Generally he shoots folks in the back."

"We found a camp shot up, Essington," Theo continued. "Most of the hides were stolen. There's bodies all over out there that so it looked like Indian massacres. Only thing is, Dupree, as you call him, slipped up. That old trapper he runs with only knows Sioux tricks."

"No Sioux been reported around here recently," Essington agreed as he stroked his mustache. "You sure—"

"Not many." Theo sipped the whiskey. "If they'd been around we'd have heard. Besides, Sioux don't drive wagons and they don't steal money. The stuff taken from the camp was taken by white men. You ever heard of an Indian not takin' a mirror or skinnin' knives? How about leaving cartridges layin' on the ground?"

"You do have a point there." Essington's eyes narrowed. "Too bad nobody saw it happen." Theo's glass got refilled.

Theo let a slight smile twist his lips. "Somebody did. He'll talk if'n he don't die gettin' here, but I'll get Gasceaux first."

"You sure Dupree and Louis Gasceaux are the same fella?" Essington asked. "There's a lot—"

"Louis Gasceaux, Henri Clement, Robideaux, Dupree—same feller. I've followed him a long way. Turns out he's been a lot of folks as it suits him." Theo shrugged and dropped one of his last coins on the bar and gathered his outfit. Waving to Essington, he went to the hotel bathhouse and luxuriated. He could feel lice dying by the hundreds.

Pulling his "mostly clean" clothes from his packs, he found his pants were worn to holes. With a snort, Theo headed for Zimmerman's new store.

Fred Zimmerman had come in with the railroad and was setting up his business. The false front of the building advertised "Guns, Pistols, Ammunition, Hardware, and Tinware." Inside was a plethora of boxes and bales. A heavily bearded man was fussing through piles of goods.

"Hello Fred," Theo greeted warmly.

"Ach, Theo Belk! You it is? Velcome! You like my new shtore?" The German came rushing up, pumping Theo's hand vigorously.

"Sure is bigger than your place in Laramie. I heard you were in Kit Carson, over in Colorado, but I missed it."

"Vel, vhat do you need here?" Zimmerman nodded happily. "I see you need new outfit, ja?"

"Reckon these britches are about gone. Before you get too carried away, I need to know if I can have credit until my load of hides comes in. Unless there's trouble they should be here in two days. Is that all right? I wouldn't want to—"

Zimmerman waved his hands as if insulted. "Ja, of course, Theo. You should know better! You I know! You are a goot man, if perhaps a little vild. Someday—"

"I reckon that shooting in Laramie sticks in your mind?" Theo grinned slightly as he watched the German.

"Ach! He vas trying to rob me, *nien*? I vas scared! Dese men here, dey vild, too." Zimmerman dismissed it. "You saved my money, Theo. Vhat you need?"

"Rough country, Fred," Theo reminded. "It's a frontier. You find rough men in rough country and tame men in tame country."

"Dis contry be tame, too. You see. Many farmers come soon." Zimmerman nodded pleasantly. He had always been a God-fearing Lutheran.

When Theo was outfitted he was the proud owner of a new pair of britches, a shirt, and boots for necessities as well as a new Sharps rifle. The Sharps was the latest buffalo rifle. Chambered for a .50-caliber bullet, it was backed by 90 grains of powder. The gun was the newest offering from the Hartford Company. Called the Model 74, it was out several years early but the company called it an anniversary special. All that at wholesale—and on credit to boot!

"I'll pay you first thing when the wagon comes in, Fred." Theo waved at the happy merchant as he walked out the door.

"Ja, you take care, Theo," Zimmerman called after him.

Theo made his way through the crowded dance halls on Front Street. He did not drink, but watched the boisterous, flushed faces that crowded the saloons and gambling hells. The demons whispered and rustled in the back of his mind as he sought to control his surging emotions. Wary of what he had done in Denver, Theo fought for control.

Nowhere did he see any sign of Gasceaux. He smiled sourly to himself. Dodge was a small town; he could feel Louis's presence just as he had that night in Denver.

Stepping out into the dim twilight, he walked down the street toward the Essington Hotel. As he started to cross, a rifle barked in the night. Theo felt the whip of the bullet pass his breast as he pitched himself to the ground. He pulled the new Sharps up, aware of the dust and manure choking the street. Lying in the ankle-deep dust, he peered into the night, seeing no one.

He gathered himself and sprinted for some horses tied off in front of the hotel. The only commotion was made by the horses. Theo got a halfhearted kick on the shin for his efforts.

A group of wagons was trundling down the street. The night was silent except for the tinny sound of music and laughter from the saloons. Dodge City—being Dodge City—was unconcerned about casual gunfire.

Theo cussed and slapped dust from his new clothing. He had had the misfortune to have landed in a fresh pile of horse manure when he took his flying dive.

Essington's Hotel was crowded. Theo wandered

into the dining room, which was divided by a partition from the saloon. Essington smiled when he walked over. "New clothes," he greeted, "and dirty already! You even managed to tear the sleeve."

Theo glared at the bullet hole in his sleeve. "I guess I'm just lucky," he said darkly. "I just got shot at outside. Somebody tried to dry gulch me. Bushwacker didn't have enough light."

Essington frowned, thinking, and his eyes widened and he cursed. "That new cook! You know, that old trapper that runs with Dupree. I hired him a couple of days ago. Sabot's his name. He just came in the back door with that battered Hawken he carries. It was still smokin', Theo!"

Essington's eyes betrayed the rage growing in him. "Said he'd shot at a coyote that's been nosin' around. He stuck the gun behind the door and I didn't think any more about it. Maybe we'd better go talk to him."

"Uh-huh, let's just do that," Theo said coldly, his eyes burning. He felt the battle lust rising in him.

"Well, if it turns out bad, try not to get any blood in the soup, all right?" Essington turned and paused. "Wait. Better yet, I'll give you time to go around the back. When you hear me enter, you step in. That'll box him."

Theo sprinted for the door. He followed around the rear of the building. As he reached the door, he could hear angry words in the kitchen. A shot rang out. Theo plunged through the door to see Essington's crumpled body. The dining room door was swinging closed. Theo made it through in time to see the gray-haired cook dashing around the crowded tables. Theo leveled the Walker but too many people were in the way. By the time Theo made it to the front door, Sabot had disappeared into the night.

Essington lay in a pool of blood. The kitchen was packed with people. "Give me some room!" Theo bellowed as he bent down near Essington. The man still had some life in him.

"It was Sabot," Essington whispered. "Didn't figger who . . . he was till now. I remember . . . what you told me. Just told him . . . told him you wanted to talk. . . ." Essington was dead.

Theo found the old man's Hawken; it still smelled of smoke. He must have reloaded it when Essington left the first time. Theo noticed something else as he turned to go to his room. There was blood in the soup.

CHAPTER 9

THEO LAY ON THE BED THINKING. LOUIS WAS OUT THERE somewhere. Either he had been missed in the crowd or he was shacked up with one of the prostitutes behind Front Street. Sabot would be there now, telling of Theo's arrival. Gasceaux would make his move tonight. He'd leave town or come hunting him.

Theo was on his feet. On a hunch, he loaded the sixth cylinder on the Walker. A piece of rawhide kept the hammer from resting on the cap but would fall away when the gun was cocked.

Theo crept quietly out of the Essington Hotel. Men were standing on the porch talking of the shooting. Essington was a popular man in Dodge City. He had been well liked. The bawdy houses and saloons were running full tilt with drunken soldiers and buffalo hunters. The hardys were being fleeced of their hard-earned cash while they bucked the tiger.

Behind the Hoover Saloon was a row of tents and cribs. Female laughter could be heard along the line and dark forms walked arm-in-arm from the dance halls to the tents.

Theo made his way from one tent to the next. Listening at the wall of one he was surprised by a large man who lurched out of the doorway.

"What the hell? What are you doin'?" the big man demanded angrily.

"Shhhh!" Theo cautioned as he tiptoed conspiratorially up to the man. "I'm lookin' fer my partner. I'm gonna pull up the tent stakes an' drop the whole kit an' kaboodle on top of 'em!" Theo snickered.

"Now that's one I'm gonna remember," the man in the dark chortled back. "Need help? I could—"

"Naw, it might take all night to find 'im. You'd be bored stiff. You'll hear the yell and be able to get in on the fun. I guarantee it."

"Huh. Well, good luck, mister. Glad I don't ride with you." Laughing, the man left.

Theo resumed his prowling. The last tent on the row sported a big sign out front. It said RUBY'S. Theo hit pay dirt.

"I tell you Louis, you don't need to bother. No one will find you here. It doesn't matter what that old trapper says. You're safe here. You're in the clear and no one can connect you with anything. You hear? Nothing at all. Sabot's just an old blowhard." The voice was deep, throaty, and obviously a woman's.

Theo smiled as he drew his Walker. With the big pistol in one hand he pulled the tent flap aside with the other. The woman was alone. She sat on the bed, legs apart, smoking a cigar, talking boredly to herself. She screamed as Theo loomed in the doorway.

As Theo pitched himself aside, guns banged in the night. Theo felt the slap of a bullet as he rolled away from the tent. He'd been hit. He pulled himself on his elbows, pistol ready. A flash of yellow accompanied the crack of a pistol. He managed two shots as dirt kicked up around him.

With a start, Theo jumped for some boxes. A bullet splintered wood as he made cover. The flash of powder gave Theo the position of one of the attackers. There were calls and cries in the night as Theo triggered two shots at the gun flashes. Another flash gave him a target. By instinct he triggered the pistol and was gratified to see a form pitch to the ground kicking.

Another flash came from his left. Theo shot and heard the bullet hit wood. The sound of running feet greeted his ears. He knelt to reload. Grateful for the faint light, he poured powder into the cylinders and rammed the balls home with the loading lever. Carefully he pinched the caps over the nipples.

Men were running in the dark, shouting. Cocking his pistol he walked up to the now-still form on the ground. The man lay face down, hands clasped to his throat. In the dark, Theo could make out the widening pool of frothy blood. He knew it wasn't Gasceaux.

"What the hell are you shootin' at?" a voice called.

"I dunno," a drunk voice returned, "just joinin' the fun. I guess."

"Well shoot the other way! You might hit somebody in here!" came the angry reply.

Theo felt a burning sensation in his back. The bullet shock was wearing off. His side was wet with blood and feeling was leaving his left arm. A wave of giddiness dropped over him like a blanket. Staggering, Theo walked over to Ruby's tent.

"Do you want to come out, or do I start shooting?" he asked conversationally.

"I'll come out, but don't shoot," the woman answered unsteadily. She pulled the tent flap back and timidly stepped out. The cigar was dead and cold in her hand. "Damn him," she sputtered. "He had bullets all over in there. Broke some of my best perfume."

Through the growing pain, Theo could smell the stuff. "That ain't perfume. That's skunk water. Where's Louis at?" Theo barked.

Ruby lounged against the side of the tent. She'd recovered her composure. She cocked her hip and looked at him insolently. "He had lots of money to spend so he stayed for a week. When I get paid, I don't mind." She struck a match and lit the cigar again. "I don't know where he went."

"How come you set me up?" Theo shouted. His balance was going.

"Hell!" she spat. "He just paid me to sit in there and talk. He told me what to say and I said it. In this business men ask you to do a lot of crazy things. You don't ask questions. You just do what they say and take their money. If you do it well, they come back and bring their money with them. That's business, mister."

"I ought to shoot you right here," Theo said in a biting, low voice.

"I don't think so," she said calmly. "You do an' they'll hang you for it—even in Dodge." She sucked her cigar and blew smoke at him.

"It just might be worth it," Theo hissed.

"I'm not worried. You look like a drunk Indian on

payday. I don't think you got the strength left to hold that piece of artillery up—let alone shoot straight. You'd better get some help pretty quick or you'll spend the night on Boot Hill. Look at the bright side—you'd have a lot of company up there. The way this town is, you'd have a lot more in the future."

"Gasceaux stayin' around?" He ignored her.

"I doubt it." She shrugged. "Sabot told him he'd murdered Essington and there was something about some killed hunters becoming common knowledge. He didn't know I knew or he'd a shot me. Still . . . a woman in my business has to stay ahead. I snuck up to the tent, listened to their war talk."

"If he comes back you get me word real quick, 'cause I just might kill you, Ruby. Or I might do worse than that." Theo turned and staggered over to where the knot of men had gathered around the body.

"Who is it?" one man asked.

"That old trapper, Sabot." A man straightened to look at Theo. "Nice shot. You blew out the front of his throat. What's this all about?"

"He just killed Essington. I got one of 'em, anyway," Theo forced the words. The world was fading in and out. He felt dazed—like it was all a dream. He remembered the Colt slipping from his fingers. It seemed such a short way to fall, yet he fell so slowly—right on top of Sabot's body. His last thought was how cool the breeze was on his cheek.

The streamer of fire burned its way slowly through Theo's side. He remembered trying to move away from it; but his numb body would not function. The pain arched up and built in intensity, stabbing deeply into him. Then, as if an echo, the pain would rebound around his body like ripples in a water barrel before blasting up through his neck and exploding in his brain.

With a groan, Theo tried to push himself up.

An irritated tenor voice snapped, "Stay down! Damn! I take all this time to patch that hole in your side and you want to go spoil all my fine handiwork. Stay still or I'll pound your head in!"

Theo allowed himself a sigh as another bolt of pain erupted from his side. The voice sounded like it belonged to someone who ought to be obeyed.

"Where . . . where am I? Who . . . are you?" Theo gasped as the searing fire laced his side again. He clenched his teeth.

"You're in the Essington Hotel. Last I heard you'd rented this room. I'm Doctor Tom McCarty, at your service," came the reply.

"You must be that new doctor," Theo grunted as another of the blinding flashes of pain was let loose.

"That's right," McCarty drawled easily, "an' I sure picked a great place to start a new practice. Seems like folks around here are so happy to have a doctor—why, they ain't about to wait for natural causes. They all want to rush things.

"If they knew how many bullets I've dug out of people since I got here, one of them Colorado outfits would start a lead mine in my office. Ah, there we go."

Theo felt another stab of pain, then it turned into a dull ache. "I get one dug out of me?" Theo asked gulping cool air.

"Sure did. Looks like a .44. Probably out of a Smith & Wesson revolver. You'd be surprised at how much I've learned about bullets since I came here."

"Why a Smith & Wesson?" Theo wanted to know. His throat was dry.

"It matchs up with the cases out back of the stable.

Henrys are rimfire—these are center fire," the doctor explained. He placed an empty brass at the side of Theo's bed. Next to it he laid a flattened slug. "Thought you might want those. I can't guarantee that slug came from that particular brass, but it might have."

"Thanks, I'll cherish 'em forever," Theo growled. "You treat anybody else involved in this?" He had a momentary hope that Gasceaux might have been hit.

"Nope, you shot too good on the one hand and not good enough on the other. You took out Sabot's throat. He'd a died anyway sooner or later. Had a tumor the size of a walnut under his tongue. Still, good shot. He didn't feel a thing."

"Just dumb luck. The one I wanted got away." Theo felt his body relax as Doc McCarty bandaged his side. The wound still throbbed.

"Not entirely," McCarty said with annoyance. "He's carrying splinters and maybe a little lead. There were a couple spots of blood on the boardwalk. Bright red, not bubbly or dark like a serious wound."

"He still around?" Theo felt a tingle of anticipation.

"Nope, stole a horse from Ham Bell's livery and lit out like a house afire. Kelly's pretty upset. It was his prize racehorse," McCarty muttered.

"Damn!" Theo gritted. "How soon will I be up?"

"Depends on you. If you'll stay in bed and rest up, I'd say a week. If you insist on pushing yourself—like most do—you could end up with a hell of an infection and be dead within days. You see . . . the bullet entered through the big muscle in your back that we call the latissimus dorsi, then broke a couple of ribs and ended up above your kidney. It didn't rupture the major artery in there, but it's probably bruised pretty bad. If you stress that part of your body, you could rupture it and be dead in five minutes.

"That's all I got to say. Stay in bed and rest. There's a chamber pot here so don't go gallyvantin'. If I say so—and only if I say so—you can go to the jakes in a few days. Rest for now, I've got you on a diet of meat and vegetables. Eat all you can hold. You'll heal quicker."

Theo nodded as Doc McCarty put his instruments in his bag, grabbed his hat off the bloody washbasin, and left. For once Theo was in no mood to argue. He stayed in bed.

Two days later, Doc McCarty was pulling the bandages off and checking the wound. Theo had been doing a lot of sleeping.

Doc said, "The wound looks good. You can have limited movement . . . but not outside the hotel. And no going up and down stairs."

The door burst open and Henry rushed in. "You Doc McCarty?"

"Yep, what can I do for you?" the doctor asked.

"You'd better hurry, we got a man downstairs that's pretty sick. If he don't get help soon, he's gonna die. He's got a bullet wound that's infected." Henry stopped and stared, then with a start recognized Theo. "Theo?" he breathed.

"Figgers," McCarty grunted. "Let me get this one bandaged and I'll be right with you."

"What happened to you?" Henry walked up to stare at Theo, disbelief in his eyes.

"Run in with Gasceaux," Theo almost cried as McCarty pulled the bandage tight.

"What's he look like?" Henry squinted his distaste.

"Don't have the foggiest idea, Henry. He got plumb away again!" Theo looked glum.

Henry breathed deeply and shook his head, looking

at the ceiling. "Too bad. After bringin' that kid in, I'd kinda like a crack at him myself."

"Load your gun first, Henry." Theo crinkled his face with a smile. "You'd need to, seems Gasceaux just don't give a man time to get set. He just up an' shoots."

"Hell!" Henry spat. "You ready, Doc?" Henry led McCarty out of the room. Theo sighed and stood up; slowly he hobbled to the toilet. He was easing himself back into bed when Dolly burst through the door.

She stopped to look at him. "How do you feel?" she asked, her voice soft. "I just knew something like this would happen. I just knew—"

"Why, Dolly! Old Louis found I made a pretty good stopper for his bullets. Doc says I'll be fine if I don't get too far out of line. I feel like Hob, though. You look a little worn yourself." Something strange warmed Theo's breast.

She nodded. "That poor man has been delirious for the last two days and nights. I kept expecting him to die any second. It wears on you. There's puss all around the wound. I thought I'd developed a pretty strong stomach, but I guess not. If he lives it will be . . . a miracle. Doc McCarty says the only reason he made it this far is because of the things you did that day on the trail. He says you did everything right. If he'd a died, I don't know what I'd a—"

"Don't worry about him, Dolly. He's Irish. When the Irish get the idea they're gonna do something, they usually get so bullheaded they do it. If the fellow decides to live, he'll do it to spite the devil." He could see her brighten up.

"I hope you're right, Theo," she agreed. Her eyes were working him over, as if evaluating the damage. She settled down in the chair and took his hand, then reached down and kissed him.

Panicking, Theo joked. "Of course I am! That kid reminds me of a time we were tryin' to bury an Irishman up in the Bighorn Basin. Confound him, he kept sittin' up in the coffin tellin' us he was fine. We finally had to tie him and gag him so we could finish the funeral and get him into the ground without him hollerin' so much." Awkward, he couldn't meet her eyes.

"Theodor Belk, you're terrible!" Dolly moaned as she tried to stifle her laughter. "I can see you'll live."

"I reckon, but I'm not the only one that's terrible. Seems to me you're here in a man's room without a chaperon. What would the good Christian folk say?" Theo muttered, his heart constricting.

Dolly looked indignant. "I don't think you're in any position to be a threat to my honor. In fact, Mister Belk, you never have been or have you noticed that?" Tilting her nose up, she flounced out of the room.

He looked down at where she had been holding his hand. Absently, he rubbed his fingers across his palms, his eyes focused in the distance while the demons rustled in his mind.

Theo watched the dust boil around the wheels of the buffalo wagons as they plowed through the gray-white powder that made up Front Street. The wagons rumbled and banged on their way to the west and the buffalo. The horses and mules listened absentmindedly to the curses and shouts of the whip-handling drivers on the hardwood seats.

He had been on his feet for two weeks now. Zimmerman had been paid off and they had increased the size of their outfit. Tomorrow they would return to the buffalo plains. Doc McCarty had pronounced

Theo fit for the trip if he rode in a wagon, but not for the hard work of skinning. The bullet hole in his ribs was healing nicely.

Theo decided on his own that by the time they made the buffalo plains, he'd be ready for anything. Doc McCarty was good—no doubt about it—but he still didn't understand Western men.

And Louis was gone! The demons prodded and jabbed at his mind. They whispered that he had lost, that Dolly had pinned him down and tied him in ropes of weakness. It ate away at his consciousness.

At least he'd killed Sabot. He remembered the final degradation of his parents' bodies. His mind saw Sabot's knife cutting his mother apart, the red blood streaking from her severed arteries.

The demons howled, urging him to take the trail to the East where Louis had run, while another part wrestled with his desire to stay with Dolly and be near her. She had spent too much time with the Irishman, who still hovered between life and death. And next trip to the buffalo range would pay well. They had four wagons now. Greed struggled with revenge and tipping the scales were Dolly and Henry. He'd make one more trip to the buffalo ranges before he pulled his stake to go off and find Louis Gasceaux. This time it would be easier, he rationalized. He'd have money enough to last a long time.

But what did he do about that Irishman? Theo had to admire his stamina. McCarty had sworn up and down he was on his last legs and it was only a matter of time. The young man kept fighting and Theo had to respect that. The man was winning against all odds. Some of the infection had started to clear.

Why did Dolly have to be the one who cared for him? She cleaned and washed, caring for his needs, a job that only those who have nursed invalids could truly understand. As a result, Theo had kept paying the man visits. Not really because he was interested, but it was the only way he could see Dolly.

Mostly, he sat quietly while she bathed his fevered head and talked about how he was doing. Her soft ministrations had built a small fire of resentment inside Theo Belk. It was a hurt he could not understand.

Once he had said something to her about it and it ended in sharp words. "What should I do, Theo? Let him die? Do you know anyone else in Dodge who would take care of him?" She'd stood her ground, fists on her hips, showing a new strength.

He'd left, feeling the old growing frustration in his chest. The demons whispered that it was obvious she cared more for a half-dead man than the likes of Theo Belk. The demons giggled wickedly in triumph. A black rage choked the bottom of his throat.

Standing on the edge of the street, he watched the sun slanting westward toward night. Well, they'd be on the trail tomorrow and things would be as they had been. Fall was here; the leaves of the cottonwoods were turning yellow.

"Theo?" Dolly called softly.

He turned to see her standing there, the sun making that wonderful red-gold in her hair. She was so beautiful—the most beautiful woman in the world.

"Hello, Dolly, I was just thinking about you." He grinned at her.

"I'm glad," she said softly. He could see something in her eyes. A worry.

"Right chipper day. Can't wait to get started tomorrow. Reckon we'll have us a pretty good trip, Dolly. We'll make out good this time around. You wait an' see. I been here too long. Been missing your cookin' at night around the fire. With these new boys Henry hired, you won't have to work so hard."

The uncertainty in her eyes grew. She was hesitant to talk. "That's what I wanted to see you about, Theo."

He felt himself tighten up at the tone in her voice. He could see she didn't want to say anything; it was hard for her.

She wet her lips and looked him in the eye. "I'm stayin' in Dodge this trip, Theo. It's the Irishman. Doc McCarty says he can't take care of him all by himself. I've got to Theo. Besides, Paw says he'd worry about the bad weather. He says that plains blizzards are no place for a girl like me. Silly ain't it?" She looked uncertainly at the ground.

Theo felt himself go cold. "Uh-huh, reckon so," he said stiffly, feeling heat rise in him and numb his mind. "You take care of him Dolly, you take care of him good. Reckon I'll do fine on my own."

"Theo please," she cried. "Don't be so darn stubborn. This isn't easy for me. I've got to, don't you understand? Why are you so heartless sometimes?" She put her hand on his arm.

"Never knew I was," he muttered, shaking her arm off and stepping into the street. "Know what I think? I think you like that damn paddy. Well that's just fine, Dolly. *You keep him!*"

"Theo! How can you say that! I don't believe it's you sayin' this." Her eyes misted.

He could see the wound he'd made from her expression. Her eyes reflected shock—and pain. It made him feel better to make her suffer for once. He left her standing on the walk.

"Theo, come back here! You know how I feel about

you." Her voice quavered in his ears. She was on the point of tears but he didn't look back. Crossing the street, he went to check the wagons again and make sure the supplies were stowed.

The wagons and the stock were fine; he already knew that. Henry had done a fine job. One thing about Henry, he did know how to put together an outfit.

Theo sat on a hub and watched the sky. A slight breeze was blowing. It seemed to him that his mind was drifting. For the first time in his life he didn't have direction. Maybe he ought to just ride out looking for Gasceaux.

"She's just like Liz!" Theo muttered, angrily slamming his fist into the wagon's side.

He was searching, trying to find his way through life. As long as he had Gasceaux, he had the path. Now the way was split, and neither seemed the right trail. He couldn't make up his mind which way to go, knowing either way would leave him feeling a loss. Why had Dolly turned on him?

Why should he care for her? She wasn't for him. That was obvious from the way she'd decided to spend so much time with the wounded man. It was plain as tracks in the snow she was not the kind of girl Theo Belk could ever claim.

The tightness built in his chest and the demons whispered loudly, drowning the sound of the town. He closed his eyes and clenched his teeth as a pounding headache beat at his temples.

Theo knew what he'd do. He stifled the desire to ride East after Gasceaux. He'd go out with Henry. At least they'd have them some good times. He liked Henry. They'd shoot as many animals as the wagons could carry. When they got back to Dodge, he'd settle his account and take off on Gasceaux's trail.

Getting to his feet, Theo felt the pent-up frustration. Why did it have to be like this? Why couldn't Dolly just understand him and be as he needed her to be? His steps had taken him to Kelly's saloon. On impulse he went in and ordered a drink, thinking it would settle his nerves.

She liked that Tom fella, he decided, as the whiskey hit his stomach. Hell, how could she? She didn't even know who he was. He could have been anybody—some paddy off the railroad. What did a half-dead man have that Theo Belk didn't?

Women! Damn women! They never knew what a man felt. They just bumbled their way through life and to Hob with any poor slob who got in their way. Kelly brought him another whiskey. Theo downed it with a passion, enjoying the feel of the liquor in his gut. Strong stuff, what a feller needed when the world was all turning soft around him.

"How's the shoulder?" Kelly asked.

"Comin' along, George. Just comin' along." Theo tilted his head to one side.

"Sure wished you'd got that fella, Theo. I'd like a chance to put a rope around his neck for what he did to my horse. That animal made me a lot o' money. Be a while afore I find another of his like."

"Uh-huh. Well, George, you're not the only one wishes Theo Belk would shot straighter that night." Theo sniffed the smoke-filled air.

"You got Sabot. Here's a drink for that. Essington was a good friend of mine. Drink that one to Sabot's soul and let's hope it rots in hell." Kelly poured another glass full.

"To Sabot and Gasceaux," Theo growled. "One in hell and the other on the way."

Kelly was called to the other end of the bar and

moved away, leaving Theo alone.

The whiskey was taking effect. It felt good. It seemed to balance the angry demons hammering at his thoughts, urging him to ride after Gasceaux now. The devils kept trying to bring up memories of the Blacks Fork and two mutilated bodies. They urged Theo to pull his gun and shoot all these damned people crowding around him just as he had done at the Citation in Denver.

Theo looked down to find the glass full again. "Take this, devil," he whispered harshly, and drank. Somewhere in his head he felt the demons give way a little. It was good to know. He searched for Dolly in his mind and found that the hurt had diminished.

"Take this, Dolly." He drank some more of the amber fluid. He snorted to himself at the thought. What a hell of a way to kill a woman!

He leaned on the bar and looked around the crowded room. "Keno, gentlemen, place your bets!" came the call from one of the tables. Men in ragged clothing jeered to each other as they placed gold coins and greenbacks on the tables.

The motley assortment included a couple of soldiers in blue pants with galluses. The others were hide hunters and railroad men. They were a sordid assortment of mankind. All were bearded and husky. In a corner, a big man with a yellow beard slept on the floor, oblivious to the din of the place. His hide pants were wrapped in burlap. Next to him lay an empty bottle.

Theo saw Ruby in the press of people. She caught his eye and walked over. "How's the shoulder?" Her husky voice was rich.

"Some folks is sure nosy," Theo growled looking at her with distaste.

"Hey! C'mon." She met his glare with one of her own. "I come over to make amends. That all right with you? I'm tryin' in my own way to say I'm sorry you got shot. You can let me buy you a drink or I can leave, which is it?" Her eyes challenged.

He paused, looking at her, then, as she started away, he put a hand on her arm. "Here, stay an' talk. First drink's on me."

They were quiet for a minute before she spoke. "Theo, I'm just curious. It's part my fault you got shot. I . . . I guess I'd like to know more about you. I feel real bad for my part in that setup. I really do." She sounded sincere.

"Yep, well, it happens to people like me." Theo relaxed a little. "You pick up a gun and you're in the game. You got to figger—well, the feller you want to kill is gonna try and kill you back. That's the law of nature, Ruby.

"It ain't like dealing with some people. You know where you stand! None of this complicated stuff." He realized he'd started to ramble, an image of Dolly in his mind.

"You want to talk about it?" she asked, meeting his hard eyes with hers. "I'm a good—"

"Nope," he answered shortly. "I'm here to forget."

"All right. I buy this time around. I can at least do that after . . . what happened," she suggested.

"Now that's talkin' my language." Theo grinned. She seemed so nice, could she really have set him up to be killed?

She tilted herself against him at the bar and signaled to Kelly. Two drinks showed up. "I guess I wanted to know . . . you know, what you think of me. When you almost get a man killed, it weighs on your conscience. I want to apologize for all those nasty things I said that night. I didn't want you—"

He started to shake his head but she stopped him. "Listen, Theo. A couple of minutes before I talked to you, you came through the flap, pistol first. That scared me. Then there were bullets flying around and glass splattering on me. Then there's more shooting and silence. I just cowered in there waiting. People were . . . There was shouting and I heard you tellin' me you'd start shooting if I didn't come out.

"I was plain frightened, and I, well, handled it the best way I could. I just tightened my cinch and tried to bluff you out of it. I knew you was hurt cause you were starting to wobble. So I teased you to keep you off balance.

"I didn't mean all those things I said. I'm sorry I blew smoke in your face. It's just that it . . . it kept me from falling apart. A person can do that when they're scared," she finished a little awkwardly.

"Reckon I understand, Ruby. I guess I've done that enough myself." Theo nodded, blinking against the whiskey. "Too bad all women aren't like you. You know? You're, uh, honest. Why is it most women can't be honest? They have to do things . . . all backward all the time. First they flirt with you then they stab something deep down inside you and . . . and they don't know they did it."

"Uh-huh," Ruby agreed. Theo was looking the other way and didn't see the look of triumph on her face as she sipped her watered drink. She bought Theo another round.

This man would be putty in her fingers when she was through with him. The thought had come to her that Louis might suspect she had something to do with Belk getting out of that trap alive.

Life had taught Ruby a lot of hard lessons. She

found that most men were simpletons who liked to believe they were kings of the world. Still, she had learned to manipulate them. She enjoyed a sense of power, taking a big, rough, tough, virile man and breaking him down to base desires.

It also had a definite survival value. There might come a time when Ruby would need to have Theo Belk on her side. He'd fought his way out of that ambush. She hadn't known that Louis was going to shoot Belk. She thought he was going to use a garrote or sap and rob the man.

Anyone who could fight his way out of an ambush like that appealed to Ruby. She might need his skills sometime. One of the rules Ruby had made for herself years ago was never to let a powerful man leave her company feeling unsatisfied. It was not only bad business—sometime it might mean the difference between life and death.

Theo Belk was ripe for her picking. He was suffering from something he didn't even know he had. Ruby knew. She knew all about men and how they thought and felt. They had been her stock-in-trade for too long. Here was Theo Belk—tough, strong, unbreakable and no doubt in a snit over that saucy redhead who stayed at Essington's Hotel. Ruby would have her way. She'd laid her plans by the third drink. She knew exactly how the evening would turn out.

Theo felt the world warming around him. The red rage was subsiding in his breast as he looked down at the woman beside him. She listened to his every word, attentive to his slightest need. At the same time, she prompted him when he was tongue-tied and seemed to know instinctively what he was thinking. Ruby was all right—a man's woman.

Ruby read his mind by his slitted stare. She smiled

warmly as his eyes settled on her breasts, leaning forward so he could see more. His arm slipped around her waist and she pushed against the hard muscle of his body.

"Ruby, I'm sure . . . glad you came . . . 'long tonight." He had trouble pronouncing the words. "I was pretty sore . . . pretty sore when I got here . . . But by damn, you sure made . . . made my world a whole bunch better."

Ruby tilted her glass toward Theo's. "Yeah, I reckon I'm glad, too, Theo. It's a problem in my business. You have to put up with all kinds. Periodically, it's nice just to have someone to talk to. Doesn't that sound strange? You'd think that a line girl would have all the conversation she could handle, but it don't work out like that. We're mostly lonely."

He'd taken it all in and nodded sympathetically. He was hooked. This big lout who had threatened to kill her was ready to beg favors. She didn't want him to go that far, but he would, she knew. There was justice in the world after all for a smart girl like Ruby.

CHAPTER 10

THEO AWOKE IN DARKNESS. HIS HEAD HURT AND RUBY'S hot body lay on his arm. He was naked and the wound in his back was throbbing. Slowly, he worked his tongue around his mouth. It felt like cotton and tasted of woman in the back of his throat.

As gently as possible, he pulled his arm from under the sleeping woman. She muttered but didn't awaken. Theo painfully dressed himself. With an oath he walked out of the tent. The saloons were doing a booming business even at this late hour. The world was unsteady as Theo made his way by feel. He felt better after he vomited a load of bile into the dust.

Boyd and Deacon Cox had bought out Essington's estate. They were now calling it the Dodge House.

Hammers banged during the daylight hours as they added rooms and a billiard hall. Theo wandered into the restaurant, realizing suddenly that he had no money left to his name.

The clock on the counter said it was five-thirty. Theo blinked. Henry came down the stairs and stopped when he saw him.

"You look like hell," Henry greeted. "Where've you been? I got the outfit put together and Hank an' Jeff are hitchin' up the stock."

"Been over t' Kelly's." Theo grimaced. "Drank too much is all."

"That 'cause of that spat you had with Dolly?" Henry asked.

Theo exploded, "Don't say it, Henry! I don't want none o' yore preachin'! What I do is my business. Don't push me!"

"All right." Henry straightened himself to his full height. "Fergit it. A man's got to let off steam every once in a while. Keeps the boiler from exploding."

Theo felt his stomach jump again. He climbed the stairs and gathered his belongings. Carrying his war bag with his free hand, he took it down and loaded it in the wagon. Finding the sorrel and the pack animals, he hitched them to the back of his wagon.

Hank Simmons and Jeff Stoner were making last-minute adjustments to the traces and rigging. The two had hired on as skinners. Lastly, Theo stowed his new Sharps on the wagon seat. He wasn't used to driving but figured he'd learn in a hurry.

Henry came out with Dolly. Theo said nothing but jumped down to check the harnesses himself. The street was becoming visible in the dim light of dawn. The east would soon blaze in red and yellow.

Henry climbed onto his wagon, shivering slightly in

the chill air. He leaned down to kiss Dolly good-bye. She whispered to Henry and stepped back, looking uncertain. Then she went to Theo's wagon.

He sat uncomfortably studying the reins in his hands.

"Theo," she called softly. "I just want you to know I care very much for you." Her eyes pleaded with his.

"Yep," he replied woodenly.

"I want you to come back to me." Her gaze was level, her voice sincere. "I want to spend the rest of my life with you." She sighed, as if glad to have made the choice. "I love you!"

"Uh-huh," he grunted shortly, failing to meet her eyes.

Dolly stood there, silent, waiting, hoping for an answer. Finally, baffled, she stepped back. "Why do you treat me this way?" Her voice trembled passionately. She whirled and fled to the hotel steps where she waved to Henry. As she looked at Theo, her hand dropped hesitantly, like a wounded bird.

Henry led the way, slapping his reins and chucking to the horses. Theo pulled out behind him, with Hank and Jeff following. The empty wagons began banging their way down the street.

"Theo," a hearty voice called. He turned to see Ruby standing on the boardwalk. "You take care out there. Come see me again when you get back."

Theo caught himself grinning and looked up in time to see Henry throw him a poisoned look. His eyes sought Dolly where she stood on the steps of the hotel. The look in her eyes reminded him of a gut-shot deer. He said nothing, wondering at the sudden hollowness in his chest.

When they halted at noon, Henry walked back to where Theo was watering his horses. "Who was that woman?" He tried to make it sound casual.

"That's the gal that set me up when Gasceaux shot me," Theo said shortly, but he could see Henry reading everything from his expression.

Moore had iron in his voice. "Uh-huh, Theo, you get me straight. I ain't about to say nothin' except, don't you hurt that girl o' mine!"

"Henry," Theo sighed. "You know what kind of woman Dolly is and so do I. She wouldn't have nothin' to do with the likes of me. She's a—I . . . I don't have nothin' to offer a girl like her. You know it, I know it, and Dolly knows it."

Henry began to bristle, his eyes becoming passionate. Then he thought better of it and took a deep breath. He raised his hands imploringly before dropping them, slapping, to his sides. He looked at Theo intently and turned to leave. He made two steps before he stopped and turned.

"You might just surprise yourself, Theo Belk. But then, you might not, too." Henry started to leave one more time before he faced Belk again. "I guess that's your decision an' no one else's. You think on that, you hear? You don't take advice worth a damn! So . . . so just consider that a suggestion before your damn hair trigger goes off." Henry spun on his heel and stomped off, dust puffing from under his flat-heeled boots.

Theo glared at the man's back and muttered to himself. Pulling his plug from his pack, he sliced off some tobacco. Working up the quid, he spit into the dirt at his feet.

A rift was growing between Theo and Henry. Their conversations were based on the necessities of travel. They no longer talked like they had in the old days. The nights around the fire were silent, the men engrossed in their own thoughts as the flames flickered on their intent faces. Hank and Jeff kept to themselves, leery of the growing friction.

Theo found himself bothered more than he liked to admit even to himself. The change in their relationship left him feeling hollow. He realized how much fun it had been to just talk about the weather, to speculate on where the buffalo were and how to go about stalking them. The old man had come to mean a lot to him, and now he really wished he could get Henry to be himself again. Couldn't Moore understand that a night with Ruby was meaningless?

Theo made the first stand. With the big Sharps he shot fifteen animals. The rest of the day was spent skinning. The old ritual was soon reestablished. Shoot and skin, shoot and skin. The mighty herds had begun to thin, surrounded as they were by camps of men and the boom of the big guns.

There were lice, stink, blood, and sweat. Fortunately though, in fall the mosquitos and ticks were not so bothersome. The plagues of buffalo gnats with their stinging bites had gone.

Theo worked with a passion. In most outfits, the shooters would do their reloading while the skinners pitched in and worked the hides from the huge animals. Teams of horses and mules would pull the hides off while skinners ran their sharp knives along the resisting connective tissue, the hot bloody bodies steaming in the cool air.

Instead, Theo did his reloading at night in the quiet camp. Sizing, priming, and pouring powder into the spent cartridges before seating the freshly cast and greased bullets in the big tube of brass, he wondered at the changes wrought in him. The dream only came occasionally and he yearned for Dolly. When he thought back to who he had been, it seemed as if his memories were those of a stranger.

Then the next day it would begin again; shoot and skin, shoot and skin. The sun ran farther south in the blue sky as November turned to December.

Sitting by the fire one night, Henry looked up. "You know, it ain't right. We shoot 'em and take the hide and tongue. The rest rots. These magnificent creatures! It's a damn shame."

"Hell," Theo grunted as he worked the lever of his reloading tool. "It's money, Henry. There's a heap more buffalo. I remember when Fletch and Skin used to talk about the beaver trade. It was the same then and there's still beaver—just not so many as before."

During the day though, Theo stared out over the vast sea of bloating, stinking, carcasses turned black with rot in the December sun. Anywhere near the herds, a putrid stench hung in the air like a curtain of death. The vultures spiraled in the sky while the coyotes and wolves, now almost tame, ran through the camps, their bellies bloated with rotted viscera.

Dead buffalo were everywhere, the bleached bones from last summer's hunt, the dessicated corpses from the fall, and the newly frozen ones from this winter. Slowly, it seeped into Theo's consciousness that death was the sum of life. He shrugged. It was God's will, the law of nature.

While the nights were cold and water froze in the buckets, the snows of December held off. One night an orange light lit the northern horizon.

"What do you make of that, Theo?" Henry asked as he scratched after a persistent, biting louse.

Theo turned to look and stopped his reloading. "Range fire, I reckon." He checked the direction of the wind. "It's about time we had one. Wind's comin' our way and pickin' up, too. Load up boys! We're moving the wagon back to the creek. Hold 'em up by the buffalo crossing."

There was no dissent. Hank, Jeff, and Henry rounded up the stock and began hitching them up as Theo piled camp utensils into the wagon box. They pulled the pegs from around the hides and pitched them on top of the wagons before they pulled out.

The bank of the creek had been used by a large herd of buffalo. The vegetation had been beaten into the gray, dusty clay of the crossing for a hundred yards in any direction. Theo directed all the buckets to be filled with water and their blankets soaked down.

"Jeff, you keep the water comin' when the fire gets here. Hank, you're responsible for the stock. They'll try and bolt when the smoke gets bad and they'll be terrified when the flames show up. If they bust loose in this, it'll be Katy-bar-the-door. I don't care if it kills you, keep 'em here!

"Henry, you and I stamp out sparks and keep the outfits from burning. When you empty a bucket, get it to Jeff. Does everyone understand? There ain't goin' t' be much time for questions when this hits us." Theo's voice was tense, his eyes lit weirdly.

"These are pretty bad I take it?" Henry asked, his face a plaster of worry.

"Yep, Henry, they are. But we've got a pretty good position here. Think of what it would be like out yonder." Theo indicated the dry, grass-covered plains to the north.

"Guess you picked us a good spot." Henry nodded. "If it'd a been me, we'd be back at the old camp watching the fireworks till it was too late." His eyes appraised Theo respectfully.

The flames advanced, pushed by a strengthening west wind. They could see the licking wall of fire virtually flying through the tall, tinderlike grasses.

"Didn't think grass could support that much fire!" Henry cried in amazement.

"Sure can, especially when there's this much wind. It's killed more men than one. The Indians use this as a means of warfare. They'll burn out each other's buffalo range to starve their enemies or smoke out a group that's forted up in a battle."

They all watched the coming fire. Already, breathing was difficult in the smoke-filled air. Black cinders were falling from the sky like some macabre, perverted snow. The horses began stamping and snorting.

Buffalo were running frantically past, along with antelope, rabbits, and coyotes. They ran together, ancient animosities forgotten in fleeing the common terror. Hank had his hands full with the horses. Jeff ran to help him as Theo and Henry started batting out sparks that landed on animals and wagons.

Each man was put to the test, stamping on coals, watering down the stock, slapping wet blankets on the dry wood of the wagons. They tried to keep damp handkerchiefs over their faces, but the hot wind dried them as soon as they were wetted. Even before the fire raged at the edge of their retreat, they were hacking and coughing.

Then it was over. The fire passed, jumping the creek to either side of the crossing and sweeping on. Still the sparks fell from the sky. They worked brutally to cool the camp and hold the horses, whose eyes were rolling in terror.

Finally, as the wind began to die down, they collapsed to the warm ground. Nothing was said. Coughing, spitting, and drawing rasping breaths of smoky air, their eyes running tears—they lay as if stunned.

"Some doins'," Hank gasped.

"Yeah," Jeff agreed. "At least you can't smell rotting meat anymore."

The men attempted to sleep where they were on the ground. When the night came to a close, the sunrise was a spectacular red-orange—a blaze of new rose-colored light streaking through the sky to illuminate a blackened landscape. The creek floated with ash. They moved out and crossed twenty miles of scorched ground. The horses' feet tender from smoldering sparks and the animals balking repeatedly, they reached the Arkansas River.

The water floated with charcoal and burned branches. The south bank was untouched. "No graze for the animals on this side, Theo. They're sore pushed," Henry said as if no one had noticed.

"Ain't gonna be much anywhere on the north bank either. That was a pretty big fire. Now you know why I insist we put the campfire in a pit. Stops wildfires like those." Theo ran a hand over his soot-blackened face, leaving streaks of smudge.

"Reckon we ought t' cross?" Henry was pensive with worry. "Them's treaty lands over there. Comanche may not like it. I wouldn't—"

"Henry, from right here, I can see a herd of buffalo. Now, I'd bet there's pretty good hunting over there. I see it like this: There isn't any graze on this side of the river for at least twenty to thirty miles in either direction. It don't look like we got much choice from the standpoint of the stock.

"Then, too, winter is comin' on. Any Comanche should have made their hunts by now and be holed up someplace in the interior. If I was in the business of shooting buffalo for a livin', why, I'd go where there's buffalo. Reckon we cross, Henry."

Henry turned. "All right, boys, fat's in the fire. Let's go. Mind yer hair and if you see anything that looks to be Injun, give a holler real quick." Henry waved them forward.

They crossed the Arkansas into the Medicine Lodge Treaty grounds that the United States government had told the Comanche and Kiowa would be theirs inviolate and for all time to come.

The hunting was good. The herds were not as skittish as they were to the north of the river. They were unused to the banging of the big guns. Theo and Henry shot as many as they could skin in a day. Soon the grasses near the wagons were littered with pegged-out hides. The stacks grew as they worked their way along the river.

Several snow flurries blew in and shut them down for a day or two, but no major storms came howling out of the north. It looked like it would be a warm winter. Spirits soared and to Theo it seemed Henry had forgotten the affair in Dodge City.

By the fifteenth of December they had some six hundred hides piled on top of the wagons. The weather was getting progressively colder and the wagons could not take much more weight.

"Horseman!" Hank called.

Theo looked in the direction the man was pointing and could make out a mounted figure approaching. It was an Indian. Theo checked his rifle and pistol before saddling the sorrel.

"Keep your guns ready!" Theo ordered. "Don't shoot unless I do. Looks like he wants to parley."

The rider was a Comanche. Theo walked his horse a short distance. To Henry's understanding, they waved their hands a lot and gobbled to each other. Theo was shaking his head and gesturing while gobbling back at the Indian. He pointed to the Sharps and the Indian grunted.

Theo backed the sorrel to the wagon. Henry's heart was pounding clear up to his throat. "What's he sayin'?"

"Says we're on Comanche ground and have shot their buffalo. He told me all about the treaty and says he wants to be paid with all the hides we've taken and he wants most of the horses. If we do that he'll let us go with our lives.

"I told him back that the fire forced us to this side of the river to get feed for the stock and the hides were taken in the north. He says we pay up or his warriors over the hill will kill us.

"I told him that we had many big guns which shoot farther than he could see. Many of his warriors would die for no reason and their women would cry and cut off their fingers. Isn't it better to let us leave in peace? Instead of war, I told him he could have coffee and flour."

"I didn't know you talked Comanche." Henry shook his head. His scared eyes were on the Indian.

"I don't. I speak Shoshoni. It's about the same. Comanche split off and moved south about a hundred years ago. Hank, bail out some of the coffee, flour, and sugar."

At Theo's orders, they left the Indian with a pile of goods too big for him to carry. "That'll keep him busy. He ain't gonna want to leave any of that out here. He'll pack it on the horse and walk back to camp. That gets us a good day's travel to make the river."

As they pulled out, the Indian did as Theo had said and dismounted trying to tie the supplies on his horse. That night, they stood double watches.

"You reckon there's gonna be trouble?" Henry asked over the low fire, his eyes glittering in the light.

"Never can tell, Henry. Kinda makes me wish we was in Dodge right now relaxin' in a warm bath. Still, we got a good strong outfit. As long as we can keep the stock, we'll be in good shape. We lose the horses and we're dead. It's just that easy." Theo could see that Hank and Jeff were drinking in every word. They were more than a little nervous, glancing into the dark fearfully, but no war whoops came that night.

Theo drew up his wagon as they came in sight of the Arkansas River. His old sixth sense began to cry in alarm. Theo watched the trees along the river intently. They would have to pass through them to make the ford. The demons gibbered softly.

A crosswind was blowing so the horses could get no scent. Henry pulled up next to him. "What are ya thinkin', Theo?" he asked around his wind-whipped beard.

"Just a hunch, Henry." Theo chewed his lip. "Pull the wagons up to the hilltop there."

They circled and ran the wagons up the hill. Theo stepped down and pulled the Sharps. Quickly he saddled the sorrel and stepped up.

"What's wrong?" Henry insisted.

"Nothin', I hope." Theo was sober. "I'm gonna ride down and check out them trees and the crossing. Keep on your toes. If I come a foggin' out of them bottoms be ready."

"Injuns huh? I reckon it's about time." Henry reached down and pulled out his Remington. Hank and Jeff unlimbered their Winchesters. "Don't tell me, Theo!" He glared. "It's loaded."

Theo chuckled to himself as he headed away from the grim-faced men who watched him. He rode slowly toward the trees. The wind had stopped. Roughly 150 yards from the cottonwoods, he pulled up. Slowly, his eyes searched the trees. Then suddenly the sorrel stamped, ears pointed as he snorted.

"So they're in there, eh?" Theo laughed. He could feel his blood start to surge. He rode in a little closer and watched the fallen logs. Through a gap in the trees he could see an Indian youth holding horses.

In Shoshoni, Theo called out, "Forget it, brothers. I see you in there hiding in the trees like old women." Throwing the rifle to his shoulder he snapped a shot at the horse holder and wheeled the sorrel before kicking the animal in the slats and racing for the hilltop.

Cries broke out behind him and a few shots rang out in the cold air. Theo raced his horse straight out. He reached the wagons as the Indians broke out of the trees.

"There's hell to pay!" Theo shouted as he pitched off the sorrel. Hank and Jeff were plainly scared. "Take your time boys. Make every shot count and don't shoot until you're sure of your target. They want the stock. If they break 'em loose, we're gone goslin's."

Hank grinned at Jeff and shrugged, checking the horses. Jeff wet his lips and hunkered down over his Winchester.

"This ain't gonna be bad. We got the edge," Theo chortled.

"Glad you think so," Henry snorted. He pulled back the hammer of the big Remington and touched the gun off. A spurt of dust rose behind the oncoming Indians. They pulled up and milled their horses.

"Don't rush your shooting," Theo reminded calmly. "Take your time. Here, watch me."

The Indians had got started again as Theo braced the rifle on a hide. He centered the sights on the first horseman and touched off the shot. The lead horse crumpled and pitched its rider. The man landed, running on his feet.

"Can't beat 'em for riding style," Henry commented with a nod of his head. He'd settled down considerably.

"Nope, sure can't," Theo agreed as he took another shot and missed. "They start learnin' to ride as soon as they're out of the cradle board."

They carried on an easy chatter as they took their shots. It had its effect on Hank and Jeff, who had relaxed.

"Thought they was Comanche," Theo growled. "From the cut of the hair, they're Kiowa." He could see them clearly now. Henry's gun boomed and another horse fell.

"Now that was a nice shot, Henry. You done good." Theo chuckled.

"Watch yer own topknot," Henry growled. "Pilgrim!"

Theo took his time, holding slightly lower on the oncoming lead rider. The Sharps pushed into his shoulder as the gun went off. The five-hundred-grain bullet caught the Indian in the chest. The man held to his horse for second before slipping lifelessly to the ground. The Indians called to each other before retreating.

"Hell! What are they doin' down there?" Henry demanded. The Indians were milling again talking to each other. The two on foot ran up to the main bunch.

"War council," Theo laughed with a wry smile. "We hit 'em too hard on their first try. Those two on foot will be haranguing the rest to hit us again. They'll loose face if they have to walk back to camp. The others are trying to reevaluate their odds. They just lost a man, which means this raid ain't gonna be a success—even if they wipe us out."

"Hell, Injun fightin' ain't so bad," Jeff chirped. "I always heard it was to the last man."

"If we'd a driven into them trees, it woulda been," Theo warned darkly. Jeff's silly grin faded.

"Theo?" Henry asked. "Now if . . . Well, what do you make the range down there to be?"

"Well, I got an idea but what would you say?"

Henry squinted. "I reckon right on four hundred yards—give or take ten," Moore ventured. "You know what the Indians say about these here buffalo guns. They call 'em 'shoot today, kill tomorrow.' "

"All right, Henry, four hundred yards it is." Theo adjusted the elevation on the back sight and laid the gun over the thick hides. Making himself comfortable, he squeezed the shot. An Indian horse jumped and bucked before falling on its side and kicking.

"Nope, it's about four hundred and forty yards, Henry," Theo returned as he levered the brass from the chamber. "I'd aimed at his head." Theo shook his head, chagrined.

Henry adjusted his elevation and shot. He was satisfied to see an Indian duck as the heavy bullet whirred past his ears.

Theo blew smoke from the barrel and inserted another cartridge. Closing the block he settled the gun on the hides. The Indians were milling in confusion. Theo set the trigger and fired. The Sharps bellowed smoke and fire as a puff of dust rose just behind the Kiowa.

"If they weren't movin' so much we'd do a sight better, Henry," Theo moaned, shaking his head as he jacked out the spent brass. The Kiowa had packed up double and were fleeing the field.

Henry sighed and took a final shot that raised dust ahead of the racing warriors. One of the riders looked back and gestured what must have been an insult. Theo's shot landed between the running horses' feet, causing some consternation.

"Some shooting that was," Jeff whooped at the fleeing braves.

"I didn't even get a chance to fire a shot." Hank sounded sullen.

"Not bad for now," Theo agreed dourly. "Let's pull out. If I don't miss my guess, we've got a blizzard comin' up. The sooner we hit the trail on the other side of the river, the sooner we get away from them Kiowa. Once the storm hits, they'll lay low."

The next day, as Theo had predicted, the blizzard struck them with a vengeance. Theo made sure they had a plentiful supply of wood. For two days they waited out the storm. Theo surprised them all by making a shelter out of the frozen hides. Then, with flakes still falling, they made their laborious way toward Dodge City.

It was slow going. The wagons were heavily laden and the snow was deep. They spent the evenings clearing snow and stripping cottonwood bark for the horses. During the day they struggled down the trail.

The drainage crossings were the worst. The wagons slid down the frozen cuts, then the stock struggled to find footing to pull the loads up the other side. On steep grades the wagons had to be half loaded and make two trips.

"Seems to me there's an easier way to make a living," Henry puffed, watching his frozen breath rising in the still air.

"Yep," Theo agreed. "Right about now, swampin'

saloons would be just fine." He slapped the snow from his frozen gloves.

It took two weeks to cover what should have been a four-day trip to End-of-the-Tracks. The Atchison, Topeka, and Santa Fe was moving right along. From there the trail was much better. Other wagons had broken the snow and travel was faster.

They pulled into Dodge just after Christmas with their hides intact and an added benefit—another sixty that had been abandoned by overloaded outfits seeking to lighten their wagons.

As they entered the city, a second blizzard was hard on their backs; snow was falling and the wind blowing as they clattered down Front Street. Theo could hardly make out the buildings in the blowing snow.

"I'm glad we missed this one," Henry grunted as they made arrangements with Ham Bell to stable the animals.

"This one is some all right," Theo nodded. "I'd bet there's gonna be froze hunters from here to hell.

"Henry, you go see how Dolly's doing. I'll handle the hides." Theo pushed the old man out the door. Henry nodded appreciatively and took off for the Dodge House. Theo asked where to find the local agent who was buying hides.

The selling completed, he found Henry sitting over a plate of stew in the Dodge House restaurant. "Henry, I got $3.60 a hide! Not only that but the man didn't even want to see 'em! He just up and shelled out the money and said my word was good on the count. Hell, some ain't worth half that much!" Theo was dancing up and down.

"You don't say!" Henry jumped to his feet. They hugged each other and cavorted around the table with hoots and cheers to the amusement of the other clientele.

"Here!" Theo pulled up a chair. Slowly, he counted out the money. There was no way to be calm. When it was all said and done they had $1,050 dollars pure profit apiece.

"That's what's left. I already paid off Hank and Jeff and what was still owed on the wagons. We done fine, Henry."

"By God! I'm rich," Henry gabbed to himself. He looked up thoughtfully. "Thank you, Theo. I owe this to you. I'd a never made it without you. Don't reckon words are good enough to tell you what you mean to me. I just thank my lucky stars for the day you walked into my life. There ain't no way I can ever repay you for what you've done." There were tears in the old man's eyes.

"Ah Henry, don't go gettin' all emotional. It did me good, too. You know, I never had me a friend like you before. Reckon that's good enough."

There was a tight place in Theo's chest. It was a welling of emotion he'd never felt; a joyful, almost bursting warmth built and for the first time in years he felt like crying.

It stunned him. Was this what friendship was all about? Was this the feeling Fletch and Skin had shared all those years? Why had he never allowed himself to experience this? For once, the demons were completely stilled in the back of his head.

He was so overcome with the feeling he didn't see Dolly walk up to the table. When he did, he saw no welcome in her eyes. The joy in his chest died.

"Dolly!" Henry cried getting to his feet. "Look! Gal, we done it! I told you I'd see to it! Theo an' me, we done it! I got us set, Dolly. No more worries! That, an' we'll go back an' get more come spring!"

"I knew you would, Paw," she said warmly, her eyes bright blue and dancing. "I always knew you'd make out fine. I can't stay. I'm off on break. I've been helping Mr. Zimmerman with his store. He and his wife have been very kind. If you'll excuse me." She bent down and kissed Henry's cheek. "Mr. Belk." She nodded coldly and walked out.

The emptiness was so cold after the glow died. Theo fought down a swallow and stifled a curse as he imagined the way it should have been. She should have been in his arms, her eyes lit for him. She should be glowing with admiration for him! The demons laughed as the pain grew. Henry's voice brought him back to the present.

"Here, Theo," Henry chortled. "Eat something, I'm buyin'!"

"Nope, not hungry, Henry," Theo said softly, a wistful note in his voice. But Henry was oblivious. "Reckon I'll take a turn about town and see what's been built while we was away."

"Suit yerself," Henry mumbled through a mouthful of food.

Theo stood, pocketed his money, and walked out into the cold, blowing snow.

CHAPTER 11

THE WIND GUSTED FROM THE NORTHWEST, WHIPPING streamers of snow around the buildings and trailing wisps from the eaves of the wooden structures. Only horses were standing on the streets, and they tried to keep their backs to the wind.

She hadn't even wanted to talk to him! The last traces of his good mood vanished as if blown away with the storm. Damn it all, if nothing else, she owed him. He'd found them ready to freeze, miles from any kind of help. He'd taught her and Henry how to make do. He'd taught them how to survive and to build an outfit that would make Henry Moore a fortune. Without him, Henry would have been swamping out saloons and Dolly'd be cooking—if they'd made it this far in the first place.

Theo felt a rising hatred. The feeling grew until he burned with a desire to go find the girl and physically beat her. In his mind, he saw his fists impacting on her soft flesh, reveling in her terror. She cowered in front of him as his fists punched into her pretty face. He saw the pain in her eyes and . . .

The image faded. He couldn't hurt her. He couldn't punish her for the hurt he felt. What had happened to him? Once upon a time he had been strong. Now he was weak. He could feel the demons stirring, chittering softly.

Frustrated, Theo kicked the top out of a snowdrift and felt the hollowness in his chest. He closed his eyes in misery. The whole situation was impossible! The demons began picking at his concentration.

The smartest thing would be for him to just ride out. He'd promised himself that months ago. He had his stake now. He could just load up the horses and be gone. Dolly had turned into another trap. Louis Gasceaux had escaped. He had failed. The dream would be back soon, he knew it. The demons rustled their agreement.

But what had happened to Dolly? It had to be that wounded man. He was poisoning the girl's mind against him. She must really have come to care for him.

"I autta kill him." His voice was harsh. The thought of Liz and the look she'd given him came back. Would he want Dolly to look at him that way? Anyway, he didn't even know if the mick had lived. Maybe he was dead and buried by now.

A bundled figure came out of Zimmerman's store. It had to be Dolly. Theo stood in her way as she shuffled toward him in the snow.

"Hello, Dolly," he said lamely, feeling all the emotions within him still to simple anxiety.

"Theo! What are you doing out here in the storm? You should be inside where it's warm. You'll catch your death." She looked fragile against the background of blowing snow.

"Would that make any difference?" he asked sourly. "I want you to . . . No, I guess I wanted to . . . talk," he continued after she was silent. He was awkward and it bothered him. It was a sign of weakness. She always made him weak.

He was vulnerable again, as vulnerable as he'd been on the Blacks Fork.

"Talk, Theo, but hurry, it's cold out here." The tone had turned cool again. She stamped her boots in the snow.

Theo felt anger stir in him. What if it was cold? "All right. Are . . . are you in love with that Irishman?" He felt better. Jaw clenched, he waited for the answer he knew was coming. But her reply put him off balance.

"That, Mr. Belk, is an improper question to ask a lady. But for your information, I am not. Now let me ask a question. Are you in love with Ruby?" She glared defiantly at him, eyes blazing indignantly.

Theo stopped cold. "Now that's . . . that's crazy, woman! Why would you say that? What possible—"

"Why do you say I'm in love with Tom? It isn't any crazier; in fact, I'd think it made more sense." She sounded so sure of herself.

"You didn't even want to talk to me in the hotel!" Theo accused. He wanted to smash his fist through the side of the building. "Hell, you've been taking care of him, haven't you? Haven't you? Y-you've been with him all this time! Why wouldn't—"

"Yes, I have!" She was defiant. "And Theo, don't

you ever dare curse at me! Tom is a very nice man and he is a gentleman. He came out of a coma last week and needs help. But that does not mean I love him." Her tone had turned soft, logical, touching him, breaking down his resistance. The demons cried out.

Theo felt flustered again. "Well, you been, uh, seeing a lot of him is all," he ended poorly, suddenly angry that she had made him a fool.

"Theo!" she cried, her hands imploring. "I was hurt. You were not exactly gallant the last night you were here. Then I hear you spent the night with that . . . that Ruby woman. How was I supposed to feel? You know—"

"That was my business!" His voice was rising in heat. "What difference does it make? Sure I was with her. Maybe I needed someone to . . . to talk to!" He felt the veins standing out in his neck. "Man's got—"

"I see." Her tone was as icy as the air around them. "You never realize how other people feel, do you, Theo? You are just about the most insensitive brute I have ever known." She fought for control.

They stood silently, glaring at each other.

When she spoke again, her voice echoed a deep wound. "I loved you, you hear? I loved you with all of my heart and you went off to . . . sleep with another woman. How can you know what that feels like to me? I just don't . . . don't want to hurt anymore, Theo." She buried her face in her hands, her iron will shaken.

Theo stood there, unable to keep the surge of anger that had sustained him. He couldn't take it any longer. Frantic with emotion, he turned and ran into the night and the soft, falling snow.

Dolly fought back the tears and wiped her eyes only to look up into the empty dark street. "God, Theo . . . come back! I need you!" she cried into the wind. She rushed out into the street, looking for his tracks in the drifted snow, seeing nothing in the poor light and track-gashed street.

No one saw him as he rode out of Dodge City that night. There were no tracks in the shifting streamers of blowing snow. The sorrel was unhappy to leave the warm stable. The packhorses balked, moving only when the man cursed and beat them into the wind-torn storm that the world had become.

In her small room, Dolly thought of what she would say to Theo. She would tell him it was all right. He was forgiven. Then he would hold her in his strong arms and soothe her, and she would be close to the man she loved. She could make them happy. Her love would change him.

In the warmth of his little soddy behind the Dodge House, Tom O'Connell tuned his fiddle. It was his prize possession. He had managed to buy it from a railroad man for a pittance. Dolly had given him the money and though it hurt his stubborn Irish pride to have to borrow, the fiddle was worth it.

Slowly, his strength was returning. Doc McCarty still called his survival a miracle—and well could Tom O'Connell believe that! Only to him, the miracle's name was Dolly Moore.

There was a knock at the door. He called and Dolly entered, bearing a plate of steaming food. Snow still fell outside. "I'm sorry I'm late, Tom. I was trying to find someone and almost forgot," she said with an apologetic smile.

"Ah, hello, lassie. What have we here? Food for a starvin' Irish lad?" His critical eye studied her face. "What's this? Girl, ye've been cryin'. Not bad word from the buffalo range I hope," Tom asked in his gentle brogue.

"It's nothing, Tom. I'm just a little upset is all." She smiled and pulled her hair straight where the wind had snarled it. "Paw an' Theo came in last night; they're fine."

"Well, lassie, seein's yore a wee bit o' down, per'aps this will add a bit o' light to yore face. Yore bright lips were ne'er made to be sad. Listen to old Tom play." He grinned as he picked up the fiddle.

"You mean you'll finally play for me? You've been putting it off for a week now. I thought you bought that thing on a lark." She settled herself excitedly.

"Nay, lassie, not a lark, but a canary instead," Tom chided. "I can play, an' well, too, if I na' be too swell-headed. But the fiddle takes some practice when ye been away from it for a whoile. I was just waitin' for the roight toime. Listen now, this is an old Irish song called *To a Wee Lassie* that I composed this very afternoon." O'Connell picked up his bow and ran it across the strings.

Dolly sat back and let herself be enraptured by the soft strains of the fiddle. The notes touched her and played lightly among her emotions. The sweet, light music brought tranquility and left a glow where only darkness had been before.

"That's beautiful," she said wistfully. "You did that just for me?"

"Aye, to make something pretty and harmonic is just a small way to repay the kindness you've showed me," Tom replied.

"To think you were fevered and sick as late as last week! You took a long time to recover, Tom, but I'll say this—when you finally got around to mending, you've done it fast," she agreed.

"Well now, lass. I do suppose a lot o' folks here aboot figgered me fer dead. Not many a mon can lay abed for six months, then come to in foine shape. Still, I be Irish and 'tis the way o' the Irish that we don't quit." Tom plunged into his food with a passion.

"That's what . . . he said," Dolly said sadly, feeling her stomach drop.

"Ah, an' who moight *he* be?"

"The man who found you. We thought you'd die, but I remember Theo said you were Irish and you'd recover just to get one up on the world."

"True i'tis." Tom nodded happily. "This mon now, he knows the Irish?" Tom's eyes narrowed as he watched the girl. "Lassie, would this mon have anythin' ta do wi' yer cryin' now?"

Dolly nodded. "That's him," she said wryly.

"Easy now lass, did anythin' happen to 'im?" Tom asked easily.

"No, that is, nothing this last trip. He just scares me is all. Tom, he can be so much fun. Then he changes and becomes something violent and terrible. There was one time I saw him kill an Indian boy that was trying to steal our horses. I just don't know how to take him." She smiled bravely, feeling self-conscious. "I . . . if . . . Oh . . ." Her hands fluttered.

"Aye, lass, 'tis a hard land we have here. Still, 'tis a land we can build. It takes hard men to tame such a land, but think, Dolly . . . think o' the opportunity. That's why Peter an' me came here. Oh, o' course, there be a little matter of a hangmon's noose, too, but we talk'd o' the wild and free land, an' we came!" Tom's voice had gone far away, speaking of a dream to be lived.

Dolly watched him with admiration. Maybe he was right.

There was another knock at the door. At Tom's call, Henry entered. "By God!" he cried. "Ain't it good to see you settin' up pretty as a picture!"

"Aye, sir, but it's only been a day or two. I still be weak as a kitten. Just playin' me fiddle took much from me. I'm pleased to meet you, sir, an' who moight ye be?" Tom looked blankly at Henry.

Dolly laughed out loud. "Tom, this is my father, Henry Moore. He helped bring you in."

Tom looked stricken. "Ah, an' I'm so sorry, Mr. Moore. I really don't remember much until the last week or so."

"Paw, meet Mr. Tom O'Connell, the man who can make magic spring from his fiddle," Dolly introduced cheerfully. "He's living proof my nursing does wonders in spite of what you think."

"Magic, eh?" Henry cocked his head. "How about makin' up a pot of gold? I heard stories about that."

"Aye, sir, would but that I could. I fear that I have some heavy debts to settle for." Tom was thoughtful.

"I don't reckon you owe Dolly or me for anything," Henry snorted. "Doc says you was just plumb lucky to make it at all."

"That's right," Dolly added. "Doc McCarty says Theo did the most for you. He did the right thing when he found you. He cleaned and sterilized the wound before he packed it. He taught me what to do."

"This man, Theo"—Tom threw a warm glance at Dolly—"I'll have to thank him, too."

Henry scowled and looked hesitantly at Dolly. "Well, you'll have to go some to do it. He left town last night."

"He left?" Dolly's face lined in panic. "Last night? In the storm?"

"Uh-huh, I went by the stable this morning to see if he was there and Bell said he pulled out last night. I wanted to talk about buying some more equipment. Bell said he just loaded up and said he wasn't coming back." Henry stopped and looked tiredly at the backs of his hands. "He didn't even say good-bye."

There was a long silence.

Henry rubbed his face, fearing to look at his daughter. "Don't know about that man. He saved us from prairie fire, Comanche and Kiowa, and kept us from freezing to death—and that's just this last trip. I can't say how much I owe him, and I can't help but like him even when he's plumb devilish. Now he's gone, not hide nor hair of him left, and he didn't even say good-bye. Damn him!" Henry's voice almost broke.

"Paw, will he be all right in the storm?" Dolly worried.

"Girl, with all the storms brewin' inside that man, the blowing snow just better take care o' itself," Henry said pointedly. Then he started and reached into his pocket. "Here Tom. I plumb fergot." He handed the man a rather worn letter.

"Ah"—Tom's eyes lit—"'tis from me brother's widow's address but . . . 'tis not her handwriting." Tom frowned and opened the letter hesitantly. Slowly, he scanned the lines as the frown deepened. As Dolly watched, she could see his face go blank as he stared sightlessly at the letter.

"Tom? What's wrong?" she prompted.

The young man sat silently, as if he did not hear. Vaguely, he shook his head, moving his lips slightly. A single tear coursed down his cheek.

Dolly and Henry watched as the seconds ticked by,

unwilling to disturb him, fearing to remain silent. As the tension mounted, she drew a breath to speak to him. At that moment, his eyes flickered to hers.

"'Tis me sister-in-law—such a lovely girl. This letter, 'tis from her lawyer. It was her way . . . Well, she lived for me brother, Peter. He was going to Denver to send for her. We'd made a bit o' money with the moine—the Shamrock 'twas called. Peter had taken the money to Denver—to send for her, ye see, when he was killed o'er a spilled drink in a local bar. I sold the moine an' . . . an' came here lookin' fer the mon that kill'd me brother. Now his woife is dead, killed herself from despair."

"Oh, Tom, I'm so sorry," Dolly whispered, as she watched the man with dry eyes. "If there's anything we can do, you must let us help! You have suffered so much! The man who caused this must be a monster!"

"No, lass, you an' yore father ha' done enough. 'Tis up to me now. I must get well an' strong and foind and settle wi' this mon—this Mr. Belk!" Tom cried hoarsely and spat the last.

"Who did you say?" Henry asked, a cold feeling in his belly.

"Theodor Belk, sir. The mon that killed me brother, then killed his foine woife wi' grief."

Something unknown, unseen, had destroyed his new world beyond repair. The demons had broken loose and savaged his mind in the night. He'd been rocked by the dream time after time while Louis's face leered at him. He almost cringed as he beat a hole through the snow and looked out at the blue sky through different eyes.

Breaking crusted ice away, he crawled out of the small cave he'd dug in the side of a drift. The chill bit through his gloves. He pulled out his blankets and beat the snow off. Then came the soogan that insulated him from the snow and any water that might have melted. Folding the bedding, he pushed through the deep drifts to the horses, walking in swinging steps.

Theo checked the stock; they were pawing through the white stuff, looking for graze. No features could be made out in the vast ocean of white. Theo dug out the packs and dusted them free of snow, then he cared for the horses, carefully cleaning the ice from their backs before saddling them and hoisting up the packs.

He pulled his bandanna up around his nose and his hat down low. Satisfied, he looked out the narrow slit that would protect his eyes from snow blindness. Then he stepped into the saddle and followed the trail east, toward the rising sun.

Meeting up with the Arkansas River, he followed its path to the East. Nothing moved in the vast whiteness. The cottonwoods were motionless, waiting for the warmth of spring so many months away. Ice had formed over most of the river, except where the water ran fast and deep.

A building lay on the southern shore, back from the river. "Nesters," Theo grunted. The country was filling with them. Building a fire, he cooked some buffalo jerky that was in his possibles. He shaved the thin strips into a small pot and added snow. As the stuff melted, he added more along with tallow. Too many newcomers to the West made themselves sick on a diet of lean meat. Theo laughed as he remembered the first time he'd made Henry eat boudins, or innards, of a buffalo they'd shot.

There was too much good healthy food in the guts.

The Indians knew—but then they usually did. Theo remembered the white men that he'd seen every so often. Mostly greenhorns, they were starving, their haunted faces despairing. They'd lost their supplies and were starving in a land of plenty. Simple ignorance had killed more men in the West than all the Indian warriors on the continent.

The long ride cleared his head. He allowed his thoughts to drift to Dolly. She had made him weak. She had made him vulnerable. Never again, Theo vowed to himself. *No woman would do that to him again.* Damn her! Damn Dolly Moore to hell. She was probably back in Dodge right now, laughing to herself about how she'd pulled one over on Theo Belk. She'd put him through the paces just like a good horse!

Now Ruby was a man's woman. She'd known what he felt and she wouldn't have made a fool out of him the way Dolly had. Ruby had appreciated him for what he was and had never tried to change him into anything he wasn't. Ruby knew her place.

Dolly was behind him now. And out there, somewhere, between the pricked ears of the sorrel, lay his future. There in the distance was Louis Gasceaux and behind him were the chattering demons, waiting, making sure he didn't fail this time.

"She was clever," one of the demons whispered in his ear, "but not clever enough."

Theo had escaped. He was free.

He'd miss Henry. The old coot was fine company. He'd learned fast. He'd pitched in full tilt until he'd become a pretty good buffalo runner. Not only that but he'd weathered the storms. If he went back to the buffalo ranges, Henry wasn't going to get caught with his britches too low.

Theo smiled warmly remembering how innocent Henry had been at first. He laughed at the thought of old Henry standing there with his unloaded rifle. That had become quite a joke between them. He'd become a survivor.

"Henry is good," one of the voices whispered. "It was the woman, Dolly, who was evil and drew you from the path."

"You saved Henry," another of the voices whispered. "That repays the debt to Washakie."

Theo nodded at the voices. It made sense. There was a divine plan that he was part of. He had become God's tool. It was his medicine—and Theo took medicine very seriously.

"Howdy!" called a big man in buckskins. He wore a black felt hat and a brace of Colt revolvers on his hip. His two companions seemed to be half-breeds. They both carried muzzle-loading rifles. The morning light filtered through a world of green.

The Indian Nations were verdant that spring of 1873, exploding in warmth, water, and sunshine. Theo'd never been this far south, but the demons drove him, as if to a destination. The winding trace of the Shawnee Trail passed through the middle of the swampy forest. Theo pulled up the sorrel, the demons whispering a warning.

"Morning," Theo allowed civilly.

"You're new to this country," the big man said sociably. His wide face took on a nasty grin.

"Yep," Theo replied. He didn't like the cocksure attitude the man had. Carefully, Theo scanned the brush with his eyes, looking for another accomplice.

"Stayin' long?" the big man asked.

"Passin' through, I reckon," Theo said softly. His senses were clear and his blood was rushing in his veins.

"Well, now, that's what we wanted to talk to you about. You see, this here's a toll road. Me an' the boys run it." The big man grinned again.

"Is that a fact?" Theo's eyes went wide. "I've never been on a toll road before. Just who are you anyway?"

"Why, mister traveler, I'm Bill Chandler." Chandler laughed loudly, waiting for a reaction from Theo. Suddenly the two half-breeds had their rifles leveled on Theo's chest. "Now, normally, for three horses to travel this road we take your whole outfit. That's our toll fee."

"I guess you got the drop," Theo smiled pleasantly. "You boys be real careful. I'm gonna step down. This here horse is pretty skittish so I can't drop anything from him. Don't shoot me, I'll go slow. Just a—

"You sure will." Chandler had turned hard. "'Cause if'n you don't, you're a dead man."

Slowly, Theo stepped off the sorrel, keeping his body onside and in their view. His hands were up when his feet hit the ground. He'd slipped the thong off the hammer of the Walker when they'd ridden into the road, and now he turned to face them.

"Why, stranger, you're just plumb accommodatin', you know that? This toll road business must' a happened to you a time or two afore. I guess now we'd like to see you uncinch that gunbelt and let it drop. Careful now! This is the most sensitive part of the business so you use your left hand."

Theo reached down and tugged at the belt. Fumbling with his fingers, it was obvious that he couldn't manage to retract the tongue. At last he looked up hesitantly. "Don't shoot, Mr. Chandler. It's gonna take two hands. I don't want you ta think I'm bein' ornery."

Chandler's eyes narrowed. "You be real slow, mister, *real slow.* I'll only tell you once . . . only once. The boys here will shoot you quicker'n a shuck."

"Yes, sir. I'll be slower than molasses in January," Theo agreed. He worked the belt loose. As it dropped, his hand flashed back and snared the big Walker.

Theo dived to the side as one of the rifles flashed fire. The horses spooked at the shot and Theo put a shot into Chandler's chest. Still smiling, the man began to fall limply from his horse. Theo spun on his heel and put another shot into the man on the left. The second youth was trying to hold his horse and level the rifle. He almost made it.

Theo rolled on his shoulder as the second rifle spoke. The ball missed him as he sighted the Walker on the young man and triggered the gun. The half-breed's eyes were wide as the bullet caught him low under the ribs.

The second man was on the ground, crawling toward his rifle. Theo stood and shot him in the back of the head. The three horses were trotting down the road.

"Christ! Christ! Y-you killed me!" the gut-shot boy screamed, a stain of red spreading over his dirty shirt. From the deep color of the blood, Theo knew his bullet had smashed the liver.

"You brought it on," Theo reminded casually, stepping into the sorrel's saddle.

"You can't just leave me here to die!" The young man looked at him with scared eyes, panic on his face. "Can't leave . . . leave me to die!" He choked on his words.

"Sure I can, kid. I can leave you here to die just like a coyote. You'd a took my outfit. Reckon you wasn't strong enough. Boot's on the other foot now . . . how's it feel?"

"I c-c-can't die," he cried, tears welling in his eyes. "I can't. I . . ."

"Sure you can, kid. We all can." Theo's face was hard as he rode up next to the young man. Little bastard couldn't have been more than twenty-one.

"D-don't l-leave me here," the man pleaded, blubbering in fear. "You can't just ride off. I'm a man." Then he screamed. "*P-please, help me!*"

Theo ignored the terrified screams as he prodded the nervous sorrel. The last he heard was the sobbing of the young man in the road. He never looked back.

As he rode, he poured powder into the cylinders of the Walker, rammed the balls home, greased the bullets, and pinched nipples onto the caps. After reholstering the gun, he wondered if he had been made to go south to kill the Chandlers. If he had, it was too bad the boy had to die so poorly. He hadn't been a survivor, not in the end.

The weather was becoming much warmer. It had been three months since he'd left Dodge City. He was tired of trees and water, and felt claustrophobic in the dense growth. The grasses were coming up bright green in spring growth. If nothing else, the horses were satisfied. The sorrel, born and raised on the northern plains, was in a verdant seventh heaven.

Two days after the shooting, Theo heard horses coming up behind him. There were a lot of them from the rolling sound of the pounding hooves. He pulled his outfit off to the side of the narrow trail and unslung the Sharps. If it was a party of Chandler's kin, they'd all have themselves a time.

The first of the horses came in sight. There were perhaps fifteen—all riderless except the last. That horse had a small, wry-looking man attached to its back. He looked up at Theo and smiled from a beet-red face.

The little fellow whistled and called to the horses, pulling up. His sharp eyes studied Theo's horse's hooves, moved to the big rifle and the thong off the pistol. His insolent smile grew a little. He was covered with short, red, curly hair, and his pug nose was peeling from sunburn.

"How do?" he greeted. "Nice day, ain't it?"

"Sure enough," Theo returned, curious. He didn't look like one of Chandler's kin.

"Name's Dobbs," the little man offered as he rode closer to Theo. He pulled up and kicked loose from the stirrup with one leg before hooking it over the saddle horn and pulling the makin's from his pocket. The man began to build a smoke.

"Folks call me Theo Belk."

Dobbs stuck his tongue out the side of his mouth as he poured the tobacco. Satisfied, he rolled the paper and licked it before he looked up.

"My pleasure, Mr. Belk." Dobbs nodded. "I'm headed back to Texas with these here hosses. Seems there was some question about who own'd 'em. Legallike, ya see. Old Bill Chandler now, he figgered possession was what put gravy on the biscuits. Clementine Thomas, he figgers different. He figgers Chandler don't know his on ox from his off. See, Thomas figgers if he bred 'em, foaled 'em, and raised 'em, that makes a hoss his—even if Chandler done swooped 'em up one night and driv 'em to the Nations. That's why they sent me."

"Huh?" Theo puzzled. The words didn't make much sense to him but the little rider didn't seem addled.

"You ain't from around here, are you?" Dobbs asked as he scrutinized Theo's outfit. "Nope, north plains or I'm a sassy greaser."

"Montana and Wyoming Territories," Theo confirmed.

"Yep, well, in Yankee talk, Chandler done stole these here hosses so they sent me," Dobbs translated. "You lookin' fer a job?"

Theo spat a stream of tobacco juice onto an unoffending caterpillar. "Doing what?"

"Why, helpin' drive these here hosses." Dobbs waved at the animals that had begun to graze along the trail. Striking a match, the little man lit his cigarette.

"How much you pay?" Theo asked, finding he was starting to like the fiesty little redhead.

"Hell, I ain't got the foggiest idear. Take that up with Thomas if and when we get them fool hammerheads back to Texas. 'Sides, I might need a man that's good with a gun by the time we get to the Red River Crossing."

"What makes you think I'm good with a gun?" Theo watched him with narrowing eyes, his soft tone noncommittal.

Dobbs looked at him with mild amusement. "Wal, if'n you ain't, somebody ridin' yore hoss sure was." Dobbs smiled smugly and took a draw on his smoke before continuing. "Somebody ridin' yore hoss done shot the daylights out'a Bill Chandler and that mangy, wuthless bunch o' kin he rides with."

"You work for Thomas?" Theo asked.

The sawed-off redhead shook his head. "Nope. I'm

what they call a Texas Ranger. We ain't really state police, like in the old days. Just a bunch o' the boys still hangin' on waitin' foah that damn carpetbagger skunk Davis t' meet his maker."

"All right." Theo laughed. "I'll help you drive your horses."

"Good!" Dobbs grinned and stuck out his hand. "You're hired. Let's get 'em movin'. Some o' Chandler's kin might want t' argue ownership an' ta be perfectly honest, I never wus nothin' at elocution."

Theo shook the man's hand as the little Texan slipped back into the saddle and started pushing the horses.

The Rangers, it turned out, were outlawed by the Reconstructionist Army and Davis had his own Texas State Police to strongarm his administration. Dobbs had a local reputation for getting things done and worked for various ranchers in north Texas.

"You mean they only sent one man to ride three hundred miles into the middle of Chandler's country and pick up stolen stock from under his nose?" Theo was incredulous.

"Why, o 'course." Dobbs looked curiously at Theo. "There's only twenty or thirty Chandlers. How many men should it take?"

They made the Red River ferry in record time. The horses seemed to know where they were headed. Three days into Texas, they met Clementine Thomas coming up the trail with some of his hands.

"Reckon I hired Theo here to help keep the stock together, Mr. Thomas," Dobbs explained.

"What do I owe you?" Thomas threw his hard eyes on Theo. From first impressions, this man was made of iron and whipcord. His thin face and sharp nose had seen some pretty tough times. He reminded Theo of a bald eagle—strong, fierce, and deadly.

"Well, sir." Theo pulled his beard and met those eyes with his own. "How about a good bait of grub?"

A twinkle showed in Thomas's eyes. "My pleasure, Mr. Belk. We got a pot of chili hung on that sour old paint back there. Tino will set you up."

Theo stepped down from the dusty sorrel and walked back to the cook's packhorse. Tino was a squat Mexican with a lame leg who wore a huge sombrero. The man looked Theo up and down, and pulled the pot off the horse.

Chili was something new. After his eyes quit watering and his throat confirmed it was still part of his body, Theo chucked down the last bowl. Checking to see if his hat was still on his head, he saw Thomas walking toward him.

"That's some pot of beans," Theo greeted as he wiped the sweat from his face. "First time I ever run into a pot of self-cooking anything! If you could sell that stuff in Montana, you'd make a fortune. Enough of that and a man could melt in a snowdrift!"

"I reckon it might take some gettin' used to if you'd never had it before," Thomas agreed, then his eyes went cold and deadly. "You a Yankee?"

Theo pondered. "I don't reckon so. To my thinking, Yankees come from back East. If I had to call any place home, it'd probably be Montana or Wyoming. I was raised there."

"What did you think of the war?" Thomas asked, measuring.

Theo squinted, meeting the fighter's eyes. "Mr. Thomas, that's an odd question. If I get your drift, you're interested in what I think of the Confederate cause. Well, I'll tell you. I don't have any opinion one way or the other. War's just that, folks fightin'. The strong live."

"How'd you like a chance to get used to that chili?" Thomas asked, making a decision.

"Sure beats the socks off any beans I ever ate," Theo laughed. "What have you got in mind?"

"Dobbs tells me you've been huntin' buffalo in Kansas. Says you're a pretty fair hand in a scrape. How well do you know the western trails?"

"Fair enough." Theo smiled dryly, a curl to his lips.

"I've got a herd about to start for the railroad at Ellsworth," Thomas told him. "I need to have those animals get through. I need men who know the country up there, and I need a man who can scout and fight if necessary. Let me make this real clear, Mr. Belk: *that herd goes through no matter what it takes.* Is that understood?"

"Mr. Thomas, I never worked cattle before." Theo was leery. "I ain't sure I'd know one end from the other."

"You'll learn," Thomas grunted. "That's more or less irrelevant anyway. Last year I sent nine hundred head up the trail and they just plain disappeared. I lost . . . lost *ten* good men and nine hundred head—gone, just like that. Nothing ever found out about it. That won't happen to me again, Mr. Belk. I don't want you for herding. I want you to make sure no one stops this herd, and I'll pay you whatever you want if you make sure there's no trouble along the way." There was an unsettled anger and pain behind the man's raptor eyes as they glared at Theo.

"Mr. Thomas, I think I might just be the man you're lookin' for in that case." Theo allowed himself to smile in satisfaction. It was a challenge. The demons shifted. This was the way to Louis Gasceaux.

"You're hired," Thomas agreed. "At least thirty-five dollars a month to start. I'll throw in a bonus when the herd is delivered." He turned and walked off.

Tino was standing watching with his hard black eyes. Theo looked at him and smiled. He belched and learned the chili was as hot the second time as the first.

CHAPTER 12

TWO WEEKS LATER THEO RODE INTO THE T-BAR RANCH. Thomas had built his ranch sixty miles north of Fort Worth on Denton Creek. The country was pleasantly rolling with brush-choked draws. The grass looked good and the pecan trees had started to leaf out. Theo sniffed, learning the sweet odor of a new land.

He stopped the sorrel and studied the pretty, whitewashed adobe ranch house. It had been built low to the ground. The windows were small, with rifle ports about a foot off the ground. A man sat in a crow's nest above the roof and was scanning the surrounding area with field glasses.

"Quite a fort," Theo said approvingly.

Thomas leaned over the saddle horn. "Yep, we

carved this ranch right out of prime Comanche territory. We've buried six of 'em up on the ridge. Buried 'em across from five of my boys and my wife. We came to stay and we done it so far. We can beat the Comanche and the outlaws, Mr. Belk. I just ain't sure I can beat the damn taxes that son of a bitch in Austin keeps makin'." Thomas spit and added, "Then there's the bank."

"Reckon you'll stay, Mr. Thomas. You're a fighter." Theo rolled his quid.

"I hope to God you're right." Thomas stretched his back. "Report to Charlie Torgusson. He'll be the foreman on the herd north. He's a good man. There's the bunkhouse over yonder, and chuck will be at sundown." Thomas waved as he rode off to the ranch house.

Theo turned his horses into the corral next to the bunkhouse and cooled them out. He rubbed them down and curried them before he let them go over and water. When he left, they were nuzzling the other horses. He picked up his packs and carried them to the bunkhouse. It, too, was built like a fort and had a commanding, flanking field of fire to support the main house.

The inside was dark but well kept. The stacked bunks were made and personal items were stowed in an orderly fashion. Three men lounged around a handmade wooden table.

"Holy Moses!" The smallest of the men whistled. "Look at all the stuff this yahoo's got!"

"You rob a store, mister—or are you plannin' on startin' one?" the second man called as he cradled a cup of coffee.

Theo leveled his gaze defensively. He wasn't used to being questioned. "What's wrong with my outfit?"

His voice was low. "My outfit bother—"

"You ain't no cowhand," the little one stated. The third man sat silently and gave Theo a thorough inspection. His measuring eyes were knowing.

The small man was redheaded and reminded Theo of Dobbs. His face was covered with a smattering of freckles that looked like they'd been thrown haphazard onto his face. The second man was tall, blond, and awkward in his movements. With a shock, Theo realized that the two insolent ones were just boys! The third man was obviously something else. He was of medium height and build, but there was a calmness about him. Blond hair hung down around his shoulders and he sported a drooping mustache. He'd been well seasoned.

"No," Theo returned, a little more at ease. "I'm no cowhand. This is new work for me." He set his packs on the floor.

The redheaded boy got to his feet and extended a hand. "My handle's Red. Never figger'd out where it come from. This here long drink o' water is Willy, my bunkie. Last, but sure not least, is Charlie Torgusson, ramrod for this two-by-twice rawhide outfit."

"My name's Theo Belk." He shook hands all around. "Mr. Torgusson, Mr. Thomas told me to report to you. Tell me what you need done an' I'll do it." Charlie Torgusson, he decided, was a tough man.

"You may be new to the cattle business, but you've seen a sight of rough country," Red pointed out, looking over Theo's packs.

"Reckon," Theo agreed. "Where should I cache my outfit?"

"How much do you want for it?" Willy asked.

"Want for what?" Theo was puzzled.

"Hol' on, Willy." Charlie chuckled, shaking his head. "Try that lower bunk there." Torgusson turned his attention to the two enthusiastic boys. "Listen, this man's from the Northwest, savvy? He's from the north plains and they talk different up there."

"Hell," Red sputtered. "How's I supposed to know he didn't savvy English?"

"What all you got in that outfit o' yore's?" Willy was amazed. "You could run a army on all that."

"Most of it's reloading supplies, equipment, pots an' pans, an ax, shovel, rope, gold pan, and too many books. You know, the necessities of life." Theo threw the packs into the bunk. He started to put the Sharps in on top of the pile.

"Holy Moses," Red sighed. "Look at that long gun! Mister, that ain't no squirrel rifle!"

"Excuse my askin', Mr. Belk"—Charlie looked at Theo curiously—"but did Mr. Thomas say why he hired you?"

Theo threw the man a level stare. "He said something about getting a herd through to market in Ellsworth, Kansas."

Charlie digested that thoughtfully. He stood and reached down a hat from a peg. He nodded at Theo and started out. Before he left he fixed both Red and Willy with a serious look.

"You boys ride this man easy, if ya get my meanin'," the honcho warned the two youngsters. "I don't think Mr. Belk would appreciate snakes in his bedroll. In short, he ain't any greenhorn an' I don't want to have to bury either of you. We're shorthanded as it is right now, and neither one of you *companeros* are worth the effort to dig a grave. *Sabe?*"

Charlie tipped his hat and walked out. Red and

Willy looked wonderingly at each other, then at Theo. He had started to arrange his bedroll on one of the bunks.

"Guess you must be pretty good with that hog laig," Red ventured.

"Hog leg?" Theo looked up with narrowed eyes. Were these boys funnin' him after Charlie's warning?

"Yes sir, that there six-shooter on yore hip," Red explained.

"Oh!" Theo grinned. "How's I supposed to know you didn't speak English?" he goaded the youngster.

"We've bunched the herd north of here on the creek," Charlie explained the next morning as they rode out from the ranch in a drizzling rain. "We ought to move them out sometime this week. It'll take a while to trail break them."

"I see. I guess you know I'm a little green at this sort of thing." Theo squinted at the verdant land around them.

"Uh-huh, Mr. Thomas said that. He also said that my job was to let you follow your nose if you got the urge." Charlie looked curiously at Theo.

Theo was amused at the concern in Charlie's eyes. "Well, Mr. Torgusson, let's just see if you can make this child into a cowhand."

Charlie looked beyond the horizon. "I can do it, Mr. Belk." He squinted into the gray morning. The air was fresh with the smell of mud and new growth.

The sorrel trotted over the slimy ground and never missed a step. The air was warm and the misty rain dripped from the brim of his worn hat. The odor of wet horse met his nose. It was a morning to feel good.

"You see, Mr. Belk. It's been hard on Texas since the war. We didn't have the fighting they had in the

East. Still, we got these damn Reconstructionist carpetbagger jackasses here. Hell, we don't need no reconstruction. Texas is fine as she stands.

"Now the trade in beef has opened up. We got a lot of beef, Mr. Belk, and the Yankees have got a lot of empty bellies that need filled. Mr. Thomas sent a herd up the trail last year and we lost it. Not a trace of it could be found. Worse, all the boys that went up the trail disappeared, too. One of 'em was Mr. Thomas's son."

"Uh-huh," Theo grunted thoughtfully, eyes moving on the horizon.

Torgusson waved. "This herd is going to go through. It's got to. If'n it don't, the T-Bar is in trouble. This herd has to make it so that Clementine Thomas can pay off a couple of bank loans or the T-Bar's chances are about as long as a baby's shirttail. That, for your information, is short and full o' brown stuff," Charlie sighed.

"We'll make it," Theo agreed placidly, working his chew. "I'm only one man, Charlie, but I'll do what I can. Don't seem like there should be much trouble this time around. Some tempers in that part of the world are still riled because of the war. You got to consider that most of them folks up there are farmers. Consider themselves Christian folk, tied to the ground. Seen enough of them on the way down here. They don't understand cattlemen, don't understand men at all!" Theo spat a stream of tobacco juice into the mud.

"That may be, Mr. Belk. Last year they wanted two dollars a head for every animal that crossed the state line. Damn Jayhawkers! Said our cattle made theirs sick. Hell, if our cows was sick they'd go down, too! That only makes sense."

There was a pause before Charlie continued, "Just another way to bleed us. They're gettin' all the money they can out of blood-sucked Texas! I tell you, Mr. Belk, we bled enough in the war. If we could of . . . But that's over. Why the hell don't they let us get on with our business instead of rubbin' our noses in it! I just hope God's keepin' his eyes on this. There's folks up there got time comin' in purgatory."

"What happens when you just ride through?" Theo asked, juicing his quid.

"Tried last year. We heard a couple of our boys got shot. Then we heard some of the stock made it to Abeline, but they didn't want no part of their bizness there. After that, the herd just dropped plumb off the face of the earth. Something rotten happened up there!"

Charlie gritted his teeth. "This herd is mine. It's my responsibility. Let me tell you. Mr. Thomas come here in '49 and scratched this place out o' Penateeka hunting ground. He built this place with guts, sweat, and blood. Then he consecrated it with his tears. If I don't get that herd through, he loses it all to the carpetbagger banks and Davis's damn taxes.

"I . . . I love that man, Mr. Belk. He stuck by me when I come back from the war, and I'll charge hell with a bucket o' water at his say-so. I'm pushin' that herd through on my honor. I'll do anything that won't weigh on my soul. I'd . . ."

Theo drawled softly, "Mr. Torgusson, with that attitude, you'll do."

A rider was coming down the slippery creek bank at breakneck speed. The boy pulled up, sliding the horse on its hocks. "Mr. Torgusson!" he cried. "We got trouble. Some grizzly come up from the river and played hell last night. Harley put a bullet in 'im, but it sure didn't slow 'im down none. Cattle's all started to scatter."

"Hell!" Charlie spat.

"Reckon I'd best start earnin' my pay," Theo said conversationally. "Charlie, you've been wonderin' what I'd do in a cattle outfit with this here Sharps. You're about to find out."

Charlie looked annoyed. "How many bear do you think we'll run into on the trail, Mr. Belk? That lodgepole may be more trouble than a Fort Worth whore on payday."

Theo smiled. "Critturs come with less than four legs, Mr. Torgusson. I know what this old babe'll do to a bull buff. I also know how much argument you get out of a man when she speaks first." Laughing, Theo spurred down the trail. That night the camp ate bear steaks.

Louis Gasceaux studied the muddy street with care. He had no desire to get his new boots covered with the thick sticky mud that was mixed with manure and night earth. Louis was very careful of such things now that he'd started his own saloon and gambling hell. He enjoyed maintaining the appearance of a dapper man about town.

Ellsworth, Kansas, was a haven. Why had he not realized the advantages of running a house like this in Dodge? Well, Dodge City was a little on the rough side. The buffalo hunters were not the kind that took kindly to being cheated out of their hard-earned money—not that they minded being fleeced so long as they enjoyed the fleecing!

In Ellsworth, the risks weren't as high. Most of the young cowmen could be bullied or were not that certain of their shooting skills. They, unlike the buffalo hunters, did not shoot for a living.

Also, it was a handy weapon to appeal to their pride and honor. To intimate to a cattleman that a certain action was unbecoming to a gentleman would stop him cold in his tracks. Having never heard the word, a buffalo hunter would cut your throat thinking the word "honor" was an insult in some unknown language.

Best of all, the drovers were mostly Texans. Louis hated Texans. As a consequence, he didn't mind taking them for everything they had. Things were going well.

Why, just last season he'd stolen an entire herd of cattle—or at least what was left after the Jayhawkers got through with it. They cut it up pretty bad. Louis had to poison the drovers, but that was of little consequence and less effort. The rest of the cattle he'd sold anonymously and for good profit. Old man Thomas had sent inquiries, but no one had known anything. Texans were too numerous to be missed.

Indeed, taking Texans was an enjoyable sport. Louis still remembered the cold nights when he'd waded through swamps the first time he'd set foot in that state. All that misery, mud, water, copperheads, alligators, and diarrhea was being paid for now and at considerable interest.

There had been no further sign of Belk either. Louis scowled. Belk had sure played hell! He missed old Sabot's company. The wily old trapper had been a wealth of information, and he had had excellent eyes and ears. That cunning old brain had been a wonderful asset.

Gods! How had Belk gotten out of that trap? They had had him dead to rights. Louis had relished the moment when the big S&W had gone off. He'd seen

Belk jerk from the bullet, but it hadn't been a fatal shot. Belk had shot back and done it well.

Louis had seen plenty of gunfights. Rarely was anyone seriously hurt, especially at night. When passions flared, accuracy suffered. Belk was a different cookie. He had been wounded. Surprised, he'd shot back so well that Sabot was dead and Louis had a permanent scar that would mark him until death. Louis fingered the hard scar tissue left by the glancing bullet that had shattered his cheekbone.

For the first time that night, Louis had felt cold, stark, encompassing fear. Belk was on his trail. If the man ever caught up, Louis was not sure he could foretell the outcome.

For the present, though, he had some ears out. If Belk should come to town, Louis would know. Then he would shoot the man, hire an assassin, or skip town until the danger passed. All were viable options. Besides, men died in Kansas, perhaps Belk would, too.

Abeline had been the start for Louis. He'd bought a small place with two rooms, one a bar, the other a gambling hell. The game had been good and Louis made money. He made enough to have retired in the East, but with pickings so good, his greed got the better of him. The money was so easy, he'd taken to following the trade from Abeline to Newton to Ellsworth.

At each place, the Texas herds were forced to give way before the farming frontier. The yeoman farmers who scratched the dirt to make a living brought their churches, schools, newspapers, and jails. Louis screwed his face up. He had no love for any of it. Some smart son of a bitch always started a reform crusade and Louis ended up being one of the reformees.

When the sheriff got uncorruptible, the end was in sight. Well, the law in Ellsworth had started to change, too. Not only that, but some damned idiot was bringing in a newspaper!

Louis looked down at his expensive boots and rubbed the scar on his cheek. He had to see Rice Goldbach about some stolen cattle. Goldbach was a good man; he'd buy anything, set anything up for the right price. A man never knew when he might need Goldbach's services.

He jumped daintily off the boardwalk and tried to tiptoe through the ooze. He grimaced each time the slimy mud squished over the tops of his flashy black boots.

With the help of Theo's scouting, they managed to have the cattle sheltered when the blue norther rolled out of the crystal sky. They threaded a cautious line between the Cherokee lands to the east and the Comanche hunting grounds to the west. Theo managed to wind them through a southern herd of buffalo that would have caused disaster if they had mixed with the cattle.

Puzzling why the buffalo were so far south, he found the answer. Comanche, making a spring hunt, were pushing the animals beyond their range. That night, they made a run for it.

The drovers pushed the cattle into a tight group. These were Texans and they'd fought the Comanche for years in bloody campaign after bloody campaign. It had been a war of raids, brutality, and inhuman torture wreaked by both sides. It had generated a hatred that burned hotter than a bonfire in the hearts of Texan and Comanche alike.

"We'll push 'em tonight," Charlie told Theo. "This way they've had the entire afternoon to rest. Tomorrow, we hold 'em again. If we push hard enough tonight, they won't be much trouble in the morning."

"Good, I can scout the back trail in case they pick us up. That sound all right?" Theo was thinking to himself.

"You mean that if they pick up our tracks you're gonna declare war on a Comanche war party?" Charlie looked at the man like he was crazy. Red was standing nearby, all ears, his eyes wide while he looked at Theo as if the man had been slightly touched in the head.

"Hell," Theo snorted. "I've shot Indians before. I lived long enough with 'em, Charlie. I know what they'll do an' what they won't. Kill four or five of 'em and they'll stop. It'll take a day for 'em to make new medicine. Then we'll be long gone."

Charlie looked unconvinced. "You may be right. Theo, you might not know one end of a cow from another, but you do come up with the damnedest ideas."

That night they pushed the cattle as hard as they could. Theo hoped that the Comanche were feasting and singing. He knew that the bawling of the cattle could be heard for a long ways in the still night. They made fifteen miles that night and the Comanche were too busy jerking the spoils of their kill.

The pace slowed down but they made more time, putting distance between themselves and the Comanche hunting camp. Theo, riding scout, pondered what had happened to Gasceaux.

"He's ahead," a demon whispered in his ear. "Have we ever steered you wrong?"

Only Dolly had led him down the wrong path. The demons were right. She was wicked, evil—and like the Christians claimed, a temptress who would bring about the fall of man. He'd needed to go to Texas. Louis must have had some connection with Texas or the trail herds. Some hand had placed him on this path. It was that force that guided his life, his part in God's plan. The demons whispered agreement.

"Charlie?" Theo asked that evening. "You ever been to Kansas? To Abeline or Newton?"

"Nope, I just acted as foreman on the ranch, for Mr. Thomas," Charlie related. "Jingo has been up here a time or two. What you got in mind?"

Jingo was called from his rounds. He was a small, wiry black man with a scar along his jawline that was curiously pink against the deep black of his flesh. He listened to Theo's questions.

"Don't dat take all, Mr. Belk." Jingo nodded. "Dey was a fella like you describe in Newton. He runned a little place up der dat sold whiskey and dey did a little gamblin'. But dis man had 'im a big scar on de side o' his face. He say'd it were a bullet what did it in de war."

"Louis never had no bullet scar that he got in the war," Theo said thoughtfully.

"Needer did dis man, Mr. Belk." Jingo had a slight smile in his eyes. "I seed him when he first go to Abeline. Dat scar be fresh den. Dat was maybe year and a half ago. Not only dat, but he talk kind like Cajun den. Now he talk Texas talk, but I doan 'member what he call hi'seff."

"Damn!" Theo exploded. "Doc McCarty was right! I did mark him!" He jumped up and down and laughed while Jingo and Charlie watched him.

"What are you gettin' at?" Charlie couldn't help but ask.

"It's Louis Gasceaux. He's the one who took that herd last year, Charlie." Theo's eyes had started to smolder.

"How do you know that?" Charlie demanded. "Can you prove that in a court o' law?"

"Probably not, Charlie. Louis would'a been too good at covering his tracks. He's pretty canny and the trail's too cold. Fits the way he operates, though." Theo, feeling lightheaded, the demons chuckling in his mind, told the story of his search for Gasceaux. When he tried to mention the dream, a demon screamed and he stilled his tongue. Charlie listened skeptically while Jingo just nodded.

"And you believe that God or Fate or whatever is makin' you follow his trail? That's kinda oddball soundin' Theo." Charlie frowned.

"Don't t'ink dat it is, Mr. Torgusson," Jingo put in. "I had me a gan'pappy what did de same t'ing onct. He say dat der be t'ings in de world dat is only understood to some men. He always be a little funny in de head dough. Don't be makin' light o' what Theo Belk tell you *Hefe,* dey's t'ings in dis world beyond you an' me."

"Uh-huh," Charlie agreed. "Maybe. Reckon I'll want to think on this one for a while. Reckon when we get to Ellsworth, we'll follow up on Theo's hunch and look up this character. I'd like to ask him some questions."

Theo's eyes were hard, his voice like spring steel. "You'll wait your turn, Charlie. I got a prior claim." He turned his eyes toward the northern horizon. There, ahead of them across the rolling hills of grass, lay Kansas, Ellsworth, and Louis Gasceaux. That night the dreams almost drove him mad.

Theo watched as ten men rode out of the little grove of trees in the creek bottom. He pulled his Sharps from its sling and spurred toward them. Charlie was angling in from the point and was going to get there first. Theo put the sorrel to a gallop to catch the towheaded trail boss. They were in Kansas now, and this looked like Jayhawk trouble.

Charlie pulled his horse up in front of the group. "Mornin'," he drawled.

"Who are you?" One of the men looked at Charlie. His eyes were black and featureless. He wore ragged clothing and worn boots, but the Colt pistol on his hip was polished. The rest of the riders were dressed in homespun and sported stubbly cheeks. They all carried guns.

"Name's Charlie Torgusson, foreman for the T-Bar ranch out o' Denton, Texas, and you, sir?" Charlie was polite and civil.

"You know where you're at?" the man demanded. "You're in Kansas. But you ain't goin' no further. Unless that is, you pay to cross our land."

"How much?" Charlie asked. He had counted the rifles; if he balked, some of his boys would die. He felt a sinking sensation in his belly. Mr. Thomas's herd was hanging in the balance.

"Standard," the man growled. "Two dollars a head. That's for grass eaten, pasture damage, water drank, and covers any of our cattle that die o' Texas fever."

Theo had pulled the sorrel up in time to hear the last of it. "Who are you?" Theo demanded, feeling his blood rise, trying to hear over the demons chattering with excitement. His thumb was on the hammer of the

Sharps, the thong was off the Walker Colt at his belt.

"Hank Torrent's my name . . . what's it to you?" The response was surly.

No one had ever taken that tone with Theo. He felt his senses clear. "Not a damn thing, mister," he hissed. "I just might like to know who I'm buryin'." A somber wave went through the Jayhawkers. Men looked grim and fingered their rifles.

"Take it easy, Theo," Charlie warned, raising his hand. "Let's see if we can't work this out without trouble. I'm sure Mr. Torrent will be reasonable with his price when he learns we're not here to take him."

"That's right, and the price is two dollars a head. No dickerin'. Pay, or get off our land." Torrent turned to Theo. "And I don't take no horseshit off Rebel scum, you hear that!"

Theo squinted an eye at Torrent. "Which outfit did you fight with? Who was your commanding officer?" The question was voiced easily. "You tell me!"

Torrent fidgeted. "Rebel, that ain't your business. What are you, a Confed'ert spy? You shut yore—"

"You tryin' to tell me you didn't fight?" Theo mocked. The answer was in Torrent's eyes.

Theo's voice cracked like a whip. "Well, Torrent, I did! Ever hear of the Wilderness campaign? Maybe Spottsylvania? Petersburg? You see, I was there with Hancock's army. Remember which side he fought for? A lot of good men died to keep this country in one piece while yellow-bellied cowards like you sat in your safe warm farmhouses away from the mud and bullets and disease. Now, Torrent, who you callin' a Rebel?" Theo's voice had become deadly with intent.

Torrent turned to Charlie, his face growing red and the veins at his temple standing out. "You gonna pay or not?" he demanded of Charlie.

"We'll—"

"You gonna get outta our way or not?" Theo asked softly, never taking his eyes from Torrent. The man squirmed under the deadly cold blue eyes.

"Easy, Theo," Charlie murmured nervously, "We'll talk this out. We can all be reasonable here."

"That's right Rebel, an' if you don't shut him up the price goes to $2.25 a head," Torrent shouted almost out of control, hooking a thumb at Theo. "An' we cut yur herd when you get through! Don't you go a messin'—"

"Get out o' my way, Torrent!" Theo hissed. The black rage broke loose as the demons droned in a siren's pitch and surged through his brain. "*Move now, damn you!*"

"You shut up, you son of a—" Torrent slapped at his pistol, his words cut off as Theo blew him in two with the big Sharps. Shifting his grip Theo pulled the Walker and calmly began emptying saddles. At each shot a man jerked under the impact of a bullet. Only a couple of the Jayhawkers got off wild shots as they turned to wheel their horses. As one, they spurred for the safety of the trees.

The Walker empty, Theo reholstered the gun and jacked the shell out of the Sharps. He reloaded and centered the big rifle in the middle of one man's fleeing back. As he breathed out and took up slack on the trigger, Charlie knocked the gun up and out of line. The big bullet whistled harmlessly through the trees.

"What did you do that for?" Theo demanded hotly.

"Christ man! You killed four and two of them on the horses are bad wounded! Let 'em go! They ain't gonna come back!" Charlie looked almost shocky.

Theo locked eyes with the foreman before shrugging

and reloading his pistol. Charlie held his gaze for a moment before he glanced at the fleeing figures. One man was being held on his horse by another. One fellow slumped over his saddle. "Four men?" he whispered faintly. "That quick?"

Red and Willy came to a flying halt. Both boys stared at the bodies on the ground. Torrent had a gaping wound that had blown his chest wide open. Willy let out a low whistle and Red turned pale, shaking his head.

"Holy Moses," Red gasped. "I ain't seen that many carcasses piled up in one place since who flung the chunk."

"You in a heap o' trouble now, Theo," Willy moaned.

"How's that?" Theo asked defiantly as he pulled the loading lever down to seat the bullets. He shot a quick, icy glance at the boy.

"Saint Peter's gonna raise the roof when them fellers come stumblin' through the Pearly Gates all at once. He's gonna be powerful sore at you." The boy shook his head slowly, his big eyes on Theo.

"Hell!" Red spat. "Ole Saint Pete's a gonna have plenty o' time. Why, Theo sent them boys upstairs at least a half second apart." He finished with a snort.

"You think he's that slow?" Willy asked in amazement. "I heard you say you was the fastest waddy in the outfit. Think you could'a done it quicker?"

Red looked at Theo and swallowed when the older man gave him a wolfish grin. "Not me," Red breathed. "I'm slower than old man Gomez comin' home on Sunday mornin'."

Charlie cleared his throat. "While you two decide who's the slowest, why don't you ride back to the pack train and bring Tino and Theo's shovels up here. Now quit jaw jackin' and move! We gotta bury Theo's handiwork."

The two boys took off, still arguing about who was the slowest. Charlie looked at Theo, who was sticking another cartridge into the Sharps. He pulled his blond beard, his eyes troubled.

"Theo, I hope you did the right thing here today. Cause if you didn't, sure as hell you'll have a lot restin' on yore mind."

Theo slipped the Sharps into the sling on the saddle and leaned over the saddle horn before he looked at Torgusson. "Charlie, they were gonna charge us too much money. Then, when it was all said and done, they'd a cut the herd. They didn't leave you any choice from the moment they rode out," Theo challenged.

"I guess," Charlie sighed wistfully. "Do you think they'll be back again?"

"I doubt it." Theo spit out his exhausted quid and ran his tongue around his mouth. "Most folks in this part of the country are dirt farmers. They're working themselves to death while they slowly starve. They try to hit up the trail herds for extra cash 'cause they ain't got any to start with. If they can't get the money, they back off. Most of 'em won't buck a hard fight."

Charlie gave Theo a hard, level stare as if he wanted to believe that very badly.

CHAPTER 13

TOM O'CONNELL PAUSED THOUGHTFULLY AT THE EDGE OF the camp. Henry Moore had done well for himself. Even a bullheaded Irish lad could see that. Henry owned five wagons and the associated equipment to run a successful buffalo camp. Fifteen men worked for the old man as skinners, including Tom O'Connell. Henry should net over four thousand dollars on this venture alone.

Tom watched the sun setting over the rolling grasslands. Absently, he kneaded his tired forearms, massaging the stiff muscles that ached from stretching the thick hides. A buffalo skinner had fingers that could crush a rock; at least, it seemed that way.

Dolly bent over the fire. Tom watched her lithe

movements and vented a heavy sigh. Such a girl. Ah, if she only knew how he felt about her. An excitement stirred in Tom's breast when she was near. He shook his head gloomily. Dolly hadn't the slightest interest in him.

Tom growled to himself. Ever since Theo Belk had ridden off, she'd withdrawn inside herself. Even old Henry noticed it and scowled disapprovingly. Dolly, however, didn't seem to care. She kept to herself and didn't share her thoughts. Tom could see the heartbreak in the girl. He wished he could put his hand out to her and help her as she had helped him.

Turning, he glanced again at the red-orange sunset and smiled at the vista, feeling the beauty of the soft light. There was peace out there in the sunset. It touched him deep inside.

As the light died, Tom walked into the camp. From his pack he took the large flat stones for sharpening his knives and oiled them liberally. He began to draw the blades fluidly over the stones in strong, sure strokes. When he had achieved the edge he wanted, he tested them on his thumbnail and began stropping the sharp steel on his strap. Concentrating on his work he didn't hear Henry Moore come up behind him.

"Supper's about ready, Tom," Henry Moore greeted. "Say, just how many animals did you skin today anyway?"

"One or two, Mr. Moore," Tom said softly as he looked up at the man.

"More like seven, Tom," Henry said gently.

"Aye, sir, seven 'twas," O'Connell admitted. "'Tis but me job, sir."

"How come you didn't team with some of the other men?" Henry was curious.

"Oh." Tom frowned in thought. "I don't know. I

suppose I was just feelin' loike workin' by meself t'day." Tom smiled and tried to shrug it off. "A'sides, Mr. Moore, I need the exercise. I still be rebuilding me body."

"Uh-huh." Henry nodded with reservation. "Your body's fine, Tom. I do declare, never seen a man recover so fast. But I think I understand. A feller has to work alone at times so's he can think. Still, seven animals all by yourseff's some doin's. Why don't you take part of the day off tomorrow and run a scout down the creek a ways? See if'n you can't cut some new buffalo sign. Buff's been gettin scarce on this side o' the river."

"Aye sir, that I'll do. T' be honest, Mr. Moore, I've seen more than me share o' buffalo hides since I been on these plains. A roide down the creek will be well taken."

"You've been kind'a quiet lately, Tom. You got somethin' under yer skin?" Henry asked, his eyes watching the expressions in Tom's face. "If I've—"

"No, sir, nothin' ta be concerned aboot." Tom kept his eyes on his knife stropping. There was a silence.

"You worried about Dolly?" Henry asked seriously. He was satisfied to see Tom start as if struck. "Well, I don't know what's got inta that gal. She's just plain clammed up an' don't nobody git anythin' out'n her these days."

"Aye, sir." Tom looked up cautiously to study the old man.

Henry sighed before he continued. "Yep, reckon she ain't been the same since Theo pulled out. Wimmen can be funny that way, Tom." Henry squinted and pulled his beard while he looked over at the girl, the old eyes a well of concern.

"Mr. Moore, perhaps I . . . I be out'a loine . . . but

she wa' in love wi' the mon," Tom reminded softly as he placed his razor-sharp knives in their scabbards.

"Reckon so, Tom. An' another thing. That ain't bein' out'a line. I . . . I guess I was foolish. I thought Theo would'a stayed around and . . . and made a husband for her. I just thought . . . Tom, my hindsight is dead on at a thousand yards, it's my foresight that can't hit the ground in three shots." Henry paused. "Ah, hell, it's probably just as well he left. He always had a mean streak in 'im. Just saved me from ever having to admit it is all. Fact is . . . aw, fergit it!"

"Aye, sir," Tom agreed. He bent his head in thought before looking up at Henry. "I don't know what t' do aboot the mon, sir. He killed me brother and me sister-in-law. Yit at the same toime, I owe the mon me loife. 'Tis a bad an' sorry state of affairs I got meself inta."

"Tell me about your brother, Tom. I heard about it after the fact." Henry hunkered down, his eyes on the violet light fading in the west.

"Ah, Peter," Tom sighed, slipping into happy memories. "He was me older brother. Took care o' me, he did, since I wa' a wee lad. Peter saw to me needs an' kept me from grief. Mind ye now, trouble an' Irish lads, they go hand in hand.

"When I was but sixteen, sir, I managed to be a wee bit o' trouble to the English soldiers that were stationed in me town. I was young an' there be a faction in Ireland that wouldn'a weep if the English were all taken t' hell of a foine day. Needless to say, sir, I wa' caught red-handed t' be sure.

"Peter, now, he wouldn'a let me hang loike the English soldiers were makin' t' do. Bless 'im for the brother he was. He come t' see me one night an' 'tis sad but true, Mr. Moore, God made whiskey so the

Irish wouldn't rule the world. After the constable was blind drunk on Peter's whiskey, he snuck me out'a the jail an' we jumped a ship that brought us t' this foine new land."

"Sounds like quite a character, Tom." Henry chuckled.

"Aye, he was that an' then some," Tom smiled wistfully. "He be a big mon in more ways than one."

Tom's face fell. "He'd gone to Denver that day to send for his woife an' little ones t' come to Colorado. He stopped in the Citation Saloon—a well-known place in Denver—an' that's where Mr. Belk killed 'im o'er a spilt drink. From what I could hear, there was a glass that Mr. Belk threw an' when Peter went o'er t' talk t' him aboot it, they scuffled an' a drink wa' spilled. Belk told Peter ta buy and called 'im a coward. Then he killed 'im. Those who saw it said there was no rhyme nor reason for it. It was just done." Tom's voice drifted off and his face was blank.

Henry nodded and placed a callused hand on the man's shoulder. "Tom, you said you didn't know what to do about Theo. I think the best thing is to just let him go. I'd hate to think about you an' him tanglin'. I think . . . I think he'd kill you, Tom.

"Not only that, but let him find his own fate. I reckon he's gonna destroy himself one of these days. He's just that way. I owe that man so much, but Tom, he just isn't made for the world of men. I think he's a little twisted in the head somehow. Leave him alone. Let nature take its course."

"Aye, sir, I been thinkin' the same, wonderin' if it be the roight thing. I just didn't know if I be shirkin' me duty ta think so. I'm glad ye told me." Tom studied Henry's face.

"C'mon Tom. Grub's on. Let's eat," Henry said at

last, his eyes sympathetic.

"Aye, sir, I can always eat." Tom stood and stretched.

"Oh, Tom, one last thing. If you get a chance tomorrow, uh, could you talk to Dolly? Maybe you could break the girl out'a her melancholy. I'd appreciate it. I can't seem to get anywhere."

"Don't know that I'd be much good talkin' t' the lass, Mr. Moore, but I'll be glad ta try." Tom met the older man's level gaze.

Dinner was an unusually quiet one. The hands had managed to wear themselves out skinning thirty-three animals. It had been Henry's record shoot.

As the dishes were stacked, Tom tried to stretch his tired body as he relaxed on a cottonwood log. A light touch of inspiration brought him to his feet and the young man went to the wagon where he fumbled through his possessions until he found his fiddle. He had not played since he'd gone to work for Henry Moore. It wasn't that his interest in music had desisted, mostly he was just plumb tuckered.

As the first soft strains of the music came from his bow, the camp stopped short. All eyes went his direction. This night Tom O'Connell played with his heart as well as his hands. The emotions that had welled up and been beaten back within him found their release in the singing strings.

Looking up from his instrument, he could see Dolly watching him with a slight smile on her lips. It was as if a greater talent than his descended and touched the bow. His fiddle made sweeter sounds than he would have ever thought were within his reach. His music gripped him and carried his soul. The Irish melodies filled him and floated in his consciousness. He played and played until of a sudden he could play no more.

Exhausted, he lowered the bow and looked thoughtfully at the polished violin in his hands. Not wishing to break the mood, he ran his fingers lovingly over the carved and shaped wood, savoring the feel of so delicate a piece of work. Finally, as if handling a baby, he placed the fiddle in its case and tied the latches.

"That was beautiful, Tom," Dolly whispered.

"Aye lassie, 'twas indeed," he said with a sort of reverence. The firelight flickered across his gentle features as he looked up. "'Twas for you girl. I'm happy and glad that you enjoyed me playing. I hope that it touched something deep inside o' you and gave you a wee moment o' joy."

"It did, Tom." Dolly sighed. She looked at him with wide eyes, as if wondering how the young man could have such an ability with music. "I'm amazed my heart didn't just jump right out of my body, your music is so wonderful, Tom. It touches the soul and few are those who cannot enjoy its gentle language. You have a gift, Mr. O'Connell, a very special gift. Thank you for sharing it with me."

She was smiling radiantly at him and Tom felt himself beginning to blush. Uncomfortable with the thought she might see what he felt for her, he turned and sought his blankets.

Dolly sat by the fire, finishing the last of the plates. She hummed lightly to herself, hearing again the soft strains of music that Tom O'Connell had played. Why, she asked herself, could some men always build while others would never cease to destroy? Absently, her eyes strayed toward the dark form of Tom O'-Connell in his blankets.

The morning after the shooting, Charlie reined in beside Theo as the sorrel trotted ahead of the dusty herd. Theo looked curiously at the trail boss as he spat a stream of brown fluid into a prairie dog hole. Charlie was spending a lot of time acting casual.

"Well?" Theo demanded at last. He'd already had enough of respectful stares from the waddies around the fire the night before. They were treating him like something special. He wasn't sure he liked it.

"Yesterday, Theo . . . Why?" Charlie asked. "Do you really think it was worth the lives of four men? I'm not makin' any judgments on what happened. I'm just curious about how you feel."

At his silence, Charlie shook his head. "Hell, life out here ain't no picnic. I know that. I lost my kid sister to the Comanche. I've shot men, too—but maybe you'd better give this some thought. Seems to me you shot those boys pretty easily, didn't you?" The trail boss's eyes followed Theo's every move, looking for an answer.

"Dyin's part of livin', Charlie. You know that. They started it an' I finished it." Theo squinted an eye at the man.

"But, didn't . . . didn't you feel anything when you shot those men?" Charlie couldn't help but ask. "It was as if . . . Hell, you had to be thinking something, Theo! You ain't made out'a stone. You're—"

"Maybe I am," Theo granted with a little amusement.

Charlie frowned. "Every time I've had to shoot a man, I've had a real hollow feeling on the inside. I've never had to shoot more than one at a time. I couldn't have done what you did yesterday. There's that little hesitation after the gun goes off when you know you did something terrible. You've destroyed a man who was like you. There's that sense of loss and futility. The men I've had to shoot usually shot at me first, like in the war. But, lordy, they were still men. Even the Indians. Men just like us, Theo." He searched Theo's expression.

"Reckon so, Charlie," Theo agreed before he cocked his eye at the man. "But I don't know what you're talkin' about by a hollow feelin'. When I rode up and faced those men, I was doin' what I had to to keep the herd in one piece. They wanted money an' I know for a fact that we ain't got any. If they'd found that out, they'd have cut the herd. They'd a been set then, Charlie. They'd a known there was a good chance for a fight. I had 'em bunched, thinkin' they had a sure thing. I had the edge and they were in my way. Now we're through and two will get you ten, we don't see no more o' them. But Charlie, I didn't feel a thing except madder 'n hell at the tone in Torrent's voice."

Charlie was stubborn. "They were livin', breathin' human beings. They laughed and cried and loved. They might have wives and kids at home. Don't you feel for them? Makes you wonder how many lives this herd is worth?"

Theo pulled up and leaned on his saddle horn, staring at Charlie. "Ain't you gettin' a little carried away by all this? Yesterday I did what Mr. Thomas hired me to do. I did it pretty well, too. Herd's in one piece and all the boys are alive and breathin'. We survived."

"But I was—"

"Now, I don't know what you're tryin' to get at Charlie, but if you really want to know how I felt when I shot them fellers, I'll tell you. I felt good. It felt the same to me as it does when you drop a running deer with a well-placed shot. Only, it felt better 'cause they could'a killed me just as easily—and would have if the tables had been turned."

Torgusson shook his head as Theo continued, "There were ten of them, Charlie. They had all those rifles and were set to use them. They wanted us to crawl for them and I don't crawl, hear? Not for Jayhawkers, not for nobody. I had to crawl once, an' I swear to God, I'll never crawl again!"

Charlie looked away, biting his lip. "It just don't—"

"Yesterday they thought they were stronger and that I'd bow to them, but they were wrong. I was stronger than all of 'em. You saw that! They tried to scare me! I was scared once and I won't be again! They ran like quail in front of a coyote. They ran from me!" Theo ended with gritted teeth and shaking fist. His heart was pounding with emotion.

Charlie sat silently on his horse, hunched in the saddle and studying Theo. Then, slowly, he began to shake his head as sorrow replaced the curiosity in his eyes. "Watch yourself, Theo. Don't let yourself lose what's . . . what's human inside you. Killin' can get pretty easy for some people. When that happens, Theo, they come after you with a rope . . . or else someone puts a shotgun in your back some night and pulls the trigger. It don't matter how fast you are or how tough you are, the odds get stacked against you."

Theo smiled sarcastically and spit.

"Theo, you may not feel the guilt I do for the men I've killed. If you don't, it's a mixed blessing. Makes your life a whole lot easier if you can forget. On the other hand, it don't say much for the quality of your soul."

"You sure any of us have a soul, Charlie?" Theo asked as he tipped his hat back.

"I am, Theo. I think we all got one. Ain't no other

reason for us to be here. I don't know so much about it as them sky pilots do, but what we do and learn while we're alive has to be for something. I worry a lot about how my soul stacks up. I don't mean that in a Christian sense either. I reckon the things a man does are either good or bad. You stack up the chips after the game's over and either you're ahead or behind and I want to come out ahead."

"Uh-huh, reckon you will, Charlie." Theo nodded, scanning the horizon. "I don't see the world working that way. We do what we have to and Fate pulls the strings. Tell you what, you worry about your soul and your debts to God. I'll worry about me." His voice was sharp as he bent his cold eyes on Charlie.

Theo reined the sorrel and cantered off down the trail. Charlie's horse shifted as he thought. The pointers headed the lead steers past his position when he shrugged and rode ahead.

A week later, Theo watched as the drovers circled the herd in the Big Cow Creek bottoms. They were ten miles from Ellsworth.

Charlie waved and smiled as he rode up to Theo. "I reckon you was right, Theo. No more trouble from Jayhawkers. The herd is here in one piece and Ellsworth is just over the divide. Damn fine job, I tell you. Sure thought somebody'd get shot over that mess down south."

"I told you, Charlie." Theo grinned back. "If they cross you, just show 'em which side the grass grows on and you don't get no trouble. That's what's wrong with these folks comin' west anymore. They don't know what it is to have to fight. Don't know life or threat or death. Weakness in 'em! Let 'em know they got a chance to die and they sort 'o fold up and melt away."

"Wal, maybe so, Theo. Sure wish it didn't have to come to that all the time though. You'd think folks would learn to make way for each other. I guess I'll always believe that way down deep. It just makes more sense to get along with folks than to kill each other. We'd get a lot more done and you wouldn't have to watch your backside all the time."

Theo laughed. "That's for Boston, Charlie. This here land belongs to the strongest. That's God's law. Works the same for us as it does for rabbits, coyote, antelope, and wolves. Don't matter how you'd be likin' it. You root hog or die. If you win, you live. If you lose, you die. Simple rules, Charlie." Theo spoke sincerely as he watched the trail boss.

"Yeah, I reckon," Charlie agreed as he stretched himself, standing in the stirrups. "It'll change someday. Them Boston rules will be brought here. When that happens, Theo, you be someplace else. I just don't think you'd make good in that kind of system."

"Don't suppose so." Theo threw the man a shady grin.

"We might just as well ride on in and see what the cattle market is like. The sooner we find a buyer, the sooner we head back to the ranch and some decent cookin'. Gawd! Don't ever tell Tino I said that. I'll spend half my time eat'n prairie dog or some such thing. Never, but never, rile the cook." He finished with a hearty chuckle, and after leaving orders they trotted across the verdant, green grass. As they got closer to town, the grasses were cropped shorter.

"Lot of cattle been held here over the winter," Theo remarked. The cow flops were obviously from winter graze.

"Yep, it does look that way don't it," Charlie said with apprehension.

Large herds were visible as they got closer to the town. The holding pens were full of beef.

' Charlie was interested in the condition of the cattle. "None of it looks as good as ours." He smiled broadly. Theo just nodded with a premonition.

Charlie dragged him through numerous hotels and saloons asking for buyers. The stories were not good. There were fifteen cow camps holding their herds, waiting on the right price. Depending on who a person talked to, cattle were selling for as little as thirteen dollars a head and as high as eighteen. Charlie's mood deteriorated.

"Hell!" Charlie snapped bitterly. "Let's stop at Brennan's for something wet. I reckon I got to think on this a while."

"At these prices are you even going to make wages?" Theo asked.

"That an' maybe a little more," Charlie grunted. "Sure won't make up for what Thomas lost on last year's herd. Reckon he ain't never gonna make up for that son he lost, but hell, the financial part is bad enough."

Brennan's was booming. Theo caught himself scanning the faces, looking for Gasceaux. While the cattle business was slow, the young men were enjoying their play. They were blowing the scanty pay they'd received. Yelling men and roistering voices filled the room. The soiled doves smoked their cigars and cadged drinks and favors from the cowhands. The faro and poker tables were packed with serious-faced men calling their bets or squinting at the spots on their cards. Grimacing, they clutched their pasteboards as the bets were thrown.

"See that fella over there?" Charlie pointed. "That's Ben Thompson. He's in your class with a gun.

Mostly he makes a living dealing poker."

"Looks like a tough gent to tangle with," Theo said, studying the lined face.

"Yep, I don't want nobody to try and put me in his league." Charlie got his drinks and handed one to Theo. Theo gulped his and hollered for more.

The faces in the crowd were familiar. Many he knew he'd seen. Others filled the bill for a given type. Men he'd known from Laramie, Dodge, Denver, Virginia City, and other places. Hard men, drifters like himself.

A thin waddy told them there had been a financial panic back East. People had been put out of work and factories had shut their doors for good. Money in the states was hard to come by. "There's folks back there ain't had no work since the first of the year," the thin cowhand told them. "Hell, they just flat can't afford to buy beeves."

"Makes you wonder who'll buy ours, now don't it?" Theo threw Charlie a calculating look.

Charlie sipped his drink and looked about with resignation. "Don't look like it'll straighten out either."

"Nope," the thin man continued. "A feller what could read the newspaper told me folks was workin' in New York ten hours a day for room an' board only. Now that's some, it is."

"Reckon we'd better sell for what we can get an' get out, Theo," Charlie decided. "I'll mosey over an' see this Mr. Baker. He's supposed to be buyin' for fifteen dollars a head. The only folks that talk eighteen dollars are dead drunk. If I can get fifteen, I'll take it. It might not stay up for long."

"That or hold 'em until the price comes back up," Theo suggested.

"Won't wash." Charlie shook his head. "Shanghai Pierce and Jim Reed held a herd here all winter. There just isn't enough graze. Also, Mr. Thomas has a loan comin' due real quick. He's got to have money. So does the outfit for that matter. They're good boys, every last one of them—and damned if they wouldn't stick it out no matter what—but T-Bar would have to pay them sometime. We give our word on that. I'm selling for what I can get. Hang around. I'll find Baker and sell. See you in a bit." Charlie headed for the door.

Theo shrugged and tossed off his drink, then he started asking about a man with a scar on his face that ran a place in Newton. Was he here? After hearing lots of different stories, Theo watched Ben Thompson play for a while. The Texas gun hand was good at it and was doing quite well. Theo could see it was just plain skill with the cards; the man didn't have to cheat.

Twenty minutes later, Charlie walked in with a scowl on his face.

"He bought?" Theo asked.

"He did, but for fourteen a head. He also said that would be negotiable if the cattle weren't in as good a shape as I told him."

"Better than nothin'," Theo tried to console.

"It was the best I could do!" Charlie raised his hands. "I sure hope Mr. Thomas makes out on that. This is gonna hurt. Reckon some good came of that shootin' after all. If they'd a cut the herd, there would have been that much less. We'd a lost the whole thing if it hadn't been for your gun, Theo. It's a hell of a thing to say, but I mean it."

"If things are so tight back East, folks must be plumb scared. Them Jayhawkers would'a known all about that. They must've meant to cut the herd from the very beginning. They knew you didn't have any money. They were real desperate." Theo was thoughtful.

"Poor bastards," Charlie said lowly. "They were. . . family men, you know."

"Most farmers are," Theo said absently as he sipped his whiskey.

Charlie pursed his lips. "Reckon we'd better get back an' tell the crew." Charlie straightened and began pushing his way through the crowd.

The news was received by the drovers with oaths. "It's another damn blue-belly trick!" Red shouted as he stomped around the fire. His outburst was greeted by cheers.

"All right!" Charlie shouted, his hands up to tolerate no more. "That's enough. Heard tell there's folks starvin' back East. They ain't got the money to buy our beef, that's all. Nobody's got money back there."

"*Si,* includin' us," Tino sputtered.

"Best beef in Texas and nobody'll buy it," Willy moaned.

With a start, Theo realized these men loved their damned cattle. It was an offense for them to sell so low. It wasn't the money that really bothered them. The thought amazed him. These kids—and they were nothing more than that—had worked harder than any crew he'd ever seen, and for scant wages. It was a wonder that none of them had been killed, and now they'd go do it all over again at the drop of a hat. Their pride was hurt worse than their wallets. They loved those stupid, pesky, tick-filled cattle!

The next morning they pointed the herd and drove toward Ellsworth. By late evening they had the cattle in holding pens. Tino and Jingo made the count with a knotted string. Baker tallied and both counts came out on the nose. Charlie took his check and the waddies lit out for town with a passion, whooping and hollering, the sting of the low price momentarily forgotten.

On the spur of the moment, Theo went in and bought another pistol. After the fight with the Jayhawkers, he had come to the realization that he was getting too many enemies. The plains were changing. A revolver and a rifle had been enough in the early days. Now there were too many people.

There was no Walker Colt to be found. The gunsmith had only seen Theo's; they had become a rare weapon. As a result, he ended up with a shiny new Remington since they had a better reputation for not jamming.

Then Theo went prowling for Gasceaux. It didn't take him long to find the joint Louis had owned. He had sold it no more than two weeks before. Theo cursed and stamped as the clientele tried to hear, all the while hearing nothing. One man said he thought the previous owner had moved on to Dodge City.

It was an angry Belk who entered Brennan's. Red and Willy had their arms around each other and were singing "Yellow Rose of Texas." They were all on the way to a good drunk and in rosy moods. Charlie was propped against the bar with a drink in his hand, a stupid smile on his lips.

Theo ordered a rye and leaned next to him. The demons gibbered and a black rage was choked in his chest. Why did he have to always be just a hop and a skip behind the man? Was it some perverse sense of humor Fate had where he was concerned? Why couldn't it be simple? Where was justice in this world?

"You comin' back with us?" Charlie asked. Theo could see Torgusson wanted him to.

"Nope. I can't. Louis's skipped out. I'm two weeks too late, Charlie. He sold out and left. The fella runnin' the place now thinks he's gone back to Dodge. He might end up in Texas someday. He'd make a great carpetbagger, but he fought on the wrong side. One of them Texans would recognize him sure as hell."

"We could use you, Theo. Sort of like Dobbs, you know. You're a hell of a hand when it comes to trailin'. Besides, old Clementine Thomas sets store by you. You could do a lot worse; the cattle business won't always be this slow." Charlie looked at Theo, the question in his eyes.

"I'll stay up here, Charlie. I appreciate the offer, though. I got to go to Dodge and see if Louis's there. I owe him for a lot of things. The more I track him the more I know he needs killin'."

Charlie shook his head again. "Gonna kill another man, Theo? Where will it end? I just don't understand you, Belk. I been around long enough to know what'll happen to you. Someday, the gun will jam, powder fouling will bind the cylinder, or a cap will get stuck. That or they'll ambush you and put a rope around your neck. Worse yet, somewhere, somebody will just walk in and shoot you to pieces when you got your back turned."

Theo smiled. The trail boss was still trying to save him. Somewhere down the road he'd be telling his grandkids about Theo Belk—the man he'd tried to save.

"Not me, Charlie. I don't trust nobody. You notice that my back's to the wall. I've seen every man in here. If trouble comes, I'm ready for it. There's only two people between me and the back door. You just got to take precautions is all. You got to—"

"Theo, yer plumb crazy. *Loco* is the word we use in Texas." Charlie had a pleading look in his eyes. "Other people don't fight the way you do. They'll back shoot you in the end! By Gawd, it's in the cards for men like you. Get out while you got the chance. Make a break—"

"Lord, Charlie," Theo spat. "Get out of my life! I done told you how I work, and you keep tryin' to make me something different than what I am. Go back to your cows and . . . and leave me be! I made my way this far and I don't need nobody tellin' me what's right and wrong! You hear? I don't need it!"

"Sorry, Theo. I reckon I deserved that. Fergit I, uh, said anything. I'm just glad I don't have to worry about havin' a bunch of folks come in and shoot me is all. It's a comfortable way to live. You know it's . . . well . . . Reckon a man's got to do what he's got to do. If you live long enough . . . come down to Texas and, well, say hello one of these days." Charlie offered his hand, his eyes warm.

"Damn, Charlie, still preachin' even when you say you're sorry." Theo shook his head and refused the hand.

The warm eyes cooled. "Yep, well, you ride trail with a man and he kinda gets special. Excuse me for carin', Theo." Charlie nodded curtly and walked off.

The words stung him. Theo spat into the sawdust between his feet. He called for another drink and laughed. It was just as well. Charlie could follow his own path but he didn't need to be riding Theo for following his. Charlie's way was safe—let him be an old man with bouncing grandchildren.

He didn't need any damn wet nurse. He'd wasted too much time with these cattle drivers anyway. If he'd just rode north when Jingo told him about Louis, he'd had him by now. So much for honor and his promise to Clementine Thomas. He'd left Louis Gasceaux to roam for too long.

It was Dolly's fault. He'd been close so many times only to be sidetracked by different people. Damn women anyway. Damn Liz! Damn Dolly! Damn Charlie and his stinking cattle. The second a man started to depend on anyone, they ran out on him.

Liz had turned him down for a storekeeper and Dolly had turned him down for an Irishman. Not only did it hurt, but it had taken invaluable time—time he had needed to catch Louis Gasceaux and make him pay.

Again, Theo's thoughts returned to Dolly. Why had she left him when she had come to mean so much to him? What had he ever done to her to make her hurt him so badly? Why had she done that to him just after he realized he needed her so?

Theo cursed and sipped at his whiskey. He felt the heat rise in his chest. He'd made the mistake of trusting too many people. Trust was a weakness; it killed. It might have killed Theo Belk—but he'd been smart enough to escape. Dolly had tricked him into trusting her so that she could destroy him, turn him from his duty.

He'd caught on. Now he was on the trail again. The devil that had sent him Dolly had failed. Louis was no longer safe from the revenge of Theo Belk. He would fulfill the obligation laid on him at the crossing of the Blacks Fork.

His brain had begun to drift. There was a warm feeling in his guts—beyond the rage that ebbed and flowed with his thoughts. Where was Henry now? The question startled him. Henry, good old Henry. It was pleasing to think of his old friend. That was it. Henry was the only friend Theo Belk had ever had who'd not tried to hurt him. Henry was all right. One man out of the whole damned world.

When he had finished with Louis, he'd look up Henry and see how he was doing. He'd sneak around until he found the old man and catch him sometime when Dolly wasn't around. There was no reason to have to see her. That way she couldn't hurt him again and cause him to feel the loneliness. The demons whimpered.

He shook his head. To be lonely was to be weak, and Theo Belk was never weak. He tossed off the whiskey and wandered out the back door to relieve himself. He found the corner of the building and leaned his shoulder against it as he lowered his britches. The night air cleared his foggy senses.

CHAPTER 14

THEO WALKED THE STREETS OF ELLSWORTH, HOPING THAT just maybe there would be a sign of Gasceaux. In his head, though, he knew it was of no use. His demons told him Louis was gone.

He stopped at the stable and checked on his outfit. He walked over and talked to the sorrel, stroking its neck and letting the horse snuffle at his hand. No matter what, he always had the sorrel. The horse was his friend and would never let him down like Dolly had.

Dolly again! Angrily, he cursed at himself for being foolish. The sorrel went back to eating, and Theo could hear the big teeth grinding the tough stems of hay. Feeling foul, he bent his tracks back to the saloon.

He'd square things with Charlie, buy another drink, and ride out.

He entered the back door like he'd left. Two men were facing Charlie. They had their hands clenched at their sides and Charlie faced them, red faced and angry. Theo could hear the heated discussion. He stepped lightly to one side.

"That's right, you and your Rebel scum murdered Torrent. Him and three other God fearin' boys. Good Christian folk and your devil worshipin' Rebels killed 'em! Shot 'em down like dogs!" the man shouted. Tino and Jingo were working their way up behind the two men.

"Where's that other butcher of yours? Where is he, Torgusson?" the second man demanded.

"Belk's gone, but I'm here. Your God fearin' Mr. Torrent—good Christian that he was—wanted to steal my herd. Nobody does that." Charlie was cool but heated. He reached forward and grabbed the man by the collar and shoved him out the door. The second man threw a punch, but Jingo's pistol barrel laid him out cold. The second man was pitched into the street amid cheers.

Charlie looked up and saw Theo. Meekly he grinned. "Friends of your Jayhawk buddies."

"Shore went out the door in a hurry," Red crowed.

"That they did," Willy hooted. "Looks like the hens went home to roost!"

"C'mon, Charlie, I'll buy you a drink for that." Hell, he really did like the Texan even if he had funny ideas. The man had just showed spunk.

The whole T-Bar pitched in and hollered. Red started singing again; it was "Dixie." The whole place picked up the tune and Theo joined in, something he'd never done before. After several more whiskeys he found he could sing as good as the rest.

The nagging sensation he felt in the back of his mind turned out to be his bladder again. He made his way through the crowded room and found his corner out back. He was a little more clearheaded this time. The revelry suddenly stopped and Theo knew it was trouble.

He ran for the door. This time ten men had Charlie backed against the wall. "We're callin' you a murderer, mister. The law won't do nothin', but we will!" They shot Charlie Torgusson to doll rags.

No one moved; the men were expressionless. Charlie's body slowly sagged to the floor, sliding unevenly down the splintered, bloody wall.

Theo ran right into the middle of them, the black rage loose. The Walker banged as it was thrust against each body. He was roaring and screaming at the top of his lungs. He cursed them as he shot them down. The Walker empty, he reached out the Remington and continued. They watched him, horror on their stupid, farmer faces.

Still they didn't move, but stood there like sheep at a slaughter, refusing to believe the wolf who killed them. One man fell to his knees, pleading, and put his hands out as Theo shot him through the brain. Another cowered on the floor as Theo calmly grabbed Tino's pistol from his hand and blew the man's head apart. It was over. The place was silent, thick blue smoke climbing in wreaths and curls to the ceiling.

Theo handed the gun back to Tino. "He was a good man. See that Mister Thomas gets the money, Tino. Jingo, you, Red, and Willy make sure he doesn't have any trouble."

"Mister!" a voice called. Theo turned to see Ben Thompson standing there, pistol drawn. Theo's guns were empty. Was this going to be it? What options did he have with empty pistols? Coldly, he looked at the man, then Thompson smiled. "You'd better make tracks. I can talk to Sheriff Whitney but nobody knows you here. That was some shootin'. My pleasure, sir." He bowed.

"Thanks," Theo said holstering the guns. "I'm on my way."

"Oh, one thing." Thompson stood and offered his hand. "What part of Texas are you from?"

"I'm not," Theo grinned, taking the man's hand and meeting those hard eyes. "I'm a Yankee, I guess. Seems I fought for the wrong side—the one that won. But these boys here are good men. It's been an honor to know them."

Theo turned and ducked into the night. The last thing he heard was someone asking who'd done the shooting. Jingo's voice rang out. "Bless me if I knows who dat be. But he shoah be som'tin' else." He found out later that no one really connected him with the famous Ellsworth shoot-out, but a lot of people suspected him.

Tom O'Connell whistled merrily as he rode his dusty horse into Henry Moore's buffalo camp. Dolly was sitting in the shade of one of the wagons, reading from a book. She looked up at Tom, a little curious, and gave him a hesitant smile.

"Have a nice ride? Did you see any buffalo?" she asked, folding the book closed.

Tom took a deep breath and held it, his eyes merry. "Sure lassie, 'twas a noice ride." He cocked his head and sighed. "But no, Miss Moore, there was no buffalo ta be seen."

Tom stepped down from the horse as the animal

nickered slightly and sidestepped. "Stop that now, ye hear?" Tom snarled at the animal, batting her sharply in the withers. She instantly bobbed her neck and worked the bit before shaking her head in disagreement.

Dolly laughed openly. "You like that horse, Tom. She's a good one."

"Aye, lassie, that she is. Just aboot ornery enough for a stiff-necked lad loike me, she is," Tom said pleasantly as he tied the horse and walked to the water keg which hung from the side of the wagon. He reached for the ladle and dipped. Drinking deeply, he sighed and looked at Dolly. "Foine thing 'tis to have a cool drink on a hot day loike t'day. 'Tis the small things in loife that make't worth livin', Miss Moore. T'gether, all the small things make loife a thing o' wonder."

"You are always so happy, Tom. Does nothing ever worry you?" Dolly couldn't help but laugh.

"Aye lassie, some things. But on a good day such as this, 'tis but fittin' that the bad things be shoved inta some corner o' yore moind where they don't get in th' way. T'day is a good day to be livin' an' feelin' the sun on yore back, the breeze on yore cheek, and the air in yore lungs. 'Tis a grand day t' look at pretty girls—which is what I be doin' now," Tom ended with a beatific smile.

Dolly shook her head, giggling. "I'd swear, Tom O'Connell, you are a poet. Are all Irish lads that way?"

Tom pulled his beard thoughtfully and studied his dusty hat before speaking. "But o'course, Miss Moore," he said soberly, then burst into laughter.

"It must be." Dolly's eyes were reserved. "What

makes you that way? Did you read poetry when you were little? Is it—"

"Poetry, Miss Moore, is not just read to the Irish. 'Tis everywhere in Ireland. 'Tis in the misty mornings; 'tis carried in the breeze and sung by the birds. The hidden places where the little people live are rife wi' it, and the cobblestones will dance with it under the full moon. 'Tis but the simple nature o' the Irish, lassie." He waggled his finger at her.

She enjoyed Tom's sham sincerity and felt her lips curling into a relieved smile. "I'm so glad that you are with us on this trip, Tom. You bring me so much happiness. Thank you for making me feel better." She wondered about that. There had been such loneliness since Theo left.

"An' yore more than welcome for that. 'Tis such a pleasure indeed t' see yore face lit with warmth." Tom grinned, the laugh lines around his eyes deepening.

Dolly looked down at her book. "I know. I've just had things on my mind is all. I need . . . time to think. It's just that . . . I need to sort some things out in my head. I can't really . . . It's tough to do. I . . . I'm sorry I've put a damper on everyone's feelings." It was her problem and she needed to solve it.

"I know, you'll do well," Tom agreed. "You're too sweet a girl to let the shadows of love stand in your way. Your spirit is too bright for that lassie. If'n I know me wimmen, which I really don't but you'll never hear me admit it, you'll come a shinin' through like the old lighthouse that stood beyond the reefs."

"He gutted me when he left," she said, the tone in her voice betraying her emotions. "I feel like I . . . I've been cheated somehow. I would have given him everything; then he just up and rides out of my life like I don't even exist. But I . . . Why, Tom? What did I do wrong?" Her eyes were far away and she shook her head slowly.

"Men be fools, lassie. Look at me, why I be the worst o' fools. I'll tell you aboot the time I was goin' to join th' church. 'Twas on a warm summer day very much like this that I—"

"Tom, please don't," she interrupted smoothly. "I don't need to laugh right now. I just need to talk to someone. Lord, how wonderful it would be to be able to make sense of it. I feel confused, frustrated! And the toughest part is that I don't know what to do. All my life I've known what I was doing. Now I'm lost as I've never been before." She looked up at the sky defiantly before shutting her eyes and breathing deeply.

Tom squatted down next to the girl. "All right, Miss Moore, we'll talk. I wasn't sure you'd want to talk to another man. I'm honored that ye'd be placing such trust in ol' Tom O'Connell. I'll do what I can to help," he said softly.

"Thank you, Tom. You are just what I need right now. I've never had anyone in my life that I could call a good friend since I was a little girl in Richmond. Isn't that strange, surrounded by people an' I don't have any good friends but you, and Paw?" She bent her head again and bit her lip.

"Well, Miss Moore, I'd be honored t' be yore friend. To be missin' someone to talk wi' is a terrible thing," Tom replied carefully, concern in his eyes.

"I know," she nodded. "But, I've always been so . . . so strong before. I always knew my mind. Then Theo came along and everything changed. I guess it was me who changed, but I didn't realize it until he left. He was a windstorm that blew through my life and carried me away 'cause, Tom, I haven't felt whole since he left. Does that make sense? When he rode out of Dodge City last year, he took part of me with him." She looked up, puzzled. "Does that make any sense at all?"

Tom studied the dirt under his feet. An ant was struggling across the sandy earth with a huge leaf. Dolly twisted the material of her skirt to a little point before smoothing the fabric and doing it all over again.

"Miss Moore . . ." Tom began hesitantly. "I'd not want you to think poorly of me, but we see Theo Belk as two different men." He looked at her hesitantly, as if afraid of her reaction.

"Yes, Tom. I know. I don't think you ever knew him like I did, though." She looked at him challengingly.

"I don't really know him at all, Miss Moore. The man leaves me with more than a little distress, too. You know that I left the moine with the express purpose of killin' Mr. Belk. Now I owe the mon me loife. Make sense o' that would ye?" Tom spread his hands in despair.

"Theo can be a problem," Dolly chuckled wryly. "He's an oddball, Tom. That's what makes him so . . . difficult—that's the right word—to deal with. For instance, if he'd a known you'd come to kill him, he'd a still saved your life and found a grim amusement in it. He would have done everything he could to get you well, then he'd a dared you to kill him . . . and given you an opportunity to try.

"He's a funny mixture of warm, friendly savior and cold, brutal destroyer. Tom, he's haunted. In his sleep he'll—"

"Haunted, ye say?" Tom looked up in surprise.

"That's as close as Paw and I can make it." She

nodded thoughtfully. "Late at night, he'd have a dream. He'd be crying and carryin' on. Then he'd wake bolt upright and the sweat would pour off him. After one of those dreams, he'd be up all night. There's something in his mind that he fears, Tom. It plain terrifies him. Then afterward . . . afterward he's hard, cold, and driven by cruelty. To my knowledge, the dream is the only thing that man's afraid of.

"Then after he blows up at something, he's the nicest person you'd ever want to meet. He'll tell you stories of the old mountain men he's known. He'll tell you about Indians and how they live and about places he's been and things he's seen. When he does that, Tom, there's a warmth in his eyes that a woman just can't help but love. At those times, you know that he's a good man."

"Miss Moore, I don't doubt that he's as good as ye say, but what aboot the other times? Lassie, could ye have lived with those? I've heard he goes berserk then. Seriously, how could you ha' dealt with that?" Tom asked, with sincerity in his voice.

Dolly sighed and looked at Tom with a trite answer on her lips. At his look she stopped. "All right, Tom. I don't know. That's the hitch in the mare's tail."

She looked away. "There was one night we camped on the Arkansas. I was teasing him. I admit it. But Tom, I was desperate to have him notice me as a woman. I was playing up to some other skinners and Theo started huffin' and puffin' around the camp. Finally he stalked out and he had that dark look on his face. It scared me. I thought sure he'd come back and kill one of the boys being friendly to me. It scared me to death.

"Instead he found an Indian boy trying to steal our stock. Theo shot him down and dragged him into camp just happy as can be. I'd never seen a fresh-killed man before. He had his head blown open. It came as a shock that Theo could do it so easy. I'd . . . I'd never seen him in that light before."

"And his whole nature changed after he shot that man?" Tom pondered.

"He went from foul tempered to happy as could be, just like snapping your fingers," she admitted.

"What does Mr. Moore think of Theo?" Tom asked.

"Paw wonders about him a lot," Dolly told him. "I guess everybody wonders a lot about Theo. And there's a real good chance that neither Paw nor I would'a been here today if Theo hadn't found us when he did. We'd a froze, died of thirst, been killed by Indians, starved, or God knows what. Paw sure wouldn't have the outfit he has today without Theo Belk. Paw knows it, too, and he's loyal to folks who've helped him. I think Theo could rob churches and Paw'd still give him the shirt off his back. That's just Paw's sense of gratitude."

"Did he ever catch up with Louis Gasceaux?" Tom looked up at the warm, blue sky. Maybe after he'd caught and killed the man, Belk would be back. Tom fervently hoped not.

"Almost. He and Louis had that shoot-out in Dodge where he killed the man who shot you. I haven't heard anything since."

"How about you, Miss Moore? What do you think you owe him?" Tom felt his heart constrict as she furrowed her brow in thought. He realized the answer to this question would be very important to him. He had stopped breathing.

"I . . . I just don't know, Tom." She shook her head and looked at him. "Something, I guess. No, a lot. But hang, I just don't know. He did so much for us. Then he ran out on me and made me feel cheap and used! Why did he do that to me?" Her eyes were strained and troubled. "Why did—"

"If he came back and asked you, lassie, would you go with him?" Tom felt his heart pounding.

"I don't know, Tom. I'm not sure I'd want to. I couldn't trust him anymore. But in the end, I . . . I guess I would. I'd owe him . . . that much at least." Her voice broke and she rested her head in her hands, her body sagging against the tree wearily.

Tom felt his gut go hollow. He reached out and lightly touched her shoulder in a reassuring gesture. Then he stood slowly and pulled the battered hat onto his head. Looking down he saw the eyes of the girl on him. He smiled warmly, belying the cold emptiness in his breast. "I'd not want you to, Miss Moore. But whatever you need to do, count on me for support."

"Thank you, Tom." She smiled anxiously again. "It really helps to have you around."

"Anytime, Miss Moore. If you get to feelin' a wee bit down, come talk to me." Tom waved at her again and mounted the horse. He rode out in search of the skinning crew. Tom O'Connell didn't whistle this time.

Louis Gasceaux leaned up against the wooden support of the veranda and watched the bustling activity on Front Street in Dodge City. With a satisfied look he reread the note he'd received from Ellsworth. Behind him was his new saloon and dance hall. Louis had been managing it for shares in the business and—after the owner mysteriously died in the night—he had assumed full shares.

He'd felt that the time had been right to leave Ellsworth. The prices were still high for businesses like his and he'd made a profit. The newspaper had started and the Christian folk had made their feelings immediately apparent.

Changes were coming to Ellsworth as they had to Abeline and Newton. The cowmen and those who preyed on them were going to have to give way to "decent" people. More and more squatters were coming into the country; all complained about Texas fever and licentious behavior among the barbaric cattlemen.

The dowdy, severely dressed wives of farmers had begun to walk the streets of Ellsworth and sniffed as the cowmen passed them. The message was plain—if still in its early stages. The cattle business would *have* to go. Louis had left while he was ahead.

Slowly, almost absently, Louis fingered the scar where Belk's bullet had passed and crushed his cheek. Realizing what he was doing, Louis snorted. Belk's shot had been fool's luck, that's all. Fool or not, Louis knew he was marked for life.

Coldly, he spat into the dust. He had convinced himself now; Belk was the son of the woman he'd had on the Blacks Fork. Somehow, he'd followed him all these years. On a hunch, Louis had written to Salt Lake City. The Mormons kept lots of records. Sure enough, they had information on Belk as well as a warrant outstanding for his arrest. That information Louis guarded, hoping that he would have the chance to use it.

He had come to terms with his worry. In his business, it didn't pay for a man to fret lest he get too irrationally frightened to operate effectively. To be wary, however, was a different thing. Caution did not mean a faint heart. It was simply good sense and kept a man's neck the same length.

Still, the gnawing fear came back, and with it the question that had formed that night several years ago in this very town. How had Belk shot his way out of that trap? He was canny and had more lives than nine cats!

Louis took the crumpled newspaper from under his arm and skimmed through the story he now knew by heart. An unknown man had shot ten men in just about as many seconds in a saloon in Ellsworth. No one would admit as to who he was, but Louis had connections. He'd heard that the man was called Belk and he'd been working for Clementine Thomas.

Louis felt that light touch of fear ripple along his spine. How in the name of God had Belk known he'd been involved with the T-Bar? Did Belk know that he had taken that first herd? How could he have put that together? It was impossible! Louis made a living gambling; he didn't have that much belief in impossibilities.

Louis watched a man he'd known pass him with no more than a glance. He'd changed since he'd been here last. He'd put on weight as a result of the life he was living. He'd trimmed his beard and, of course, there was the scar. He passed that off as a wound received when he rode with Wheeler's cavalry. It made the Texans like him.

Now there was just Belk. Louis smiled again at the note in his hand. He savored the words on the short missive. Belk could be handled more than one way, and Louis was a master at intrigue. The note had been sent to him from Goldbach. The man had received his instructions and was at work. He expected payment later. Louis smiled an oily smile.

* * *

Theo Belk stared into the glowing coals of a near-dead fire. The night was almost finished. With bleary eyes, he watched the eddies of breeze play across the coals and ripple away. The dream had been bad this night. Since the shooting in Ellsworth, Theo had not been able to sleep. Either he was at the Blacks Fork or he saw Charlie sliding down the wall, a baffled look in his pleading eyes.

Theo worked his way slowly toward Dodge City. He felt helpless. He was going nowhere, the quest for Gasceaux was the same as always. He didn't seem to be making any progress whatsoever. For the first time Theo knew desperation. He was not sure he'd ever catch Gasceaux. It was as if the Fates toyed with him. The demons gibbered in his ear.

He'd convinced himself he was a plaything of the forces that directed him. The powers kept him and Louis apart—yet so close. They were laughing at him, baiting him like a fighting cock. The Fates would let him get close, but never, never would they let him strike the final blow. Something was nourishing itself on his hope, anger, and frustration.

Theo Belk was a puppet. The dreams would not allow him to escape their machinations, and yet when he got close to Gasceaux they'd skate Louis safely out of the way. Theo felt his emotions rising. There was a rush of adrenaline and a surge of futility for his life.

Theo looked at the stars and screamed his defiance. The sound ripping from his throat was an agonized cry that echoed in the quiet night. The sorrel watched him alertly, unused to such behavior.

He was trapped! The thought pounded at the core of his brain. All he could do was play—or go totally mad. Or get himself killed. Perhaps in death there would be an end to the supernatural comedy into which he'd been cast. Perhaps death was the inevitable end to this long ride. Watching himself in his mind's eye, he could see a little Theo Belk jerked around a stage by ghostly, dark forces that laughed as he came close to an ephemeral Louis Gasceaux.

Charlie would have loved that—dear old Charlie, so concerned with good and evil. What could a man see as morality when the gods themselves were capricious tricksters? Charlie would know by now. Perhaps he was the lucky one. He'd been played, too. All his beliefs of fairness and good had been for nothing as the gods slapped him down in the ultimate irony.

And what happens, Theo wondered, if I die and this continues through eternity? What if I have a soul and the gods make me chase phantoms forever? What did I do to deserve this? The question begged at his thoughts.

He turned his face to the night skies. "Why?" he cried hoarsely, cursing, his voice breaking. "Why have you bastards done this to me?" He sobbed at the last, feeling the convulsions of the tears racking his body.

Slowly he curled into a fetal position in the dust, trying to protect himself from the universe, trying to withdraw into himself and regain that invulnerability he'd had before he questioned. His sobs were uncontrollable, and each sputtering breath he drew tore deeply at his consciousness.

He felt pain, then he felt guilt, anger, despair, and through it all came weakness, filtering through his mind, his blood, his bones. He could feel its soft tendrils creeping deep into his guts.

"No!" he screamed. "Leave me alone, damn you to hell! Leave me alone!" He cried harder then, feeling the tears running down his face. He cried until he had no fiber of resistance left. Spent, he lay on the ground moaning, oblivious to the world around him, shamed by his display.

He could feel the ghosts of his parents standing there looking down at him. He could feel Charlie's eyes on his huddled, frail body. Terrified, he couldn't look up at them. He couldn't face them knowing they'd see his weakness. They'd look into his soul and know that he couldn't survive, that he was losing. He started trembling again, just as he'd done that day at the Blacks Fork.

Something pushed at his shoulder and Theo stiffened with a little whimper. Hot air blew on his face. In horror he clamped his eyes tighter, fearing the wind of hell. The soft push came again, fluttering down his sleeve. It was real, not part of his imagination. *The ghosts were real!* Afraid he would foul himself in his fear, he had to look up.

The sorrel stood looming over him. As he moved, the soft nose pushed in between his arms and legs and the warm breath was expelled over his face again. Theo gasped the cool air of the night, pulling it deeply into his lungs, and sighed, stroking the horse's nose lightly until it pulled away.

He watched the red-orange sun crawl over the horizon, bringing a new day to the land, and wondered what had been real and what had been imaginary in the night. The birds bounded from branch to branch, chirping their welcome to the new day. Their wings whirred through the air and the day warmed. The leaves of the cottonwoods clattered as the morning breeze rustled the grass. Untouched, the haggard man sat and stared absently at the backs of his hands.

His thoughts revolved around Charlie. This was a

sunrise he'd never see. Charlie, who'd come to see him last night. A man who'd believed in humanity and had been shot down by those he pitied.

The damn dirt farmers had done it to him. What right had they to come to the Western lands and fill them with their plows, pigs, corn, and kids? When it was all done, the wolves would be gone and snot-nosed kids and bleak, dirt fields would be all that was left of the wild trails.

They were weak, these farmers. They came at a man in packs like that day at the border. Then when they were routed, they snuck away with their tails between their legs waiting to sneak back in a pack like they'd done in Ellsworth. Cowards, they hid behind their plows and their churches and their holier-than-thou morality—cowards who killed good men like Charlie.

Theo swore and grunted, realizing he hadn't eaten. To hell with them! He despised them! He put together a fire as he thought about the farmers. They were the enemy. Instead of fighting the Comanche and Kiowa, the hunters and soldiers should be killing off farmers for the plague they were.

Even if men and their passions were playthings, God had made the world for the strong. Louis Gasceaux was an enemy, but Theo could respect him even while he destroyed him. It was God's one simple law: Only the strong could even be good amusement for the Almighty.

The Kansans were attempting to drive the Texans from their towns. They'd succeeded in Abeline and Newton. Ellsworth was going the same way. Strong men like Chisum, Rath, Johnny Riney, Charlie Reynolds, Fletch, and Skin had built the land with their blood, sweat, and strength. These farmers had sweat, but where was the blood and the strength?

Theo spat into the new flames that licked around the kindling. The whole damn world was going to hell. That was what the ghosts had tried to tell him last night. What kind of world would it be when it was filled with homesteaders? Where would his people be then? The dog packs of farmers would kill them, just like they'd killed Charlie. Theo's red eyes narrowed and he sighed. How was a fellow supposed to fight them? It would be like killing grasshoppers with a branch.

Eating a quick breakfast of rabbit, Theo groaned and pulled himself to his feet. He put his outfit together and threw the packs on the animals. Checking the loads in his pistols, he swung into the saddle. He hadn't ridden for fifteen minutes before he started dozing.

As he began to dream, he saw Charlie against the wall as the Kansans hammered bullet after bullet into his body, as if in slow motion. He saw the Texan's frame shake under the impact of each slug. Charlie turned to look at him, pleading with his eyes.

Theo felt himself reach for the pistol, but his arm was made of lead. Slowly, so slowly, he grasped the walker, each finger searching for the smooth grip, thumb on hammer, index finger to trigger. He pulled at the pistol but it wouldn't yield. The worn leather held it like a vise.

Slowly the big gun came loose as the Kansans laughed and continued to shoot into Charlie. In horror, Theo watched as one of Charlie's arms fell to the floor as if dropped in water. The severed arteries spurted blood on the rough-cut planks.

Theo cried in despair; he could not lift his too-heavy arm and his thumb didn't have the strength to pull the hammer back. At last, the gun was free, but so heavy. The Texan watched as a bullet split his head. The eyes pleaded hopelessly.

Theo struggled to get the gun up. The hammer clicked in place as Theo sweated to level the gun. Gravity kept pulling it out of line. He triggered it and watched in fascination as the hammer crept forward. Slowly it slid into the receiver and onto the cap. Theo waited for the booming concussion. Nothing! The gun wouldn't fire!

"Theo," Charlie whispered softly. "Are you sure you want to live with the burden of the men you've killed? You didn't have to kill me, too."

"It wasn't me!" Theo screamed. "It was them! Them damn, weak farmers!" But there was nobody there. The room was empty except for Theo, his smoking pistol, and Charlie's body which had slowly slumped to the floor.

"Charlie, I didn't do it," he pleaded. "They did it! Come back and fight, cowards! Come back! You tricked me, damn you! Damn farmers tricked me, Charlie! Just like always! I won't be tricked again, Charlie. I swear it to you. I didn't kill you!" Then he knelt on the bloody floor and cried.

He was still crying when the sorrel jerked him awake.

CHAPTER 15

THAT EVENING THEO SET UP HIS SMALL CAMP ALONG THE Arkansas River and relaxed near his fire. He watched the evening come and heard the train headed east from Dodge City with ricks full of buffalo hides and some cattle. He'd almost finished a stew of jerked meat and cornmeal when he heard the soft thumping of a horse's hooves on the dry ground.

A man rode up to the edge of the camp on a blood red Morgan. He let his eyes run over the packs and equipment. He noted the animals on their pickets. The pot was boiling on the fire and the old, soot-streaked coffeepot steamed. The black packhorse whickered slightly.

The man stepped off his horse and ground reined it.

He was thin and dapperly dressed. His high, English-style riding boots were polished. He was clean shaven and wore a derby hat over a narrow, pale face. The stranger walked to Theo's fire and squatted down as he rolled a cigarette. He reached a twig out of the fire and lit his smoke.

"You want to tell me who you are and what you're doing?" a low voice called from the brush to the man's left.

If the man was startled he didn't show it. "My name's Rice Goldbach." He spoke casually. "I'm trying to get in touch with Theo Belk. I'd heard he was in this part of the country. If you're not him, I'll ride."

"What makes you think this is his camp?" Theo called softly.

"Well"—Goldbach grinned—"this is his horse right here. Heard that he rides a sorrel and the pack animals match the description."

Theo stepped out of the brush, the Walker in one hand, the Sharps in the other. "You found him. What do you want?"

"You are Theo Belk?" Goldbach ran his eyes over Theo's tall frame. "Yes, you must be. Not that many Walker Colts in this part of the country."

"What do you want?" Theo repeated shortly.

"I need to know if you are for hire. I need a man to do some work for me. It won't take more than a day, and I'll wager the pay is better than any you've ever made in your life." Goldbach showed no concern over the big pistol pointed at his chest.

"You know an awful lot about me. What kind of a job?" Theo asked. He was curious. This man was no run-of-the-mill farmer or cattleman.

"I see reloading equipment in your pack. I've heard that you shoot well. In fact, you've been a buffalo hunter for quite some time. I hear, too, that you made history in Ellsworth, shooting ten men. I heard they were all nesters who'd killed a friend of yours." Goldbach's eyes never wavered. Even though such allegations might compromise his life, he was cool as could be. Theo let him continue.

"There is a man who is presently living on some land of mine. This man is akin to those who shot Charlie Torgusson in Ellsworth. Does that make a difference?" Goldbach looked at Theo with flat eyes.

Belk spat into the fire. "No difference," he said.

"Suppose there was a thousand-dollar difference," Goldbach continued with a slight smile. He'd seen Theo's interest. "Nesters, Belk. One man that makes me a big problem. He's a damn dirt farmer with an Eastern law, a bunch of pigs, and a newspaper to back him. It would be worth a thousand dollars to have him, shall we say, moved."

"Why not do it yourself?" Theo asked shrewdly.

"Mr. Belk, two years ago I would have. This is 1873 though, and the damned nesters have brought their Eastern law with them. If I 'moved' him today, they'd have me in jail tomorrow. They'd pick a jury the next day and hang me the day after.

"I need you Belk. I've always fought my own fights, but life was simpler then. Times change and we all have to adapt. The nester is sitting in the middle of a very lucrative deal for me. He built his damn farm right on my water. He won't sell for what I consider to be reasonable money and, damn it all"—the gray eyes were hard—"I was here first.

"The gist is, Mr. Belk, I have to be in town, where a lot of people can see me, when that man is shot. Then I'm clean. I offer condolences to the widow and everything works. That makes it worth the money to me," Goldbach finished.

"What about me?" Theo asked cautiously.

"You get five hundred now. Don't worry, Mr. Belk, you've been in this country a long time and your word is good. If you say you will do the job, you will. I trust your reputation. When the deed is done, there will be another five hundred in the bank in Dodge City. You will have a voucher signed by me to release the money. How does that sound to—"

"No!" Theo said evenly as he watched Goldbach. "You want me, you do it my way. You send the money to . . . to Denver and I have a year to collect. If I start these kind of business dealin's, I don't want to have to stick around to pick up the rest of my cash."

Goldbach frowned slightly before he nodded. "All right. It makes it a little tougher for me in the beginning, but it might work out better in the end. If I'm ever connected, I can say the money is for mining stocks.

"Incidently, Mr. Belk, I know that your word is good. You don't know mine is, but remember, if I welsh on the deal, I know you can always find me. It's a problem with men who . . . do big business—we can't just pack up and run. That's your security.

"Further, if this works out to be acceptable to both parties, I will no doubt be employing your services in the future. I intend on having a place in this new country we're making, *and by God, I shall!*"

Theo reholstered the Colt and sat back on his haunches, the boiling stew forgotten. It was a simple job. Find a man, line up the sights, squeeze the trigger, then look for Louis Gasceaux and make tracks for Denver picking up more money than most men made in ten years.

Theo still had his stash from the hide hunting as

well as his payment for the cattle drive. The ugly rumors of Black Friday and a financial-crash in the East were circulating through the trails. Jay Cooke's railroad empire had failed and factories throughout the East were closing their doors. A solid piece of change might be real handy. He might have to use that money to find Louis Gasceaux.

All for killing some damn Kansas nester? Goldbach had said the target was kin to the farmers who killed Charlie. Just like the ones who tricked him in his dreams. If he killed this one, the dream might go away. Maybe then Theo would get a full night's sleep.

"Where do I find him?" Theo asked at last. He felt uneasy for a second as Goldbach smiled and pulled out a fat wallet. Theo counted the bills as the thin fingers peeled them from the roll.

He spent the next two days scouting the little shack. At dawn of the third day, Theo worked along the brush-lined drainage. He was relaxed and rested for the first time in weeks.

He found his stand, downwind from the soddy the nester lived in. The birds had begun to sing in the trees as Theo settled himself behind a split cottonwood. Carefully, he raised the Sharps and checked the load in the gray light. A rooster began to crow hoarsely, greeting the morning. An ash-colored cat crept across the corral pole before dropping silently to the ground and trotting behind the house.

An hour later, low voices could be heard from the house. Theo came alert. Another five minutes passed before a man unlatched the door and swung it wide on the leather hinges. He was young, muscled, but gaunt in the belly. He met the description Goldbach had given.

As the man yawned and stretched in the morning

light, Theo set the hair trigger. The target scratched his sides as he looked around and Theo increased the pressure on the trigger. The big rifle pushed into his shoulder with recoil as the boom broke the morning stillness.

The nester jerked under the impact of the bullet, bounced off the wall, and pitched into the dirt. Theo calmly ejected the spent cartridge, pocketing the brass, and inserted another before he coolly shouldered the weapon and shot the man through the head.

As Theo trotted back to his horse, he heard a woman scream and the sound of crying children. With an almost audible sigh of relief, Theo knew the dream of Charlie would never return to haunt him. Deep in his mind, he had evened the score with the Jayhawkers. The demons were nodding happily.

Mounting the sorrel, he kept to the creek bottoms where there would be no tracks and headed west toward Dodge City and Louis Gasceaux. For the first time in a long time, he knew he'd found himself again. He was strong now—invincible.

"Did you read this crap?" Henry thundered as he paced the room, his worn boots hammering the plank floor. "How can they slander a man like this? This is a free country! This ain't England, or Spain, or one o' them places. They can't do this!" Henry's nose was red with anger as he finished his tirade.

"I don't believe it!" Dolly cried in his wake as she put the worn newspaper down. "It's a pack of lies!"

"Theo may be a little on the rough side, but he ain't no dry-gulch killer!" Henry roared.

Tom O'Connell sat and said nothing. His perspective of Theo Belk was a little different than the one shared by the Moores, but it had bothered him when he first read the story. His first impulse had been to throw it away before Henry or Dolly could get a hold of it, knowing it was going to upset them. The story about the shooting at Ellsworth had already worked its way down the trail.

Henry's rage continued to build. "I can see him shooting those Jayhawkers. Damn it, they killed his friend. They shot first and Theo finished it. I'd a done the same thing in his shoes. That's the sort of thing Theo'd do, step in for his friends! This other, though, ain't him. Bushwackin' a man in his front door for no apparent reason. There just ain't . . . naw, I'll be damned if I ever believe that!" Henry was shaking his fist. The veins on his neck were sticking out and his beard was bristling.

"That's the trouble." Dolly was shaking her head. "A man in this part of the country gets a reputation with a gun and all of a sudden he's a vicious killer!"

Henry stopped in his tirade and looked at Dolly in amazement. "That my daughter talkin'?"

She shot him a defensive glare before turning to O'Connell. "Tom, do you believe this?" Her eyes pleaded with him but he remained silent. "I guess you do," she said in misery.

"Well, it seems to me that . . . I guess . . . Dolly, there's no evidence that he did, lassie. I'll hold my judgment until they know. They just say in the paper that he be suspected is all," Tom said, but he could see his words made no impression.

"Tom! You can't—"

"Aye," he continued. "I see Mr. Belk in a wee bit different light than you and yer father. I'll not soon forget lowerin' the body of me brother into a grave. Whoa, before you say anything, the mon also saved me loife. It makes for . . . I'll not condemn him, but I will wait for more evidence." Tom ended positively.

She bit her lip. Sighing loudly, she went to the window to stare out at the street, arms crossed tightly across the stretched cotton cloth at her chest.

The cattlemen had come to Dodge City. The open range cattle industry had been pushed ever westward by the farming frontier. The cowboys mixed on the streets with buffalo hunters and soldiers now. They, too, played the same rough games of drinking, dancing, shooting, fighting, and whoring. A growing concern called Boot Hill was well established on a terrace outside of town. It was said that folks were dying to get in. Good folks including Christians, storekeepers, merchants, and wives were still buried down at the fort cemetery. Now, though, the soldiers were pulling out.

One of the big wagons banged and thundered by under the window. Instead of hides, the big box was filled with merchandise. Another followed in its path, then another.

"Charlie Rath is pulling out," Tom muttered absently. "He's on his way, moving his whole outfit to Texas. Strange, Charlie's been in Dodge City since the beginning. Things are a changin' to be sure."

Henry stopped pacing and sighed. He looked at Tom, his mind only half on the conversation until the words sank in. "The herds are getting pretty thin north of the river," he agreed.

"Next trip, we're going south. We got ta get hides where there's buffler. Just no two ways about it. It's treaty lands or nothin'," Henry snorted. Dolly still stood by the window.

"Mr. Moore . . . " Tom fidgeted in his chair, dreading what he was about to say. "I think I'll not be goin' wi' ye this next trip." His voice, as always, remained calm and left no doubt as to his sincerity.

"Tom?" Dolly looked at him, stricken. "Why not? If it's money, we can make some sort of arrangement. You know you're Paw's right arm out there. The outfit couldn't run without you." She walked over and put a hand on his shoulder. Henry had stopped short and was staring with a look of almost panic in his eyes.

"I'm tired of it," Tom said levelly, his eyes on the girl's. He watched as her lips trembled. "I can't stand the butchery anymore. It's a waste. Do you know how many of those animals we've killed in the last season alone?

"Something always cries inside me when I see them great creatures bleed and fall and all we do is pull their hides off and leave the rest to rot. What rots every day out there would feed Ireland for a week! And we just cut oot the tongue and leave the rest to t' flies, maggots, an' vultures.

"The injustice of it goes to me heart when I ride by an' see a brown pile o' meat filled wi' maggots and the smell o' corruption. We've no right to do this, an' I fear in me heart that one day we'll ha' a comeuppance for't." Tom sighed with relief; he felt better having said his piece.

Henry clasped his hands behind his back and continued his pacing. He studied the floor between his feet as he walked. He stopped, cocked his grizzled head, and looked at Tom. "I've thought that a time or two myself. I remember sittin' on a ridge and counting the carcasses. There was the ones that was rotting and the white bone piles from older kills, and I wondered how long it would last.

"I guess that I been so carried away makin' money that I forgot what I felt when we first got started in this business. It seemed a shame. 'Course Theo was around then an' what he taught me give me the edge on a lot o' the competition. Still I came out here to make a stake, not spend the rest of my life livin' with fleas, blood, lice, ticks, grease, gunsmoke, freeze, and thirst."

Dolly sat down across from Tom O'Connell and started figuring on a piece of paper. Henry frowned and paced over to the window where he took Dolly's station just in time to see the last of Rath's wagons rumble out of sight.

"Tom, what do you think the going price for one of those wagons is today, outfitted complete?" Dolly's forehead crinkled as she chewed the end of the pencil.

"With the newcomers pourin' in every day a tryin' t' go to the buffalo range, 'tis hard to say, but I'd venture a minimum of four thousand dollars for a small outfit." He watched her return to the figures. Dolly's whole attitude had changed from one of anger to studied efficiency. Tom shook his head in amazement. She had completely reordered her world.

"That's it!" she cried. "Paw, let's sell out! Figure that we're at peak right now. Sure, hide huntin's got a long run yet, but buffalo are getting scarcer and the overhead is getting higher, traveling to where the buffalo are and back to a shipping point. The competition is increasing, too.

"Also with the economy the way it is back East, we know that the only direction hide prices are going is down. There's a real strong market right now for outfits, and I don't think it'll ever be this good again. Too many people want to go buffalo runnin'. It's the only thing in the country where a fella can make a livin' right now. It won't take long before they figger it ain't so, but in the meantime, we can sell for a whole lot more than we paid out and make a killin' on the profits."

"Huh?" Henry frowned, "You think so? What would—"

"Come look at my cipherin', Paw! See it in black and white," she challenged.

Henry bent over the paper, his eyes squinting at the pencil marks. He grunted and humphed to himself before nodding. "Maybe so, then what?" he asked.

"You could go back to freighting, Mr. Moore." Tom shrugged. "We're buildin' a new land here. A man with your experience would do well an' I'd be more than happy to stay with you for such a job as that." He threw a look at Dolly to see how she'd taken it. Bingo! Her eyes were bright and she nodded in affirmation.

"Somehow that all sounds real good," Henry agreed. "I been thinkin' about goin' south of the river. To be honest, that scares me the hell outa my wits. The Comanche and Kiowa just ain't good ta mess with. The Sioux and Cheyenne might come a ridin' by and shoot a few arrows and run off some stock, but Comanche have a mean streak a mile wide.

"I always thought down deep inside that we got off easy that first time. 'Course, Theo was along to smell out the ambush. This time we might not be so lucky. There's been a lot o' stories comin' up from south o' the river about outfits bein' wiped out and hunters mutilated.

"If we sold out and went ta freightin', you'd stay with us, Tom?" Henry finished.

"Aye sir, I can drive, as you well know, an' freightin' now, that takes bullheadedness t' be sure." Tom laughed.

"You can't beat it, Paw." Dolly shook her red hair

over her shoulders. "We've made more money runnin' buffalo than you made in all the years of runnin' freight in Virgina. Not only that, but I figure with the economic situation, we'll be able to buy up equipment for cheap, new wagons and harness, not the old stretched out, patched up stuff we've been using."

"I'm sold. We go into the freightin' business. Tom you're in." Henry nodded to himself with satisfaction. "I'm sure tired of the stink an' blood an' vermin. I've never been so cold, so hot, so thirsty, or so tired in my life as on the buffalo plains. To be honest, a freight office would just suit me fine."

"I know a man that will buy the outfits," Tom ventured. "He's got a plan cooked up. He thinks he'll give an outfit to a party and supply them. They shoot and skin and he transports the hides and sells 'em. In the meantime, he outfits other parties to do the same thing. He does not have to do the hard work, just make the initial capital outlay. He needs outfits badly. You can practically name your price if it's within reason."

"Well, quit sittin' there," Henry growled. "Go see the feller." Tom sprinted for the door and was gone. Henry turned to Dolly. "You sure you want to sell the wagons?"

"Yes, Paw. They're worth more in Dodge than it will cost to replace them." Dolly was firm.

"How about Colorado?" Henry asked. "I'd not like to think I was beat by that place, and the country is nice around there."

"Colorado, again?" Dolly lifted her eyebrows as she looked speculatively at her father. "You said you'd never go back."

"That was then, this is now. I guess Theo taught me how to succeed out here. I'll go back girl. And once

I'm there, I'll make it work. You must love your old father, gal, you sure done stuck with 'im through thick and thin," Henry finished with a shine in his eye.

"I do," she admitted standing up to hug him. "You needed the hard work and a teacher. Now you are the man that I grew up knowing and loving. When Mama died you went to pieces, Paw. Then the war came and you lost your head—fifty years old and you wanted to fight?" She shook her head as she watched him.

"Well I guess I needed to feel wanted, child." Henry studied the backs of his hands, blackened by the plains sun.

"I know, Paw," she said knowingly. "But I always needed you. When the business collapsed and the Confederacy took all the wagons, it broke you completely. Coming out West was the best thing you could have done. I declare, men can be so bullheaded sometimes. I admit, I've spent more than a little time wondering if any of you ever grow up."

Henry allowed himself a slight chuckle. "What if we don't? What other choice have you got?"

"I could be a spinster and raise cats for company." She threw him a cool look, raising an eyebrow.

"Well, gal, I've wondered a time or two if that wasn't where you was headed. You never gave much time to the boys that come acourtin' in Virginia.

"Then Theo showed up and I'll admit I got my hopes up that you'd marry him. I reckon, now that I look back on it, that it sure would'a been a mistake. You're sharp, gal. What do you make of Theo, seriously?" Henry asked, seating himself on the edge of the table.

Dolly crossed her arms and leaned against the table as she thought. "I don't know, Paw. I've thought about it a lot. He was always two people. He could be the most fun and exciting man I've ever known, but it was always for too short a time.

"It was as if he'd realize he was enjoying himself and clam up tight. Then there were the dreams. We both know about them. Something eats inside his mind, Paw. For awhile I sat around and thought that if he'd let me I could have helped him forget whatever it was. Together we could have beat it. I guess I was just being starry-eyed.

"He'd a made my life miserable, Paw. I can see that now but, you know, if he ever came back into my life again, it would be real hard not to fall in love with him all over."

"Do say?" Henry was surprised. He tilted his head curiously.

"Uh-huh, I do, Paw," she admitted seriously, a frown on her face as if she, too, didn't understand. "You know the way he smiles sometimes and his whole face lights up? His eyes twinkle and those lines around the corners of his eyes draw together. Well, Paw, that look just makes me feel real safe and secure.

"Theo also has a lot of style. It's the way he carries himself and how you know that no matter what might come up, he'll be able to handle it. He's not like most men, Paw. Whether they want to admit it or not, most are just too fragile and shallow. Theo wasn't anything like that. It ain't to say he wasn't always smart though. I don't know"—she shrugged, slapping her hands to her sides—"maybe I'm just in love with an image."

"You know," Henry added, "Tom's pretty interested in you."

Dolly stopped short. She cocked her head and looked at her father in surprise. She was skeptical and an eyebrow raised slightly. "Paw, he's just a good friend! What would he see in me?" she asked seriously, somewhat off balance.

"Damned if I know!" Henry grunted. "But every time you look at him his eyes get all soft—like he's about to turn into a pile o' mush." He bent his knowing gaze on his daughter. She was getting flustered. Why wouldn't she admit to it?

"Tom is my best friend, Paw," Dolly stated positively. "He really is. I tell him things that I don't even tell you. I don't know what I'da done without him during the months after Theo left. But I . . . I don't feel about him the same way I did about Theo. I don't get all . . . all stirred up inside. When Tom's around I just feel real comfortable."

"Huh!" Henry snorted, working his jaws with disgust.

Dolly gestured with her hands. "For example, he's like that old pair of boots you're wearing. Love should be like a pair of custom-stitched Mexican boots, all shiny and decorated," she finished, searching his eyes to see if he'd understood.

"Uh-huh, reckon you don't know as much about men as I thought you did," Henry grumbled with a tired sigh. "No, I take that back! You don't know as much about you as I thought you did. That scares me a whole lot worse."

"I know me pretty well, Paw," she defended.

"That so?" Henry said slowly, mocking astonishment.

"That's so," she asserted, hands on her hips, chin thrust forward, eyes glaring.

"Then you think about this, gal," Henry challenged. "Which ones do you want to walk through life with, that old, comfortable pair of boots that won't let you down or that fancy Mexican pair that pinches yer toes and raises bleeding blisters on your soul?"

Henry shook his head as he grumbled to himself and pushed the door open. "I'm gonna go find Tom and sell the outfits."

Dolly stood mutely and watched him go. For several minutes she pulled her thoughts together. Then, frowning, she went for a long walk in the August afternoon.

Theo Belk followed the dusty road that paralleled the Atchison, Topeka, and Santa Fe Railroad tracks. Twice a day the AT&SF chugged, whistled, and wheezed its way past. The engine bellowed smoke as the cars clattered along the slim ribbons of steel, first headed for Dodge and End-of-the-Tracks, then coming back hauling hides and cattle. Even with all the commerce, the line wasn't doing well. It was said that the AT&SF was having trouble paying the tracklayers.

The dreams had subsided. Once again, Theo slept at night. He never worried about shooting the nester. He'd done plenty of that sort of thing in the war and this seemed no different. And anything would have been better than the constant dreams about Charlie. The score was even now and Charlie's ghost could rest in peace.

The dream of the Blacks Fork still woke him in the night. He could feel Gasceaux ahead of him. The old confidence was back. He'd survived and his time with Louis would come.

As he neared Dodge, he wondered how Henry was doing. It would be good to see the old man again. He'd heard Henry was doing well in the hide business. He couldn't think of him without thinking of Dolly. He remembered how the sun shone in her red hair and how the fine bones of her face gave her a classic beauty.

Theo made good time, much better than he had the last time he came over this trail in the middle of that frozen waste of blowing snow. In the warm August sun, it seemed a different world. There were more homesteaders' soddys now. Wide-eyed children watched him ride by, and men plowing virgin fields waved from their work. Theo felt his skin crawl at the sight. They were raping his land!

Theo pushed on, wondering where it would all end. They'd turn the country into one giant farm from the Atlantic to the Pacific. But, on the other side of the Kansas border were the high plains of Colorado. He'd give them a pound of gold for every bushel of corn they'd raise in that high, dry land!

If he could find Louis in Dodge, he'd still play Hob getting to Denver before the really cold weather set in. That was all right; he had crossed the continent in the icy grip of the winter wind more than once. Pilgrims feared and dreaded winter, but not Theo Belk.

So, he asked himself, what would he do after he found Louis? He'd never given it much thought. Free from the dream, what lay ahead of him? When the debt of blood had been paid, could he lead a normal life? A small thought began to bud.

Maybe he'd go look up Dolly and take her away from that Irishman. That was just a right fine idea. If he had any money left, he could either buy a place or go back to running buffalo until he had built up his stash. Riding out on the buffalo plains with Henry again would be just the ticket.

After that, he'd load Henry and the girl up and head

for Montana. He could do a little hunting and trapping, selling to the mining camps. Not only that, but he had experience with cattle now and the success of Nelson Story and his Montana herd was legendary. He could go into the beef business as well.

Then, too, he'd found another occupation that paid better and didn't involve the risks. He could always go snipe down homesteaders as he'd done for Goldbach. Killing paid well, and with care, it could become a very profitable profession. Of course, he couldn't let Dolly or Henry know what he was doing.

However it worked, he'd have a home. He marveled at the word. Home! A foreign concept. Most of his life, home had been the hurricane deck on the sorrel's back. It had almost been the same when he was riding the country with Henry. The wagon had been home then. Then there was the skin tipi that he'd lived in with Fletch. The only time he'd been in one place for very long was with the Mormons, and that had hardly been a sterling experience.

Curious, he wondered what it would be like to have a permanent place to stay. How would he deal with having to be in one place all the time, day in, day out? Somehow, it didn't seem like the way men were supposed to live. There was something unnatural about it. He chuckled to himself. Most whites lived exactly like that. It couldn't be too tough if so many people did it.

He passed a collapsed soddy. He wouldn't have a home like that to bring Dolly to. He'd have himself a nice frame house built all out of wood. He'd paint it white so that it would stand out from the surrounding land—a monument to himself and all he'd accomplished. It would be trimmed in red, with a big yard and straight fences for his stock. It would be situated in the foothills so he'd be close to trapping and hunting.

In his mind he could see Dolly waiting for him at the door when he came in from a long day on the trail. She'd be there, her slim body outlined in the yellow light. He could see her bright blue eyes welcoming him back. She'd rush out and hug him, raising her soft lips to his. He'd enter the house and there would be a steaming plate of elk on the table with soup on the side and a big plate of biscuits.

There too would be his children. Theo smiled. He'd have a son. No, several sons, and daughters, too, who could wear little white dresses. With enough money to go around, Theo would be the talk of the territory.

Best of all would be Dolly. She'd be there to cook for him, warm his bed at night, tend to his needs, and bear him sons. So much was within reach now. All he had to do was kill Louis Gasceaux and he could obtain all those things. How blind he'd been! Two weeks ago he'd just been following the old trail. Shooting that Jayhawker had opened his eyes to all kinds of possibilities. All those years had been spent training for such an occupation.

With the money he had now, he might just go ahead and marry Dolly anyway. Then he could find Louis and kill him and be that much farther ahead. Goldbach might have some more work for him, and if not, he probably knew someone who did. If Dolly asked him what he was doing on his long rides, he'd tell her something. A woman shouldn't meddle too much in a man's affairs anyway.

In the meantime, if they had to scrape a little, Dolly would do fine. There were plenty of jobs she could take on, she could cook, wash clothes, or even waitress. Why, if things really got desperate, she could run a boarding house or some such thing. Surely, she'd do that for him.

A load lifted off Theo's chest. For the first time he knew he had the world by the tail and it was all going his way.

CHAPTER 17

LOUIS GASCEAUX FINGERED HIS SCAR AS HE WATCHED THE crowded room of his gambling hell milling with a mass of humanity. At last the trail herds had started coming to town. Dodge was going to be the biggest and best of the shipping cow towns to date. Farmers would come here someday, too, but for the present they were still over the horizon. Now it was all boom and buck, even if cattle prices had fallen.

Louis watched gold and greenbacks shuffling across his tables. He sighed with joy as two of his ladies walked out with a couple of cowmen who had bought his liquor. It was a foolproof system, with less risk than anything he'd ever been involved in.

Louis poured himself a shot of his best whiskey.

Goldbach had come through. Theo Belk had bought it all, falling into Louis's trap. Louis had managed to snuff one of the rabble-rousers who had driven him from Newton, and Goldbach had himself a new set of clothes and a good chunk of change. Tipping the newspaper was a master stroke. They'd hunt Belk now.

If he came to Dodge, Louis could have him arrested. If not, he could be made a tool to destroy Louis's opposition. To turn Belk's violence in his own favor had been but another example of Louis's finesse.

Hopefully, the man was on his way to Denver. It was worth a thousand dollars to have Belk on his hook. The man would be out of the territory for at least six months while he went to pick up the money. It was a priceless solution, and best of all, Belk had suggested it himself.

At first, Louis had thought of killing him when he came to Dodge to pick up the cash. He would have been a local hero to the genteel folk for eliminating a ruthless killer. They might have elected him sheriff, a plan Louis was even now aspiring to. He'd learned a lot from Henry Plummer.

Indeed, Louis Gasceaux was in charge of an excellent thing in Dodge. He'd never have to do his own dirty work again. The stash was growing, hidden beneath the false floor of his room. When the farmers came to Dodge, he'd retire with enough money to be a king.

And tonight . . . ah, yes, tonight Ruby would give him all of her attention. She would make him a happy man as he lost himself in her sensuous body. Perhaps he was seeing too much of her, but she was the best he'd ever known. She was so accommodating to his needs and feelings. He never left her without wanting her more. She drove him wild. Perhaps someday he'd marry her? Non! Never that far, *even for a woman such as she!*

He chuckled at the thought. Phillip, his bartender, looked at him curiously before turning back to the boisterous press that shouted at him to refill their empty glasses.

He was still chuckling as another group of Texans whooped their way through the door. The three were obviously flush with money. One was a loudmouthed boy while the other two seemed to be in their twenties. Louis called to them and waved them in. They drawled an answer, smiling as they pushed to the bar.

Louis still hated Texans with a passion. They were loud, uncouth, and barbaric. He remembered the time they'd brought a mummified Comanche head into one of his places. They'd skewered it on a pole as a mascot for their outfit. It had even made Louis despise the southern accent he'd affected to facilitate his business. He hated Texans more than any other human beings on earth!

As much as he despised doing it for Texans, he ordered a round of drinks on the house for the new bunch. That cost, true, but it kept his clientele coming back for more. It was good business and these boys brought their money to places that treated them well.

Besides, there were only three of them. They would tell all their friends about Louis's Place and how the first drink was free. Advertising paid in the long run.

Gasceaux turned his attention to other things. He went to his private room, opened the window to get some fresh air, and began going over the books. He stopped for a moment and stared at the throw rug covering his small cache of loot.

Times had been good and he had almost thirty

thousand in that hole in the floor, on top of his account in the bank. He'd have a couple of hundred thousand by the time he got out of Dodge City in the next year or two.

He was on the verge of investing in a scheme that would make him a million dollars. He'd need a few thousand more before he could set the deal up. When he had that cushion, he'd bilk French farmers for all they had.

He'd sell them prime farmland in America's great West. They'd buy farms for which Louis held no title. After Louis made his move, he'd own all their savings and they'd be in Dodge City, finding the land was free to anyone, but Louis would be long gone. It would be the ultimate swindle. Maybe he could bilk the French government at the same time. Why not?

After Louis had made his entries and counted the receipts, he paused to think about his plans. They were all coming to fruition. Grabbing up his hat, he checked his appearance in the mirror and, satisfied, returned to the main room.

Phillip, as usual, was watering down the drinks of the inebriated customers. He was a good man and knew how to keep a man drinking for as long as possible. The new Texans had split up. Two stayed at the bar talking about cattle prices and their trail drive. The youngest boy, about fifteen if Louis could guess, was involved in a game at Jenks's table.

Good man, Jenks. He'd be sure the boy was skinned clean by the time he was through. Louis had a system. Notable men were allowed to win enough at his tables to make sure they spread the word. That included trail bosses, cattle buyers, local merchants, and an occasional cowboy for good advertising.

The average waddy, fresh from a drive with his

pockets full and a pint of whiskey in his craw, would be busted flatter than the alley cats prowling the cans and garbage out back. It was a good system, and Louis was proud of it. It gave his place a reputation for straight play.

"I ain't so drunk I didn't see that!" a high-pitched voice shrilled. The Texas kid stood up. "Damn you!" he yelled again. The two men at the bar turned to stare at the boy and Jenks, who was looking up mildly. "That was a damn bottom deal!" the kid declared.

"I beg your pardon," Jenks said softly and intently. Louis could see his eyes narrowing as he neared the table.

"Is there a problem?" Louis asked smoothly.

"Damn right!" The kid was red-faced and getting madder by the minute. "This double dealin' skunk cheated me. He threw a bottom deal. My pap taught me that years ago. This place is crooked! Yer a four-flushin'—"

"That's a lie!" Jenks stood up menacingly. "I could kill you for that!"

Louis was deciding if he should cool them off when it happened. The boy, young though he was, pulled his pistol and shot Jenks through the chest. Louis had never seen a pistol produced that quickly.

"Called me a liar . . ." the kid started as he turned toward Louis with his pistol. Louis shot him. He spun on his heel and saw one of the other two bringing out a gun. Louis snapped a shot at him. Louis's third shot took the man in the left breast. He turned in time to see the last Texan burst through the door, pulling the hinges loose as he went.

Louis ran to the sagging door and was satisfied to see the Texan pounding away, his horse at a gallop. Louis allowed himself a small sigh. He would have to inform the sheriff and all the statements would have to be made and printed up in the paper. The mayor would have to win a couple of hundred dollars some night soon, and the whole thing would be forgotten.

"See to Jenks," Louis ordered as he checked the boy. His shot had been good. The second man lay propped against the bar with his jaw clenched, sweat beading on his face. "Get the doctor down here!" Louis hollered. Most of the other patrons went back to their drinking or playing, talking about the shooting.

"You got more trouble comin' than you know, mister," the wounded man gasped as Louis leaned over him. It looked like he was going to live.

"He called my man a cheat and shot him," Louis reminded. "Then he pointed his pistol at me. It was self-defense. What could I do?" He straightened and snapped the Smith & Wesson open, ejecting the brass, and began inserting new .44s.

"That boy is old man McHattie's son. McHattie owns the Concho outfit. You'd better leave while you're able. He'll hang you for killin' the kid," the man whispered fervently.

"Relax, don't strain yourself," Louis soothed. It didn't matter a damn if the man lived or died, but it was good for his image when lots of people were listening. Louis noticed the place was clearing out and men were whispering to each other as they left.

"Boss?" one of Louis's dealers asked as the wounded man was taken to Doc McCarty's.

"Yes, Jim?" Louis turned to the man, raising his eyebrows.

"That was part of the Concho bunch. The wounded man said you killed McHattie's son." Jim looked him straight in the eye.

"So?" Louis asked simply, scowling at the blood on the floor.

"We got trouble. They don't like their men gettin' shot, boss. They come from over in the thicket and most of those boys are kin; they ride for the brand. The family is one of those Tennessee clans with Scotch ancestry. I'll repeat, they are trouble." Jim was serious. "If you got my time, sir, I think I'll find other work for a while."

Louis stared into the steely eyes, not believing what he was hearing. "I had no idea that you would run at the first sign of trouble, Jim," Louis said softly. What did Jim know of the Concho boys that made him so leery? In other instances, Jim had pitched in and cleaned house. The big man was not a coward.

"When it's that outfit, sir, I don't stand in the way. I was in Nacogdoches one night when one of them got shot, or knifed, or some such thing, by a Mexican boy. When it was all over, they'd burned a couple of jacals and hung three greasers back in the trees, including the boy." Jim hadn't flinched. "There's other things I heard, too, and none of them make me want any part of 'em boss. I'd urge you to skip out for a while."

With a shrug, Louis handed the man more than his time and watched the broad back disappear out the door. The bodies had been hauled out. The saloon was almost empty now. New sawdust was already on the floor. Louis noticed some of his people were missing. Two more men asked for their time in the next half hour.

Louis was concerned. The last of his men had just left when horses pulled up outside. Louis stood back from the window and looked out. He counted fifteen men. The leader was a white-haired man with a well-trimmed mustache. His eyes were as cold as those in a rattlesnake's head. A noose dangled from the man's saddle. Louis's stomach turned. Gathering his nerve, he smiled and walked out calmly. As he passed through the door, he had a premonition that he'd made a mistake.

"May I help you, gentlemen?" he offered in his best drawl.

"Damn sure can," the leader called back in a rusty voice. Hard eyes settled on Louis, and he felt himself shudder involuntarily. A snake had warmer looks. "My name's McHattie, Bob McHattie, and we want the man that calls himself Louis. We want him now, you hear?" Bob McHattie bellowed, his face turning red.

"I am the man you are evidently looking for," Louis said seriously, allowing a pained expression to cross his face. "But I'm not sure you've heard the story of what happened here." Louis hoped he sounded reasonable. "The young man in quest—"

"I heard enough, mister! You want to come easy or hard?" was McHattie's deadpan response.

"Your young man had a misunderstanding with one of my employees. Allegations were made that the man was cheating and the boy shot him. Then he turned the pistol on me, and in self-defense I was forced to shoot. Your other man is at Doc McCarty's right now, of course I will bear any medical expenses. They had all been drinking; there was nothing I could do."

The cold eyes didn't waver. There was no change of expression.

Louis waved. "Two men are dead, Mr. McHattie. One of mine and your son. I am deeply disturbed by this whole affair. I think that two dead men are price enough for a misunderstanding. If you would care to dismount and come inside, perhaps we can proceed as if none of this had happened." Louis had put all the eloquent polish on his talk he could, his voice oozing sympathy.

McHattie's hard eyes never even quivered. "We done gave you a choice, gambler. You gonna come easy or hard? You can hang alive or dead. It don't matter to us." Two rifles were pointed at Louis. The men behind them didn't even waver, their grim faces had all the give of granite. His stomach muscles crawled, waiting for the impact of a bullet.

"None of your talk's gonna bring my son back, gambler," the white-haired man rasped.

This was it. The loudmouthed kid was this cold-eyed snake's child, and he was out for blood. Hell! Louis was a dead man unless he did something fast. The very air seemed to still.

"Well!" Louis grinned. "Here comes the sheriff, he may have something to say about this." Louis let his gaze go beyond the mounted men. He made the fastest draw he'd ever made in his life as some of the heads turned.

He was so fast his first two shots were off before he could align the pistol. They were clean misses. At the same time he leapted for the door with bullets splatting into the wood of the frame.

Pitching through the door, Louis slid on the tobacco-soaked sawdust, tearing his shirt on the rough-cut planking. Someone slammed the door shut and shot the bolt as the windows exploded in a rain of glass. Bullets grooved the tables and pattered into the walls. A staccato of gunfire accosted his ears.

The inside of the saloon was chaos. Men who'd hung around to see the action were diving under tables and hugging the floor. Some were pulling guns, others were grabbing bottles. In a less serious situation, Louis might have found it amusing, even if it was his whiskey!

Pitching to his feet, he ran through the building to the back door. Bursting through into the daylight, he sprinted for the tents his girls used. A horse rounded the corner of the saloon, ridden by a youth with a flushed face. He spied Louis and leveled an old pistol.

Louis slid to a stop and took careful aim. The horse raised its head as Louis shot. The animal reared as the bullet hit above the animal's eye and it collapsed in a heap. Kicking and squealing, the animal died. The rider rolled across the hard ground, the pistol discharging in the process. The youth screamed as the gun emptied into his leg.

Louis continued his dash. He vaulted some empty whiskey barrels. As he landed, his feet slid out from under him in mud created by saloon habitués who couldn't make the outhouses. A bullet whacked by his head as Louis went face first into the goop.

Gasceaux scrambled on all fours and pulled himself out of the way. He got his bearings and fired at a second man who'd ridden around the building. The man flinched as the bullet whizzed by his head, and Louis ran full tilt for Bell's Livery.

A saddled buckskin gelding stood by the door. The animal waited, ground hitched, as the stable hand was tightening the cinch, checking the hooves, and making the horse ready.

Louis made a flying leap for the saddle, got lucky, hooked a foot in the stirrup, and somehow caught up the reins. The stable hand shouted something as the horse, recovering from the shock, exploded out of the yard and down the street, Louis trying desperately to catch the other stirrup with the offside foot.

The westbound AT&SF, a mile down the tracks, was chugging relentlessly for the End-of-the-Tracks. Louis pounded the ribs of the already-scared animal. The train might be the only hope. Glancing over his shoulders, he saw the remains of the Concho outfit rounding the corner of Bell's Livery and hollering as they saw him. Thirteen riders stretched out behind him.

Running the terrain through his mind, Louis thought about the bridge. The tracks crossed a steep-walled, deep arroyo. It was some distance upstream before a crossing could be made on a horse. The only problem was the train might make the arroyo before Louis did. If that happened, he would be a very perforated corpse in Doc McCarty's office before the day was over.

He was riding the animal along the tracks now. He could hear the occasional crack of a rifle or pistol, and dust spurted from the ground ahead of him. The shots were wild, hoping for a lucky hit. Slowly, the caboose grew closer. The train was still picking up speed. Louis spurred the horse with all his might in a last, frantic effort. The caboose was close now.

The arroyo loomed ahead; for a brief moment Louis felt sure he wouldn't make it. Then he was beside the platform. Throwing out a hand, he caught the railing. It was enough, he kicked loose from the stirrups and flopped. He caught a foot in the step and was aboard the train.

The horse, relieved of its burden, slid on its haunches trying desperately to stop before it slid onto the bridge, but the momentum was too great. The hooves clattered over open ties and the animal flipped over, a foreleg catching between the ties. The leg bent, the bone snapping loud, as the horse somersaulted through the air over empty space. The buckskin hung, dangling over the chasm, held by the twisted leg and shrilling loudly with pain and fear. Then the leg pulled loose.

Too bad, Louis thought. The horse had saved his life. But after all, horses *were* expendable. Sighing heavily, he sank to the deck of the platform and calmed his pounding heart. The pursuers slid to a stop at the edge of the arroyo and shook their fists. Several parting shots were fired at the train with no effect.

Louis smiled weakly. One of the men stepped down and walked to the edge of the arroyo. He shouldered his rifle and shot into the drainage, putting an end to the buckskin's misery.

With a sigh of relief, Louis straightened his tie and slapped as much of the mud as he could from his stained, torn clothing. He smelled like urine. Opening the door of the caboose, he made his way forward.

It cost him a little of his roll to buy the conductor off. With a start, he realized all he had on his person was three hundred dollars. The rest of his loot was still under the floor in his office.

The only clothes he had were on his back! Well, the money would stay hidden for a long time, at least until the building was torn down. If he went back now, he'd be a dead man. The Concho outfit would have feelers out all over the country trying to find him.

"Where am I gonna end up?" Louis demanded of the conductor.

"Granada, just like the rest of the train," the conductor growled, wryly wrinkling his nose at the smell of Louis's shirt.

"Then where?" Louis asked, thinking McHattie

would undoubtedly send a rider looking for him along the train's route.

"You want to go to Denver?" the conductor asked.

"I might as well." He wouldn't live long in Kansas if McHattie had his way! Louis thought again of the money in his stash.

"Then it's only fifty miles from Granada to Kit Carson. You pick up the Kansas Pacific from there and it takes you right into Denver," the conductor related.

"Fine!" Louis growled. "And how do I get from Granada to Kit Carson?"

"Mister, it seems to me like that's your problem, now don't it?" The conductor grinned sardonically and walked away. Gasceaux seriously thought about shooting him in the back, then decided against it.

"Hell!" Louis spat as he leaned back into one of the seats. So close to reaching his goals, had the world by the tail, did he? Now there was a death warrant out for him in Dodge City. "Damn Texans, anyway!"

Theo rode into Dodge City as the sun dropped below the Arkansas River uplands, a big, red-orange orb that seemed to sink into the ground. The high clouds blazed in a fury of pink, red, and purple. For a sunset, Theo thought, admiring the sight, it was some indeed.

He pulled his horses up to Bell's and stepped off the sorrel. He walked in the delicate, swaggering steps horsemen take after a long ride, as if to prove their legs were really made for walking instead of acting as a clamp around a horse's slats.

Ham Bell came out of his livery into the failing light to squint at a worn bridle's stitching. He looked up and inspected Theo's outfit before he recognized the rider. "Theo Belk!" he cried. "Long time no see."

"It's good to be back, Mr. Bell," Theo agreed, pulling his dusty hat from his sweaty head and slapping the grime out of it.

"Where all you been since I seen you last?" Bell asked, an almost childlike curiosity in his eyes.

Theo squatted down next to Bell and shaved some tobacco from his plug, offering Bell some before loading his lip. He related all of his travels.

"Sounds like quite a time. Any of it pay better'n hide huntin'?" Bell laughed.

"Nope, can't say as it did, an' a lot of it was harder work by a damn site," Theo grunted back, letting his eyes roam down the street. Some of the buildings were the same, but Dodge was bigger now and bustling.

A cool breeze blew up from the river in the September evening. Bell looked at Theo with questioning eyes. "There's talk about you, Theo. They say you dry gulched a nester over by Newton. It was even in the paper."

Theo met the man's eyes with a hard squint, his mind working over the information. How could anyone have suspected him? It came as a surprise. "Do say?" he asked, startled.

"Uh-huh. Didn't say in the paper who it was thought you done it. Just said you was suspected," Bell related, as he fingered the bridle absently.

"Folks talk, I guess. Had me some trouble with Jayhawkers on that cattle drive. What do you think, Mr. Bell?" Theo snorted as he juiced his quid. *Only Goldbach knew!*

"Ah, they're crazy. Them old hens just been a settin' in the sun too long is all. It don't seem like your kind o' doin's. Not to shoot an innocent man fer nothin'." Bell looked at him thoughtfully. " 'Course, if a fella wronged you once upon a time, you might do it, but that changes the color of the cat you're skinnin', don't it?"

"Sure would," Theo agreed, feeling nervous.

"Most of that talk comes from over across the street. Most of the straitlaced folks remember you was a buffalo runner and you had that shootin' that time. Now they heard you rode with a Texas herd and to some folk's notions, that means you done it." Bell shook his head then looked at Theo.

"Huh!" Theo grunted. "Maybe I better walk easy. It seems that them pious Christian folk can get pretty quick on the trigger when it comes to judging their fellow man." Theo was sardonic.

Bell nodded in agreement and snickered. "Hey, I'm one o' them," he said with a note of surprise. "I go to church of a Sunday."

"Uh-huh, there's a difference, too, Mr. Bell. I think you read between the lines." Theo changed the subject. "Old Henry Moore still around?"

"Nope, he's gone like most of the old buffalo runners, moved on. Funny though, he sold the whole outfit first. Said he was goin' inta freightin' in Colorado. Made a bundle, too. You know, he always had the best wagons in the business and he kept his stock up. That man was some with a team."

Theo's heart dropped. His mood was changing. What kind of damn luck was his anyway? He was feeling black on the inside when he had another sudden thought. "Tell me, is Ruby still runnin' her place?"

"Sure is," Bell told him agreeably. "She does right well, too. I keep reckonin' she's just gonna up and leave one of these days. I think she's a little smarter than the rest of the girls on the line."

"Well, Ham, keep them horses ready. If the Christian folks is a passin' judgment, I may just need 'em in a hurry." Theo laughed, slapped his thigh, and tossed Bell a coin. Ham would have them ready at a moment's notice anyway, but the gold engendered goodwill.

"I won't keep 'em too ready," Bell said soberly. "I had a horse stole last week. Some cow outfit ran a gambler out of town and the damn fool rode the horse into the arroyo west o' town catchin' the train."

Dodge was all new and still the same old place. The names on the buildings had changed. Theo read them as he walked down the street: The Lone Star, The Alamo, Sam Houston's, and others appealing to the drovers. It was the atmosphere that remained constant. It was still Dodge City, curly and unkempt.

Walking around a raucous-sounding bunch in front of Peacock's Long Branch Saloon, Theo headed for Ruby's tent. The place was empty. Lifting the flap, Theo saw most of Ruby's belongings were gone. Worn clothing, empty bottles of perfume, and assorted other things, easily replaceable, were scattered about.

"Hey," Theo called to a man. "How long's Ruby been gone?"

"Saw her wander into Louis's Place a couple of minutes ago," the fellow related. "If she's still there, her buggy will be hitched out back."

Theo strode off toward where the man had pointed and found a clapboard structure. Louis's Place? Could it be? He grinned and hurried his pace. The buggy was hitched out behind and Theo noted it was packed full of bags and boxes.

The back door burst open. "Leave me alone!" Ruby's gravelly voice ordered.

"Ah, c'mon, Ruby. I ain't had a lady in three weeks," a voice slurred. Theo stepped into the growing shadows. It was almost dark.

Ruby pushed her way out into the dusk and shook off a restraining hand. "I ain't interested, Hardy. Not tonight. Even I get a night off every once in a while. Is that too much to ask?"

"I'll throw in another five bucks," the voice offered.

"No!" Ruby was adamant. "Go find Sally!" The door slammed after a curse and she hurried toward the buggy with a large satchel in her hand. At that instant, the door flew open again and a man staggered out.

"I changed my mind, Ruby. I want you. Sally stinks." He stumbled after her.

"Hardy, I said no." Her voice was like a whip in the night.

"I pay," he said insolently. "I want you. You gonna put out or not?"

"Not tonight, I told you," she insisted vehemently.

"You bitch!" he cried. "I'll force you. Ain't nobody gonna care if a whore gets forced." He lunged and caught hold of her arm. She struggled, dropping the satchel.

The man cried out. "You knifed me!" he shrieked, letting her loose and sucking at his cut hand. "I'll kill you for that!"

The man staggered back a couple of steps as Ruby retrieved the satchel. He pulled out a pistol. Ruby's eyes went wide. Theo's pistol barrel thunked hollowly against the side of his head and Hardy dropped.

"Thank you so much, mister," Ruby breathed, her

chest heaving. Theo kicked the gun away.

"Anybody see you come out here with him?" Theo demanded.

"Yeah, of course. The whole saloon is full of people. Do I know you?"

"Is Louis in there?" he demanded.

"Hell no! He wouldn't come back here if the devil made him. The Concho outfit has a five-hundred-dollar reward out on his head. Who are you anyway?" She peered through the night, trying to make out his face. "Don't I—"

"Was the Louis that owned this place Louis Gasceaux?" he asked.

"Yeah, that was him. He killed a kid from Texas and the boy's father is huntin' all over the country for him. Louis's long gone if I know him. He'd get his neck stretched if he stuck around.

"Look, I gotta go. Hardy might have some friends in there that'll come out to check. He lives on the other side of the street with his good little wife. My word wouldn't be worth a damn against his." She turned and climbed into the buggy.

"You know where Louis might have headed?" the calm voice asked, stirring her memories. Who was it that had known Louis as Gasceaux?

"No, he left so fast you can bet it was anywhere away from here. McHattie and his Concho outfit are after him. Say, I know you, what's your name?" She was puzzled; he seemed so familiar.

"Theo Belk," he said softly.

"You!" She looked around furtively. "Look, Theo, you'd better clear out of here, too. They want you for shooting some farmer. It was in the papers. I'll see you again somewhere—but don't hang around Dodge. Thanks again for coolin' Hardy out for me." She slapped the reins and the buggy shot away into the night.

Theo shook his head. It looked like Louis was a step ahead of him again. He'd heard of the Concho and McHattie. He was supposed to be a feuding terror in east Texas. Louis probably wouldn't come back to Dodge. At least not for quite some time.

For as coolly as Ruby had started out, she'd sure fallen apart quickly when he told her his name. What did she know that he didn't? He grunted and started up the street for the Dodge House to get dinner and think over these new developments. Louis was out of his reach again. This time by only a week!

It was strange to be back in Dodge City. Louis escaped, Ruby taking off for someplace or another, and all kinds of warnings from old friends to leave town.

The familiar surroundings brought back memories of Dolly. He could see her standing on the walks. There was Zimmerman's store, where he'd tried to talk to her that night in the howling storm. There's where they'd parked the wagon that first day in Dodge. Things had been so different then. He'd been happy, but he hadn't really known it. Would he ever be happy again?

Theo rounded a corner and almost walked into Charlie Bassett.

"Evenin' Charlie," Theo drawled a greeting. He saw with some interest that Charlie had a star pinned to his chest.

"Theo? Is that you?" Bassett squinted in the dark.

"Sure enough, how you been? Looks like you got elected sheriff." Theo smiled at the man. Things had changed.

"Uh-huh, I did, Theo. You stayin' around for long?"

Charlie's voice dropped.

Theo became wary. "No, I'll be leavin' soon. Why?"

Bassett hesitated, then spoke. "All right. Listen, Theo, I gotta ask. Did you shoot that nester over t' Newton?"

"What do you think?" Theo asked softly; the thong was off his pistol, his hand on his belt.

"Yes or no, Theo." Bassett was firm.

"If I say yes?" Theo queried. He cocked his head and studied Bassett's posture in the night. What would the man do?

"If you say yes, I gotta take you in. We got a warrant for your arrest, Theo. In Newton, they think you done it." Bassett was shaking his head, not liking the situation. "They want a man to hang over there real bad. That nester was pretty popular with the reform crusade and circumstantial evidence points right at you."

"Goddamn farmers!" Theo spat. "If they want me, why don't they send one of their dog packs after me? Hell, that's how they hunt wolves an' bears ain't it?" Theo felt his anger rising. Charlie backed up a couple of steps, keeping his hands away from his guns. Theo's pent-up rage burst loose.

"Sure, I shot him!" Theo hissed. "He was just like that dog pack that shot Charlie Torgusson in Ellsworth. Damn them! Damn them all!" Theo clenched his fists. "You ain't takin' me in, Bassett. Not to give to their damn dog pack!"

Charlie Bassett was a good peace officer. A peace officer differs from a lawman. Lawmen live to enforce rules. If the rule is in black and white, the lawman will lay down his life for it. The peace officer makes his calls as he goes. His duty, as he sees it, is to protect people and property and to maintain order. He will see to the safety of the community even if he has to bend the rules a little to do so. Charlie Bassett made that decision.

"Theo, will you leave town peacefully if I ask you? Will you give me your word that you'll leave the Dodge area?" Bassett asked quietly.

"I reckon," Theo fumed.

"Between you and me, Theo, I don't think I can take you with a gun. I want you to know though that if it becomes necessary, I'll try it. If you don't push me and just get on your horse and ride out, I'll look the other way, 'cause I ain't about to put together a dog pack as you call it. If you push me, I'll try and take you in and that scares the bejesus outta me. If it becomes my duty, I'll do it and be damned the consequences. You hear? I'll have to do my job if you hang around." Bassett's voice was level.

"Damn, Bassett." Theo grinned. "You sure are more than most of these fools deserve. Hell, yes. I'm leavin' right now. I give you my word I'll stay shut of Dodge, too. And one more thing, Charlie. After the way you just said that, I reckon I wouldn't want to face you either. So long, friend, see you along the trail somewhere." Theo disappeared into the dark.

Bassett watched him long enough to see Belk turn his steps toward Bell's Livery before leaning against the side of the building and wiping the sweat from under his hat brim. There were times that being sheriff was plain hard on a man's peace of mind.

True to form, Theo's horses were fed, watered, and the saddles were on, though the cinches weren't tightened. Theo chuckled as he waited for the sorrel to blow before he pulled the rigging tight.

"Hello, Theo, leavin' already?" Bell called as he swung down from the loft.

"Yep, thanks for doing such a good job on the stock. They was ready ta go just like you said."

"I figger'd that if you weren't back by midnight, I'd strip 'em down, let 'em roll, and have them ready for you in the morning around light," Bell told him as he hung some tack on the wall.

"Don't you ever sleep?" Theo looked at the man.

"Off and on all day and all night. Livery business takes a different schedule than sellin' hammers down to Zimmerman's," Bell said lightly.

"Be seein' you, Ham," Theo told him as he offered his hand. "It appears that Charlie Bassett would rest easier if I never came back to town."

"Take care, Theo. It's the times, I guess. A lot of changes are comin'. I don't know if I like 'em or not. There are good things on both sides. I guess I'll just ride 'em out and make do."

"I reckon you will, Mr. Bell." Theo tipped his hat and led his string of animals into the night.

CHAPTER 27

IT WAS EARLY EVENING AND THE NIGHT WAS COOL. THEO stopped to dig his old, worn-out coat from the packs. Winter would be here soon. The grasses had turned brown. The leaves had darkened to a deep shade of green.

He'd learned a lot in Dodge. Louis was gone again, and the gods laughed as they pulled the strings. Henry and Dolly had gone freighting in Colorado. Ruby had pulled out for places unknown. He was a man wanted by the law for killing the nester. Lord knew how they'd learned that; unless it was Goldbach who'd told—but why would he? Theo shrugged.

Always the trail, and this time, he knew that no matter what, he couldn't go back to Kansas. They'd kill him. These new farmers were different. They played by different rules. Collectively, they were stronger than he was. There was a survival value in the dog packs and their strange morality.

Damn the nesters anyway! They were a plague, like locusts upon the land. Making men like Bassett do their dirty work proved it. What horrible world would they build out of Kansas? Why, next thing a fella knew, there wouldn't be a drink of whiskey in the whole state and they'd outlaw the line girls to boot. *Lord, were they even human*?

There was no way he could declare war on them and win. Worse, they were headed west and he'd just have to stay ahead of them. How in the name of hell did they fit God's plan?

Dodge had been a disappointment. He'd hardly got the reception he'd anticipated. Henry and Dolly were gone. There was no redheaded girl to rush into his arms or be by his side as he hunted Louis Gasceaux. She was somewhere ahead, between the pointed ears of the sorrel; so was Louis.

Theo finally moaned himself to weariness. He made a little camp in the evening chill and rolled out his bedroll. That night, the dream came again. He woke in terror, pulling himself from the dream only to stare as he had so many times at the few, glowing embers in the fire.

He was on the trail before sunrise, passing through an increasingly brown land. After sunrise, he passed a wagon of immigrants. The farmer, wearing a dirty, white shirt, waved cheerfully only to be greeted by Theo's fierce scowl.

No more than an hour later, he passed another wagon full of them. The squat farmers called to him happily and made Theo's mood worse; he spurred the horse to a canter as he passed them. Theo was grim as he thought of what he'd told Bassett. He'd do the man one better. *He'd be damned if he ever set foot in Kansas again*!

At the head of a draw in front of him, he could make out a vehicle lying on its side. More damn farmers, he growled to himself. The driver had caught a wheel and flipped his outfit. He could see a figure working to right the wagon. It seemed to be a woman and the wagon was a buggy!

Theo laughed as he rode up. He pulled the sorrel to a stop as he guffawed in the saddle.

"You want to move your ass off that mule-headed horse and help me?" Ruby glared, red-faced, at Theo. Her ample breasts were heaving from the effort she'd put forth. A pile of her belongings were next to her.

"What in hell did you do?" Theo wondered aloud. He hooked a knee around the saddle horn and pulled out his plug of tobacco. Shaving some, he chewed the hard stuff.

"You son of a bitch," Ruby panted as she went back to trying to lever the buggy upright with a cottonwood branch. Each time she got a good purchase, the tip of the branch would break off, dropping Ruby on her firm backside. This action was accompanied by a string of curses that brought a smile to Theo's lips.

"If you don't get off that horse, Belk, I'm gonna shoot your lazy ass off," Ruby threatened.

Theo grinned and shook out his rope. Dropping the loop on a hub, Theo sidestepped the sorrel and lined out. When he reached the right angle, the buggy righted onto its wheels.

"My pleasure, ma'am." Theo tipped his hat to the

woman. She shook her head and began rehitching her team. When she had driven the buggy from the arroyo, she piled her belongings into the back, putting the satchel Theo had seen in Dodge on the seat beside her.

"You didn't stay long in town." She looked at him from under lowered lashes.

"Seems Charlie Bassett was just plumb uninterested in my company," Theo admitted. "Said he'd just as soon I left rather than tryin' to take me in for that shooting at Newton."

"You did that?" She stopped short, staring at him curiously.

Theo shrugged. He moved the quid from one side of his mouth to the other and spat a brown stream at an ambling stink bug. On impulse he stepped off the horse and rearranged the suitcases in the back of the buggy so they'd ride better.

"Looks like you was ready to leave long before that run-in with Hardy."

She grunted, settling herself into the driver's seat. "Which way you headed? West?" she asked.

"Colorado, I guess." Theo stepped into his saddle. "Which way you goin'?"

"I was headed west, maybe Colorado. Least I was till you showed up—now I ain't too sure." She threw him a wry look.

"Why was you leavin' Dodge?" Theo was really curious. "You had a real fine setup there."

Ruby eyed him speculatively, her mind racing. Theo could read the indecision in her eyes, then he could see a choice made. "In case Louis came back."

"You following him now?" Theo's eyes had grown thoughtful.

"No, I ain't!" She glared at him. "He's about the last person on the face of this earth I'd want to see right now! That man's a damn viper!"

"You're goin' the same way he is," Theo pointed out.

She shook her head in amazement. "Belk, did it ever occur to your dim-witted brain that west might be the only direction I can go? If I ever set foot in the eastern states again they might just make an exception and hang me in public," she snorted sarcastically. "Men! For the love of mud, there's times I wonder how humanity's made it this far. Hell, men are more stupid than sheep."

"So where do you think he went?" Theo asked, ignoring her outburst.

"Anyplace where he could get out of reach of old man McHattie. That's a lot of country, Theo. One thing's sure. He didn't go east and he didn't have a lot of money with him. He's got the shirt on his back and whatever he had in his pockets. He'll go to the nearest city and try to wire for some of his funds from Dodge if I don't miss my guess."

"Damn!" Theo cried in anguish. "Why can't I ever catch up with that bastard!" He pounded his fist into his palm.

"You know you've got him runnin' scared don't you? Who do you think set you up for that nester shootin' and then spilled it to the papers?" Ruby watched Theo's face contort. "You ruined his beauty for life with that bullet that night outside my crib. You come close to breakin' him. He don't have the self-confidence he used to."

"Lot of good that does me." Theo was sour. "I just want to have him in my sights for a second. That's all it would take. Just a second." Theo went silent, seeing in his mind's eye the bullets impacting on Gasceaux's body.

"What did he do to you?" she asked. She'd wondered that since the night of the shooting in Dodge.

"That's my worry," Theo said shortly, and swung onto his horse. He watched as Ruby slapped the reins and pulled her buggy onto the trail. Behind them rattled and banged the wagon full of immigrants, cresting the hill as they left.

"You decided where you're going?" Theo asked after some time.

"Colorado, I guess. I don't know all the whys and wherefores to gettin' along in New Mexico. Colorado has more promise for a girl like me. There's more men with money. I can handle miners I guess, but I'm not sure about Mexicans. Ride along if you like, Theo." She smiled. "I might drive this contraption into an arroyo again."

"Why, Ruby, I just might at that. I ain't had nobody to talk to since they shot poor Charlie over to Ellsworth."

The sun was high in the blue, cloudless sky as Ruby looked over at Theo. "You know, I ain't never driven a buggy through the wilderness before. To be honest, it scared the hell out of me. Men may be insecure, dumb creatures, but by God they can be comforting to have around when a woman's out on her own.

"Don't you dare believe for an instant though that I couldn't a done it by myself!" She glared at him.

"Nope." Theo smiled. "Not this child. I'd never a believed that for a minute, Ruby."

She chuckled at the sham seriousness in his voice.

That night, Theo found them a place to camp. They were away from the river and he located a sheltered spot below a butte. Theo set up the camp and cooked the supper. Ruby, he found, had never been camping and in her later years had never been out of a town. She had no concept of camping or camp chores. He arranged the packs, built the fire, picketed the horses, and saw to cleaning up afterward. Lastly, he began to build a bed.

"Theo?"

"Yep."

"Two separate places, please."

"Huh?"

"When I left Dodge, I quit that business." She was firm.

"Hold on now! You mean that I'm supposed to travel halfway across Kansas and most of Colorado and not touch you. Damn you, name your price!" Theo bellowed.

He turned to face her and found himself staring into a nickle-plated Sharps derringer.

"I'm serious, Theo. By damn, I mean it. I got just as much mean and evil in me as you got in you. If I tried to push you too hard, Theo, you'd beat me half to death on a bet. You try to push me too hard and I'll kill you. Now, have we got an understanding?"

Slowly, he lowered himself to his haunches. The woman was dead serious; it was in her eyes. Theo spent several seconds estimating his chances to knock the gun from her hand and force her before deciding against it. She was too wary, but there would be other chances down the road. Satisfied, he shrugged and separated the bedrolls. Besides, she would have to sleep sometime and then he could take her.

"Theo," she said softly, "if you try while I'm sleeping, you'd better never trust yourself to sleep again." She smiled wickedly. Cuss it all, Theo thought, did this woman read minds too? Then he rolled into his bedroll to seek sleep.

Ruby shuddered as she watched the heat waves rising on the horizon of the baked land. Every bone in her body creaked and threatened to shatter at the next jolt of the buggy. The shimmering horizon appeared to be made of water.

Squinting caused her sunburned cheeks to twitch in pain, but it helped her raw, aching eyes. She winced as the buggy rattled across a small drainage in what Theo called the trail. Somewhere ahead lay a place called Kit Carson. The Kansas Pacific Railroad was there, and there was a trail that went straight west to Denver.

On the verge of tears, Ruby reached under the seat and pulled out the water sack. She fumbled it up to her cracked, scabbed lips. The water was hot and brackish. She swallowed only enough to wet her throat and redistribute the foul taste in her mouth.

"So this is success," she croaked to herself. A thin smile opened a cut in her chapped lips. Absently, she worried it with her tongue. The thin, white, powdery dust stuck to her mouth as soon as she relaxed her lips. Without thinking she wet her lips and was rewarded by the feel of her gritty teeth.

"Damn!" she growled to herself. Even her nose was plugged with dust. At night when they made camp she would drop her bedroll on the ground to see a cloud of dust rise in a puff.

Ruby was physically miserable. But mentally, she spent her days in rapture. For the first time in all of her long, painful life, she was free. Never again would she have some drunk man, stinking of sweat and lust, pressing himself against her body. There would be no more pawing, slobbering men breathing fetid breath in her face. Never again would some lout thrust hotly into her as he moaned with pleasure. Never again would she fondle some man and discreetly spit his semen into a handkerchief.

No indeed, she thought as she patted the carpetbag at her feet. Her future lay in that bag. She was saved forever from the misery, the slavery, the abuse, and the fatigue of working the line. The sum total of the savings accumulated by Louis Gasceaux lay in that bag. Now it was all hers—so long as Louis didn't find her!

She'd come so far from that little dogtrot cabin she had called home as a girl. The memories of her parents were so faint they seemed almost a fantasy.

Then came the war. She remembered the troops who had come to take her brothers away at gunpoint. The soldiers called it conscription, but when her old father had gone out to argue, the gray-clad men had shot him and left him lying in the dirt. Her brothers had marched obediently and wide-eyed from the farmyard. Absently, she wondered if they'd lived. She might have even had one of them somewhere on the line but she'd never have known.

Mother had died soon after that, leaving her alone. Barely eleven years old, she'd dug a shallow grave with a kitchen knife and rolled the earthly remains of her mother into her final resting place and covered it with the rich, Kentucky earth.

How long had she stayed there, waiting for her brothers to return? Then Markus had come. Sick and feverish, she had fed him and nursed him back to health. Markus, the Yankee deserter. Eighteen years old, cold, and hungry like herself, he had been scared he'd be captured and shot. Together, they fled north.

At first, she had thought of him as another brother.

Then came that terrible night. He'd lifted her ragged dress and taken her. She remembered the pain of her first time. She remembered the feeling of degradation and self-disgust. Most of all, she remembered the shattered trust she had placed in him. She'd never trusted another man after Markus.

For two years they were together. Most every night he'd mount her. He never took long, but it always shamed her. She'd hated him, but there was no place else to go, and he threatened to kill her if she ran away. Worse, he said she'd starve because without him, who'd steal food?

All the time she stayed with him, she hated and feared him more, still acquiescing to his physical needs. It didn't seem so bad now after all she'd been through.

At fourteen, she had felt the life stir within her. She had hoped the feeling would go away, but it never did. Then Markus had seen the swelling of her belly. He'd thought she'd been hiding food to become so fat! Furious, he'd beaten her!

Bruised, bleeding, and aching all over, she had cowered on the wet muddy ground of the deserted barn and sworn she hadn't held back. No, in fact she was carrying his child. Crying, she'd looked into his smoldering eyes.

"By God!" he'd cried, fear in his eyes. "How in hell can we feed a child? I can't be tied down with a squalling baby. If the army catches me, I'm dead, you hear? I ain't gonna be slowed up by no baby! What did you go and do that for anyway? Why did you do this to me?" Then he'd kicked her in the belly, hard, before he ran, cursing, into the cold rain.

First came the blood, then the raw red fetus, followed by pain. She didn't remember the people who found her and took her to Cincinnati and left her at the Charity House. She remembered the sisters telling her to pray for her soul and to seek forgiveness for committing sins against God and nature.

Bewildered, she had fled. Scavenging a pile of garbage, she was found by Aunt Hilda, who fed her and took her to a place that was warm and nursed her back to health. All that if she would only cater to the needs of the men who arrived at Aunt Hilda's door after dusk. Since the sisters claimed that her soul had already been lost, she'd done as she was bid.

"Men!" Aunt Hilda had told her. "They are animals. Watch them, learn them. Remember, when you have them panting at you, you have them in control. He has come to you, and don't you ever forget that! Any woman can control any man if she uses her wits and her body. Always know what they think before they think it and enslave their passions, Ruby. The world is made for the clever.

"But have a great deal of caution and care about how you use this strength. They must never know you have used them and to rub their noses in it is the worst mistake. They will destroy you. You must be cunning, it is the only advantage we have against them."

Ruby had learned well. From that day on she had never but once let a man know he was her tool. That once had almost killed her and ended with two men shot, one by her in an alley back of Olive Street in Saint Louis. She had fled to the West after that. A warrant for her arrest was in effect in Missouri.

Those years were over now. Almost thirty thousand dollars were hers. All she had to do was get to San Francisco with the money.

At the moment, she was not worried. She had found the easiest way across the plains. She had a guide, scout, Indian fighter, buggy repairman, horse wrangler, cook, and camp tender all rolled into one.

She smiled, grimacing at her cracked lips as she watched the broad back of the man riding ahead of her. She had enjoyed watching the desire building behind his eyes. He wanted her more than any man had ever wanted her before. Well, Louis Gasceaux had come close, but she no longer had any need for Louis.

To see his face when he bent over that empty hole in the floor would almost be worth the fortune. How he would rave and curse. Then he would settle down and put his mind to work. When that happened, he would know who to look for.

Her first plan had been to dump Belk in Denver, catch the spur line to Cheyenne or Laramie, and ride the cushions west on the Union Pacific railroad until she reached San Francisco. Now, as she watched, the rider pulled up his horse, unslung the big Sharps, and shouldered the weapon. The big rifle boomed and an antelope some 350 yards ahead of them dropped. Ruby smiled; she would add bodyguard to Theo's duties.

Why did the drifter hate Louis so much? What ancient wrong had Louis done the man? They were at least ten years apart in age, more likely fifteen. Their backgrounds were diverse. Belk would kill Gasceaux at less than a drop of the hat. Such passion could be invaluable if Louis ever found her, but that meant having to put up with Belk for a long time, possibly even years. Ruby scowled to herself as Belk rode over to gut the antelope.

The thought of Clementine Thomas's trail herd and the McHatties came to mind. Then she thought of the trap Louis had laid for Theo Belk. She smiled to herself, content. If the *Rocky Mountain News,* for example, got the story of Louis's actions and, say, the Dallas and Fort Worth papers as well as Kansas City, what would become of Louis's activities? She could drop a line to the army at Fort Laramie, too. She'd learned a lot about Louis.

It would work, she decided. Louis had accumulated too many enemies. There would be a certain amount of time though before the information got out, she'd need to have a stopgap along the way until all the hounds could be put on the trail. Her stopgap was riding to catch up with the wagon, an antelope across his saddle. Yes, Belk would do fine.

That night around the fire, Ruby looked at the man. "Theo, why hasn't some woman tied you down? That antelope smells magnificent."

He squatted over the fire, turning the meat on the glowing coals. He threw her a fast, measuring glance before he shrugged. "I been on the move too much, I reckon. Never had time for a woman and never found one that had time for me."

"What about Dolly Moore? I thought you were, well . . . close?" Triumph! Look at the pain in his eyes! He must still think he loves her. Ruby cackled silently to herself in glee as she threw Theo a comforting glance.

"Aw, I reckon she'll come around," he told her. "I heard in Dodge that she's gone to Denver with Henry. I'll look her up when I get there and maybe marry her."

He sounded so positive! Men! My God, they have no sense at all, she told herself with amusement. "Theo, I don't know how to tell you this," Ruby began as if hesitant, "but I'm sure you remember Tom O'Connell? The boy you saved? When Dolly left Dodge, she and Tom were pretty close. Now they didn't come right out and say they were engaged, but, well . . . you know."

Theo's eyes burned into hers. Careful, she thought, his temper is rising. She put her hand out and laid it on his arm. The muscle under the thin fabric was bunched like steel. He would have to be handled very carefully indeed, lest he get violent. If that happened he might jump on that ugly little sorrel horse of his and ride off, hell-bent for Denver.

"Theo," she whispered softly, "she never knew what she had. I can see that you are building up to be pretty mad, and I don't blame you but listen to me. I want you to think about what I'm going to say very carefully.

"Have you ever thought about what life would be like with her? I am not trying to run Dolly down, Theo. She's just not the kind of woman who would understand a man like you. I think you know that way down deep inside.

"For example, think of this. If someone, say Louis Gasceaux, was trying to kill you and you were laid up, say with pneumonia, do you think she could kill him if he walked into your room? I don't, Theo. She's not that kind of woman. When did you ever see her shoot anything?"

Belk glared at her, but she realized the glint in his eyes was part grief and part anger. They were conflicting emotions for the moment. Time had come to use another weapon.

"Theo, you didn't take time to think about that did you? I understand because I'm a woman and I know Western men. Women can do such terrible things to men. They hit 'em below the belt by using their hearts against them. No man can fight that, but at least you know what happened to you now."

"Damn her," Theo growled darkly. "Just like a woman. Hell's full of women!" He stood up, his huge bulk looming against the night sky. Theo took a deep breath before leaning his head back and sighing. The soft breeze rustled the fringes at the sleeve of his coat.

To Ruby, he looked magnificent, and she thought that about few men. There was something magnetic about the way he stood staring defiantly at the sky; for the first time in a long time, she felt herself stirred. Easy, not the right time for that, she warned herself.

Standing, she walked next to him and laid her hand on his shoulder in a manner suggesting nothing more than friendship.

"Don't hold it against her, Theo." Now was the time to take the sting away. "She just came from a different world is all. We ain't nothing more that what God makes us. She can't help her bein' raised as she was anymore than you can help your upbringing. Theo, it's just how life works and it ain't fair." She ended up using a maternal voice.

Victory! The tension was leaving his shoulders. Now would come the despair stage. She would feed off that and begin rebuilding his self-confidence. Men were clay and the greatest power in the world was to understand, manipulate, and mold them.

"Huh," Theo grunted, fooling Ruby with a small chuckle. "Guess I've known that all along. God made life so the strongest survive. Keep fergittin' when I think of that girl. I ain't dead an' I been down a lot of hard trails with either my butt froze or my scalp sizzlin'. Reckon you have, too."

She studied him intently. Was he avoiding the despair? Indeed, he'd completely relaxed. His mind worked very differently. Unlike most, he'd accepted her words without a single pout. She'd have to be very careful not to expect him to react in a normal way. It fascinated her.

Again she could see desire for her in his eyes. She fought down a half temptation to indulge him. Well and good, as long as it didn't get too far out of hand. She needed him to need her, and he would try another advance soon. She would have to give a little. If she remained steadfast, he might get mad and leave her out here.

Alas, she sighed to herself as she sat down, life ain't no bed of roses. Yet if the bed of life wasn't filled with roses, it might have to be full of Theo Belk a time or two to keep him tame. It would be a small price to pay, and it wasn't as if he hadn't had her before.

This time though, he'd work for it first. By the time she gave herself to him, he would think she was the best thing in skirts between New York and 'Frisco. The more he needed and wanted her, the greater her power over him.

"Yeah, life is somethin', ain't it, Theo." She smiled graciously and somewhat conspiratorially. "Makes a body wonder what two lonesome souls like us have to do to get along. Here, come sit by me and let's talk."

She dragged the man down on the saddle next to her. At least he's a handsome devil, she thought. "You know, Theo, we've never had the chance to just talk and we've been traveling together for some time now. You've been pretty quiet. Why?"

"I've just never talked to a woman—except maybe to Dolly, and there was something about talking to her about serious things that made me nervous. You know"—he laughed—"like reachin' under a rock without looking first to see if there was a snake or scorpion under it." He chuckled as he turned the meat.

"You never had a woman as just a friend?"

"Nope, nary a one. 'Ceptin' maybe Shasty, but she was more like a mother. Never knew a woman that cared a lick about me. I always thought women were different somehow. Then there's the prostitutes and they don't care how a man feels—they just want his money." Theo pulled the meat from the fire.

"Don't be too hard on 'em, Theo. They're all on their own, too. Think of how it is for a girl on the line. If she takes a shine for a fellow, it affects her job. Some girls have even fallen in love with a man, quit their work, and had him run out 'cause some sweet young thing came to town and he decided at the last minute to marry a 'good woman.' That don't seem very fair either, now does it?" she told him coolly.

"Nope, but life ain't supposed to be fair. If it was, I'da killed Louis Gasceaux years ago. His damned body would be rotted to maggot meat by now." Theo scowled into the light of the dying fire as he and Ruby ate the tender meat.

"What did Louis do to you that you've been after him for so long?" she asked, casting him a sideways glance to monitor his reaction. How would he take the question?

Theo didn't react. His face was blank and his eyes stared emptily at the lump of meat simmering on the end of his knife. They sat like that for several minutes while he was lost in thought, and Ruby wondered what tack would bring her the greatest return.

"Killed my folks," Theo snapped suddenly, causing her to jump.

After a pause she added, "That doesn't surprise me. Folks don't last long in this world. Not for the likes of us. I lost mine when I was eleven." Here's another handle on him she thought. Theo just nodded; the facts stood by themselves and didn't need comment.

"Makes us more similar than I would have thought, Theo," she added softly, attempting to sound absent-minded.

"I reckon so." His eyes had a haunted wistfulness when he looked at her. "The way the world is made to turn, you got to be strong, Ruby. Never depend on nobody. Keep your pistol at your side and never leave your backside uncovered.

"I remember Charlie Torgusson telling me how wrong I was. Then they shot him to pieces. He thought he was going to live to a ripe old age. I hope I can live long enough to find Louis and put a bullet in him. You tell me where the right of that lay?

"Charlie liked people and respected them. Saved a man's life once, and damned if the fellow he saved wasn't one of men who killed him.

"You've made it on your own, Ruby. That's some. I don't think from watching you that you take anything for granted, either. You're a survivor. That counts a lot in my book. You're strong, Ruby, that's good. I don't think Dolly is." His eyes were hard and he appraised her with a strange look.

She wondered what that look signified. It was unlike any look she'd seen in a man's eyes. It bothered her, and worse, it mystified her. She did not like unknown quantities in men. They made her nervous.

"Thanks, Theo," she said softly, to let him know she understood the compliment. At least he was no longer scorning her for not letting him bed her. She had won her right to be respected by him and he was considering her as a potential friend. Now, how long would it take to make him completely hers? Or worse, could she really control him at all if push came to shove?

He was watching her again with that pensive, intent look. Nervously, she wondered what he was thinking back of those cold blue eyes and why it bothered her so.

Louis Gasceaux squatted in the dark. With knowing fingers he worked the floorboards loose. Quietly he laid them aside, listening to the man snoring in the next room. He'd been gone less than three weeks, riding to End-of-the-Tracks and hiding out long enough to let McHattie's men lose interest. Then he'd ridden the train back.

The McHattie outfit was still holding a herd on the grass outside of town. Louis would have to be careful. He grinned to himself in the dark silence of the room. He'd at least recoup the loss of his money. His building had already been taken over by another man, but so what? That was Dodge City. No one thought he was coming back. It would do him good to move on anyway. He couldn't stay in Dodge after the McHattie fiasco.

His fingers reached down. What? Nothing! Louis groped at the loose dirt. He felt around as far as his hand could reach, nothing! With his fingertips he could feel the outline where the satchel had rested on the dirt.

Gone! Someone had lifted his cache!

But who? Who would know the money was there? Feeling panic followed by anger, Louis stared into the darkness. Could it be the present owner?

Making his way across the floor on cat feet, Louis felt along a shelf. His questing fingers located what he had hoped was untouched. A little stack of candles met his hand. Lighting a candle, Louis spilled some wax and stuck it to the floor next to the hole. Then he opened the office window and placed a chair on its side underneath. He retreated to a second chair near a stack of boxes. Banging the chair on the floor, Louis dived behind the boxes.

"Who's there?" came the cry from the next room. "Speak up!" the rough voice demanded. There followed a rustling of clothing followed by the click of a gun hammer. Fingers fumbled at the door before it opened.

"What the hell?" A bearded man blinked his way into the room. He stopped and stared at the hole in the floor, then glanced owlishly around the room. The man slowly bent over to stare at the candle then he peered into the hole taking the candle to look around under the floor. Curiously, he glanced at the open window with the chair placed suggestively under it.

The man shook his head looking puzzled. "Huh! Looks like ole Louis had him a cache here. Damn! All this time there musta been a fortune right under my feet! Damn!" he growled. "Wait till the boys hear about this." He closed the window and took the candle back to bed with him.

Some time later, Louis slipped from behind the boxes and ghosted to the door and outside. Scowling, he stole through the dark streets. The new owner hadn't taken the loot. That was obvious from his reactions. Who would have known of the location? Gasceaux leaned against a wall and thought rapidly. Each of his acquaintances was reviewed again. Only Ruby had had access to the inner sanctum. Only Ruby might have guessed the location of the stash!

Of course, Louis cursed to himself. Ruby was the one! Damn him for a double-dyed fool! Louis felt himself go cold as he crept through the night. At Ruby's tent, muffled giggles and muted male laughter greeted his straining ears. Louis felt his heart skip a beat—the voice was not Ruby's.

Numbly, Louis crouched in the dark. His temples pounded as he cursed himself and the whore who'd left him destitute. Wild, he ripped the tent flap aside.

"Hey!" the woman cried.

"Who the hell do ya . . . ?" the man began as he focused on the barrel of the Smith & Wesson.

"Where's Ruby?" Louis demanded quietly. He felt a muscle in his crushed cheek begin to twitch with the tension.

"She's gone," the woman replied slowly.

"Where? When?" Louis grated.

"A couple of weeks ago. She bought a buggy and left. Took off right after you was ru . . . just after you left." Her eyes wavered as she swallowed rapidly.

Louis shifted his position and the woman gasped. The man on top of her flinched.

"Where did she go?" Louis almost shouted.

"I don't know," the woman moaned. "West is all. Somebody passed her on the road. He just said she was headed west and wasn't any too sociable. Honest, that's all I know."

That was it! Louis knew it. He raised the gun, enjoying the terror in their eyes. The woman watched him wide-eyed while the man closed his eyes and shuddered waiting for the impact of the bullet. Tears began to streak the woman's face as she spoke silently to herself.

"Have a pleasant evening," Louis said softly as he backed away. Making his way to Bell's Livery, he stole another horse and left town riding west.

CHAPTER 18

HENRY STOOD AT THE EDGE OF THE BOARDWALK, ARCHING his back with his thumbs stuck into his belt. The warm September sunshine cast a golden glow to the rising buildings on both sides of the street. Hundreds of people rolled past in a stream, with a babbling of voices reminding Henry of a brook. They rolled like a series of rapids around the piles of refuse and huckster stands. The hustle and bustle of Larimer Street was indeed pleasant after the long days on the trail.

He was back, returned to the city he had left in disgrace. Henry smiled wistfully to himself. He'd made good after all. Lord alone knew how he would have done had it not been for Theo.

At the thought, Henry felt a vying of emotions

within him. Remembering Belk brought a warm, soft memory of nights around camp fires. He recalled the chiding look in Theo's eye as he'd taught him how to hold and shoot his rifle, and the almost fatherly way the younger man had taken him under his wing and taught him the ways of the wilderness. They had been the best of friends, as well as partners.

Mixed with those warm thoughts were cold, fearful reminders of the violence that tainted Theo's trail. Never during their time together had Henry felt completely comfortable with Belk. It was like living on a keg of powder. A feller just never knew when a casual remark would set off a conflagration so full of brimstone that old Bug himself would move to a cooler climate.

Curious indeed, Henry thought. How could emotions as diverse as love and fear be vested on a single, curly wolf of a man? No matter, it would be good to see Theo again.

Then, of course, there was Dolly. How nice that she and Tom were starting to make moon eyes at each other. Tom. Now, there was a good lad—Irish though he may be. Henry laughed out loud. The Irish were something of a problem. Denver was now full of them. They, along with the Chinese, had come to work the railroads and were everywhere. They were not well liked by the Protestant townsfolk, but they managed.

Things would level out; they always did. The Irish and the Chinese would make their place in society by hard work, sweat, and character. Fifty years from now, nobody would know the difference. Hell, his own grandfather had come from England as an indentured servant!

Tom would make a good husband for Dolly. Henry felt a slight sorrow; he'd always hoped that she'd turn

Theo around. Well, that was a fool's notion. Nobody could shut down the west wind, and Theo was a full-blown Chinook.

Returning his thoughts to the present, he pondered. What was he going to invest his money in? Henry scowled at the crowded skyline and squinted at the carpenters and masons who toiled to build a city. A beer wagon banged and clattered down the rutted street bearing cases and kegs. Two Irish lads sat balanced on the back of the wagon, laughing as they swayed with the rocking vehicle.

"Mr. Moore?" a well-modulated voice asked. Henry turned to meet the intent stare of a medium-built man with piercing eyes.

"Yes, what can I do for you?" Henry responded cautiously, his hand slipping around toward the butt of the Remington at his waist. He carried a lot of money in his belt and Theo had taught him about how the world worked. The greenhorn who'd driven off into the teeth of a blasting Colorado snowstorm had vanished somewhere along the trail.

"I'm Walter Cheesman, sir." The fellow introduced himself and offered his hand. "I have heard you are interested in venturing capital. Perhaps I might be of help. We are looking for solid citizens to make an investment in our future here."

"I see." Henry grinned. "Well, I'm in the market. I made a modest stake on the buffalo ranges and now I'm ready for a change. People say you're the man to talk to about investing."

"I can only hope that I can live up to my reputation then, Mr. Moore." Cheesman laughed. "Come, let us go and get a cup of coffee and we'll discuss this. Perhaps I can give you some leads."

"Denver is changing," Cheesman began as they sa

down. "She's building, growing, maturing. A few of us have always had faith in the town. There are Chaffee, Dave Moffat, James Archer, Fred Salomon, Henry Wolcott, William Evans, and me that have always worked to build this city.

"Oh to be sure, we've had our hard times. In the early sixties we fought with Auraria and Golden for the capitol. We won. We fought for industry and we got the smelters. Now we are trying to change this town from a frontier camp into a real city that not even New York can look sideways at."

Henry nodded. "From the looks of it out there, you're doing it. I had a freight business in Richmond before the war. I've seen cities, Mr. Cheesman. Denver will make it all right. The worst is over. Your baby has made it past childhood—all you have to do now is ride out the growing pains."

"I'm glad you agree, Mr. Moore." Cheesman sipped his coffee. "Now, what sort of investment did you have in mind?"

Henry grinned. "Well, now that's the hitch in the mare's tail. I've spent all my life running a freight outfit—that is, until the war. After that I drifted out here. I lost my hide in a poker game here in Denver. I decided to go for broke hunting buffalo and made it. I suppose that a freight outfit would be just the ticket again."

Cheesman frowned. "You know the railroads have had a considerable impact on the freighting business here. They have taken over most of the major freight routes. The Union Pacific ran a spur line in here two years ago, and the Kansas Pacific main line terminates here. The Denver and Rio Grande Western is building south, the Colorado Central has built up to Blackhawk.

"All this railroading has freed up the freight wagons for smaller runs. The competition is rather fierce, if I do say so. However, on the bright side, there are new mining camps springing up every minute all over the state. If you could get in at the ground level on one of these new camps, you might make a tidy fortune."

"I see." Henry rubbed his bristly chin with his stubby, sun-blackened fingers. He scowled at the marred tabletop before looking up at Cheesman. "That would entail a lot of legwork up in the hills, wouldn't it?"

"Most likely," Cheesman agreed. "Keep in mind that it all hinges on being at the right place at the right time. After news of a strike gets out, you will have plenty of competition."

"I'll have to admit, Mr. Cheesman. I'm just gettin' too old to go a traipsin' all the time. That and I have to think of Dolly, my daughter. She hasn't had a home all her own since they burned our place in Richmond. Seems to me that a woman ought to have a house. She needs a place to light for a spell."

"I see," Cheesman said absently. "Have you ever thought of investing in buildings, utilities, or merchandising?"

Henry looked curiously at the man. "Mr. Cheesman, my expertise was in freighting. At my age, I'd better stick to what I know. I'd hate to have to make the mistakes necessary to learn a new occupation. I got lucky with the buffalo hunting. I had a teacher that just couldn't be beat.

"With a string of wagons, I know how to set up the books, maintain the equipment, develop a schedule, and care for the stock. There's genius in a well-run outfit, Mr. Cheesman. I did real well at it in Virginia."

"I daresay you would, and I agree with you."

Cheesman finished his coffee and wiped his mouth with the napkin. He leaned forward. "I'll tell you what. Let me ask around. I hear you are staying at the Planter's House. I'll be in touch. There's a man I know of who might have just the thing."

"I can't say how much I appreciate this, Mr. Cheesman," Henry began.

Cheesman gestured negatively. "My pleasure, Mr. Moore. We want development. I believe that you will do just fine. You're a stayer, Mr. Moore; exactly the sort of man this country needs. Don't worry about the bill and wait to hear from me before you do anything."

With that, Cheesman stood, adjusted his hat, and left at a brisk walk. Henry finished his coffee and started down the street to find Dolly and Tom.

The Planter's House stood at the corner of 16th and Blake Streets, built originally as a depot and post office for the Central Overland, California, and Pike's Peak Stage Company. Dolly stood on the second-floor balcony watching wagons, men, and machinery rumbling past. She was wearing a white dress and shading herself with a parasol. Spotting Henry, she waved.

"Come on up, Paw," she called. "It's a delightful afternoon. Tom's gone to check on the stock, but he said that he'd be back in time for dinner."

Henry took the stairs two at a time. "I talked to Walter Cheesman, Dolly," he greeted. "Mr. Cheesman said he'd ask around." Henry related the gist of the conversation to the girl.

"Well, it sounds good, Paw," Dolly replied after Henry paused. "Do you really want to stay here in Denver, though? After Dodge City and the buffalo range, this here's pretty tame."

"That it is, girl." Henry raised an eyebrow and

glanced at his daughter. "Might be that you'd be a needin' a house sometime soon. Just think lassie, some lad might want to marry you."

"Paw! You never give up do you? To my knowledge, nobody's asked me yet." She blushed slightly then stared absently at the dusty street below.

"Dolly," Henry started softly. "I think Tom will be a askin' you before long. He's got that look in his eye. I've never told you what to do with your life, but I'd approve of that young man. He's fine, strong, gentle, tough, and smart. Even if he is Irish, he's a good man and most of all, he loves you."

Dolly pursed her lips and began twisting the fabric of her dress idly through her fingers. "I know, Paw," she whispered.

Henry patted her shoulder and bent over to kiss her softly on the head. "Mind if I ask what you will say?" he queried.

"Reckon I'd say yes if he asked me. That's sure more than Theo ever did. I reckon I've learned my lesson. If you can't get the man you love, take one that loves you." Dolly tightened the edges of her mouth and sighed.

Henry shook his head. "That ain't the way it's supposed to work, girl. For as smart as I know you are, you can sure be damn dumb. Maybe you'd better think on that afore you go and make a fool of yourself."

Henry stood and stomped through the doorway seeking his room. "How in the name of Hob has the human race ever made it this far, Lord?" he asked, looking at the whitewashed ceiling.

That evening at supper the waiter entered, bringing Walter Cheesman and a short broad man in tow. The man's face was wrinkled and worn, his gray hair standing like straw below a derby that had been mashed onto his bullet head.

"Mr. Moore," Cheesman greeted. "David Moffat asked me to introduce you to Mr. Iza Hayman, here. I believe that Mr. Hayman and you might be able to be mutually beneficial to each other. Mr. Hayman currently owns a freighting outfit in the city of Cheyenne, just north of the territorial border. His health requires that he return to the States, and he is interested in selling his company."

"Indeed, Mr. Moore, such is the case. When Walter said that he knew of a man who had both the desire and experience to run a freight outfit, it was like an opportunity from heaven." Hayman smiled.

"Do sit down then, sirs," Henry offered. "I would like to introduce my daughter, Dolly, and Mr. Tom O'Connell, who functions as my supervisor."

The meal proceeded while Hayman detailed his business and its operation. At the present time, he had a government contract to haul supplies from the railhead at Cheyenne to Forts Laramie and Fetterman on the North Platte River. Hayman had developed an ailment which required specialized medical care; the result being that he could no longer manage his company and would need money for his treatment.

Later that evening Henry strolled back to the hotel with his daughter on his arm. "Do you think we should take Mr. Hayman's deal? Cheesman vouches for him so I'd guess that he's honest. This might be just the thing, Dolly.

"There's war talk in the North. The papers are crying that the Sioux should give up the Powder River Basin and the Black Hills. There are several mining companies that would like to get into that country and you saw how the Medicine Lodge Treaty slowed the whites down in the South. The Fort Laramie Treaty will be just so much paper, too."

"Well, I . . . I don't know, Paw. I—"

"We would do well hauling for the army, Dolly. The depression back East will generate a whole new batch of gold hunters come next spring, and the Black Hills will be the place they want to go. The papers are already calling for the removal of the Sioux and you know they won't go willingly."

Dolly began, "Making money off any war don't seem right. Still, I reckon that if somebody's got to make it, it might just as well be us. I'd like to see Wyoming Territory. That's where Theo grew up."

"All right, girl, I'll call on Mr. Hayman tomorrow morning and we'll dicker price. Who knows? Cheesman started as a druggist, maybe I'll be a high roller in Cheyenne before this is all over."

"You just might at that, Paw," Dolly murmured as she hugged him. "I can't think of a better high roller than you. Why, I might be able to put some meat on your skinny frame after you make our fortune."

"Huh! That'll be the day," Henry grunted then started for his own room.

Ten minutes later there was a knock at the door. Dolly opened it to greet Tom.

"Good evening, Dolly," he began hesitantly. "Now would ye be at all intrest'd in walking wi' an Irish lad for a while?"

"No, Tom, not interested—I'd love to!" Dolly laughed. "Paw was just here and we discussed Mr. Hayman's offer. Some air would help me think."

"Aye, an' that be a foine thing, Dolly." Tom grinned but seemed preoccupied. "'Tis both an honor and a pleasure ta be your escort, Miss Moore."

Dolly took his arm and they walked down through

the doors and into the street. The evening was cool as they walked. The streets were lined with young saplings that had been planted in hopes that someday Denver would have shade from the hot plains sun.

"Now tell me, lass, what did yore father decide? Will he make Mr. Hayman an offer?" Tom began carefully.

"Looks like it, Tom. He'll be happy for the first time since the war. I think it's the best decision. I gather from listening to Mr. Hayman that he will spend most of his time in Cheyenne. But, Tom, there is a catch. Paw thinks the army is about to go to war with the Sioux. It could be dangerous."

"Aye, 'tis always dangerous, Miss Moore." Tom smiled warmly. "Still, 'tis much better than runnin' buffalo. Runnin' freight for the army will mean armed escorts to protect the shipments. 'T wouldna' be good business on the part o' the government to lose their supply to the Sioux, now would it?"

"I guess not, Tom," she agreed. "But, war means somebody gets killed, and I hope it isn't you or Paw."

"I see," Tom started then stopped. "I, uh, Dolly?" he stammered.

"What's wrong, Tom?" She turned to see his face better in the light. "You are coming with us aren't you?" She felt her heart begin to pound and as he continued to stare into the dark. She was holding her breath.

"Maybe not, Dolly," Tom whispered to the dark. He jammed his hands into his pockets and began to scuff the toe of his boot into the dusty roadbed.

"Tom!" Dolly cried. "What are you saying? You heard Paw tonight. He wants to make you the supervisor. He needs you, Tom. Paw can't do everything anymore. He needs you to ramrod the company. You can't walk out on him now!" She stood glaring at him defiantly.

"'Tis not that, Dolly," he started softly. "I . . . I'm afraid, I—"

Dolly blurted, "Then what is it? Paw needs you!"

"Aye, perhaps he does. I'd loike ta work for him. He's a foine man. But lassie, I just . . . I couldna' work in the same office with you. Not day after day and week after week." He sighed and clenched his jaws. "D'ya see what I'm saying, lass?"

Dolly began to speak and caught herself. Then she ventured, "Did I do something to you? I didn't mean it, Tom. Just tell me what I did and I'll apologize. I can't . . . You are the best friend I have. I wouldn't hurt you for all the world. I swear, Tom. What did I do?"

He smiled his warm smile at her and gently took her shoulders. "Ye've done nothing wrong, Dolly. 'Tis I that have done the wrong. Don't worry that lovely head o' yours. 'Tis Tom O'Connell who's ta blame, an' b'cause 'tis him he'll take 'is medicine an' go now."

Dolly shook loose and stepped away only to turn back, tears streaking her face. "Why? God, are all men like this? I don't . . . Theo ran out on us, too. I thought you were better, Tom. You're not! You're just like Theo! Why do men insist on . . . on hurting the people they are closest—"

Tom reached for her again and caught her as she tried to break away. His voice was choked. "Don't you ever compare me to that man, Dolly!" He found himself shouting. "Don't you ever think of Tom O'Connell and Theo Belk in the same manner!"

"Then why are you running out on me just like he did?" she spat back.

"Because I love you!" Tom flared. "I love you so

much it's killin' me heart, Dolly. Killin' me! Now do you understand?"

She stood silently, her mouth open to voice a reply but no words came. Slowly, she began to shake her head in amazement.

Tom took a shallow breath and sagged, shaking his head slowly, sadly. "I'm sorry, lassie. I'd no roight ta say that ta ye. I . . . I'd a nay left wi' you thinkin' blackly aboot Tom O'Connell, but me temper and me big mouth be but the legacy o' the Irish. I'll understand, girl, if ye niver forgive me . . . 'cause 'tis likely I'll niver forgive meself."

He turned to walk away. He made three steps before she called to him. Turning, the girl was in his arms.

"Tom," she murmured, "I love you, don't you ever leave me, you hear? I want to marry you, love you. Be with me, Tom! Please!"

"Aye, lassie." He smiled his warm smile at her.

Theo sat his sorrel and watched the building thunderhead to the northwest. The brilliant white cloud towered to the top of the sky, billowing against the deep blue. The storm was moving slowly in their direction. Idly, Theo wondered whether or not he was going to get wet.

"That coming this way?" Ruby called from her buggy.

"Hard to say, Ruby," Theo granted. "This time of year they build up and kinda wander across the plains like a blind buffalo bull. From the size of this one, though, it'll drop a good three or four inches of rain or hail depending on the luck of whatever's under it."

"Damn!" Ruby groaned. "That just beats the britches off the banker, now don't it?"

"Hell, Ruby, it ain't even here yet an' you're already

soaked," Theo taunted. He artfully ducked the boot she threw at him and prodded the sorrel on down the trail. In the distance he could see the tracks of the Kansas Pacific glistening in the brassy afternoon sun.

"Hey," Ruby called. "Get my damn boot, huh?"

"It's your boot!" Theo chuckled over his shoulder as the sorrel began to trot. Good thing he'd unloaded her little four-shot Sharps hideout gun late one night while she slept. Ruby wouldn't want to get rid of him just yet, but she did have a fair temper and might have shot him before she thought it over if she was mad enough.

The billowing white clouds continued so high that they seemed ready to flatten their tops on the deep blue of the sky. The puffs of cloud were rounded and brilliant against the sky, while the bottom of the formation was flat, leaving the shadow underneath almost black. The stringers of rain under the cloud were plainly visible.

True to form, the storm was headed their way. Theo reined in the sorrel and glared at the menacing thunderhead.

Ruby pulled up next to him. "Coming this way, isn't it?"

"Yep," Theo mumbled as he worked his chapped lips over each other.

"You know," Ruby said thoughtfully, "I'm so hot right now it might not be so bad."

Theo met her wry eyes. "You never been through a gullywasher like this one's gonna be. The temperature drops about thirty degrees in minutes and the wind blows harder than an Irish washerwoman on Saturday morning."

Ruby cursed and began scanning the horizon, squinting against the sun. "So close to the railroad tracks and I don't see nothing that looks like any sort of shelter."

"Nope," Theo agreed. "I reckon we'll just have to tough it out. Mind you now, keep a close hand on the reins. I wouldn't want your team to bolt in the middle of this. Not only that, but there's always lightning, too."

"Theo," Ruby said, her spirits dropping, "I think I'd do almost anything to keep from getting wet and cold. I've baked out here for weeks now. I've drank water I pretty near had to chew that was swimming with little crawly things and tasted like the bottom of someone's foot. You ain't never heard me complain. But this time, I'm tired, hot, and dirty, and I just don't want to get cold and wet." She looked at him pleadingly. "Can't you do something?"

He laughed, grinning at her reaction. "I reckon. You hop on down and unpack your outfit. I need that canvas you got in the bottom of the buggy."

He swung off the sorrel and stepped back to the packhorse before unlashing a shovel. Ruby was busy piling her belongings on the ground, never far from the carpetbag that she claimed held her private things.

Theo unhitched the horses and tied them to the buggy, then picketed his own animals. He eyed the storm, dug a trench around the vehicle, and draped the canvas down, packing the excavated earth around the bottom before lashing the material to the sideboards.

"Isn't that a lot of dirt to hold the canvas in place?" Ruby asked frowning at the deep trench.

"You don't know how the wind blows when these thunderheads hit," Theo replied, then turned to look at her as he leaned on the short shovel. "If you want though, I can shovel some of that out."

She gave a brief shake of her head, noting the quiet amusement in his eyes. "I trust you," she granted.

Theo stuffed the packs in next to the canvas just as the first fierce gust of wind hit them. Ruby staggered and grabbed at her hat. The buggy was rocking while the horses tried to put their tails to the storm.

"Better crawl in," Theo shouted as he gave the horses a final inspection. She lost no time scuttling under the buggy. The first large spatters of rain were landing in the dust.

Ruby was huddled against the packs, looking skeptically at the buggy bottom rocking over her head. "You weren't kidding," she whispered. "Sorry I said anything about the job you did."

The rain began to come down in sheets, chattering against the thin boards of the buggy over their heads. Several rivulets of water had worked their way through the cracks overhead and puddled on the hard, white ground.

"Ouch!" Ruby cried as she shifted to miss a new leak. "Cactus! Why did you have to put the thing in a cactus patch?"

"Can't say as I knew there was any here," Theo growled in return. "Do it yourself next time."

She looked at him and met his fierce eyes. "You don't have to snap at me." She lowered her eyes and began biting the spines from her palm.

Theo watched her strong white teeth sliding behind red, sunburned lips as she pulled at the spines, then turned her head to spit the small needles outside. Idly, he noted the skin around the spines was now clean.

Just like a woman, he thought; first she wants him to make a shelter so she doesn't get wet; then she cusses because there's cactus. He'd done a lot for her these past weeks. He'd made camp, cooked, guided, kept her from trouble, and now what was coming? The tracks were just up ahead.

"Which way are you going when you catch a train?" he asked suddenly.

She turned to study him. "Denver, like I said. Why?"

"Just wondered," Theo replied guardedly. "Reckon as how you're probably going to send me packin' as soon as we reach some sort of civilization is all." He picked up a dried stem of grass and toyed in the dirt with it.

She watched him speculatively. He was sharper than most men. She'd been playing her hand pretty close to her vest for the last week. She had thought she knew him now and gained at least a little control over his actions. Could he see so clearly that he wasn't in her long-range plans?

It worried her. From the way his eyes studied her, she knew he could leave her or stay. He was wavering on the thin line of deserting her. There was still Denver, and after that, Cheyenne. Louis could be at either of those places. She needed Belk.

What should she do? Although she'd told him that she needed time before she slept with a man again, he had seemed to know exactly what went on in her mind. If he balked, she might have to play her last card.

"Theo," Ruby began slowly, "I ain't sure that there's a whole lot of future for the two of us in the long term. Still, I want you to go to Denver with me." She watched him for a reaction. A cold shiver sent its way down her back. What would happen if Theo did up and leave her out here? Could she make it on her own? What if Louis was waiting in Denver? He'd never believe that she was bringing him his money.

No. He'd ask for his loot. Then, at first opportunity, he'd kill her!

She had come to like Belk, but the last thing she wanted was to have him around full-time. Still, for a man, she could almost respect him. He hadn't raped her yet, although the want was in his eyes.

Deep inside, she knew she would never be any man's wife, not, that is, unless he was a thoroughly weak man with lots of money—enough money to make it worthwhile for a lady like Ruby to marry him and put up with his slobbering embrace.

"I see," Theo said after thinking for a minute. "I should have known. Seems like every time I help somebody, they get what they can from me an' run off. You're just like Dolly and Henry."

He turned his cold blue eyes on her and watched intently. She could see the little muscles at the corners of his eyes begin to tighten.

"No, Theo," she replied firmly, "you didn't listen to what I said. I said that there may not be a life for us together down the road. For now I want us to be friends is all. I never said there wasn't a chance. Do you understand? Give me time, Theo. I'm not up to a man yet, I need to . . ."

It wasn't working. The little muscles were still tight and his jaw was clenched. The damn fool was going to leave.

"Reckon I'll be on my way, Ruby. There's the tracks over yonder. You just follow them on west and you'll be in Denver. That, or you can abandon the buggy and flag a train and ride the cushions in." He started to crawl from under the buggy.

Ruby felt fear building deep in her gut. The silly fool was going to leave her! Panicking, she grabbed at his arm. "Theo, no! Don't go!"

He attempted to shake off her grip.

"Theo," she pleaded, "I need you! You understand?" Almost with joy she realized that a tear was creeping down the side of her face. It made her that much more convincing.

He turned to look at her and noticed the tear. "You need me, huh?" he said somewhat sourly. "Then what? Denver and you leave? What, Ruby? Why should I believe you need me?"

"Because I need your strength, Theo. I need a friend. I've never had a friend until you. Do you hear? You are my first friend. I want you to stay with me for a while, you understand?" She searched his eyes for any comprehension. There seemed to be a glimmer, then with another thought she could see him close his mind to the possibility.

"Woman usually knows how to let a man know she wants him to stay," he replied, while his predator eyes watched her intently.

It was on the line. Ruby felt herself sigh way down deep inside and reached up to kiss him. It was time to ante up or get out of the game, and she needed him for a couple of hands in the future. She felt the heat of desire in him as he responded. Then she felt his strong hand working along her leg.

Theo let himself fantasize about the two women when he was spent. He remembered the way Dolly walked and how she smiled and laughed. He remembered dancing eyes as she listened to his stories. He could see her as she bent down at the camp fire. There had been a definite grace in the way she handled the pots. He thought of the way she would roll her tongue across her lips as she concentrated on some task.

Theo wondered what it would feel like to have her

body close against his. What would having her as his woman be like? He could see her meeting him at the door of their cabin. Standing there warm and soft, waiting on him as he stripped the saddle from the sorrel.

He would come up to her and she would reach up and softly kiss his lips before telling him about what their children had done that day. Then they would go inside and there would be a hot meal on the table, but first she would hand him a cup of coffee. Strong black coffee, fit for a man.

He would have a chair by the big stone fireplace. She would come and sit near him while he told her what he had seen and done that day. The children would play on the plank floor, and then come and hug him good night. Dolly would pull him to his feet and they would go to their bed. A bed in a separate room.

He imagined what she would feel like. How they would be with each other.

"Happy?" Ruby asked. "You smile any wider and your mustache will curl."

"Just thinking is all," Theo mumbled, feeling miffed that the image in his mind was fading.

"That can kill a person," Ruby allowed solemnly.

"You ever thought of having kids, Ruby? I mean have you ever thought of what it would feel like to have a real honest to God family?" Theo asked distantly.

Maybe if it all worked out right, he'd marry Dolly and Ruby might just set up a house in the vicinity. Now, that would be some, it would.

He felt Ruby squirm to look at him. "Don't you go gettin' mushy on me now, Theo. I told you how I feel." She was defensive.

"Naw, Ruby. Get off your high horse. I was just

askin' cause I wanted to know. I wasn't thinking of you in a family way." Theo ended up with a chuckle.

Ruby sniffed and realized she was slightly angry. Who did he think he was? She could have a family if she wanted! It irked her that he would think she was incapable. It really bothered her that any man should think he knew who she really was.

That's one, Belk. She promised herself. My day will come and you just see if you know who I am and how I'm going to act. Just see, mister!

He tried the same fantasy with Ruby but it was all different. Where Dolly was a perfect wife, Ruby was a perfect friend. He could see himself riding to town when he needed to talk. Dolly couldn't understand his needs the way Ruby could.

He could tell her things and she would listen then give him the best advice on how to proceed. If there was trouble, Ruby would be there, ready to back him up. She was all woman, Ruby was. You could take that to the bank. No matter what, she would be there.

"Reckon we ought to go on over to the tracks?" Ruby asked.

"Almost dark, Ruby," Theo responded. "By the time we get packed up we'll have to unpack. Might just as well spend the night here. I'll rustle up some of that antelope, but there isn't a whole lot around here that looks anything like wood, and buffler chips will be wet.

"Still, you'll do, Ruby. Jerked antelope ain't a gonna hurt you none. You'll do." Theo turned to look at her and nod his head in approbation before scuttling out from under the buggy.

Tarnation, she thought, the big ox thinks I'm fit to ride the river with! She was surprised to find that that, too, upset her.

In Kit Carson they found the cost for transporting the stock by rail was going to be prohibitive. Ruby knew that Theo would never abandon his sorrel horse. She could have paid enough to have bought the whole train, she thought smugly, but the last thing she wanted was for Belk to know how much money she had.

Reaching the trail, she did pen several letters to the papers she thought would do her the most good and posted them. It was a weight off her mind and would set the wheels in motion. At least she was not helpless. The papers would have the stories about the same time she made Denver, and, of course, the *Rocky Mountain News* would have it first. Denver might be hot for Louis when he arrived.

They rode into Denver two weeks later in the middle of an October snowstorm. Ruby swore that she'd never be that cold again!

"Theo, let's rent a room. Someplace where can we stay warm for a change," she asked, thinking only of being comfortable. There was a chance Louis could find them easier if he knew she'd taken the money, and if he knew which way she'd gone. Had he ridden, they would have met him on the trail. If he'd managed to take the train, well, who knew?

Registered at the Planter's House as Mr. and Mrs. Belk, Ruby relaxed in the big bed. Theo had awoken early and run some errands. She felt rested and safe for the first time in a long time. She smiled again as she read the article in the paper and chuckled to herself. Now all she had to do was get to Cheyenne.

Belk was on her line. She just had no idea how well the hook was set. She'd been dropping subtle hints that he was the man she'd been looking for. She'd casually suggested things that they might do together and pumped him for information.

When he told her of places he'd been, she would look seriously into his eyes and hint of how nice it would be if he would take her there sometime. Many of his dreams were fantastic nonsense. Her, go trapping in the Absaroka Mountains of Montana? Ridiculous!

Ruby sighed as she pulled back the covers and began packing her things. Theo had had enough time to be out of her way. This was it. She was on her own and the gamble had to be taken. If she ran into Louis, it was all over. Taking a deep breath, she checked outside for Theo. He was nowhere to be seen. As a final touch she left the note she'd penned the night before on the bed. Clutching the train schedule in her hands, she put her bags together and left the hotel.

CHAPTER 19

THEO SCANNED THE NOTE, FEELING FRUSTRATION, ANGER, and amazement.

Dear Theo:

Amy Schwartz just came in to see me. She is an old friend from the line. She says that Louis is in town looking for me. It would be too easy for him to find me here. Amy has some friends who are on their way to Cheyenne and I'm going with them.

Theo, my love, I'm scared to death. If Louis finds me he'll kill me. I can't stay in Denver any longer. I'm going to hide out until I know I am safe. Please Theo, believe me. I need you very much. In the last months I have come to love you and I never thought I'd love any man.

Meet me in Cheyenne. It may be a month or more before I know I'm safe. One last thing, Theo—I don't know how long it will take me to get there. Promise me you will wait!

I know now
that
I love you,
Ruby

Louis was in town! Deep inside he felt a building satisfaction. This time, there would be no passionate mistake. Louis was his. Smiling, he turned and trotted down the steps to begin searching the streets.

He made his round of the cribs searching for Amy Schwartz. No one seemed to know of her. It puzzled Theo, but perhaps she'd quit the business. He prowled his way through the saloons and gambling halls asking for a man with a scar on his face.

Four days later, no closer to finding Louis Gasceaux, he had seen the paper and read the article. Right there in print was the story of Louis's most recent escapades. Theo grinned, wondering how his old nemesis was taking that. Maybe he'd seen the story first and run? That sounded right for Louis. It had to be, but where was he?

Worse, since Ruby had left the dream had returned. He'd awakened every night reliving the horrible day at the Blacks Fork. There had been no sleep. On the trail he'd had the dream once. When he woke in fright, Ruby had held him and soothed him. They'd made love, and for the first time he'd slept in peace afterward. It was a sign. He needed a woman.

Theo cleared his mind and thought, waiting for some hint from the demons who had always pointed him to Louis in the past. They wiggled in the bottom of his mind. A nagging part of his brain kept thinking of Ruby. Was she even now waiting for him in Cheyenne?

Theo pulled the note from his pocket and reread the already-memorized lines. He remembered the way that she'd looked into his eyes. Could a woman who'd held a man like that have lied? Could she even now be laughing at him? He refused to believe it. She couldn't have held him so close, loved him so thoroughly, then left him. She'd wait for him in Cheyenne. She really needed him.

Stopping to eat, Theo watched the people. Denver was a real city now. It was huge! The town was bigger than anything he'd seen since the war. Louis could be anywhere. Picking up the paper, Theo skimmed through it and stopped. There was a notice that Henry Moore had established himself in Cheyenne and was hauling army freight.

He leaned back in the seat thinking to himself. It was all coming together. The plan was working. He'd have to go to Cheyenne. That was what he was being told. The demons chattered happily.

Theo chewed as he let his mind wander. He'd go to Cheyenne and wait for Ruby. While he was there, he'd see Henry and Dolly. That would be fine. Idly, he wondered if Dolly would hold him after he had the dream. He imagined her warm arms pulling him back down under the bedding, her soft voice telling him it was all right. Well, what if Ruby never came back? There would be Dolly. It was all according to the plan. The Fates wove well. And, deep inside, Theo knew Gasceaux would be in Cheyenne, too.

Smiling to himself, Theo finished his meal and paid the bill. He stood, stretched, and made tracks for the

Planter's House and his belongings. Three hours later he was on the trail north to Cheyenne.

His thoughts returned to Ruby. Would she be there waiting for him? He could see her standing there in the street smiling as he rode in. Then his mind saw her melt into Dolly Moore. He tried to separate them, but they'd become one. Perhaps that was how it was to be. In the end, they would both be his, just like the dream he'd had outside of Dodge.

Then he remembered Ruby's words. What if Louis showed up sometime? How would Dolly deal with that? Ruby would know what to do, but Dolly? He saw her again as she'd been that night in the buffalo camp, her eyes wide and sick at the sight of the dead Indian boy. She was so delicate, he thought, so frail. He remembered the analogy of the flower that he'd thought of on the buffalo plains.

Theo grunted to himself as he tried to sort out the conflicting emotions he felt for each of the women. He imagined again what life would be like with one then the other.

His heart went cold. What if Dolly had married that Irish boy, Tom? He felt himself tightening inside. He'd deal with that. Dolly would leave the man. Theo was stronger than any Irishman. He'd prove it to her. Hell, it didn't matter to Theo Belk if she had to leave her husband. She wouldn't even need to divorce him.

"And if she wouldn't go?" a demon whispered.

That was absurd. Of course she'd go with him! Their life would be like it was on the buffalo plains, only she would do things for him like Ruby had. Henry would know that. Henry was his friend and he could be trusted. Good old Henry! He'd tell his daughter what to do. He owed Theo Belk and there was no way the Irishman could mean more to Henry than Theo did. He knew that deep inside.

And what the hell, there was always Ruby. After he talked to Dolly and Henry, he'd look up Ruby. However it worked out, Louis Gasceaux would be coming to Cheyenne—and to Theo Belk!

Deep in his mind, he knew everything was coming together. The debt of blood would be paid in Cheyenne. The feeling was stronger than it had ever been. Never had he felt so sure that Louis was going to be his!

Henry Moore looked up from the long list of figures and sighed. Tom should be in late tonight with his jerkline string of wagons. Henry looked at his watch and pulled his glasses off. He closed the big ledger book with relief. The company was a good one. Hayman had run his outfit well.

Henry stood, stretched his weary old frame, and reached down his coat. It was a short walk home, but the December night was cold, with the west wind blowing strongly across Sherman Hill from the Laramie Basin. There were wisps of snow swirling outside the window as he blew the lamp out.

He cinched his new hat down tight against the tugging wind and locked the door. He could see a man riding down the street leading three pack animals. There was something familiar about the way he sat his horse. The stranger pulled up in front of the building and squinted at the sign in the darkness.

"Can I help you?" Henry called. The wind tried to take the words to Nebraska.

The man looked at him measuringly and spit a stream of tobacco onto the ground. "Reckon so, Henry. Got a cup of coffee handy?"

"Theo!" Henry cried, running into the street.

"Theo! It's you! Goddamn! Am I glad to see you! I been wonderin' what happened to your ornery old soul. Come on, follow me! The house is just down the street. By God, it's good to see you! Can't wait to hear tell of what you've been up to!" Henry started to lead the way.

"Hold your horses, Henry. Where's your place at? You got room for the horses?" Theo called.

"You ever heard of a freight outfit that didn't? There's a big barn out back," Henry said almost with disgust.

Theo followed Henry to a neat frame house backed by stalls. A larger structure sheltered equipment and repair wagons. In the barn, Henry lighted a lamp as Theo dismounted stiffly.

Henry walked up to him and looked fondly into his eyes. "Aged a little Theo," he remarked. "Tad bit o' gray in your hair."

"Been down a trail or two, Henry. You're lookin' pretty chipper. Not only that, but that little belly you had's comin' back," Theo noted in his slow, wry voice.

Henry gave him a bear hug as a silly grin pasted across his features. "Where'd you ride in from? Must a been a cold trip."

"Reckon so. Come up from Denver. Saw in the paper you'd gone back to freightin'. Give up runnin' buffalo?" Theo asked, his breath visible in the cold air.

"Yep, sure did. Come on up to the house. I'll build a fire in the stove and fix you that cup of coffee. Dolly's downtown and won't be back for a while yet. You eat'n?" Henry was tugging on Theo's coat.

"Better see to the horses first, Henry. They come a long way today." Theo turned and stripped the animals while Henry helped curry them out and pitched them some feed. Making sure of the water supply, Theo finally let himself be led to the house.

Henry lighted a couple of lamps and built a fire in the range while he chattered happily about the freighting business. When he had the coffeepot on, he sat down next to Theo.

"Now tell me where all you been?" Henry demanded. "I ain't heard nothin' but what the newspaper printed, an' I never believed that."

"Yep. Turns out that old Louis Gasceaux set me up for that." Theo had a sour expression on his face. "I left Dodge an' went down through the Nations into Texas. I'd never been there before. Trailed north with a cattle herd and kicked around with the Texans for awhile. The Jayhawkers shot the trail boss in Ellsworth.

"Funny thing, Henry. Been trying to understand why that happened. To the fella they shot, all folks were good people. He'd even saved the life of one of the men who shot him down. He always figgered I'd be killed before he would. Kept tryin' to tell me to change my ways. Said always havin' to watch my back would get me one of these days, but he was shot first."

Henry shrugged. "No tellin' how things work out and where God's hand is Theo. Things just have a habit of ending different than any of us expect is all. I reckon you do the best you can and hope it comes out right. You ever settle up with Gasceaux after he framed you?" Henry's eyes were serious. There was none of the old Henry behind them now. He had toughened considerably.

"Nope." Theo laughed. "Everytime I get close, he's gone by a week or two and I have to sniff him out again. Last time was in Denver a couple of weeks ago.

There was an article in the paper that got to him before it got to me. Afore that, he was driven out of Dodge City by a rampagin' cattleman. Hell, he was probably there before you left. Set up a saloon called Louis's."

"I remember." Henry nodded. "Big fella with a hell of a scar on his cheek."

"Yep. That was Gasceaux. Turns out I gave him that scar the night he shot me in Dodge." Theo settled back in the chair and looked around. "Pretty nice house, Henry."

"Yep, it's what I wanted all along. The buffalo business was at a peak, and it's gonna play out one of these days soon. The time was right, so I left. Now it looks like there's gonna be war with the Sioux an' Cheyenne. The freighting should go like hotcakes. Not only that, but I ain't had a louse or flea since I left the buffalo range."

Theo nodded. Henry stood up and poured coffee into two cups. He sliced some potatoes and put them in a pan with lard. Then he went outside to the icebox and brought in two steaks and put them on the fire.

"Part of all this is yours, too, Theo," Henry said as he sat down again. "Wouldn't a been none of this without you. To this day I never have figger'd why you stayed with us when you could have just ridden on. I thank the Lord every night for what you've done."

"Don't make no difference, Henry." Theo waved absently. "Somebody had to keep you from grief. Besides, I liked your company." Theo's eyes got serious. "You know something, Henry? You were the first friend I ever had."

Henry nodded. "You where the best friend I ever had," he said, a catch in his voice. He looked at Theo with longing in his eyes. "Reckon it hurt when you rode out of Dodge that night, but I guess it had to be." He spoke in a whisper.

"Reckon so," Theo said lowly. "Me an' Dolly wasn't doin' too well an' Louis was gettin' away. Never made much sense of how my head was workin' then. Still don't, I reckon."

"Still havin' the dreams, Theo?" Henry watched him with concern.

"Yep. Had it again last night and the night before." He looked down where his hands clasped the coffee cup. What the hell was he doing talking to Henry about it in the first place? "There's demons in my mind that stir up the dream, Henry." He met the old man's knowing eyes.

"What's the dream, Theo? Is it the same one over and over?" Henry studied him, leaning forward over the table. "Gasceaux have anything to do with it?"

In an unstemmable rush, he began telling the whole story, unable to clamp down and kill the urge. The demons screamed as he told of the ambush, rape, and mutilation of his parents and how he'd hidden in the sand.

Henry watched him with understanding, nodding now and then. The old man's eyes clouded, as if on the verge of tears. Theo could see love in Henry's eyes and it frightened him. Why was he telling this? The fear grew but he couldn't stop. It was like a flash flood pouring down an arroyo. He just couldn't stop no matter how the fear welled within him.

He could feel himself becoming vulnerable. Another person knew the secret! He'd betrayed his trust with the plan. He could be hurt by the knowledge that he now loosed. When he finished the story, he was trembling. He was naked now, defenseless. Henry knew what made him strong. The fear built, feeding on his sudden insecurity. God help him, what of the Fates? Had they decreed this? The demons gibbered anxiously.

Theo wanted to cry and fought the urge to run. He shot a frightened glance at Henry, but the old man was lost in his own thoughts. Panic pounded in Theo's breast. It was as if it would burst. Henry looked up to meet his eyes and Theo saw the strength there.

"Wish you'd a killed him years ago," the old man said softly.

Maybe it would be all right. Henry was his friend. Henry was the only man he could turn his back on. He'd told that to Charlie. He knew it was true even if the demons screamed no.

Anger began to build in him to counter the fear. He was scared again. Silently, he cursed himself for a fool. He had made a mistake coming here. Henry had tricked him somehow.

No! It couldn't be! Henry was his friend! Henry would not turn against him!

"Wish I could have," Theo heard himself say. Again, he beat down the frantic urge to run, to find the sorrel and ride out and hide himself in the blackness of the night. He needed to run from this man and this town and the knowledge that another knew his secret. There was a frantic feeling inside him now, and he fought to control his fear.

Be strong, he told himself. The world is made for the strong and the clever. You will survive! You must survive! But all the training and the shaping that the Fates had put him through hadn't strengthened him for this.

"Think Louis is in Cheyenne?" Henry's voice was soft and soothing.

"He'll be here soon, I reckon," Theo agreed, struggling to bring all his mind back to the conversation. He fought to push the fear and the anger away, to stifle the demons with it. He worked to wall it all back.

Henry stood and turned the steaks and the potatoes, throwing more wood in the stove and adjusting the dampers. Theo shrugged out of his coat and sipped the coffee. He was winning. The panic was held back.

Henry was digging plates out of the cupboard. He turned and looked at Theo. "I always thought it had to be something like that. Surprises me how you've made it this far. Maybe I can understand the rages you used to fly into." Comprehension was in the old eyes along with admiration.

"Reckon," Theo said shortly, nervously.

"Theo, if you need anything, you always know where I'm at. Like I say, I could never done this without you. I don't fergit." Henry motioned to the house around him. He set the plates on the table.

"You don't owe me for nothin', Henry. You did this on your own." Theo was irritated by the implications.

"Nope," Henry snorted. "I'da been dead out there on the plains somewhere. Me and Dolly both. Even if we'd a made it to Dodge, I woulda been a laughing-stock. We owe you a lot." Henry's lined face was a mask of sincerity.

"Huh," Theo grunted, picking up his fork and knife. He shoveled the hot food into his mouth, chewing thoughtfully.

They ate in silence, each thinking to himself. The fear and anger began to break out, and Theo felt helpless to deal with the burning in his breast and mind. The demons were picking at his control, testing the wall he'd built to hold them back.

He looked up to see Henry's old eyes on him again.

The man was deep in thought. What was he thinking? Oh God, Theo's mind shrieked, why did I tell him about the dream?

Because you trust him! he answered back.

You never trusted nobody in your life!

Trust is weakness, he thought in return. The world is made for the strong. That's God's law, the one law, the simple law. There's the strong and the live, and the weak and the dead. Just like hunting buffalo or shooting a man in war. It all works the same.

Henry had been weak and now he was strong. He was no obstacle for the survivors. The obstacles were the worst. They didn't have the grace to die. They just hampered the survivors. But where was the distinction? How did a man tell a survivor from the wreckage that infested humanity?

He thought again of the Kansas farmers—a collection of obstacles banded together in a dog pack, killing the strong. Where was the sense in the simple law? How many times had he wondered what God had meant by allowing them to kill Charlie Torgusson?

He had quieted that ghost. He'd done right by that. Charlie rested in peace. Now all he had to do was deal with the ghosts of his parents, and that meant killing Gasceaux. Fearfully, he wondered if he'd compromised his power to do that by telling Henry of the dream.

How could he get his power back? What could he do to undo the damage? He threw a worried glance at the old man. The fear rose again. Had telling Henry ruined his chances to kill Gasceaux? Just like the Indians he'd lived with, he knew that his medicine was bad now. He felt the fear, anger, and frustration building.

They had finished eating. Theo was still trying to understand what had happened to him, fighting for control.

"What are you going to do now?" Henry asked, his kind eyes curious.

"I don't know, Henry. I just don't know. Look around town for Louis, I guess. Then there was someone I was supposed to meet here. After that, I guess it just depends on what happens if I find Louis."

There was indecision in Henry's eyes. Theo felt the fear rising in him again. Then Henry looked up firmly. "Ever thought about driving a freight wagon?" Again the doubt came to his eyes.

"Nope, never have, Henry. Don't reckon that would sit too well with my disposition though." Theo saw a wave of relief flood Henry's eyes. Why? What about Theo did he fear?

"Army's gonna be needin' scouts for the fighting sometime soon. That might be right for you," Henry said thoughtfully. He was nervous now, Theo knew. It was as if he'd suddenly realized something and was unsure of himself.

Maybe he had thought about something in the dream? The fear and panic began to rise again.

There was the sound of a door opening and a rustling of clothes from the other room. "Paw? I'm home," Dolly's voice called. Henry's eyes looked even more frantic.

"Dolly! C'mon in here! We got us a guest for dinner. See if you can recognize this fella." There was a false heartiness in Henry's voice.

Theo felt his chest was about to burst as she walked into the room. He started up, thinking to make for the door, but she was there before him. Theo looked at her, his heart pounding. He felt as if he was trembling and almost shook himself in an effort to force calm.

She came in with a smile on her face, but when she saw him she stopped and her eyes widened. She gasped a little as she drew in a breath. He could see the joy leave her eyes to be replaced by wonder and pain.

"Dolly," he greeted and nodded.

"Theo?" she returned, and took a step closer. "It's you?"

"Reckon so." He was cool on the outside, but he felt nervous. His bowels had that distinctly runny feeling. Again the anger built at his inability to deal with these people.

"Coffee's on," Henry suggested. "Why don't we go into the front room and relax."

"Sounds good, Paw." Dolly smiled. She'd regained her composure. "Come on, Theo, this way."

He followed her to the front room. It was finished with overstuffed furniture, and he found himself in a plush chair while Dolly bent down to start a fire in the fireplace.

"How have you been, Theo?" she asked as the kindling started. Was she heavier or was that just her clothing?

"Been gettin' along, Dolly. How about yourself?"

"Just fine. Things here have been going real well. Paw's happy and I'm keeping busy doing the office work. I'll tell you, it sure beats pulling hides of buffalo by a long shot. I even get a bath every night now." Her voice was even and melodious.

She stood and shook her head a little while she looked him over. "You seem pretty fit, Theo, if a little leaner. It looks like you've been seeing your share of long trails."

"Been around," Theo agreed. He told her about Texas and the Nations while Henry brought out the coffee.

There was a knock at the door. Henry opened it to a man Theo didn't know.

"Howdy, Frank. Meet Theo Belk. Theo, this is Frank Wilder. He's one of my drivers."

"My pleasure, Mr. Belk." Frank nodded, then he turned to Henry. "That wheel team mare is havin' trouble. I thought you might want to take a look at her. She's lamed up something bad."

"All right." Henry nodded. "Be right out. Excuse me, Theo. Horse trouble." Henry went to the kitchen to get his coat and left.

Dolly looked at Theo as she seated herself with a cup of coffee. "Where you off to now, Theo?" she asked. "More long trails, or are you going to be around for a while?"

"Don't know, Dolly. I'd guess it depends on which way the wind blows. Louis Gasceaux is supposed to be coming to Cheyenne."

Her eyes hardened a little. "Last time, he almost killed you, if you'll remember." She sipped her coffee and studied him intently. Her face looked fuller, as if there was a healthy flush.

"He can't be lucky all the time," Theo said whimsically. She was still beautiful. Her long hair hung in red ringlets, offsetting the light skin of her face and her red lips. He could drown in those blue eyes.

Theo felt his heart getting tighter in his chest. He had an almost overwhelming urge to go take her up in his arms and kiss her.

She sighed. "Theo, there's times I just don't know about you. You have so much potential, you . . . you can't go on driving yourself like this! One of these days, you're going to end up shot . . . or hung. Why don't you give it up?" She looked at him seriously.

"Because I can't!" he snapped. He stood up and took a deep breath. Would this woman never understand? She'd seemed so level-headed on the trail. Theo ran his eyes over the room. It was tastefully decorated. He smiled. There next to the kitchen doorway was Henry's old Remington rifle. He wondered if Henry still kept it loaded. The sight of the gun brought back other memories of their times on the buffalo range.

He turned. "I was wondering"—he met her cool eyes—"maybe we could spend some time together. I been missing you, Dolly." The admission made him nervous. He felt the tightness in his chest expand. What was he saying?

She sighed, looking at the floor. Slowly, she shook her head. "It can't be Theo," she said softly. "What's gone is gone. So much changed that night you rode out of Dodge." She looked up at him sadly. "I . . . I'm a . . . married woman, Theo." She blushed slightly. "Our first baby—Tom's and mine—is due in a few months. Don't show much, but it's—"

"You're married?" He felt the passion rising through his chest rage seeped at the back of his mind. The demons laughed. "To that mick? To that Irish . . ."

"*He's my husband, Theo!*" she exploded angrily, her arms straight at her sides, her face red with sudden anger. The muscles along her jaw stood out, rippling as she glared defiantly at him.

He ignored her outburst. The baby complicated things. "You don't have to stay with him, Dolly. I spent a lot of time thinkin' about . . . about us. I reckon maybe we'll go up to Montana and I'll build us a house up in the foothills an' I can hunt and trap and run some cattle."

He shifted into his daydream. "There'll be a nice frame house, with red shutters and separate bedrooms for us and the kids. You'll have a big yard with straight fences for the stock." He stopped, watching her as she shook her head.

"It's too late, Theo." She stood up and faced him. "That's what I wanted to hear from you a year ago. I'm different now. I don't think I could live with you. Theo, I don't love you anymore. Not only that, but I don't think I could if I tried."

"But, Dolly, there'll—"

"Do you know how badly you hurt me that night? I don't think you do. Oh, Theo, I don't think I could ever trust you. Living with you would be like living on top of a powder keg. A person never knows when you're going to get all moody and blow up. I made my choice and I took Tom. He's kind! He's . . ."

"Why, you can't just up an'—"

"I'm not saying these things to hurt you. I can see you're getting mad, but just listen to me. Too many changes have occurred, and I'm not the same person I was back then. I have different goals, Theo. I'm goin' to have Tom's baby! He's kind and gentle and he loves me for who I am. He's not going to go out some night and . . . and get shot!" Her eyes pleaded with him.

Theo stood, tight lipped. He could feel his heart pounding, and the black rage was rising within him. Hell, he ought to just take her right now! He felt the urge building.

All the things he'd planned to do for her were crumbling to dust and rotting in his mind. He felt the pain surging through the caldron of fear and anger in his mind. It built and welled in him.

He could see Dolly backing away from him, a worried look in her eyes. He didn't care. His thoughts were riding on the growing tide of anger and frustration. Did nothing he ever did come out right? He'd offered everything to this woman, *and she'd thrown it right back in his face!*

"You owe me!" he gasped hoarsely. "I done everything for you. *I would give you anything I had!*" He heard Henry enter the room and stop at the kitchen door. *"Why did you do this to me?"* he demanded.

"Because, I can't go with you!" she flared back. "It was over a long time ago Theo, as if it ever even existed." Her eyes were hard as she stood up to him. He could see the anger in her.

"Go on," she prodded. "Go find Louis Gasceaux and kill him! What's another body on your back trail?"

The wall broke and the black rage was loose. He hit her. He didn't even remember starting the fist for her; then she was rolling on the floor.

He remembered throwing Henry off with one arm. Vaguely, the old man's cries penetrated the red haze. He picked the girl up and glared at her again. Her eyes burned into his as he pulled back the fist and started it forward to smash her mouth to a bloody pulp.

Then he was on the floor. He put his arms under him to lever himself up. He attempted to bound up and reach the girl, but nothing happened! He kicked his legs around but they didn't move. Dumbly he looked down and kicked again. *His legs didn't move!*

Dolly's eyes were wide with terror. She lay where she'd fallen, then looked up as Henry walked over, the Remington in his hands. There was a wisp of smoke curling out of the big barrel.

Theo looked up from where he lay on the floor.

Henry was shaking his head slowly. There were tears streaming down his lined cheeks. The gun dropped from his numb fingers and thumped hollowly on the carpet.

Funny, Theo thought. He hadn't heard the shot. Henry must have missed since he hadn't felt the impact of the bullet. Again, he tried to get to his feet, only to flop about the carpet. He reached for the corner of the couch and pulled himself up to get his feet under him, fell again, and rolled over. There was blood on the rug where he'd lain.

"Dolly, get the doctor, quick!" Henry ordered. Theo saw her stagger to her feet, a large red spot on her cheek where his fist had hit her. The anger was gone now, and there was a funny blurring in his mind.

Henry bent down and put a hand on his shoulder. "Easy, Theo. Easy, please. I . . . oh, God . . . I . . . Relax, don't move, you'll be all right . . . all right! I . . . Dolly's gone for the doctor."

"Why?" Theo asked numbly. "I'm all right, Henry. You missed. I'm all right! I'm fine! Can't feel a . . ."

Henry shook his head. Theo looked into those eyes, drowning in love, concern, sympathy, and something new—guilt!

"I had to Theo. I had to, you understand. That was Dolly and you were . . . were hurting her. I . . . I tried to stop you first, I did. *Oh God Theo, why did this have to happen?"* The old man broke down to tears.

"Where am I hit?" Theo asked slowly, the realization creeping into his brain.

"In the back, Theo," Henry whispered through his tears.

Theo reached a hand around and felt; it came back red with blood. "I'll be damned," he muttered, voice rasping.

"Henry, is there an exit wound?" Theo asked softly. The old man was still sobbing. "Henry?" Theo shouted. "Tell me, is there an exit wound? Where did the bullet go?"

Henry pulled himself together and looked over Theo's back. "I can't tell, the shirt's all . . . shirt's all bloody."

"Well, rip the damn shirt off, Henry!" Theo cried. He could hear the material tearing.

"Oh, my God!" Henry sobbed. "My God! My God, Theo, your whole back's laid open. There's chunks of bone stickin' out. Dolly's gone for the doctor. Theo, we'll get you fixed up. I promise." The old man's knobby hands were bloody and shaking as he knotted them miserably before his weather-beaten face.

"It's all right, Henry," Theo whispered hoarsely. "You done right. Don't know what happened. The way I felt just then, I . . . I mighta killed her. You done right! Hey, my friend. Come here and hold my hand. You did the right thing. I lost my medicine is all."

The room was getting hazy in front of his eyes. He could make out the form of Henry crouched over him. He could feel the old man's hand in his. He could sense Henry's suffering. The old man seemed suddenly so frail . . . so old. He had to explain, to salve the hurt.

"There was power in the dream, Henry. It's my fault. I shouldn't have told you." It was getting hard to talk. "When I told you . . . I lost strength. It weakened me . . . weakened me, you understand. You had to do it. It was my fault!"

"Theo." Henry's voice came softly through a mist. "Don't talk, Theo. You got a lot of strength. I want you to relax. Take it easy, just rest . . . rest now. The doctor will be here soon."

"All right, Henry. I'll rest. Don't think I'm . . . gonna be around . . . much longer anyway. Things is gettin' . . . real . . . fuzzy. Hazy like . . . It's hard to. . . think. Reckon I might . . . die now."

"Oh God, Theo, forgive me!" Henry's voice was pleading, hysterical with pain.

"You're forgiven, Henry," Theo whispered, then he laughed. "Henry . . . don't forget to load your . . ." Then all sensation slipped away.

CHAPTER 20

THEO STRUGGLED TO PULL HIS EYELIDS APART. HIS EYES felt sandy and gritty—glued by rheum. The throbbing ache he'd been conscious of in his disturbed sleep became pain. He was lying on his stomach. He tried to turn over. He couldn't. Something held him down. When he moved, the pain became worse and he groaned.

"Don't move," came a soft deep voice. "Ye've been bad hurt, Mr. Belk. The doctor says if'n ye be movin' too much, it'll be th' worse fer ye."

"Where am I?" Theo heard himself ask. The scratchy voice didn't seem to be his.

"Ye be 't Mr. Henry Moore's house. Mr. Belk, ye've been shot. Y've got to rest."

"Who're you? You sure don't sound like Henry." Theo struggled to place the voice.

"I be Tom O'Connell. Ye saved me loife once on the Arkansas River trail, Mr. Belk," the soft voice continued.

"I remember," his voice rasped. Theo tried to swallow; his throat was dry and his tongue stuck at the back of his mouth. He managed to pull his eyes open: the world was bleary. "Any water?" he croaked.

He could see an unfocused form loom close and place a cup to his lips. It was difficult to drink from the position he was in. Most of the water spilled. The man wiped it up and brought more. It took several trips before Theo felt some relief.

"Where am I shot?" he asked as he blinked his eyes clear.

"The bullet crossed the small o' yor back, Mr. Belk. You are . . . goin' t' live." There was a hesitation in the voice.

"How come I can't move?" Theo asked stupidly. He could move his arms fine, but the rest of his body seemed firmly pasted to the hard bed.

"They've got ye strapped down, Mr. Belk. It's t keep yer spine in place," O'Connell told him.

The memories seeped back. Theo had thought it but a dream. Henry, Dolly, Theo's anger, the way he couldn't get off the floor, the tears in the old man's eyes—the images haunted him.

"Where's Henry?" Theo growled to hide the panic rising in him. How helpless was he?

"He's gone to Fort Laramie on business. He'll be back in a coupl' o' days," O'Connell told him. Theo looked up into the man's soft brown eyes. He could see the strength there and there was something else too—a dark conflicting of emotions.

"When can I get up?" Theo asked, still feeling his panic. There was something here he didn't understand.

Tom's eyes wavered and he didn't speak, his lips pursed. The man looked away.

"Tell me, damn it!" Theo ordered hoarsely.

O'Connell met his gaze and he could see pain in the man's eyes as well a burning of something else, hate?

"You may niver walk again, Mr. Belk. The doctor says the bullet smashed yer spine just above th' sacrum . . . which be a bone in yer hips." The words were spoken slowly and deliberately.

Theo let his head sink to the mattress. The words repeated themselves in his brain. It meant that he was crippled, paralyzed, maybe for life. Against his will, the implications began to form.

Never again would he walk through the evening dusk, his rifle in hand, searching for a glimpse of deer. Never again would he ride the sorrel down new trails or know the joy of a warm fire in the night. He'd never throw a pack on a horse. He'd never see the sunset from the top of a mountain or wake in a frosty camp.

He'd never see the antelope running, fleeting and quick as they seemed to float across the sagebrush. He'd never climb through the rocks, or break another horse. He was a lump of clay now, a no good pile of meat—useless.

"Mr. Belk, the doctor said that there moight be a wee chance. It all depends on how yor back heals. There be quite a bit o' damage to the spinal cord, but the body o' the vertebrae still be connected," O'Connell continued, watching him neutrally.

"How long?" Theo asked, his blue eyes boring into the man.

"He said 't would be years," Tom told him.

"Damn," Theo whispered hoarsely. The panic surging through him tore at his brain, but he could only lie there, helpless. There was no vent for his feelings. He felt the tears slowly welling in his eyes in spite of his effort to control them. The loss began pounding at his consciousness. Then anger followed, mixing with pain and fright. What would happen to him?

"Don't worry, Mr. Belk. Ye've a place ta stay . . . and care." Tom leaned forward, his concern masking the other emotions that boiled behind his eyes.

"Why here?" Theo cried, almost in terror. "I want to ride again. I want to go. I still gotta find Gasceaux. It's the dream, don't you understand? I can't stay here. This can't happen ta me!" He gritted in anger, fighting to overcome the panic that ebbed and surged within him.

"Damn it, Belk!" O'Connell spat at him. "Be a mon now! C'mon, laddie, don't make it worse on Henry than 'tis already!" There was unbridled anger in O'Connell's voice.

The sudden hostility startled Theo and the panic vanished as he glared at the man. No one had ever lectured him like that!

O'Connell continued in a harsh voice. "Ta be honest, Mr. Belk, I'd no real use fer ye afore this happened. I'd gone to Kansas ta kill ye! Yer friends Gasceaux and Sabot found me first. Then ye saved me loife an' I decided that you could go, but it didn't really even me debt. Then ye hit Dolly an s'far as I be concerned, ye could die an' good riddance ta ye.

"But Henry Moore, now, he sees ye in a bit o' a different light, Mr. Belk. Right now, he's holdin himself responsible fer ye bein' this way. He has a great deal o' r'spect fer ye, Mr. Belk. An' I ha' a great deal o' r'spect for Mr. Moore. He'll take care o' ye and so will the rest o' us. Dolly's been worried sick aboot ye.

"Now relax and rest. Ye've got a chance ta recover, mon. It's a matter o' years . . . but ye got a chance. Hear me?" Tom finished and sat himself in a chair.

"Why'd you want to kill me?" Theo asked, wishing he could get to his feet and teach this paddy a thing or two. "What did I ever do to you?" He frowned up at O'Connell. "You jealous over Dolly?"

"No, Mr. Belk. I suppose that meet'n' Dolly is something I'm b'holdin' to ye for. If ye hadn't found me on the trail and saved me loife, I'd a niver knowed her.

"Mr. Belk, ye killed me brother in Denver. Ye shot 'im down loike a dog in the Citation Saloon o'er the price o' a drink." O'Connell's voice was like a whip. "As a result o' that, Mr. Belk, his foine wife died o' grief, an' I've not been able to foind out what become o' his young children. That's why I trail'd ye ta Kansas." O'Connell finished and sighed, never letting his eyes leave Belk's.

"Why don't you just kill me now?" Theo stared balefully at him. "That way you'd do us both a favor."

"No, Mr. Belk. I couldn't. I couldn't because I owe you me loife. An' Henry loves you. It'd nigh kill the old mon o' guilt if ye'd up an' die on him. He be blamin' himself fer this," O'Connell repeated.

Theo sighed. "Henry was right. He did what he had to, O'Connell. I was out of control. I might have killed her. Damn me anyway. Never did have no sense. Reckon I'da done the same thing if I were in his place. Guess I'da shot a little straighter though." He felt the grief building in him and fought to cover it.

"Aye, an' I'm glad ta hear that, Mr. Belk. I don't suppose you an' I can e'er be friends. There be too much blood owed b'tween us, but I'll not be holdin' a grudge. I don't know how God works his hand, but he must o' had a reason for all o' this." Tom looked at him with his eyes soft again.

"Reckon so. It's the Fates that done that in Denver. There's devils that make men do what they do, O'Connell. I done had more than my share of 'em is all. Look where they . . . brought me." He heard his voice crack. Theo closed his eyes and breathed deeply.

He'd been a puppet on a string all of his life. The demons where laughing at him again. He could feel their ironic humor. Why had they chosen him? What had he done in his young life to have deserved all of this? Why had they chosen him to be their plaything?

Damn them all! They'd made him suffer ever since that day on the Blacks Fork. Why couldn't they have let him die there in the sand? It would have been over then. Instead they'd sent him to Fletch, who'd taught him so well. They'd given him the dream and pushed him. They'd sent him off to the Mormons, who'd imprisoned him.

He'd been shaped. He'd learned among the Mormons. Then he had been forged and tempered during the war. He had been strengthened in his pursuit of Gasceaux. Everything that happened to him had a purpose.

Now he was crippled, useless, and to what end? The Fates, God, or the demons, whoever they were, had spent so much time to shape him for his destiny and now what? He was forsaken and discarded—a broken tool.

Baffled and angry, he strove to make sense of it. Everything in his life pointed to something. He had been made the perfect warrior. Where had he failed? He had to have failed! Where was the flaw? What had he done wrong? Again the rage washed him with desperation. What part of him didn't meet up to expectations?

Emotions changed and surged in his chest. The despair grew in his belly, making it empty and dark. It expanded as if to fill him and burst his ragged body. He choked on it.

It was misery he felt now. Pure, unpolluted, raw misery, worse than any he'd known in his violent, tumultuous life. Always before there had been the quest, the hope that he would find Louis Gasceaux and kill the dream. Now there was despair, loneliness, emptiness, and rage he could not vent. Even fear had deserted him.

The empty husk that had been Theo Belk felt Tom's hand on his shoulder. "I've got chores to attend to, Mr. Belk. The window is open. If ye be needin' anything holler good an' loud an' I'll come a runnin'. Ye need ta think fer a while. T'will do ye good. Remember though, ye've friends aboot you here. Dolly will be in later this afternoon."

Theo didn't even open his eyes as he heard the man leave. Left alone, he allowed himself tears. He cried and tried to live with the emptiness and futility until his frayed mind and injured body sought oblivion in sleep.

The dream came again. The rock-capped Uinta Mountains rose to the south and the Church Buttes thrust above the gray-white banded clays of the Blacks Fork terraces. The wagon stood there between the dunes while Louis Gasceaux threw his mother to the ground. Sabot and the other men jeered and laughed while his father bled.

The whole dream repeated, and Theo lay cowering on the small dune. Then as Sabot cut his father's body apart, the bloody head lifted and looked at Theo with pleading eyes.

"Do something, son." The haunting voice echoed hollowly through Theo's mind. He shook his head in terror and Sabot pulled the bloody scalp from his father's head.

Then Sabot went to his mother and began his work. "Do something, son," his mother echoed his father's words. It sounded like Dolly's voice.

"I can't!" Theo screamed, feeling his vocal chords straining. "Oh, God, I can't!"

Louis Gasceaux looked up at him and laughed. Then Sabot threw him a wicked grin as he held his mother's hair up in his bloody hands. Gasceaux laughed again and again. Theo could only grovel in the sand and scream.

Then they were gone. Irish O'Connell walked toward him over the cobbles. The big miner watched him with curious eyes. "An' ye called me a coward, mon? Where be ye now? Look at ye alayin' there. Ye be no more than dirt, Belk! Fer I be the one who broke yer back an' laid ye low. Now, buy me a drink! *Buy, damn you!*"

Theo dug himself farther into the damp sand and tried to move, to run from this demon of the dead. He looked down in horror to find the sand damp from blood—deep, dark, red blood. He tried to kick out, but his legs wouldn't work.

He heard laughter and looked up to see Sabot laughing through the torn remains of his throat. As he laughed the blood sprayed in tiny droplets onto the soaked ground and onto Theo.

"Easy, Theo," Charlie looked down on him. "They're gone now. I sent them away. But Theo, where's the sense in it? I asked you before—how's your soul stack up now?"

"How does it?" asked another voice. Theo looked over his shoulder to see a nester with a gaping hole in his chest, his head all bloody.

"Theo?" Charlie called hollowly. His back was to the bar in Ellsworth. He was sagging while bullets pounded into his flesh. Charlie's arm fell slowly to the floor. "Why'd you kill me?"

Theo tried to close his eyes. "I didn't, Charlie! They did! They tricked me!" He felt his voice straining with emotion. "Damn them! Go away! For God's sake! Just let me die!" He ended sobbing into the sand—the red, bloody sand—of the Blacks Fork.

Through it all he felt a hand on his shoulder. "Theo?" It was Dolly's voice. "Theo?"

No! He hadn't hurt Dolly! She was fine! He hadn't hurt Dolly. He'd loved her!

"Theo!" Her voice was sharp now. "Theo, wake up!"

He gasped and shook himself awake. The bed was wet with his sweat. It was Henry's room. Dolly bent over him.

"You had a bad dream, Theo," she said softly. "Are you all right?"

He swallowed and nodded, breathing deeply. "Happens on occasion," he growled defensively.

"I know." She brought him more water. Greedily, he drank it. "I closed the window. It was getting cold. Looks like it will snow again tonight."

"Huh," he grunted. He looked around the room, as much as he could see from his point of vantage. His clothes were stacked on the table in the corner of the room. He could see the handle of his old Walker Colt. Sitting on top of the pile was his worn hat. With resignation, he wondered if he'd ever wear it again.

Dolly came back and looked him over. The bruise on her face was almost gone. He shut his eyes, too tired to cry, too tired to do anything but lie there limp, in total exhaustion.

"How are you feeling?" Dolly asked with kindness as she seated herself by the bed.

"'Bout like a bag of lead," Theo whispered wearily.

"Did Tom tell you what the doctor said?" she asked, her bright blue eyes were pools of concern.

He could see the swell of her belly, growing with new life—new hope for a future now gone sour.

"Yep," Theo muttered. "Said I was crippled. Guess I done played hell, Dolly. Ain't much left for Theo Belk now." His mind was blank and foggy, as if it were not his own.

"Can't say that yet, Theo," she reminded him.

"The dreams are back," Theo said listlessly. "All of 'em. Did Henry tell you about the dreams?"

"Yes. Theo, I'm so sorry this had to happen. Paw's real upset. He's being awful hard on himself." Dolly placed a cool hand on Theo's forehead. "You're hot, Theo. Want me to take some of the blankets off?"

"No, leave 'em on," he mumbled, lost in his thoughts of the dreams. "Tell Henry not to worry. He did what he had to. It was in the plan. I did it to myself, somehow. It had to be. I failed, Dolly. I wasn't strong enough. I was vulnerable, too soft!" He spat the last.

"Theo, don't talk like that. You are one of the strongest men I've ever known." Her voice was warm and caring. It hurt him to hear her speak like that. There was something in her voice that reminded him of his mother, and he'd failed her like he had Dolly.

"How's your face where I hit you?" he asked absently.

"Fine, Theo. I had quite a shiner for a couple of days. It's almost gone now. Tom was scared to death that you'd hurt the baby. It don't matter though." She actually ended up with a laugh.

"Reckon it does." Theo blinked his eyes in an attempt to rid them of the gritty feeling.

"Theo, don't do this to yourself." Her voice was stern. "Folks do what they think is right is all. I guess I could have been a little more tactful. I'm sorry. I had to tell you those things."

He could hear the guilt in her voice. "You did what you had to. Don't try to make me feel any better. If we could go back, nothing would change. I did what the demons told me, and you did what you thought you had to. Nothin's changed, Dolly. You're still you and I'm still me. Don't spend the rest of your life tryin' to fool yourself. You hear?" He glared at the girl, and she straightened at his harsh tone.

"That's better." Theo nodded. "Life is too real to spend any time on a lot of sweet, meaningless words. Things are as they are. That's all."

"All right, I can accept that, Theo," she agreed. "You never were much of one to mince words, were you?"

"Reckon not." He sighed. "If you never learned anything else from Theo Belk, remember that people do what they gotta do."

"I know that, Theo." She nodded. "I really knew that a long time ago. I guess I spend too much time searching for the motives."

"Sometimes there ain't no reason," Theo told her. "There's times when you just got to follow what your mind and emotions tell you is right. Just like last night, when Henry did what he had to."

"That was last week, Theo." Dolly met his startled

stare. "You been unconscious for awhile."

"A week?" Theo looked puzzled.

Dolly dropped her eyes. "Theo, there's something else, too. I've been all over town. There's no trace of Ruby. We found the note in your things. No one has seen her. Ida Hamilton has put the word out that you're looking for her. She isn't in Cheyenne."

Dolly hesitated, her jaw muscles clenched before she added, "One of Ida's girls did see her at the station a couple of weeks ago. She rode one train in from Denver then boarded another westbound. She wasn't in town more than three hours."

Theo felt his belly sink even lower. All those looks, all the time they'd spent together, were a sham! He remembered the time he'd decided to leave and she'd kept him. Damn her, she'd used him the whole time!

"I'm sorry, Theo," Dolly told him as she saw the misery build in his eyes. "Maybe she did what she had to." Dolly's voice was toneless.

"Reckon," Theo mumbled weakly.

It surprised him a little to find that he'd had a slight ray of hope that Ruby would come to him. He'd really believed she loved him. Lord, he thought, how many times have I deluded myself. The hurt Ruby had caused sank down and melted into the greater pain that welled in his mind.

"Can't I do anything right?" He looked up, his eyes bitter.

"Theo, stop it. Don't do this to yourself," Dolly whispered. "Torturing yourself over what's past won't do any of us any good. You'll destroy yourself and . . . Paw, too. Please, don't. Things will be better. I promise you that." She sat on the chair, her eyes searching as if to see into his soul.

There were steps in the hallway and the door opened. From where he lay strapped to the bed, he couldn't see who entered.

"Good day," a deep voice greeted. Theo could see a puzzled look on Dolly's face.

"Good day. Do I know you?" she asked with a slight frown.

"Ah, I am looking for Theo Belk. You might say I'm an old acquaintance of his. I think I have found him, no?" The baritone was slightly amused.

Theo searched his mind to try and place the voice. He could see Dolly's eyes go wide.

"Who are you?" she gasped, a worried look on her face. Theo felt a thrill of fear as his mind cleared.

"I have been many men, Miss Moore. Indeed, you are very beautiful. Perhaps we can have a chat when I have asked Mr. Belk some questions," the baritone continued.

"You don't need to ask questions with a pistol," Dolly pointed out coldly. "Theo can't hurt you. He's been shot!" There was scorn in her voice.

"Indeed, so I read in the papers. Accidental discharge, they said." There was a low laugh. "That is rich indeed, Miss Moore. I, however, take no chances with this man. He is never to be underestimated. Is that not so, Mr. Belk?" the baritone asked.

"Louis, step over here where I can see you," Theo said between clenched teeth.

The big man walked over while Dolly backed into the corner off to his side. "Do not try to leave, Miss Moore. If you do I shall shoot you down. I've come too far and too much is at risk. Stay where you are," Louis ordered.

Theo nodded to her as she shot him a quick look.

"What do you want, Louis?" Theo demanded.

"Where is Ruby?" Louis demanded, his dark eyes glittering.

"I don't know." Theo glared back at him. "She run out on me."

"Indeed." There was amusement in Louis's eyes. "She has done that to both of us. Did she perhaps have a large carpetbag with her?"

"Uh-huh, that she did. Why?" Theo watched the man, feeling his hatred rise. What could he do? How could he kill him now? The pistol was over on the table. He felt a cold flush run down his back and despair washed over him again. He was going to fail yet another time!

"The carpetbag held all of my savings, Belk. There were almost thirty thousand dollars in that bag," Louis hissed. He did not, however, move the barrel of the Smith & Wesson an inch either way from where it pointed at Theo's head.

Theo began to laugh. It was uncontrollable. He laughed so hard that knives of pain speared up his back. Louis turned white and stepped forward, slapping him across the face. Dolly tensed up, crowding against the table, her eyes darting to the door as if estimating her chances.

"You . . . you laugh, imbecile!" Louis snarled, his scarred cheek twisting horribly.

"Yep, I laugh, Louis. You been had by your one weakness. Let me see," Theo searched his mind. " 'Sacré, Louis. Women, they be zee death of you yet!' Those are the words. Remember who said 'em?"

"Sabot! When did you hear them?" Louis looked puzzled.

"On the Blacks Fork, Louis. Remember? You shot my father, then raped my mother. I saw the whole thing, Louis, an' I lived with it. You hear, you son of a bitch? *I lived with it!"* Theo spat hoarsely.

"Too bad." Louis shrugged. "Had I found you that day, I could have spared you years of discomfort. But tell me, Belk, how did you follow me all those years? I had to have lost you so many times." There was interest in the big man's eyes.

"The demons told me, Louis. Maybe God's justice, for all I know. The demons drove me! They hounded me. It was God's plan, and the Fates pulled the strings. But I let 'em down. I wasn't good enough, so they broke me right when I had you. I knew you were coming here, Louis! I could feel it!" Theo thundered, venting his hatred.

Louis shook his head. "Interesting to be sure, but there is no plan . . . no God. You are a madman, Belk. There are no demons, just the ones you have put into your own mind," the voice sneered, and was so positive.

Theo just shook his head. He closed his eyes and willed his legs to move. He had to get up, to make one last try. He pushed himself up with his arms, forgetting about the straps. The pain shot up his back and he cried out, falling limp. It was no use, he could not move. He could see Dolly shaking her head no, her eyes wide and dry.

"Pity," Louis said, laughing. "I read that your back is broken, Belk. You can do nothing." He put his head back and laughed maliciously.

Then he shook his head. "It is too bad, mon ami. I had hoped to put you down in your prime. Now I must do it with you offered up on a platter. It is really a shame you wrote those stories for the newspapers. I must kill you now. You know too much."

"What about Dolly?" Theo asked. "Let her go first.

She knows nothing about you." Theo's voice was hard.

Louis walked over and felt the straps holding Theo down. "Non, Theo Belk. She knows too much now. Ah, but you are strapped down! How good it is. Your first knowledge of me was when I took your mother. Your last shall be as I take this young flower." He turned to Dolly, who watched him with fierce eyes.

"No!" Theo cried, struggling to rise again. "Damn you to hell, Gasceaux. *She's with child! No!"* He watched in horror.

"Theo, stay still," Dolly ordered him. "You keep struggling and you'll hurt your back!"

Louis absently smashed his fist into Theo's wound as he lay helpless. The pain shot into Theo's mind like white-hot fire. He heard himself cry out.

"Like that, lady?" Louis asked reasonably.

"You damn *bastard!"* Dolly spat, hatred glowing in her eyes.

"Hah!" Louis laughed and leered at her. "There is such a pleasure in breaking a woman of spirit, cheri. I shall take you and fill you. Perhaps . . . to tease the new life within you, eh? So long since I have had a woman in your . . . delicate condition!" Louis began to close on the girl a step at a time.

"No! Damn you, Gasceaux!" Theo cried, feeling tears of rage in his wet eyes. "Damn you!" he ended in a passionate whisper. There was no more he could do. Louis had won. Something in his mind was starting to let loose as it had done that day so long ago.

"Don't you lay a finger on me," Dolly threatened. "Leave this house at once! If I ever see you here again, I shall kill you!" Her voice was firm. Theo looked up to see her standing before Gasceaux, her hands behind her, her eyes meeting the big man with defiance.

"Kill me, eh?" Louis laughed again. "Very well, when I am done. If you can kill me, so be it!" He was standing before her now. He holstered his pistol and reached for the girl, crushing her into the corner. Theo saw his clothes slide off on the floor, his old hat rolling under the bed.

Dolly didn't utter a word, and Louis bent over to kiss her neck.

The muffled roar was loud in the room. Louis staggered, looking stricken. Dolly calmly leveled the smoking Walker Colt and shot Louis Gasceaux again as he pawed for his pistol. She pulled the hammer back yet again as he fell. There wasn't a tremor in her body as she shot him between the eyes.

She stood there, a grim look on her face, as the blue smoke rose slowly to the ceiling. Then she looked at Theo. "Are you all right? How's your back?" she asked, swallowing hard, her chest heaving as she drew deep breaths.

"I'll make it," Theo grunted wearily.

"I couldn't take the chance on shooting him before, Theo. He had the pistol pointed at you the whole time. I had to get him to holster it first." She sighed and wiped perspiration from her forehead. She looked at the man on the floor with regret.

Theo could see the blood welling out onto the gray, painted boards.

"I guess you did what you had to do," he said tiredly.

They could hear someone shouting in the yard. There were running steps and Tom burst into the room. The rest became hazy, and Theo didn't remember losing consciousness.

CHAPTER 21

HE COULDN'T GET HIS BREATH! HE TRIED TO KEEP RUNNING, but his legs were wooden. Like gutta-percha, they wobbled under him and finally refused to carry his weight any farther. His fear tight in his breast, Theo felt himself sink slowly to the ground. In agony, he ripped at the pistol on his belt and pulled the Walker up, waiting, knowing he had been somehow crippled.

They came softly, shouting back and forth. He saw the first one creeping through the winter-stark gray trunks of the cottonwoods. The farmer grinned, his stubble-bearded face twisting. "Got him!" the man called.

One by one, they ghosted through the cottonwoods, surrounding him, cutting him off. The pistol raised involuntarily in his hand, the hammer clicking loudly as his thumb pulled it back. And they closed their circle tighter.

Theo gritted his teeth, centering the blade of the sight on the grinning farmer, knowing how many there were, knowing he only had five shots!

"Back!" Theo cried. "Get back! Get away!"

And they closed, shotguns, pistols, and clubs in their hands. Above him, in the leafless branches of the tree, Charlie Torgusson laughed hysterically. Theo triggered the gun. The click was loud in the still air and the Kansas farmers laughed, their chuckling tormenting his very soul.

"No!" Theo screamed, triggering the empty pistol again and again.

"No!" He jumped as the farmers reached for him. . . and jerked himself awake, a sharp stitch of pain in his back. He swallowed dryly in the cold blackness of the room, feeling the sweat trickling down his hot face.

A light danced in the hallway before Dolly entered bearing a lamp. "Theo?"

"I'm fine," he gasped, fighting to still his frantic heart. His body rushed with fear. "Just a dream, Dolly."

She placed the lamp on the table and pulled her robe about her. She settled awkwardly in the chair, her swollen belly making it difficult. "That's the second time this week, Theo. Can't we talk about it?"

He reached for the water pitcher they left by the bed. Pouring a glass, he drank gratefully. "Farmers!" Theo spat. "They come after me in a dog pack. Gun won't fire. They surround me. Like a cornered wolf. In the dream I can't ever get away."

She studied the floor before her. "Paw says it used to

be Louis who came in the dreams."

"He still does," he told her, blinking. "Can't sleep anymore, Dolly. When I do, they come. I see 'em all. Toddy Blake, Charlie Torgusson, Sabot, Kansas nesters, Irish O'Connell—all the ghosts. Then there's my folks. They come and stand around the bed and look down and whisper to themselves. And the demons still talk in my head. I can't hear what they say anymore. It's like . . . like they was in another part of my mind. *I . . . I can't find me anymore!*"

She looked up at him, her face hollow in the yellow light of the lamp. "Theo, you can't keep torturing yourself like this."

He looked at her dully. "What's real anymore, Dolly? Is it what I see awake, or the ghosts and demons?" He looked into the shadows and shook his head. "Charlie asked once if the men I killed weighed heavy on my soul and I . . . I laughed at him. Now, every time I close my eyes, they're there, staring, whispering about me. Even Louis! I see him staring, looking up from the floor, blood running out where he was shot."

She bit her lip. "You didn't just do evil, Theo. You saved Paw and me and Tom. Don't know if any of us would have been here without you. We owe you—"

"Nothing, Dolly!" He settled his chin on his hands and listened to the slow sigh of his breath in his lungs—one of the only feelings left to him. The lower half of his body was dead—maggot meat! It was official now—he'd never walk again. The sudden dribbling of water into the pan under the bed shocked him. He felt the flush and looked away, unable to meet Dolly's eyes, miserable with embarrassment, betrayed by his broken body. There was no dignity or control left—awake or asleep.

"Theo," Dolly called, ignoring his evacuation. "Tom and I have been talking. The baby, Theo, we want to name it after you. We—"

He spun his head, his eyes searching hers. "Why?" he asked, nervous, feeling his confusion.

She smiled softly. "I guess . . . well, I guess because of Irish, and because it wasn't all evil. I don't know. Maybe it would heal something. It'll be a new life, Theo. New things are full of hope and it'll mean that Irish didn't die for nothing. Don't you see? Something new to mend old hurts. And when the baby gets big enough, why, you'll be able to teach it like you did us. Think of the stories you can tell and the lessons you've learned. It's hope, Theo, and the future!"

"Named after . . . me?" he repeated. The memories of his twisted dreams came back. "Hope," he whispered, thinking of the future and what that meant for him, for a baby.

She fought her off-balanced way to her feet. "Need anything, Theo?" she asked, smiling at him and patting his shoulder.

"No, thank you, Dolly." He looked up at her and ground his teeth as she resettled the blanket on him. His eyes followed her as she left, her shadow looming weirdly in the light of the flickering lamp. After several seconds, he heard her door click shut and huffed a sigh. How long could he live like this?

They were naming the child after him? A warm glow built inside his chest. Now, that was some, it was. Hope? The future? What was his legacy? A broken body and too many demons? What lessons could he teach a young child? What could he give a young human being? He heard his water dripping again and closed his eyes.

Out in the night, as if hearing his anguish, the sorrel

whickered plaintively. The sound triggered something deep in him. Snatches of memories, sights of open trails and free wind mixed with images of warm fires and the smell of sagebrush and pine. Never again. The hollowness grew under his heart.

And they would name a child after him? So, maybe it wasn't all for nothing. Maybe there was a reason for his existence, after all. He'd had an effect. He'd saved them all in one way or another. A child . . . his child by name if not body. A legacy. He reached out from under the blankets and let his fingers run over the smooth grips of the old Walker.

"Man could do worse," he whispered. His thought went to Henry, still shuffling glumly around, blaming himself. "Had me a true friend. Huh, the only person I could turn my back on. How about that, Charlie?" Yes, a man could do worse.

So, even out of the wreckage of his life, some good had come. Louis was gone and with him the debt owed. The ghosts hovered around in the darkness waiting for him.

"Just don't let the kid grow up to be part of the dog pack, Dolly," he whispered as his fingers stroked the pistol, heavy in his hand now. He ran his fingers down the cold steel. Outside, the sorrel whickered again, as if ready to travel free once more. It would be a long ride home, but he was ready now.